Jakob's Ladies

Stan Parks

*To Linda
Enjoy
Stan Parks*

Jakob's Ladies Second Edition
Copyright 2016 Stan Parks
All Rights Reserved

No part of this book may be reproduced or transmitted in any form or by any means, electronic or mechanical photocopying, recording, or by any information retrieval or storage system without the express written permission of the author except in the case of short excerpts used in a critical review.

This is a work of fiction, Names and characters, places and incidents are a product of the author's imagination or are used fictitiously. Any resemblance to a real person, places or locales is entirely coincidental.

Interior and Cover Design by: Russel Davis

SBN-10: 1-946882-03-8
ISBN-13: 978-1-946882-03-5
LCN: 2017942681

Bratcher Publishing
P.O. Box 66
Chattaroy, WA 99003
www.bratcherpublishing.com

Dedication

This book is dedicated to the lady of my life who had faith in me and encouraged me to write this book:
My Lady Norie, my First Mate and Only Mate.

Part I

Chapter 1

Headed for the West

"Here you be, Doc" drawled the stage driver, with a big toothless grin across his face. "Sheridan, Wyoming. Greatest town in the West." The door to the stagecoach opened and Jakob slithered out of the tight space he had been crowded into the past half day. He strained and stretched to straighten himself out. The stage driver took his suitcases and lockers from the top of the stage and placed them on the porch of the Sheridan Inn.

"That's got em all, Doc. Ya jes mosy inside an they take care of ya." The other passengers on the stage had already gone into the hotel. "Lots a luck, Doc. Maybe I'll see ya nex time I'm through here." The driver hoisted himself to the driver seat, slapped the reins and yelled "git," and the horses responded.

Jakob turned around and faced the hotel. He mused, *That's a pretty fancy hotel for a frontier city.* Before him was a large stately building of three floors, with dormers on the upper floors. The large veranda across the front of the building with rockers and chairs was filled with men and women in Western dress. Except for the clothes and the horses hitched in front of the wooden sidewalk, this could have been Milwaukee. With no one to help with the luggage, Jakob brought his belongings inside the hotel. The big hotel desk was against the far wall of the entry, with its key rack for one hundred fifty rooms behind the registration desk. To the left as he walked in, was a huge stone fireplace which occupied most of that wall. Next to the hotel desk was a large hallway to what looked like a very fancy bar on one side and a big dining room on the other. The smiling hotel clerk was waiting for Jakob, who moved slowly across the entry with his luggage and boxes. Jakob introduced himself while he signed in for a room.

"I'm Henry Clayton" the clerk said. "At your service, Doctor. We're happy to see you here. How long do you plan on staying with us?"

"Well, I'm not certain at this time, but it will be for a while. I am a dentist and I plan to practice dentistry here in Sheridan."

"I'm happy to meet you, Doctor. Welcome! The Sheridan Inn is, by far, the finest hotel built in the West. We just recently opened for business, and one of our owners is the famous Colonel Bill Cody. I'm sure you have heard of him. We mean this to be the finest hotel you could ever find out West.

"You say you're a dentist. Well, now, may I tell you this: we shore do need a dentist here in Sheridan. So I must say we are happy to have you come here and stay with us. I have a very nice room for you on the second floor, Room 204. I'm certain you will be pleased with it. I see you have a great deal of luggage and I'll be glad to help you with it. You can see our famous bar to the right, which is also the finest you can find anywhere west of the Mississippi."

Henry Clayton's weathered face and mustache, together with his personality, made him perfect for his job. He picked up some of Jakob's bags and started up the stairs with Jakob following him, also carrying luggage. With all the luggage and boxes now in the room Henry Clayton turned to Jakob.

"I'm going to highly recommend dinner in our dining room. Lukas, our chef, is the finest in Sheridan. If there is anything you need, please don't hesitate to ask for it. I'm at your service." Smiling, he shook Jakob's hand and departed.

Jakob looked around the tastefully decorated room and noticed the fine furniture and carpets. It even had an expensive horse hair mattress for the bed. Jakob shook his head in amazement and thought, *This is as fancy as the Stevens Hotel in downtown Milwaukee. Wait until I tell Mom and Dad about this place.* There was even running water, and he poured himself a glass of water to wet his parched mouth. He took off his coat and hat and shook the dust off. Sitting down in the upholstered chair by the window, he looked out on to the street. Wagons and horseback riders moved up and down the street, and people of all descriptions walked the sidewalks. To the right and across the street there appeared to be a saloon, as well as several other saloons, farther down. The swinging doors had people constantly moving in and out. The sign above said Lucky Lady Saloon. It didn't look too fancy; but neither did any of the buildings down the street, except for the hotel. *Don't they paint their buildings here? It looks like some of them could just about fall down.* Jakob observed the movement of people, as his thoughts drifted off recalling his journey from his home in Milwaukee, Wisconsin.

This is sure a long way from Milwaukee. He remembered taking the Milwaukee Road to Chicago, and then the long ride on the Chicago Burlington and Quincy Railroad to Burlington, Iowa where he boarded the Burlington Missouri River Railroad to Crawford, Nebraska: the end of the line. The rest of the way was by dusty stagecoaches, to Sheridan. His back still felt cramped and sore from that ride.

I wonder if I did the right thing coming all the way out here, he thought. He remembered his graduation from the Chicago College of Dental Surgery and how he felt going up the stairs to the stage to get his diploma from Dean Brophy, and being congratulated. *Doctor Jakob Miller.* This was a strange new sound to his ears. He spent one long year in that large four story building in Chicago. He saw his parents, from the stage, as he crossed it with diploma in hand.

They were really proud of me. I hope they aren't too disappointed with me for not going into practice with Dad. I know he really wanted me in his office with him. Maybe I should have gone in with him. I guess by now I'd be on my way to success, but here I am. I haven't even started. They were really angry with me when I even suggested

I wanted to go out West, instead of staying in Milwaukee. I hope Dad didn't think I just didn't want to be with him.

"Oh, my gosh! They threw that guy right out of the saloon. He looks mad." *Well, I better get going. I can't just sit here and look out the window for the rest of the day. I'm in Sheridan now and I have to get down to business. There's a lot I have to do. First, I better learn something about this town so I can get to work. I better wash up, and then I'll go down and talk to Henry Clayton, and, ...maybe I should look into that Lucky Lady and see what's going on over there.*

Jakob stopped at the hotel desk.

"Well, Doc, all settled in? What can I do fer you?"

"Mr. Clayton, I am planning on opening a dental office here in Sheridan and I need some of your advice and input. Is there any office space available in Sheridan?"

"Now Doc, I jes want you to call me Henry. You jes ferget that mister stuff. Well, now, I can't rightly say. I jes don't know of any, but ya might ask one of the business people, like Elmer Findley at the general store or maybe the banker, Harold Stevens, at the First National Bank on Main Street. Or, you might try Edgar Wright, at the *Sheridan Post*. Those guys might be able to fill ya in on what's going on in town."

"What about the town doctor? Who is he? Maybe he might have an idea as to where I might find an office to practice dentistry."

"Well, that be Doc Kelly. His office is also on Main. Yes, you could talk to him. He is one helluva good doc. Saved plenty of folks around here. I bet he's been here about ten years. You be sure to stop in and see him. Nice guy. Tell him I sent you over. He's a mighty good friend of mine, that doc." Jakob thanked him and bid him goodbye, put on his derby and went outside to look around.

Standing on the porch he looked over the street. To his left was a large building which looked like it might be a train depot being built. To his right, on the veranda, were some of the people who were watching Jakob. They now craned their necks to see the dude who just arrived in his fancy black and white hounds-tooth check suit and derby. Some of the ladies smiled at him and a couple men mumbled a *howdy*. His outfit made Jakob a standout. He walked down the stairs and headed toward the Lucky Lady. As he crossed the street, dodging some of the riders and a wagon, he approached the swinging doors of the Lucky Lady. Hearing the piano player and the noise inside, he pushed open the swinging doors and stepped inside. Looking around, he saw the crowded barroom. Jakob walked up to the bar. The bartender promptly introduced himself to Jakob.

"I'm Andy Meeks. Welcome to the Lucky Lady!"

"I'm pleased to meet you. I'm Doctor Jakob Miller. I've come to Sheridan to start a dental practice."

"Dentist, huh? Gol darn, we shore do need one here. Ain't had one here for at least four years. Last dentist we had here died in the winter of '91. Nice guy that Doc Foley was. Shore glad to see you." Placing a bottle in front of Jakob he poured him a glass of whiskey. "Here ya be, Doc. This'en is on the house.

"Hey, everybody! I want you all to meet our new dentist in town, Jake Miller. Sorry Doc. Folks, I mean Doc Miller." Jakob, now Doc Miller, was instantly accepted. People came over and started introducing themselves to Jakob and telling him how glad they were to finally see a dentist in Sheridan. Some asked him when was he going to be open for business, because they needed to see him. Jakob was amazed at the friendliness of the people in the Lucky Lady and now knew he had better find a place to set up his office soon. He stayed and talked with the people, and asked several where he might find office space, but was told there was none available they knew of.

Jakob decided to go see Doc Kelly, the *sawbones*, as he was called, and maybe he might be able to help. He had to walk over to Main Street where the doctor had his office in a wood false-front building, next to a big feed store. Jakob introduced himself as a fellow professional man and told him he was planning to open a dental office. Doc Kelly was an older man, partially bald, with some gray hair, a beard and glasses. He seemed gruff, but friendly enough. Doc Kelly had a green vest over his white soiled shirt with cuffs turned up, a string tie and a stethoscope around his neck. Jakob noticed the slight odor of horses inside the office but thought nothing of it. He told Doc Kelly he was anxious to open up an office and asked him if he knew of any space available in town. Doc Kelly scratched his head thinking and said he didn't know of any.

"But, I might be able to help you for the time being. I do have some spare room in my place which is a store room. I could it rent to you. It ain't very big, but you could use it until you found a place of your own." Jakob thought it was a great idea and he would take him up on his offer. So now, Jakob had an office location to start with. He told Doc Kelly he would be moving in just as soon as he could. Doc Kelly suggested the best way to get known around town would be to put an ad in the local newspaper, so Jakob went to the *Sheridan Post* to place an ad in the next edition of the paper. He met Edgar Wright, the editor, who shook his hand with vigor and welcomed him to Sheridan.

"You'll be glad you came here. This city has great potential. We'll have the train arriving here in just a few months and then this city will really grow. Let's get a good ad in the paper for you. I'll also make up some posters and fliers for you, to put around town, and we'll have you working in no time." Edgar laid out a fine ad for Jakob.

Jakob's Ladies

Now hear this, Sheridan
At Doc Kelly's Office on Main St.
Prepared to do all your Dental Work
By the latest and approved Scientific Methods
Crown and Bridge Work a Specialty
All your Dental Needs Filled
Graduate Chicago College of Dental Surgery
Chicago, Illinois
Doctor Jakob Miller, D.D.S.
Is Open For Practice

The following week one whole page ad appeared in the weekly *Sheridan Post*. He also made up some fliers for Jakob to post around town. Jakob moved into Doc Kelly's office with all his equipment. It was pretty small but Jakob managed to get everything in. He now needed to get a dental chair, and was lucky enough to find a barber chair that Herman Gibbs had and wasn't using. One of its arms was broken, but Homer Johnson, the blacksmith, said he could fix it.

Jakob was all set up and ready for business at Doc Kelly's office but no one showed up until the following Saturday. There was a big fight in front of the Cowboy Saloon. Jakob was in the Lucky Lady at the time when one of the townspeople came into the saloon to get him. He said his friend had a bunch of busted teeth and was "a hurten".

They took him over to Doc Kelly's office. Jakob hurried over to his office and was all set to help the poor guy out of his pain. Zeke, as he was known, was already sitting in the barber chair waiting for Jakob. The man was a mess, with all those teeth broken and blood all over his face. None could be saved so he had to take them out.

The patient was ready, but he was also "three sheets to the wind." He didn't need any more booze to sedate him. Jakob went to work, with a couple of the guys helping hold Zeke down. He took his forceps and with root elevators started digging out the roots and broken teeth. Zeke may have been "three sheets to the wind" and sedated, but he started moaning and yelping as Jakob did his surgery. Jakob worked as fast as he could, and had those teeth out before Zeke could even catch his breath. He stitched him up, sopped up the blood and wiped him clean.

Bleary-eyed, Zeke looked up at Jakob and said, "Gee, thanks, Doc," and pulled out some paper bills from his pocket. Stumbling out of the office with his friends, he went back to the Cowboy Saloon and up to the bar to show the gang how he now looked. "Didn't hurt a bit. I tell you that Doc Miller is okay," he said as he put his head back and drank down the shot of whiskey.

That was the start of Jakob's dental practice. Soon there were others who came by to have their teeth fixed and false teeth made. Saturdays, the cowhands from the surrounding ranches would stop by to relieve their tooth pain and of course, there were always fist-fights and sometimes even gun fights, but Doc Kelly or Digger O'Rilley, the local mortician, usually took care of those situations. His office was small, but it worked out just fine. Sometimes it was hard to get a seat inside Doc Kelly's office with both of them working, but they made do. He had been lucky to find the old barber chair, that Homer Johnson fixed, and with the SS White drill, which was foot powered, they satisfied his patients' needs. Doc Kelly came in and complained when there was "holler'n" by some of Jakob's patients.

He would get requests from some of the surrounding ranches to bring his equipment and take care of the owners' and ranch hands' dental problems. Jakob then would rent a rig to go out and take care of those patients. Things were starting to work out well for Jakob. Business was good and he opened a bank account at the First National Bank. The city of Sheridan accepted Doc Miller.

Winter was now approaching and soon snow would be falling. Wyoming winters are bitter cold, and snow on the ground made travel very difficult. His practice had been successful so far. But with winter arriving, Jakob's dental business was slowing down to almost a standstill, so he had a lot of time to do some thinking. Jakob saved some of the money he made, and started making plans for his future. Up to now, he didn't have time to be homesick, but in the dead of winter Jakob thought of his Milwaukee home and, of course his girlfriend, Alice.

He remembered the day he met Alice in Carter's Drug Store, where they had their ice-cream phosphate. As he shared his dream of becoming a frontier dentist, Jakob could still hear her blurt out, "But, I thought we were getting married after you finished dental school and we would live here!" Tears flowed as she shared her disappointment and continued to flow all through their walk back home. As she opened the door, she turned to Jakob and said, "Goodbye, Jakob. Don't expect me to wait for you while you go . . . go somewhere out West." The door slammed in his face as he stood dumbfounded. He tried to see her the next day and every day after, but the door remained shut for him.

He still loved Alice and thought he would like to marry her; bring her out to Sheridan and share his life out there with her. He even thought of buying some property and building a home for her where they could start a family. His dreams still remained with him.

The cold nights and deep snows gave him time to think about his dreams and make plans for his future. He kept as busy as he could but the occasional patient didn't give him enough to do. He often found himself in his room at the hotel reading or studying. He would occasionally visit his friends at the Lucky Lady and play some cards.

The long winter nights eventually grew shorter and the snow started to melt. Here and there wildflowers and greening grasses started to arrive with the spring. With the stage now making regular runs and the train resuming regular service, Jakob decided to make plans to go back to Milwaukee to see his family and hopefully bring Alice back with him.

He didn't write and tell his family he was coming back, because he wanted it to be a surprise. And it was a complete surprise. His parents asked him if he came back for good as they had hoped. Had he gotten this foolish adventure, this folly out of his system? No! But he did come back for Alice. His mother and father were happy to see him, but disappointed he was planning to return to Sheridan with Alice, if she would have him.

The next day he stopped at Wagner's florist shop where he bought a big bouquet for Alice, with the hope he could convince her to marry him and accompany him back to Sheridan. With a spring in his step, he was off to see Alice. He took the steps to her house two at a time and rang the doorbell. Alice's mother answered the door. Jakob was standing in front of her.

"Hello, Mrs. O'Malley."

Startled, Mrs. O'Malley answered, "Well, Jakob, how nice to see you. What a surprise this is! Come on in. I'll see if I can find Alice."

Some minutes passed and Alice was in front of Jakob. He immediately thrust the flowers in her hands. Jakob couldn't wait to tell her and blurted out, "Alice, I love you. Will you marry me? I've come back and I want to take you with me to Sheridan, Wyoming."

Alice's mouth opened to speak but no words came out. After an eternally long moment, Alice's lips started to move. "Jakob, I told you I didn't want to go out West with you. I thought you understood. I'm sorry but I am now engaged to Freddy Schultz. You know Freddy, he was in our high school class. He is the son of the Milwaukee Bank president."

Jakob was crushed. He stood with his mouth open but could say nothing. Then after a long moment, he turned slowly and with shoulders slumped, walked out the door. Jakob walked down the street in a daze and past Carter's Drug Store. Realizing he had passed the store, he turned around and went back and into the store.

Mr. Carter saw him. "Jakob Miller. You're back in town. How nice to see you. Are you planning on staying in Milwaukee?" Jakob shook his head and declined to say any more, but he ordered a soda and sat at a table staring into space mulling over what had happened. He sat there until Mr. Carter was getting ready to close the store. Jakob nodded goodbye to Mr. Carter and left. He slowly walked home to tell his parents of his plight and informed them he would be going back to Sheridan without Alice, to take up where he had left off. Alice was now a thing of his past.

Jakob's mother felt she should try to solve his problem by reminding him he had left Alice to go to Wyoming. Understandably, she had to find a new life for herself. "Was going to Wyoming worth it, Jakob? There is so much more for you here. You can still stay here and maybe get Alice back. You don't have to go back there."

"Mother, I love my life in Sheridan. I don't want to come back to Milwaukee. I am doing well in my practice and they need me in Sheridan. You should come out and see what life is like out there."

Jakob's father came forward and put his arm around Jakob. "Margaret, let Jakob do as he wishes. He is doing what he wants to do and I'm proud of him. He'll do well and maybe Alice isn't the right wife for him. Let's spend the rest of his visit here enjoying his company. Jakob, I want you to go to my office with me tomorrow and I will share with you some of the new developments in our profession." Margaret didn't share her husband's feelings but did not persist.

That night, Margaret lay in bed thinking about her son and his future, but remembering he did have a mind of his own. She reminisced how well he had always done in school; he was the perfect child. Then her thoughts went back to the first day, when she took him to school. *As they walked up the steps to the Allen Public School, sullen Jakob looked both ways and broke loose from her grasp, turned around and ran down the steps and on to the sidewalk. She was aghast at his rebellion. He was such a good boy and always so well behaved. All her friends marveled at his behavior. Embarrassed at the turn of events, she faced several of her friends accompanying their children. They broke into laughter as Margaret pursued the escaping boy. "Jakob, you must stop. Come back. Do you hear me?" she shouted, but Jakob kept running. She never realized the boy could run so fast. But Margaret was no slow poke. Breathless, she caught up with the boy and firmly holding his hand, they marched back to the school.*

"I don't want to go back," he cried. "I want to stay home with you. Don't make me go back. Please." And then he started to cry uncontrollably. It took a while to quell his objections to going to school. Finally, his sobbing stopped and she was able to communicate with him. They walked back into the classroom, leaving the child to the teacher. Margaret remembered Jakob as a good student who learned quickly and was well liked by the teachers. Her memories of Jakob finally brought on sleep.

Jakob spent the next several days thinking about his loss of Alice O'Malley. He had never thought his move to Wyoming would affect his budding romance to this extent. He really cared a great deal for Alice and they had made plans for their future together. Now he was truly heartbroken; he faced his future without Alice.

He achieved his dream of becoming a dentist, and found his way to that Western frontier. However, the price he paid was the loss of his sweetheart. He wondered if he should try harder to resurrect his romance with Alice. However,

Alice was adamant and she was now engaged to Freddy Schultz. No, it was over, and he had to put Alice out of his mind. He needed to complete his plans for the return to Wyoming, without Alice.

He gathered more of the belongings he had left behind when he left Milwaukee the previous year, and bid all his good friends goodbye. The last days home were enjoyed by the Millers, and it was time for Jakob to return to Wyoming. His parents were sorry to see him leave again, but lovingly bid him goodbye and wished him luck in his new-found home. They parted company and Jakob began his long trip back to Sheridan.

Chapter 2

Terror on the Trail

A heartbroken Jakob boarded the train for Chicago's Union Station. Leaving Chicago, he took the Chicago Burlington and Quincy which took him west across the Mississippi, where he would board the Burlington and Missouri for Sheridan. The railroad was now completed and extended all the way to Sheridan, so he would no longer have to take the rough and dusty stage ride. It would be faster, even though the train would make many stops to reload coal and water. The train swayed back and forth on a hot summer day. With the windows open, he inhaled a waft of smoke mixed with the hot outside air. Jakob was now more anxious than ever to get back to Sheridan and to move on with the life he had chosen. As he looked out the train window, he tried to put together some plans for his future life out West. His thoughts drifted.

I've got to move my office out of Doc Kelly's place. I need more room for my practice. It's growing and I have to grow with it, so I have to find a place of my own. I also need a place to live. I've had enough of the hotel room. It's too small and expensive to live in.

I miss not being with my new friends. They are genuine people. Wyoming is my new life and it is exciting and growing. Just last year, the train didn't go all the way and I had to take the stage with that long dusty run. Now the train is going all the way to Sheridan. Sheridan is growing fast and is becoming an important city and I can be a part of its success.

The changing landscape started to look familiar, and he realized it wouldn't be long before he arrived in Sheridan. Jakob could hear the whistle as the train started to slow down, and then the bell, as it chugged to a stop. The conductor called, "Sheridan, Sheridan, Wyoming. End of the line." Local people were milling around the new station as the passengers and luggage were unloaded. There weren't too many people on the last leg of his trip. The car was more than half empty during the last couple hundred miles. Jakob had talked with some of the passengers. Various railroad contractors were on the train, who would now be working to extend the line north of Sheridan to Billings. There were other business people, and even some ladies who were coming out to get married. Jakob noticed a pretty lady school teacher among the passengers, who was going to teach in the elementary school.

Jakob stepped off the train and was greeted by a number of people who recognized him immediately.

"Hi, Doc. Glad to see you back, Doc." He got pats on the back, and one old sot wanted him to look at a tooth that has "just been killin him." Jakob told him to stop by the office in the morning. He got his baggage together and made arrangements to have it delivered to the hotel. He then walked to the hotel.

A smiling Henry Clayton greeted Jakob as he came up to the desk. "Sure happy to see you back, Doc. You know there were some folks that was saying maybe you wouldn't be back, cuz it's too tough liven out here. But, I knew you'd be back. Thought maybe you'd be bringin' back the little lady you talked about. Didn't she wanta come?"

Jakob glossed over the Alice affair, got the key to his room, and settled in. It felt good to be back and Jakob thought he might meander over to the Lucky Lady and see some of his friends and Andy Meeks, the bartender. When he walked in, there was a lot of whooping and hollering from the guys in there. "Hey, Doc. Glad to see you back." Jakob got a lot of pats on the back as people came up to welcome him home. As he stepped up to the bar, Andy Meeks put down a shot glass and poured him a whiskey.

"Good to see you back, Doc. I didn't expect to see you back quite this soon. Did you bring anybody back with you?" as he asked with a big wink.

Jakob made little talk about the affair as best as could, then concluded with, "I don't think she would have fit here in Sheridan. Enough said."

"Hey, Doc, did you see the place they just finished up, next to the bank on Main Street? Might be a good spot for the office you been wantin'."

"I'll have to take a look at it." They continued speaking about the current events and then it was time for Jakob to go see if Doc Kelly was in.

He walked down to the bank and saw the new building getting finished. All the buildings on Main Street had false fronts, with a regular building behind. A canopy usually extended over the boarded sidewalk and people would bring out stools and chairs and sit in front of the buildings. He looked over the possible office space. Most of the building was going to be a boot and shoe store. Jakob thought the rest of it would work out perfectly for his dental office, if it was available.

Walking over to Doc Kelley's place, he thought about how great it would be to have his own office. Passing by Mrs. Howard's boarding house, he saw the new school teacher coming out and walking toward the school house. *Hmm. She looks nice*, he thought. Doc Kelly wasn't in his office. He had a sign that said *Gone on a call*. He then checked out his own office and found everything was just as he had left it. He heard the office door open, and thought it might be Doc Kelly coming back. Opening his door was Zeke, his first patient in Sheridan, grinning with his toothless smile.

"Heeard you was back, Doc. Shore glad to see ya. Ya know, I been a thinken'. Maybe I could get me some of those store teeth they been talken' about. Ya know, ya kin take em in and out. Do ya think you could make me some? I ain't got much cash, but maybe we can work out a deal."

Jakob smiled and said he'd be glad to make him some *store teeth* but wondered how he could pay for them. "What do you mean by a deal, Zeke?"

"Well, now, maybe I could do sumpen' like take ya out huntin'. Ya ever been huntin'?"

"Well, no, but."

"I knows lots bout huntin' and take out some of the dudes that come here fer huntin'. They's lots of elk out there in them Bighorns and Doc, ya ain't been huntin' till you gits an elk. I could take ya there and git ya an elk. I'll pervide everthin' ya need: horses, grub, guns, you name it."

Jakob's ears perked up and he got to thinking he had not done anything like that since he had been in Sheridan. If he got an elk, the rack might look good on the wall in his new office. "Okay, Zeke, you're on. Sounds like a good idea. When do you want to go?"

"Tomorra?"

"Well no, but how about sometime next week?"

"I'll git everthin' rady fer next week and Doc, believe me, I'm gonna get ya an elk." Zeke left and Jakob stood there thinking about what he was doing. *I've never been elk hunting. Dad and I went duck hunting, but elk? Wait tell I tell Dad about this.*

He closed the door of the office and went back to the hotel and told Henry Clayton about the elk hunt. Henry thought it was a great idea, and assured Jakob, Zeke was a good guide. "People from out East come out for elk and Zeke guides for them.

The week was busy for Jakob. He saw some of his patients and finally found the owner of the new building. They talked and Jakob got his okay for his new office. Philip Richardson owned the building and was happy to rent him an office in it. He even agreed to put up a couple walls so he could have privacy in his operatory and it would also give him space for a laboratory to make his false teeth in. This was too good to be true. He told Mr. Richardson he was going elk hunting and Mr. Richardson wished him luck and told him he would probably have his office ready for him shortly after he came back.

Monday morning came and Jakob was having an early breakfast in the hotel dining room when Zeke arrived. "Have some breakfast, Zeke?"

"Don't mind if a do." Zeke finished up a big breakfast of steak, eggs, potatoes, hot bread and plenty of coffee. Jakob, watching Zeke eat thought, *How could he ever be able to eat a steak without teeth, I will never know?* "Got everythin' rady Doc. Best we git a move on. It's starten' to git light and we gotta be on the trail."

Jakob had some of his belongings packed and Zeke went out and placed them on the pack horse. Zeke had two riding horses and a pack horse loaded with gear for the hunt. Jakob's horse had a bedroll and a scabbard with a hunting rifle in it.

Jakob mounted the horse and Zeke yelled, "Let's git gone." They slowly moved out along Main Street to the end of town. Zeke then followed a trail toward the mountains to the northwest. The sun was just coming up in the east and they picked up the pace toward the Bighorns. There were roosters crowing in some of the yards and the townspeople were up and moving about. Soon the town was in the distance, and all that could be seen were wisps of smoke from the chimneys and the glare of the rising sun. The sun warmed the cool air and they crossed Big Goose Creek. Zeke kept an endless chatter as they moved across the dried landscape. Other than the occasional hawk soaring high and the chatter of Zeke, everything was quiet. Zeke pointed out an old Indian battlefield. The trail took them through the foothills towards the mountains as they loomed higher. Jakob marveled at the natural beauty of the landscape. He'd never seen such colors and variety of textures of green and rock.

"We want to get to the other side of these mountains 'fore dark." They camped for the night in an idyllic spot alongside a small stream. A campfire and a hearty meal made by Zeke were enjoyed by both, as the sun set in the distance. This made way for the darkening sky, followed by stars shining faintly first and then getting brighter and brighter. Sleep was not difficult as both men were dog-tired. Jakob suddenly awakened from a sound sleep and found Zeke moving about the campsite putting wood on the dying embers of the fire, but then fell back asleep.

The first light of dawn had arrived. "Best we git up. I'll have breakfast rady in a few minutes. I wanna git out eearly. Not too far from here they's usually a herd a elk." Jakob got ready for a sumptuous camp breakfast. They cleaned up the campground and put out the fire.

"Time to move out." They moved out of the campsite and traveled a short distance over rough terrain, when Zeke said, "Best we git out on foot now." They tied the horses to some short trees and cautiously worked their way toward a grassy clearing. Zeke stopped to examine some hoof prints. "They's been here. No noise now and keep low." They slowly moved and Zeke looked down again and examined some more prints and slowly looked up. "Bar!" He seemed perplexed as he moved along. They reached a rise and climbed up, and then he spotted, in the distance, elk.

"They's here. Look." Sure enough no more than a couple hundred yards away was a small herd of elk. They continued quietly and moving slowly in their direction, keeping themselves concealed from the elk until they were about fifty yards away. Zeke nudged Jakob. "Git rady." The elk appeared nervous as Jakob hesitated. "Take un, Doc." Jakob raised his rifle and hesitated. He had buck fever. Zeke whispered, "Hurry up, Doc, or you'll lose em." Jakob aimed carefully and slowly squeezed the trigger. A loud sound reverberated through the area and there was a smell of gunpowder. The animals scattered except one that remained motionless and then crumbled to the ground.

"Ya got em, Doc. Ya got a good en." The two moved quickly out of the brush to the downed animal. "Hey, Doc, he's a big un." Jakob looked on in surprise and was momentarily stunned as he examined the antlers of the downed animal. He now smiled and thought he could proudly display them in his new office. Zeke said, "It's a real good un, Doc. I'll go back an git the horses. You stay here."

Jakob was elated as he carefully examined the downed animal and thought about the event and how he killed him, with just one shot. *Wait till I write home and tell Dad about what I have done.* Some time had passed since Zeke left for the horses, and Jakob could not be more elated about the event. He laid his rifle against the elk and moved around to the other side of the animal to see where the bullet had entered the body. He was amazed at the elk's size. The others in the herd had left. Time passed slowly as he waited for Zeke's return.

Suddenly, out of the brush charged a big bear. Jakob grabbed for the rifle he had propped up against the elk but it fell to the ground. It was too late. The bear's large paw hit his raised arm with great force as he tried to ward off the blow, and he went spinning down a small hill. Jakob was stunned and looked up to see the bear looming over him. His teeth were bared, and his mouth was frothing. Large eyes were staring down at him and the bear was roaring. Paralyzed with fright and dazed, Jakob's only thought was that this was his end. The roaring of the bear was terrifying beyond belief, as he just seemed to hang there above him, ready to pounce on him for the kill. Then, the bear seemed to move back slightly and quiver as Jakob heard gunshots, and the bear was motionless above him. Suddenly he crumpled from the impact of Zeke's bullets, with his head falling on Jakob's legs. Zeke came running up.

"Doc, Doc. You okay?" Jakob winced in pain, as he looked down at his arm which was bleeding profusely. Zeke pulled back Jakob's shirt to see a gaping wound, gushing blood.

"My belt, my belt, take off my belt." Zeke took off Jakob's belt and as he directed, placed it above the wound, tightening it to stop the bleeding. He then told Zeke to use one of his shirts for a bandage to cover the gaping wound on the arm and to tie it tightly. Jakob was now sweating profusely, panting and nauseous and experiencing vertigo, as he lay slumped on the ground.

Zeke managed to bandage the arm. "Doc, what else kin I do?" Jakob was quiet and his head rolled back and forth and finally stopped. Jakob's eyes opened.

"Give me some water, please. I'm thirsty" He raised his head as Zeke pressed the canteen to his lips. He drank and coughed some. Looking at the bandaged arm he winced in pain. "Zeke, can you move the bear's head off me? It hurts my legs."

"Sorry, Doc. I'll git him off." As he slowly moved the beast's head, Jakob was able to pull his legs free. Jakob placed the bandaged arm up over his heart and told Zeke to take another shirt out of his clothes bag and make a sling. Following

Jakob's instructions, Zeke made a sling he put around his neck and under his bandaged arm. Having him bandaged and with a sling for support, Zeke helped him sit aside.

"Doc, what else can I do fer you?" Zeke then helped him get up. Jakob was in great pain as Zeke helped him to lie down next to a large tree. He placed a bed-roll under his head and gave him some water to drink. His pain seemed overwhelming as he closed his eyes. "Doc, is there anythin' else I kin do? Jes tell me." Jakob shook his head.

"Doc, I gotta take care of the critters." He took his knife and immediately started skinning the bear. This was a large animal and it took him some time to skin it. Jakob seemed to lose consciousness. Zeke later came back to check on him and to make sure he was comfortable; he treated him tenderly. His hands were covered with blood. Jakob felt nauseous, as he looked at the bloodied animals but he laid still. Zeke carefully covered him with a blanket and held the canteen for him to drink some water.

"I'll be back, Doc, but I still got lots to do." He went back and removed the antlers from the elk, then cut some meat they would take with them and later fry. Finally, coming back to check on Jakob who was now laying quietly, Zeke grinned his toothless smile and remarked, "Looks to me, Doc, like youze gonna have a bearskin rug for that new office, and the antlers."

Chapter 3

The Healing Process

As he opened his eyes, Jakob felt a terrible pain in his arm. Things seemed blurry, and then he remembered the terror of the bear hovering over him, the shots and the weight of the bear's head across his legs. It all came back. The hunting trip with Zeke, the elk he shot and while he was examining his trophy, the bear confronting him. *Am I alive?* he thought. *I must be alive.*

"Oh, my arm, my arm. It's throbbing so." He looked down at his left forearm and saw the bloody bandage covering it. His fingers felt numb and his arm hurt terribly. Then he remembered, Zeke had wrapped his belt around his upper arm to stop the bleeding. Zeke tore his shirt and wrapped it around the arm. He remembered the skin laid back and he saw the muscle and bone exposed before Zeke tightly wrapped the arm with the shirt-made bandage. *Why is it hurting so? I don't think the bone is broken.* He felt dizzy and his vision was bleary. *Where am I?* He looked up at the sky and moved his head around and realized he was near some trees. Zeke helped him into the shade of a tree after he dragged the bear head off his legs. Then he saw Zeke some distance away skinning the bear. It was an awful sight, that bear body and all the blood. He was so thirsty. *If only I had a drink of water. Where is my canteen?*

"Zeke!" he called but he didn't hear him. Then he screamed as loud as he could.

"Zeke come help me." Zeke looked around and saw Jakob moving. He dropped his knife and came running.

"Doc, how you doing?"

"I need water." Zeke gave his canteen to Jakob who gulped down the water, coughing. Finally he handed back the canteen to Zeke.

"Doc you must have been out a couple hours."

"Zeke you have to take off the belt from my arm. My hand is numb." Zeke carefully loosened the tourniquet. They watched the bloody bandage but it seemed to be controlling the bleeding. The throbbing stopped. "What are we going to do Zeke? We have to get back. Doc Kelly has to see this arm or I could lose it."

"Doc it will be dark soon. We got ta stay put. I'll make camp here. I skinned the bar and cut us a couple of elk steaks. I'll cook up some chow. When it gits mornin' we kin start back. We jes can't leave now. This place will be okay fir now." He helped Jakob sit up. Zeke had cut some branches off the trees and made a shelter for them. He had a fire going and started the meal. As the sun went down, a stiff breeze came up and it got cooler. Jakob didn't feel much like eating but the hot coffee revived his interest and he took a piece of the roasted elk and started chewing on it. It was pretty tough and he had to work hard on it. The fire burned bright and warm and the sky was filled with clouds and stars, with a sliver of the moon now showing. Jakob's arm hurt a lot but he made no mention of the pain. Zeke looked at him and realized he was in pain.

"Got somem' fer ya Doc." He pulled out a bottle from his saddle bag. "Have a slug of this. It'll make ya feel better." Jakob leaned back and took a swig of the whiskey. He coughed after he swallowed it and then lay back, pulled a blanket over himself and was soon asleep. He awoke later in the night. The fire was still bright and he could hear wolves howling in the distance. The horses were nervous at the sounds of the night and the winds seemed to pick up and he noticed a light rain. Zeke woke up and looked around the campsite checking on the horses. He put some wood on the fire. In the distance he could see flashes of lightning and hear muffled thunder. Zeke mumbled something and went back to sleep. Jakob lay awake. His arm was hurting a throbbing pain. As he lay there, he thought about the day. *Why did I ever do this?* he thought. *That bear could have killed me. I'm not out of this thing yet. I could lose my arm. Oh Lord, help me get through this nightmare.* Any movement he made caused the arm to pain more so he lay as still as he could. Over and over in his mind he thought about the bear and how lucky it was that Zeke had come back when he did and shot the bear. *What if he didn't get back when he did?* He shuddered and could still feel the swat of the bear that had laid him down; he remembered the ear piercing roar and the paralyzing fear he experienced. Finally, he fell back asleep.

Jakob awakened to the sound of Zeke moving around the campsite. He looked up at the sky, which was getting lighter. There was a chatter of birds in the brush. *Oh my God, what if there is another bear out there?* he thought. The fire was burning hot and he could smell the coffee boiling. Zeke looked in the shelter.

"Ya up Doc?" Jakob answered and Zeke handed him a coffee. "Rain's gone, looks like we'll have a good day. How ya doin'?" Jakob's arm hurt as much as when he went to sleep, but he didn't say anything. He tried to get up and Zeke noticing his difficulty, helped him up. Now he noticed he had pain in other places on his body. Must have been when he went rolling down the hill. He walked with some difficulty, but was able to get around the camp. Zeke fried a couple eggs for him and burnt a piece of the tough elk for him to chew on. While Jakob was eating his breakfast, Zeke was breaking up camp. He had to get the antlers and the bearskin on the pack horse and some of the elk meat he had cut.

"Best we leave Doc. We gott'a fir piece ta go." He put out the fire and they were ready to go back. "Let me give ya a han Doc. We'll get ya on da horse." With great pain Jakob mounted his horse. Zeke adjusted the sling on his arm and they slowly moved out.

As the horse slowly moved along, Jakob's arm pained him terribly. He tried to position himself so that there was a minimal amount of pain, but nothing seemed to help. They moved very slowly. At this speed it was doubtful they could make it to town before dark. It was an agonizing trip for Jakob. They made numerous stops to rest, although getting on and off the horse was more brutal than just riding. Past mid-day Zeke noticed some riders in the distance, and shot his gun into the air, but to no avail. As the day progressed Jakob's pain increased and he grew weaker in the saddle. Some riders again appeared in the distance and Zeke tried to signal them. They must have noticed his signal, because they turned and came toward Zeke and Jakob. Three riders came up. Zeke knew one of them and explained their predicament. One of them said he would go back and try to get a wagon. Zeke and Jakob plodded along slowly and just before dark, one of the townspeople arrived with a buggy. They carefully got Jakob off the horse and on to the buggy. Jakob was more comfortable but was noticeably weaker. It was after midnight when the buggy pulled up to Doc Kelly's office. A crowd had gathered awaiting Jakob. A couple of the guys from the saloon carried Jakob into Doc Kelly's office, and put him on the table.

Jakob was still in considerable pain. Doc gave him some water and noticed he was feverish. He mixed some white powder with water and gave it to him to swallow. With a room full of people looking on Doc Kelly took the bandage off the arm. They gasped when they saw it and Doc looked at the bunch and told them to go home and he would take care of things. Some of them left, but there were some that stayed. Mrs. Howard from the ladies boarding house moved to the back of the room with the other ladies. They were visibly upset and sat down whispering to each other. It looked bad and it was still bleeding some. Doc cleaned it up and started sewing it back together. Jakob's pain seemed worse but he held up well. The arm was just oozing blood as Doc Kelly finished up. Finally, Doc placed a new clean bandage over the wound and tied it tightly. The bleeding seemed to have stopped.

"Well Jakob, I did the best I could. That bear really mangled your arm. Lucky he didn't break it. It's going to take a while for you to recover. You can stay here tonight if a couple of you ladies will stay with him, to put some cold packs on, to tend the fever." Mrs. Howard and another young lady pressed forward next to the table. Mrs. Howard said she would stay the night with Jakob and one of her ladies from the rooming house also said she would be glad to stay with Jakob. Elizabeth Jensen the new school teacher would help Mrs. Howard. They were already wiping Jakob's brow trying to make him comfortable. Doc Kelly chased everyone out but the two ladies and Jakob soon fell asleep. The two ladies sat next to him, taking turns wiping his brow with a cool towel. He slept intermittently and sometime moaned. The night went slowly but the ladies tended the patient diligently. There was a dim light in the room from the lamp and soon Mrs. Howard fell asleep, as Elizabeth sat close to Jakob.

The sound of a distant rooster crowing awakened Mrs. Howard. The sky was just beginning to lighten.

"Elizabeth, why don't you go back to the house and try to get a couple hours sleep. You have to teach those children. I can handle this until Doc Kelly gets back here."

"Mrs. Howard I don't mind staying." Just then Jakob started to stir and they both stood up on either side of him. Mrs. Howard gave him some water and then dissolved a powder Doc left for him and gave it to him. His fever seemed to have subsided and he had less pain. He meekly looked up at Elizabeth and smiled.

"What's your name?"

Elizabeth blushed and answered, "Elizabeth, but you can call me Liz. I hope you are feeling better." He weakly nodded. Just then, Doc Kelly came in and thanked the ladies for their help.

"Well Jakob you sure look a lot better than you did when I left you. You were in pretty rough shape. When a couple of the guys come over we'll get you back to your room at the hotel."

It took several weeks of tender, loving care with the ladies from town coming over to visit Jakob. Each one would spend time talking to him and bringing treats of cookies and cakes to medicate his injured arm. The guys from the Lucky Lady would stop by, and some would even come over for a friendly card game. It was a couple weeks before Doc Kelly took off the bandages and removed the sutures. Doc Kelly would keep telling Jakob to get off his butt and get going. Zeke came by to see how Jakob was doing and to find out when he was going back to work.

"I gave Lukas them elk steaks, so he kin fix em for ya. I shouda brought back sum a that bar meat, but we den't have much time fir me ta cut 'em up. You wus moanen' and groanen'."

Jakob felt he had recovered enough to go back to work. At least that's what Doc Kelly said. He didn't realize that Jakob's left arm wasn't much good for anything. He could barely hold anything in it. His wrist would drop if he held it up. But, with Doc Kelly prodding him, and his forcing himself to do things, he was getting better. If it wasn't for the ladies in town attending to his needs and coming by his room bringing him his meals and cookies and cakes, he might have healed sooner. At least that was what Doc Kelly said. He didn't have the motivation to hurry up the healing process with the ladies giving him so much attention.

Chapter 4
Getting Back to Work

The Sheridan Inn had never been busier, with a steady stream of ladies attending to Jakob and making a fuss over him. Henry Clayton chuckled, as he related the story of the parade of ladies visiting Jakob. Besides putting on some weight, Jakob was getting bored spending his days in the hotel room. Zeke was constantly checking on Jakob, to find out when he would be getting his *store-bought* teeth.

"Now don't ya hurry, Doc, but I was jes' wondern' when we could get me some teeth." Jakob was feeling well enough to be out. However, his left arm, though looking better on the outside, was not really completely healed. When the bear had swatted him, he raised his arm to ward off the blow, so it caught the brunt of the blow. The sharp nails had torn open the flesh, injuring the muscles and nerves. Fortunately, the bones were not broken. But the injury left him with a wrist drop from nerve damage. Doc Kelly told him it would take a long time for the muscles and nerves to heal, that is, if they would heal.

Jakob took a piece of wood and shaped it for a splint to support the wrist, then wrapped it with a bandage. But Doc Kelly told him to take it off and massage and exercise and work it as best as he could, to keep the muscles from shrinking. Jakob would religiously take it off and try to exercise it. It still hurt a great deal to use it, and the more he would try, the more it hurt. It was difficult for him to work. Most everything he did required the use of both hands. Liz, the school teacher, would come by and help him with his exercising after school, and he did feel there was some improvement although his fingers were still numb. Jakob was very much aware of the possibilities of permanent injury, but was determined to overcome his present disability. The time had come for him to carry on. He closed the door to his room and went down to the lobby. Henry Clayton, the hotel manager was the first to greet him.

"Hey, Doc. Glad to see you up and about. Are you going back to work?"

"This is the day, Henry. I got to start paying my bills again."

"Not to worry, Doc. I know you're good for it." Just as soon as he went out, a crowd of the townspeople gathered around him. There were all kinds of greetings as he walked over to Doc Kelly's and his own office. Doc Kelly's office was filled with people, so he went into his own office. He looked around at his dust-covered equipment. It had been a couple months since he left on that ill-fated hunting trip. He started dusting and cleaning up when the door opened and one of the boys from the Cowboy Saloon walked in.

"Boy, am I glad to see ya back. This tooth, uh, back up here has been killin' me. Up here, Doc, kin you see the one?" As Pete put his head way back, with his mouth wide open, he pointed to a shell of a tooth. "It's been given me fits for the last couple weeks, Doc. Kin you git it out? I couldn't even sleep last night." Jakob wanted to get back to work, but this was a little too fast for him. Pete got into the chair and opened his mouth wide.

"You see it, Doc? You know which one, don't ya?" Jakob could see it and it was really rotten. But, could he take it out? Was he ready? With the splint on his arm, he could not use his left hand at all. But Pete was really in pain, so he had to help him out somehow.

Jakob reached for a bottle of whiskey and gave him a couple slugs. "You just sit there while I get a couple guys to help me." He didn't have to look too far; there were a couple cowboys looking into his office window.

"You guys. Give me a hand. I have to take out a tooth for Pete." They walked in and laughed.

"We can handle him, Doc." Jakob had his forceps ready and then realized he had the splint on, and couldn't use his left hand to pull back Pete's cheek. He put down the forceps and took off the bandage and splint. His wrist dropped and he could barely raise it. He realized he had little control of his left hand. *I've got to do this,* he thought. He then hooked his fingers into Pete's mouth to hold it open and with the other hand, placed the forceps on the tooth.

"Keep it open, Pete, and hold still." He started to remove the offending tooth, squeezing as hard as he could. Pete let out a yell as the tooth started to come out. The two guys holding him down strained with the struggling Pete. "Well, there it is," he said. Jakob looked over the tooth to make sure he had it all, and breathed a sign of relief to find it all there. Pete was still groaning as he bit down on a chunk of gauze.

"Gall darn, Doc, dat sure hurt."

The two guys, laughing said, " Come on Pete, let's go down to Ginger's place. That'll fix ya up."

Pete reached down in his pocket and handed Jakob a dollar bill. "Thanks, Doc, I'm startin' ta feel better already."

"Keep the pack in for another hour, Pete, and no spitting. Understand?" They left the office laughing and cussing. The people waiting for Doc Kelly were laughing.

Jakob started cleaning up the mess. Then he began to fully realize it was going to be very difficult for him to work with the injured arm. But, he was just going to have to do the best he could. Just then, Doc Kelly came in.

"That sure was some commotion in here. You scared away half my patients with all that yelling." Jakob laughed and became serious.

"You know, Kelly, I'm worried. Taking out the tooth was a real challenge. I guess I never realized how much I needed both my hands. I don't know what I would have done if the tooth had broken and I had to take out the roots separately."

"Jake, you can and will do it, but it won't be easy. Buy you one over at the Lucky Lady when you're finished cleaning up here. Just give me a holler." Doc Kelly went back to his office while Jakob finished cleaning up after the surgery. His thoughts laid heavy on the handicap he now had.

He stopped by Doc Kelly's and the two went to Andy Meeks' place. The stage had just come in, and Hank Murphy gave them a wave. The mail was in and they both had letters. Jakob had one from his mother, and all of a sudden he started to feel sheepish. He hadn't written home since the accident. *I bet I'll catch hell from Mother for not writing,* he thought. *I guess I should have written.* He read her letter as they slowly walked.

Dear Jakob:

    We haven't heard from you in two months. You know how I worry about you. You must be more attentive to your father and me. We are all well here. Your father is very busy. He could sure use your help. I don't know why you had to go so far away. Father has been elected to the Lodge vice presidency and that will take a lot of his time. I really wish you would come back here to help him. You could certainly make a great deal of money here and live the life of a professional man. Oh, yes, I met Mrs. O'Malley the other day at the church social. She was telling me Alice has broken up with that Freddy Schultz. I thought they were engaged but I guess Alice was unhappy with their engagement; something about his card playing and running around with his boyfriends. She kind of hinted maybe Alice would like to get together with you. She is such a nice girl and comes from a good church going family. She would make a good wife. Maybe I should give her your address so she could write to you. Not much else new, except that Aunt Maude had one of her spells the other day. Don't forget to write because we miss you and worry about you.

Your loving Mother

Jakob laughed. "Kelly, you know my mother still can't understand I like it here in Sheridan. She wants me to take up with my old girl friend Alice O'Malley. Nice gal but I don't think she could handle Sheridan."

"Jake, what about that Liz gal? You know, the school teacher. She spent a lot of time looking after you when you were recovering."

"Well, I still have a lot of recovering to do. You know, money."

"You still going to move your office to the new building you were talking about? I'm not trying to push you out, but I could use the space. It sounded like you would have a nice place there and I know you need more room."

"Yes, I'm sure it's ready, because Mr. Richardson stopped by when I was laid up and told me I could have it whenever I wanted to move in. So for now, I really don't have time for any ladies." They pushed open the doors to the Lucky Lady and made their way to the bar. Andy Meeks had a big smile on his face, as he brought over a bottle of whiskey and placed a couple glasses in front of them.

"Good to see you Docs again. How's this for starters?" They clinked their glasses and laughed.

Chapter 5

The New Office

This was moving day for Jakob. He was anxious to start work in his new office at 6th and Main next to the new Bank of Commerce. He enlisted the help of a couple of the boys from the Lucky Lady Saloon to help him move into the office. There wasn't too much for him to move from his small office except for the old barber chair, his various pieces of equipment and the foot-powered drill, some benches and other pieces of laboratory equipment.

Jakob was still recovering from his run-in with the grizzly. It seemed like everything was healed over, but periodically the skin on his forearm would get red and would swell, forming an abscess which would open and drain. Sometimes, it would hurt terribly and he could hardly move his arm. He had a difficult time taking care of patients. He wore his splint most of the time because the hand would drop at the wrist. Although weak, he could now move his fingers and control them. At first, he had really worried he would lose the use of his arm but Doc Kelly had faith it would heal and he would get full use of it again.

"Use that arm and exercise it, or you'll lose it," he would say. The arm looked terrible with the large scars that had developed, so he kept it covered with the sleeve of his shirt. The bear's claws left a track of scars when it tore into his arm. He placed hot and cold packs on it and massaged it regularly, as well as exercising it. Liz, who became more than just a friend, attended to him with concern. Since the bear attack, they saw a lot of each other and she would help him with this self-induced therapy.

The new office was coming along quite well. The elk horns adorned one wall and the bear skin and head occupied another wall. They were grim reminders of his ill-fated hunting trip. Patients who came in for treatment always brought up the story of the bear attack. Sometimes Jakob thought about taking down the "gol dern bear." It had too many bad memories. But, it became a talking point and distracted some of the patients from their own problems. As much as Jakob wanted to work, he sometimes found it almost impossible because of his disability. He put off as many people as he could, but occasionally there was a patient he saw suffering and he would do the best he could to help. Old Zeke was in several times a week hoping to get his store-bought teeth. He became somewhat of a pest to Jakob, and he was anxious to take care of Zeke and get him out of his hair. But limited movement of his left arm made it impossible to do a lot of things.

It seemed little by little, Jakob noticed improvement and more strength in his left arm. He found he could raise his wrist and hold it up a while, so he made himself a new splint that allowed him more movement in his healing arm. He found ways to make do, and his fingers now allowed him to grip things. The numbness lessened. Jakob was finally on his way and felt soon he would be able to use his left arm and hand to do most of the intricate work of a dentist.

Zeke got tired of coming to see him to check on the progress of Jakob's recovery. He would just look sorrowfully at Jakob through the window. Jakob felt he was finally ready to start making his dentures and one day motioned for him to come into the office. Zeke flew in with his big toothless grin on his face.

"I think I can do the job now, Zeke, but you will have to be patient with me. I'm still having trouble with my left arm."

"Hell, Doc, I can take it. Remember da day when Big George put his fist in my face?" Jakob laughed as he adjusted that old barber chair for Zeke. He opened his cabinet drawer and pulled out a metal tray.

"Open up, Zeke, and let me try this in your mouth." Zeke opened up and Jakob started to place the tray in his mouth. Zeke grabbed his hand and started to gag, but Jakob was fighting back while also trying to check the size of the tray he would use for the impression.

"Come on, Zeke, I'm just trying this for size. You have to hold still for me."

"Sorry, Doc, I jes thought ya was gunna push da dern thing down my throat." Jakob tried another tray and got a little bit more cooperation. "Hey, Doc, what are you going to do with da thing?"

"I am going to take an impression of your jaw so that I can make teeth to fit in your mouth."

"Will I be able ta eat with dose teeth?"

"Of course. That's why I'm making them for you."

"Goll dern, Doc, I dint know dat. Will I be able ta smile like I used to?"

Jakob now had a bowl with some white powder in it, then added some water and mixed a creamy concoction.

"Zeke, I'm filling this tray with the plaster and will take an impression of your mouth. Now, you have to sit very still. Do you understand? No grabbing of my hand. Do you understand? Hold still now." Jakob put the creamy mix into the tray. "Open now and hold still." Jakob started to put the tray into Zeke's mouth. Just as he put the tray into his mouth, old Zeke tried to grab his hand. Jakob had a headlock on him as he worked to keep the tray steady. Zeke started to gag and retch as Jakob fought to keep the tray in place. After what seemed like an eternity, Jakob loosened the tray and removed it from his mouth.

"Goll, dern, Doc, I dint know ya was gunna put da stuff in my mouth," Zeke said as he spit pieces of the plaster from his mouth. "That stuff is lousy." He flicked pieces of the hardened plaster from his beard and lips. Jakob inspected the impression and was satisfied with it, then placed it on his cabinet.

"That one is good. Now we have to get the lower impression."

"Hey, Doc, come on. Please! Hey, not agin!"

"This one is easier, Zeke. Anyone who can stand up to a bear like you did shouldn't be afraid of having a little impression taken of his mouth."

"Oh, no, Doc. Please don't do it agin. I almost tossed my cookies." They discussed the matter for some time before Jakob tried the lower tray with Zeke's cooperation. He again filled the tray with plaster and put it in place while wrestling Zeke in the old barber chair. Again he removed the tray as quickly as possible, as Zeke let loose with some of his breakfast into a bucket next to the chair.

"Goll dern, Doc! Goll dern, Doc. If I knew ya were goen ta do this ta me, I'd a let that bear have you."

"Now, Zeke, just you wait. When you get the teeth you'll wish you never said that. Why, the girls at the Cowboy Saloon will smile and say nice things to you." Zeke got out of the chair and left in a huff, picking more plaster out of his beard.

Sitting in the waiting room were a couple of his buddies, laughing. "Which one of you guys is next?" They looked at each other.

"You go first, Ham."

"No, you go first, Mike."

"Okay, whichever one decides who comes first let me know: I'll be around." Jakob went back into his operating room and cleaned up the mess made by Zeke. Ham finally poked his head in and decided to come first.

"Hey, Doc, ya aint gonna do that to me are ya? I jes got dis tooth dats been killen me. Yank it out, will ya?" Jakob got his buddy to hold him down and obliged by taking it out. Jakob felt good at his attempt using both his hands taking care of Zeke and Ham.

A week later, Zeke got over being upset over the impression taking and decided to come back for his teeth. After all, it was part of the deal. The hunting trip in exchange for a denture. He was all set to get his new teeth until Jakob told him there was more work to do before they could be made.

"Oh, no! Ya mean day ain't raddy."

"No, Zeke we have to take some measurements and do some other things before they are ready. But, the worst is over." Jakob made bite rims of wax to do the measurements. He carefully placed them in his mouth while explaining what he was doing and reluctantly Zeke cooperated without too much fuss this time. "Next time, Zeke, we will try in the teeth before I finish and deliver them." Zeke left the office muttering and shaking his head.

As he left, Liz arrived and came into the office. She had come by to see Jakob. "I hope I haven't disturbed you. I see you have been busy. How is the arm doing today? Are you able to use it?"

"I'm sure glad to see you, Liz. Yes, I am finally able to do more than just one-armed dentistry. I guess I never realized how important it was to have two arms to do my work."

"School is recessed for lunch so I thought I'd have lunch with you. I brought you a chicken sandwich and a piece of cake for dessert. I made the cake last night." Jakob spent a lot of time with Liz since the accident. She helped nurse him back to health. Liz was just a little younger than Jakob and had gone to Normal College in Iowa to get her teaching certificate. Her beautiful brown eyes flashed as she told him about her students and how they learned their lessons. Her smile was warm and her cheeks dimpled. She loved her work and you could tell she greatly admired Jakob. Even though, there was no intimate contact with Jakob, you could see she had strong feelings for him. Finishing the meal, she gathered up her lunch basket, tablecloth and leftovers.

"Time to get back to my little darlings. Teacher can't be late." And off she scurried to the schoolhouse. Jakob followed her to the office door smiling, watching her as she hurried along. He went back to his laboratory to continue working on Zeke's teeth when he heard some commotion in the waiting room, only to see the room filled with Indians. It was a rarity to have Indians come to see him, and when one came, the whole family usually came along. When Jakob came out, his presence was greeted with silence.

"Well, now, what can I do for you folks?" The silence soon ended and they began to jabber with one another. Finally a squaw came forward and started to talk, but Jakob didn't understand what she said. He tried a little sign language but they didn't seem to understand. Finally, they pushed a skinny boy to the front of the group. He must have been 16 or maybe 17 years old; it's hard to tell an Indian's age. Jakob now knew why they were there. The boy's face was swollen, bloody and had lacerations that showed the need for emergency treatment. He looked like he was kicked by a horse; in reality, he was. At least, that's what the Indians indicated. Jakob helped him into a chair and tenderly touched him. He took a pan and poured some water into it and placed a towel in the water. Carefully wiping the blood and mud from the face he cleaned the wounds. The boy winced at the pain but did not move. There were deep cuts that bled profusely. They would have to be stitched. His mouth was also bleeding. The front teeth were broken off, and as he examined the other teeth he noted the lower jaw might be broken. What to do first? He pondered the possibility of a broken jaw. It seemed the movement was minimal. *Should he attempt to wire it or just immobilize it and hope it would heal?* The fractured teeth showed nerves. They would have to be removed first. He enlisted a couple of the men and instructed them to support the boy. Quickly he moved the forceps from one tooth to the next and had three roots laid on his table. The boy whimpered but sat still. The family looked on grimly as Jakob tended to the boy. He then instructed the boy to close over a piece of bandage to stop the bleeding. Next came the sewing of the lacerations on his face. He closed the wounds quickly. The boy winced in pain as he put the suture needle through the skin but he made no moves. His family looked on grimly as he did his work.

Finished, Jakob smiled at his patient and told him he was a brave man. He took some white powder and dissolved it in water and had him drink it. With sign language and pidgin English he gave the mother instructions for his care. Finally, he took a bandage and wrapped it around his head to keep his mouth closed and keep his teeth in alignment, and told them not to remove it until he came back the next day. The Indians grunted and shook their heads leading the boy off.

While all this was happening a crowd stood outside Jakob's office. Some came into the office as the Indians left to find out what had happened. Jakob answered their questions as he cleaned up the office. A couple of them said, "You shouldn't have done anything for the savage." Others were sympathetic to the boy's plight.

When the crowd had left, Jakob went back to his operating room and sat in the chair thinking about what he had done. He worried he may not have done enough for the boy. The possible fractured jaw should have been treated in a hospital, but this wasn't Chicago or Milwaukee. *What if it does not heal? He is young and there was no displacement. Maybe it isn't fractured. I'll see him tomorrow.* His thoughts were interrupted by a big lout who came in with a toothache, and his day continued.

The day ended with more patients and more problems. Jakob left his office as the sun was going down. Thinking about the day and the Indians, he suddenly realized they did not pay for his service. *Oh well. I just hope the kid will be all right* he thought. He was exhausted. *Think I'll stop by the Lucky Lady for a bracer before dinner.* He walked through the swinging doors into the noise and ruckus, and up to the bar. Harry was tending bar today.

"Hi, Doc. Tough day? I got just what you need," Harry said, and poured him a whiskey. Jakob took it down and laid the money on the bar. "Stoppin' back for some cards tonight, Doc?"

"I don't think so, Harry. I have lots of catching up to do. My vacation is over and I have plenty of work ahead of me."

Jakob was in his office bright and early the next day. He had to finish Zeke's dentures, so he spent all the time he could preparing the teeth for the try-in of the denture. The Indians came back later in the day. The injured boy looked better and they were happier. Jakob felt his swollen jaw and felt it was not broken and it would be all right. The family brought with them a ceremonial buckskin woman's dress. Real fancy. Jakob accepted it but wondered what he would ever do with it. He was satisfied the boy was improving after his serious accident.

Zeke came back the next day to see if he could have his denture. Jakob told him it was not ready to be tried in, and asked him to come back in a couple days.

The day arrived and they looked and fit good, so Jakob handed Zeke a *lookin' glass* and Zeke just couldn't stop grinning. He saw for the first time his new look. Zeke was amazed. His appearance was that of a younger man and he was anxious to show off his new look to his friends. He left sadly when he was told they weren't "rady" for him to take home. He left the office shaking his head and mumbling about not understanding why he couldn't take them with him. Jakob had to finish the setup denture made of wax, which had to be converted into a vulcanite material that would withstand the rigors of chewing food. But Zeke still couldn't understand.

When the day finally came Zeke was waiting anxiously for his teeth. He came in squeaky clean, having spent two bits for a bath at the Cowboy Saloon. Jakob placed the dentures in his mouth and adjusted them as best he could. Zeke couldn't wait to see them and Jake gave him the *lookin' glass*. Zeke was in his greatest glory and couldn't wait to go back to the Cowboy Saloon and show all his friends the new Zeke. Jakob, at last had repaid Zeke for the ill-fated hunting trip. After Zeke left, Jakob pulled up the sleeve of his left arm and viewed the still-bright-red scars on his arm and wondered if the trip was worth the high price he paid for it. He was reminded again and again each time Zeke came in to complain about his teeth, until he finally got used to using them. Zeke's friends at the Cowboy Saloon soon got tired of him talking about his teeth as he took them in and out to show them off, but everyone thought Zeke "shore" looked a lot better.

Chapter 6

The Traveling Dentist

Margaret Miller was a woman who would not be deterred. In her letters to Jakob she would always include something about Alice O'Malley. To her, there was always a glimmer of hope Jakob would return to Milwaukee and restore his romantic relationship with Alice. She would keep him informed about Alice and all her accomplishments. In the latest letter Margaret informed Jakob about Alice taking singing lessons, and said she was going to have a concert for the O'Malleys' friends and associates. The O'Malleys were part of the high society in Milwaukee and had been good friends of the Millers.

She kept thinking it would do Jakob a lot of good to marry into such an influential family and thus bring his family into high society. But Jakob had other plans, even though he had been romantically involved with Alice at one time. She was beautiful, talented and had many fine attributes. But when she chose Freddy Schultz over him, because she didn't want him to go to Wyoming, he also found she was rather shallow and a bit smug in her attitude. No, he did not want to restore a relationship romantically with her. Besides, he really liked Wyoming and Sheridan, and he had been readily accepted by the people there. They were friendly, unpretentious and very kind to him, especially when he was recovering from his adventure with the grizzly. As far as girls were concerned, there were plenty to have a relationship with, but he was not interested. However, now there was Liz, who filled a special spot in his life.

Jakob was a handsome young man, twenty-four, tall, dark haired, athletic, intellectual but not overbearing, with an infectious smile, a hearty laugh and just an all-around pleasing personality. He was kind and had humility and compassion. Everywhere he went he made friends. He wasn't making much money yet, but he had enough to keep himself self-sufficient. Ginger over in the Sheridan Inn had made overtures to Jakob, but they were only good friends. Then there was Marge at the Golden Dome who had tried her charms on him. She used to tend bar there and Jakob occasionally stopped to visit. She was a good listener and they would spend time talking, sometimes long into the night. And there were others who would have liked to have a relationship with him but he wasn't ready.

Liz was kind of special to Jakob, but she was also a very busy woman. As the teacher at the Sheridan Elementary School she was dedicated to her pupils, and they really loved her. The school kept her busy with their lesson work, and of course there were the parents she had to deal with, as well as various school activities. She took her job seriously and the pupils came first in her life, except maybe for Jakob.

Reverend Henderson came to Sheridan about the same time Jakob did. He was fresh out of the seminary and was a dedicated Congregational minister. In fact, Reverend Robert started the First Congregational Church in Sheridan. They started by meeting in the back of the general store, then later had meetings at some of his church members' homes before they built the church. It wasn't a very large church, but the Reverend attracted quite a few people and the building was always being added to. Liz was a churchgoer and even interested Jakob into going to church with her on Sundays. Jakob was a Catholic and found himself lukewarm toward Reverend Henderson and his church, but he felt he should go to church. Reverend Henderson was a single man and he took a special liking to Liz, but she was somewhat oblivious to his presence. The church did have various activities on Sunday and she was always present, with or without Jakob.

The summer was a hot and dry one and fall was approaching. His dental practice kept him quite busy but then there were times when he felt he could have been busier. He tried to fill those times with fishing and hunting. He anticipated the coming winter as a lean period in his practice. Wyoming winters were bitter cold with a great deal of snow. The ranchers and their hands didn't come into town much during the winter, which meant it would take a very bad toothache before someone would ride into town to see him. Even the townspeople didn't like going out to have their dental work done. Jakob had an idea that kept coming back to him, over and over, about expanding his practice to some of the surrounding towns. He noted some of his patients would come to see him from as far as Sundance or Buffalo, or Ranchester; maybe he could take his equipment with him and visit some of those communities. If they wouldn't come to him he would go to them. As long as he had some time on his hands, he would try doing this before the winter set in.

Jakob spent a lot of his time in Sheridan, so he didn't really need any transportation; he just did a lot of walking. When he needed a horse or rig, he would go down to the Sheridan Livery stable and rent a rig. Old Wilbur Riggs would get something together for him and off he would go. When he returned the rig he would square up with Wilbur. In fact, Wilbur still owed him money for the dental work he had done for him. Only problem was, Wilbur would always remind him about the molar he put a crown on.

"Doc, that dang thing still hurts. Especially when I get something cold on it. Ya wanta take a look Doc? Will it always hurt that way?"

"It may take a while, Wilbur, but it will stop hurting eventually. Just be patient." Later, Jakob found out from one of his other patients that Wilbur went out of his way to show off his gold crown, and told him the tooth never felt better.

Jakob decided to go to Buffalo, Wyoming, for his first traveling trip. He packed his equipment in a couple trunks and started out early. Buffalo was about forty miles south of Sheridan. There was a bit of rivalry between Sheridan and Buffalo from way back. It seems Sheridan became a commercial and railroad center and rather prosperous. However, Buffalo was the county seat of Johnson County. The wagon-train traffic passed through Buffalo but it sort of got left behind commercially when the railroad came into Sheridan; it jump-started Sheridan's growth and there became a rivalry between them.

It was a crisp autumn day with the sun shining brightly when Jakob left for Buffalo. Approaching Buffalo late in the afternoon, he saw the trading stores that displayed their goods on barrels and on pine counters, or clothes lines stretched above the counters along Main Street. There were a lot of saloons along Main Street but only one hotel—a giant extended log cabin. The Occidental Hotel's clerk was also the bartender. In the same large room with the office and bar was a gambling house. Jakob checked into the not so luxurious hotel. While he was checking in, he told the clerk-bartender the purpose of his visit. The clerk-bartender led him over to the bar and put a bottle of whiskey and glass in front of him.

"Glad to meet ya, Doc. I'm Harold Peters, at your service. We're sure happy to see you. Heard you were a damn good tooth carpenter from some of the folks who went over to Sheridan. You gonna set up here? We sure can use a dentist." Jakob explained he was over for just a short time but that he would probably be coming over regularly in the future. He wanted to know where he could set up. "I got a room where you can set up next door. We gonna have to move some supplies out but it'll make ya a good place fir you to fix teeth. When do you wanna start?" Jakob told him he could start the next day if he could get it ready for him. He yelled to a big guy over at the faro table to come over.

"Howard, this here is Doc Miller, the dentist from Sheridan, who wants to fix teeth here. I told him he could use the storehouse next door."

"Good idea Harold. Shore glad to meet ya, Doc. We shore can use a dentist here. I kin have the place rady for ya the day after tommara. Ya know, I am shore glad you're here. I got me a hole in this here back tooth that hurts whenever I eat. Think you kin fix it?" Jakob assured Howard he could take care of him, and told him he would be his first patient. He brought out a bunch of fliers he had printed back in Sheridan. All he had to do was to write in the place where the office would be. He asked if he could put them up. Howard assured him he could post them wherever he wanted.

"No problem Doc." Howard grabbed him by the arm and dragged him into the gambling area, got up on a chair and yelled for everyone to shut up because he had an announcement to make. The room got quiet. He grabbed Jakob's arm and held it up. "This here is Doc Miller. He comed here from Sheridan to fix teeth. Office is gonna be next door. We shore lucky ta have him." The room broke into a loud applause with people coming forward and introducing themselves, slapping him on the back and telling him, "We'll be in to see ya, Doc." And then, as fast as the room had quieted down, it was back to business as usual with loud talk and the piano playing.

Jakob asked a couple of the guys at the bar to help put the equipment in his room and took his rig to the livery stable for storage. It was a long day for Jakob and he was ready for dinner. He stopped first at the bar for a drink, then found a table in the dining room and was faced by the waitress.

"What ya want?" Before he could answer, "How bout a steak an taters?" she said. "It's all we got today."

"Then, I guess that's what I'll have," he meekly answered. His dinner was interrupted by people from the gambling room stopping by to meet him and tell him they would be in to see him. Jakob's fliers would let the citizenry know where his office would be so the people there would know where he was available and something about his credentials. He had these signs printed.

Dr. Jakob Miller, D.D.S.
Graduate of the Chicago College of Dental
Surgery, Chicago Post Graduate School, Licensee of the States of Wisconsin, Illinois, Montana and Wyoming.
Prepared to do all Your
DENTAL WORK
By the latest and most approved Scientific Methods.
Crown and Bridgework my Specialty
Testimonials available for your inspection and Recommendations for my work from satisfied patients Consultation and Examination Free
Office Next to Occidental Hotel

He spent the next morning going around meeting people, and posting his signs in as many places as were available. He was generally well accepted by most of the townspeople. A few of his former patients came forward and told him they had made the trip to Sheridan just to see him. Some asked him why he hadn't come over sooner so they wouldn't have had to make the long trip to Sheridan. Jakob hadn't decided how long he would stay but he thought he would stay as long as there was work for him to do.

He checked on the office space prepared for him. There was only one room and it was pretty plain.

The back part of it still had some barrels and crates. It was big enough for the barber chair he managed to find at the Buffalo Barber Shop. He promised Harley, the barber, he would fix a couple teeth for him in trade. There wasn't much room for the trunks he had brought over with the equipment so he moved a couple of the boxes and used a barrel to put his instruments on. The chair from the town barber was in rough shape. It was broken and had been sitting in the shed behind his shop for a long time. It didn't pump up, which made it somewhat inconvenient to work with, but it was a chair he could use. Jakob was now all set to work.

A few people stopped by but Jakob asked them to return the next day. He had put in a hard day getting his office ready and it was already getting dark. It was time to eat supper. Shutting the door to the office he walked to the hotel entrance. The place was full of people. Noise and piano playing greeted him as he opened the door. He was glad the noise was muffled by the heavy log wall between his office and the bar and gambling casino. Harold Peters welcomed Jakob as he walked in, as well as a few other people he had met before. The word was out that a dentist was in town.

Jakob realized, his clothes already made him different from the rest of the crowd. He was a professional man and so he dressed the part, with his black derby, winged collar shirt, black tie, and the black and white checkered coat. But he got to wondering whether he should change his dress to fit in with the people there. He found the general store and bought himself some Levi's and a denim shirt. There was a hat and boot store just down Main Street where he also bought a fine pair of boots and a Stetson. Now he looked just like the rest of the people. One of the first patients who came in remarked he looked better now that he didn't dress like a city slicker.

The restaurant was situated in one end of the large room, across from the bar. The menu in the restaurant was still limited: the same tough steak and fried potatoes, hot black coffee and hard bread, with a piece of pie for dessert. The lady who waited tables was a matronly woman who was efficient enough, but definitely on the gruff side. The walls of the restaurant were painted blue with streaks made by water that leaked in. There were always a few townspeople occupying some of the tables. Occasionally, a staggering gambler ambled in and out. The noise was deafening at times.

With his dinner finished Jakob started to leave, when one of the pretty ladies with a short skirt motioned for him to sit near her at the bar. Not wanting to be too aloof, he took her up on it. He had a drink with her but was not interested in purchasing any commodities she offered him. With that, she got up and reminded Jakob she was available any time he wanted to have an enjoyable evening.

The next weeks proved to be very profitable for Jakob, as he was busy doing the dental work for the people of Buffalo. He made many friends among his patients there. They wanted him to stay and set up a permanent practice, but Jakob felt Sheridan was the place to live. Amy, who had previously solicited his interest, would often stop by and attempt to develop a closer relationship with Jakob, but eventually realized he was not interested in her wares. Dentistry was his business and the only business he was interested in.

He looked at the calendar one day and realized it was late November; it was time for him to leave Buffalo. He had done a lot of work here, more than he had anticipated. It was definitely worthwhile for him to come but he probably stayed too long. Winter had arrived.

Chapter 7

Sheridan Winter

Jakob was bundled with buffalo skins as the horse plodded through the snowdrifts. The winds drove the snow into a fury. He had waited too long to return to Sheridan. His trip to Buffalo brought him more business than he anticipated, and he extended his stay until December 1st. Snow was already on the ground in Buffalo, and rather than returning alone using the rig he had rented in Sheridan, he decided to leave the rig, and hire the stage-driver and sleigh to take him back to Sheridan. The stagecoach wouldn't be running for some time and he wanted to get back before the heaviest snows started; however, he miscalculated, and he left on the day of a heavy snow storm.

Walter Jenkins was the stage driver who agreed to take a load of mail from Buffalo, along with Jakob, back to Sheridan. However, he decided to use the sleigh instead of the stagecoach. The first few hours on the trail were tolerable, but the further they went, the more difficult it was to travel. The snow soon accumulated into windblown drifts making travel very slow. Jakob had a fur coat, hat and boots, plus the buffalo skins piled on and he was still cold to the bone. They were on the trail for eight hours before they made the first stagecoach stop: a lonely cabin with shelter for the horses and a bed for the night.

Jakob stumbled out of the sleigh, walked through the drifts and entered the smoky cabin. The warmth of the fire in the big fireplace started to take the chill out of his bones. He removed his furs and approached the hearth. Bill and Anne Franklin manned the station and poured Jakob a steaming hot coffee. Walter had taken care of the horses and came into the cabin with a blast of snow and cold. Jakob's face was sore from the wind and cold. His feet and hands started to throb. He faced the fire, as Walter and Bill talked about the storm. Anne had a pot of stew in the fireplace. She filled plates with the steaming food. They sat by the table and ate heartily. Bill and Walter spoke incessantly. Bill was anxious to talk. It had been some days since anyone had come by and he craved any human contact.

"What the hell are you doing on the trail in this weather?" he asked Jakob. Jakob told them he wanted to return to Sheridan before the winter closed in on Sheridan. "Well," said Bill, "it's closing in right now." They all laughed but Jakob was not exactly happy. His face and hands were still paining him from the cold. They talked well into the night, with the wind howling on the outside of the cabin. The warmth of the cabin and time made them drowsy and soon they each dropped off to sleep.

Light filtered through the frozen windows and Jakob was awakened by movement of the others inside the cabin. Anne already had a pot of steaming coffee on the table as the others moved around. The wind outside seemed to subside during the night. Walter went out to the barn to check on the horses. After feeding them, he returned to the cabin. A rush of cold air came in as he opened the door.

"All's well. The horses did okay during the night. It might be good to get an early start. We still have a long way to go before we make Sheridan. It's not snowing now but I don't know how the trail is. There's a lot of snow out there." Anne had bacon and eggs on the table and they gorged themselves; it might be a long time before they would eat again. Walter went back to the barn to get the sleigh hitched and ready to leave. Jakob put on his boots and furs, then he and Walter paid their keep and out into the cold they went. The wind was down but it was bitter cold. The sky was gray with just a faint show of sun coming up over the hills. Jakob was covered with the buffalo blankets, so only his eyes showed. The horses plodded along the trail with steam coming from their nostrils. The snow wasn't too deep along the trail so they moved right along, until they came to a dip in the trail where the snow had drifted in. When the drifts were too deep, they got out of the sleigh and walked alongside the horses to prod them on. They made good time and the sun was now up, but it didn't do much good as far as warming the travelers. The Bighorn Mountains loomed snow-covered, to the west. They passed a lone Indian village but no activity was seen, so they continued onward with hope they would make Sheridan before nightfall. They made short stops to rest the horses in sheltered areas. Toward the latter part of the afternoon, the wind picked up a little and blew snow into their faces.

The sun was going down when they first saw cabins with trails of smoke in the distance. As they drew closer to Sheridan, they heard the faint sound of a train. They entered the nearly deserted snow-covered Main Street just as it grew dark. Lights filtered out the windows, as the sleigh stopped in front of the Sheridan Inn. Stiff and sore and frozen, Jakob trudged into the Sheridan Inn.

Henry Clayton was at the desk. "Doc, is that you? Wher'en the hell have you been? We gave you up for lost. I didn't think you was ever coming back. Welcome home, I still got your room here." He pulled out a glass and a bottle of whiskey from under the counter and poured a half-frozen Jakob a glass of whiskey. "Here you are Doc. This will help you to start getting warmed up."

Before even saying anything, Jakob took a swig of the stuff, sighed and then began to tell Henry his story. As he momentarily stopped, Walter blew in. He had taken the sleigh and horses to the livery. Henry took out another glass, filled it and offered it to Walter. The two related the tale of their trip from Buffalo and the three all but finished the bottle. Their innards were warmed, but their faces, arms and feet were still frozen. There was no one in the restaurant and Henry left to tell the cook to make dinner for the two frozen travelers. When he returned he gave them room keys. Walter had brought the baggage into the hotel, which included Jakob's dental tools. The three of them took the items into the rooms. Walter also had the mail bag he would deliver the next day to the post office. Jakob's room seemed like it was only a shade warmer than the outside. He turned the heat up, but it would be a while before the room would be warm. They left their boots and furs on until the room began to warm, then went downstairs to eat.

While sitting in the dining room, Lukas, the cook, brought in a pot of hot coffee and some warmed bread he had just made. People started to come into the dining room. The word was out that Jakob had returned. All wanted to know where he had been. There was a general merriment in the dining room as the room filled with people who started ordering dinners.

"Glad to see you back, Doc," "Where you been Doc?" "I thought you were just going away for a few weeks, Doc." There was a party in the making, and more people from the saloon came in when they found out Jakob had returned. Lukas really outdid himself with a sumptuous meal for Jakob and Walter. The partying lasted well into the night. Several people told Jakob they were in need of his services and would be coming in to see him.

It had been a long day. The cold trip left Jakob exhausted. His skin felt like it had been burned and he wondered if he hadn't suffered some frostbite in his toes. The drinking had left him with a glow on, but Jakob decided to call it a day. He stumbled down the hall and opened the door to his room. The room had warmed some, but it was still chilly. He removed his clothes and buried himself in the feather-bed and soon fell fast asleep.

He opened his eyes; light filtered into his room. The room still seemed cold but tolerable. His head was pounding from the results of the partying. It was hard for him to convince himself to get up, but he knew he had to do it. He threw off the covers and quickly dressed, pulling on his heavy woolens. There was pounding on the door and he opened it to find Walter, the driver.

"I was jist wondering when you would be getting up?"

"You don't have to wonder, Walter, I'm up."

Jakob finished dressing, then met Walter in the dining room for coffee. The dining room was still disheveled from the party the night before, but Lukas had a pot of coffee on the table. Soon there were the bacon, eggs, and potatoes to complete the breakfast.

"There's nothing like Lukas' cooking," Jakob related. "The food in the Occidental Hotel had a lot to be desired and the waitresses were downright miserable." Walter was talking about returning to Buffalo after he delivered the mail, maybe the next day. Jakob asked if he would help him move his equipment over to his office on Main Street first, and Walter agreed. He brought the team and sleigh over to the hotel and they soon moved his equipment over to the office.

The snow had drifted across the door and it was closed and stuck. Jakob borrowed a shovel from the bank and finally got the door open. It was cold and damp in the office and he had to start a fire in the stove. Emptying the trunks and putting things back where they belonged took him the rest of the morning. It was nearly time for lunch when he thought about Liz. Maybe he would stop by the school and see if he could have lunch with her.

I haven't seen her for quite a while, he thought, as he trudged through the snow over to the schoolhouse. The steps were covered with snow. *That's strange, and the school door is locked.* So down the stairs he went, and walked over to Mrs. Howard's rooming house.

Jakob knocked on Mrs. Howard's door and was greeted by her. "Jakob, how nice to see you. Come in out of that cold."

"Is Liz here? I stopped at the school and it's closed."

"Why Liz had left for a visit to her home in Iowa, just the day before yesterday, Jakob." Jakob was visibly surprised and disappointed. He chatted with Mrs. Howard and she offered him lunch. She was obviously happy to see Jakob, but he was disappointed not to see Liz. Mrs. Howard put out a nice lunch for Jakob and assured him Liz would be back after the holidays. Jakob thanked her for the lunch and then went back to his office. The place was still cold but he put his instruments into their cabinets, straightened things, and dusted. He was now all set to see patients and decided to stop and see Doc Kelly. Kelly seemed glad to see him and chastised him for staying away so long.

"You know, kid, money isn't everything. You're lucky you made it back. You could have been frozen stiff in a drift, and they wouldn't dig you out till spring. This should learn you a lesson—don't mess around with Wyoming snows." Jakob felt a little stupid for having miscalculated the weather. Doc Kelly was right: he had no business waiting so long before he came back. Doc Kelly was just sitting around in his office, so Jakob offered to buy him a drink at the Lucky Lady. Kelly looked sternly at him.

"Now that's the smartest thing you could do, instead of messing around in the snow. Let's go, Kid." Doc put on his buffalo coat and boots and they trudged down to the Lucky Lady. You would think the place would be almost empty in that kind of weather, but tables were mostly filled and they had to push their way to the bar.

"Doc, I heard you got back." Andy Meeks put glasses in front of the two and filled them. "What in blue blazes did you do, waiting this long to come back from Buffalo? Those gals over there better'n ours? Or was it the big bucks you were making which kept you there? Don't you know you got friends here? I can't understand why anyone would want to go to Buffalo." Laughing, he said, "Why just the other day, Ginger was asking about when you were coming back from Buffalo." Some of the other guys were joining in on the roast; Jakob was somewhat embarrassed but took the ribbing in good sport.

The rest of the afternoon was spent in bringing Jakob up to date on the news in Sheridan. It was cold and snowy outside but it sure was warm in the Lucky Lady. Doc Kelly got himself into a card game and Jakob went off to the hotel. Jakob saw Walter and settled up with him. Walter delivered and picked up some mail at the post office for his return to Buffalo the next day.

In spite of the weather, during the next few weeks he was busy with patients. The cold weather and snow didn't stop many patients who came to see him, since he had been gone for the last several months. He also spent time with some of his friends and went to the Lucky Lady for cards and refreshments.

Christmas was approaching and there were festivities in town he was invited to attend. There were Christmas decorations put up around town, and people were going into stores and carrying out packages. Kids coming into his office were excited about the special day. He had received a few Christmas cards and, of course, a letter from his mother. Jakob also received some packages from Milwaukee. But Christmas is a time for families to get together and Jakob's family was a long way from Sheridan.

On Christmas Eve, Jakob was in his room at the Sheridan Inn. He hadn't been invited to anyone's house for dinner and a feeling of melancholy overcame him. He went down to the dining room and Lukas had roast goose on the menu. Lukas came into the dining room and sat down with Jakob to chat for a while. But they were pretty busy, so he went back into the kitchen and Jakob was sitting alone again.

After finishing dinner, he began to think about his family back in Milwaukee and he remembered the festivities of the holiday there. The home was always decorated with garlands and flowers. A large Christmas tree was in the living room, with its ornaments and candles and all the gifts piled beneath. There was warmth from the hearth, with the logs burning brightly. He remembered how he could smell the evergreen when he stood next to it, and hear the laughter of children running through the house. The dining room table was adorned with the finest silverware and his mother's special china. Behind the door from the dining room, in the warm kitchen, he could see his mother and her sister preparing the food which soon would be served. Turkey just out of the oven, browned and fragrant, and sweet potatoes covered with brown sugar and butter were now ready for the table. His thoughts took him back to the library with his father's large red leather chair. His dad standing next to it talking with his brother-in-law with a cigar in one hand and a glass of eggnog in the other, and laughing. On the other side of the room were the Kramers. The doorbell just rang. It was Grandmother and Grandfather Miller. They had just come in and as he looked around the house from room to room he realized he was not there.

There was a long moment of silence in his thoughts and he was lonesome and overcome emotionally. He was lonesome, for his family and friends in Milwaukee. And then there was Liz. She came into his thoughts and he could see her beautiful, serious, and smiling face and he felt more than ever alone. *Oh, why isn't she here with me?* He had been seeing a great deal of her before he left for Buffalo. She had become something special to him, although he did take her for granted. Liz was just there, whenever he wanted her. The realization came to him that she had become important in his life. He also realized he had not heard from her since he left for Buffalo. *But then, how could she get in touch with me? She didn't have a mailing address from me,* and he realized he hadn't written to her. *Well, I was real busy. But, I guess it's my own fault. I should have written her.* The more he thought about Liz, the more he found himself missing her. The thought of her not coming back until January 1st really bothered him. What would he do? And then, suddenly, the realization came to him: Liz was more than a friend and his feelings were really strong. *I miss her. I really miss her. I guess… I guess maybe…. I wonder, could I? Do I love her?* He sat silent thinking about Liz and then decided to go into the bar. Bill, who regularly tended bar, greeted him.

"What will it be, Doc?"

"You know, I've been thinking about home, in Milwaukee. After dinner, we used to sit down and have a glass of brandy. Do you have any brandy back there behind the bar?"

"Of course I do. What kind of a bar do you think this is? Ole Bill Cody would sometimes drink brandy after dinner. I got a good French brandy I can give you." He took a large snifter and poured in a generous amount. "Here you are, Doc, just like in Milwaukee."

Jakob smelled the aromatic spirits and slowly tasted it. "Very good, but we're not in Milwaukee." He sat on the stool silently reminiscing about his days in Milwaukee and sipping brandy. People came and went from the ornate Sheridan Inn bar but Jakob sat there sipping brandy. The heat and smell from the blazing fireplace set the stage, as Jakob relived his life in Milwaukee. The room had cleared, leaving Jakob as the last one to leave. He picked up his coat and headed for the door.

"Merry Christmas, Doc," said the bartender.

"Merry Christmas, Bill."

Chapter 8

Christmas In Sheridan

Christmas Day

Jakob had been invited to the Findleys' to spend the day's festivities with them and their many friends, and to enjoy a sumptuous dinner. Ella Findley was a fine cook and Elmer, the general store owner, was known to put out a big spread. Jakob was happy to have been invited, and his lonesome feelings were somewhat allayed. He had been invited before to other parties at the Findleys', and they were always great.

Christmas was a special day and Jakob felt the need for friends to fill in for his family whom he really missed. He also longed for his special someone, whom he now realized he cared for but would be missing and was constantly on his mind. He had stopped at Mrs. Howard's to find out if she heard from Liz since she left Sheridan.

"She just said she would be back after Christmas, and she also said school would re-open after New Year's Day," said Mrs. Howard.

The thought even passed Jakob's mind: *Maybe Liz might not return.* Jakob began to wonder if maybe she had enough of frontier life. *Perhaps the children weren't paying attention, or maybe the pay wasn't sufficient, or she missed her family and friends. But she told Mrs. Howard she would be back. Liz wouldn't lie. I'm just being foolish*, he thought. *I just have to be patient and she will come back.*

The invitation to the Findleys' on Christmas day was at two. Jakob put on his best suit and covered it with his buffalo-skin coat and boots. It had snowed the night before and the temperatures held to sub-zero degrees. A light snow began in the afternoon as Jakob trod up the steps of Elmer Findley's home. It wasn't a pretentious place but it was one of the bigger homes in Sheridan on Louckes Street. Others had come before him, so he wasn't the first to arrive.

Elmer opened the door with a hearty "Merry Christmas." The house was filled with people. Jakob was no stranger to the jolly group, as he had seen most of them in his office, in church or just around town. His hand was grasped for greetings from the crowd of revelers. There was, however, one stranger he recognized whom he had met only briefly on a couple occasions. His white hair, mustache, and beard were a giveaway. It was William Cody. Elmer brought Jakob over and introduced him to the famous Indian fighter.

"Bill, I don't know if you have met our dentist here in Sheridan, Doc Miller. Doc, this is Colonel Cody, better known as Buffalo Bill."

They shook hands and the Colonel replied, "I certainly do remember meeting Doc Miller some time ago, but it has been a while." They had some small talk and were soon interrupted by an admirer of Bill Cody, and Jakob was left momentarily alone.

The group was having a good time and Elmer even had Harry, the bartender from the Lucky Lady, serving the drinks. The conversations ran from the current cold spell, news from Washington, to even some rumors of Indian problems. There was lots of loud conversation when Ella came out to announce dinner would be served.

The dining table at the Findleys' was a big one, but not nearly big enough for the crowd assembled. Mrs. Findley also had several smaller tables set and the food was served. Jakob was instructed to sit at the big table. There was a constant buzz of conversations. Colonel Cody, of course was the center of most conversation. He was a great storyteller and held the attention of most of the people. The meal was truly grandiose: Turkey, wild foul, elk, venison and even bear meat were on the menu, plus sweet potatoes, vegetables and, of course, pumpkin and mince meat pies. The crowd ate to their hearts' content. Conversation was light and happy as they celebrated the birth of Jesus. After dinner there was the port wine, brandy and cigars.

It had been a long day of conversation, drinking and eating and Jakob felt himself being worn out. To top off the festivities, Christmas carolers came by and sang a variety of carols. In the more quiet moments, Jakob's thoughts always went back to Liz. *Wouldn't it have been great if Liz had been here with me?* The time was getting late and some of the guests started to take leave. Jakob was also ready to go. He said his goodbyes to the hosts, who had put on an unforgettable holiday party, and he even got some kisses from some of the ladies who enjoyed his company. Colonel Cody was still surrounded by a group of his admirers. He was really quite a showman.

Putting on his buffalo coat and boots, Jakob went out into a cold, snowy and windy night. It wasn't too long a walk to the Sheridan Inn, but the deep snow and wind made it difficult. There were sleighs pulled by horses moving up and down the streets and one assisted Jakob. Finally he arrived at the door of the Inn, which was blocked by a small drift he had to shovel before it could be opened. Inside, the big stone fireplace was ablaze and the warmth from it thawed Jakob's frozen face. The Inn was decorated with garlands and ornaments, and a large decorated Christmas tree. It was all very festive. Henry Clayton took a long look at Jakob standing next to the fireplace.

"Kinda cold out there, eh Doc? How was the big party?" Jakob told him about the festivities and the great meal that Ella made.

"Too bad you couldn't be there, Henry."

"Aw, that's okay. I got a full house here and someone had to be at the desk. Was the old windbag Cody there?" He let out a laugh. "Never mind, that's just between you and me. Here, let me pour you something to warm you up." They had a drink together and Jakob, tired from his long day, excused himself and went to his room. The farther he was from the fireplace the colder it got. His room was not too warm, in spite of the hot-water pipes radiating heat. It seemed like they just couldn't warm up the room when the weather got below zero. Jakob left his buffalo coat on. Sitting on the bed he once again began reminiscing of past Christmases and thoughts of Liz came back. In spite of the cold, he hung up his coat, prepared for bed, and crawled under the heavy down covers. He was soon asleep.

He awoke early, with rays of sun shining through the ice-coated window. The room was cold and he just couldn't get himself out of bed, so he just lay there thinking about the party. *I wonder when Liz will be back?* he thought. *I guess I better get out of bed and get going.* While waiting under the covers, he also thought about the day he faced. Going down to breakfast he could hear the clatter of dishes and talking of the guests. The dining room was quite full; Christmas visitors filled the tables. He finished breakfast and then went over to his office. He had a couple appointments scheduled he wished he had not made, but the rest of the day would probably be light. That cranky Mrs. Reading insisted on coming in to have some fillings done. Mrs. Reading was in the chair when the door opened and Mrs. Howard came in, smiling and holding an envelope in her hand.

"The mail arrived and I received a letter from Liz. I thought you wanted to know when she would arrive, and so I came right over." She handed the letter to Jakob who quickly opened it.

"She's coming in Friday at 3:30. That's New Year's Eve." He was smiling from ear to ear.

Mrs. Howard said, "I just knew you wanted to know the news, so I brought it over right away." Jakob thanked her and gave the letter back to Mrs. Howard. He could hear Mrs. Reading in the operatory announce that she still had housework to do and hoped he could finish her soon.

"Yes, Mrs. Reading, I'll have you finished in just a short time. Please be patient." Jakob's spirits had been lifted as he went back to work. He completed his afternoon and went over to the Lucky Lady to visit his friends.

"Doc, you look mighty happy today. Did somebody pay their bill?" Andy laughed.

Jakob grinned and laughed with him. "Even better than that. Liz is coming back Friday."

"Hey, what's going on between you and Liz?" Jakob just smiled. He thought, *She will be back in five days. How can I possibly wait that long?* The following days seemed to just drag for Jakob. He was surprisingly busy in the office, even though the weather was very cold and snowy. Now, he also faced some problems with his friends. They were now onto Jakob and his romance with Liz and teased him incessantly.

December 31st arrived cold and bright. The sun shone brightly in a cloudless blue sky but it was still bitter cold. He had closed the office early for the day because he felt nobody would be interested in coming in for dental work on New Year's Eve. However, Harold Fleming brought his wife to the Sheridan Inn looking for Jakob. Her face was swollen to a point that her left eye was almost shut, and she was in pain. Henry Clayton got Jakob out of his room just as he was getting ready to go to the train station to meet Liz, who was coming in on the Burlington Missouri at 3:30. Seeing Mrs. Fleming, Jakob knew she was in real trouble and directed the Flemings to meet him at the office. He attended to Mrs. Fleming and gave them instructions on her care.

"She should be much better by tomorrow. If you have any problems or if this should get worse, let me know." Jakob looked at his watch. It was 3:00 and Liz was due soon. *I better hurry over to the train station*, he thought, as he put on his buffalo coat and closed the door to his office. He stopped over at the livery and picked up a rig from Wilbur Riggs to drive over to the station and pickup Liz. The streets were covered with ice, and snow, and with deep ruts, as he bounced along. He didn't hear the train whistle, so he wasn't too concerned about being late. At the station, he tied up the rig and walked to the tracks. There was no sign of the train as he looked off into the distance, just the ribbon of rails that ended with the horizon. He went into the station to warm up. The station-master saw Jakob was anxious about the train, so he let him know the train would be late; it might be an hour before it arrived. Jakob stayed inside and chatted with some of the other people waiting anxiously, and kept checking the time. The bright blue sky was dimming with the sun going behind clouds that had developed in the western sky. He again viewed the ribbon of rails disappearing in the distance, but saw nothing.

There was snow that reached the low clouds and a stand of woods about a half mile to the right of the rails, and then some houses with wisps of smoke coming from their chimneys, but no train. Hardly a soul could be seen in this landscape. It was quiet, oh, so quiet. Then he could hear a faint sound that grew louder and louder. It sounded like a train whistle, and looking down the tracks to the horizon he could see a mere wisp of smoke moving toward him. The whistle got louder and now he could see the outline of what appeared to be a train. As it got larger, there was more smoke and a louder whistle. In spite of the cold, Jakob stood by the tracks and peered into the distance, watching the train moving in what seemed like slow motion. Jakob's heart pounded as the train slowly approached the station with its bell sounding loudly.

The station-master came out and people gathered and milled around close to the tracks. The train, huffing and puffing steam and smoke came to a stop. There were only two cars and the conductor came down from the second. It had become almost dark and the station area was filled with lanterns. The passengers began to disembark the car. Jakob moved toward the passenger car and awaited Liz. She didn't appear and his thoughts got panicky. *Did she miss the train or change her mind?* Then he caught a glimpse of Liz behind two other passengers. She had on a long brown fur coat that reached down to her boots, and wore a fur hat that came over her ears. As she stood at the top of the stairs, she saw Jakob and a big smile came across her lovely face, along with a surprised look. Her arm raised to wave as she started down the stairs to a waiting Jakob.

"Jakob, what a pleasant surprise." Jakob said nothing but put his arms around Liz and pulled her close to him.

"Oh, Liz, you don't know how happy I am to see you," he said as he tenderly kissed her on the lips. He held her closely with their lips together.

When they parted Liz exclaimed, "Jakob, what are you doing to me?"

"I missed you so very much, Liz," Jakob answered.

"Jakob, what a surprise. I hadn't heard from you since you left for Buffalo in September."

"I know, I know, and I'm so sorry, Liz. I don't know what was the matter with me. I guess I didn't realize how much I missed you until I came back from Buffalo and realized you weren't here." Jakob drew her tightly and again kissed her, this time, even more passionately.

They stood there motionless in an embrace for some minutes. Finally Liz drew back and, looking at Jakob said, "Jakob, if we stand here any longer we may freeze to this spot. Why don't we get my luggage and we can head for Mrs. Howard's and continue where we left off here?" They both laughed as he picked up the luggage and placed it in the rig. The horse was puffing and stamping its hoofs in the cold air. Jakob helped Liz into the rig and they slowly moved off to Mrs. Howard's. It was almost completely dark as they bumped along the rutted street. Mrs. Howard's place was just a short distance away from the train station and they were soon there. Jakob helped Liz down from the rig, and removed the baggage and brought it quickly up to the house. Liz opened the door and Jakob brought a small trunk and a couple bags into the entry of Mrs. Howard's comfortable home. Mrs. Howard warmly greeted Liz and Jakob, and they talked briefly. Jakob interrupted the conversation and said he didn't want to leave the horse out in the cold too long, so he'd better take the rig back to the livery. In this cold, the horse should be tended to.

"I'll be back as soon as I can and then maybe we can go to the hotel for dinner. Lukas, the cook, will be serving something special tonight." Jakob carefully walked down the slippery steps, untied the horse, and was off to the livery stable. He left the rig with Little Henry, the stable boy who was Wilbur Riggs's son.

"Henry, please take me back to Mrs. Howard's before you put the horse away." They went back to Mrs. Howard's and Jakob thanked the boy and told him to return later. He quickly went up the steps and into Mrs. Howard's. Liz and Mrs. Howard were still talking when Jakob joined them. Liz was relating the events of her trip home then finally asked to be excused so she might clean up before they went out for dinner. Jakob said he would bring her luggage to her room, then started carrying it back there. After he brought the last piece in he turned to Liz and put his arms around her, and they kissed again.

Liz broke up the embrace and said, "You better get out of my bedroom or Mrs. Howard will get the wrong idea," and she giggled. "I'll get ready as soon as I can." Jakob sat across from Mrs. Howard in the comfortable parlor, with a cozy fireplace across one wall. The walls of the parlor were papered with a flowered pattern. Large chairs and a couch occupied the room. Mrs. Howard was a widow who had lost her husband in an accident. She was left with some money and the large house. So, she decided to rent out rooms to single women in Sheridan as a way to support herself. Mrs. Howard was very strict in who she took in, and kept the rules strict. Although there was room for three women, Liz was her only boarder at this time. She offered Jakob tea and biscuits while waiting. It seemed like forever for Jakob to keep up conversation with the talkative Mrs. Howard who told him all about her former husband and where she was from. Jakob heard the door from Liz's room open. Looking up, he saw a very beautiful woman emerge from the hallway.

"Liz, you said clean up! Well, you did a lot more than just clean up." Liz was fairly tall, with long blonde hair. She was slim and filled out the satiny green gown seductively. With the high-button beige boots, she was incredibly beautiful. A white boa adorned her graceful neck and wide-brimmed hat, which made her look like she was a picture from an Eastern fashion magazine. Not since he had left Milwaukee, had he seen such a beautifully dressed lady. He was taken aback with her beauty as she approached him. Her slight fragrance made his heart beat faster. This wasn't Liz the plain school teacher he had taken to the church hay-ride.

"I hope I didn't take too long, but this is New Year's Eve and I thought I should dress appropriately."

"Elizabeth Jensen, you look absolutely, beautiful," exclaimed Jakob, who was thrilled at the beauty he would spend the evening with.

Mrs. Howard chimed in, "Liz, I've never seen you wear that dress before. It is beautiful and you look absolutely ravishing."

"That's because I never had a special occasion to wear it, and a handsome gentlemen to be with," laughed Liz. They laughed and joked but Jakob was overwhelmed by her beauty.

"It's time we go, or we may have a hard time getting a table in the hotel dining room. I told Lukas we would be by, so he is expecting us." Little Henry came back with the rig and Jakob helped his beauty into it. The ride to the hotel was cold, but not too long. He helped Liz out of the buggy onto the walkway. It was somewhat cleaned of accumulated snow. Liz had on that long fur coat she wore earlier and had tied a scarf around her hat to keep it from blowing away. The wind gusted and snow swirled as they moved as fast as they could down the walkway. Jakob helped Liz along and finally they reached the hotel. You could hear music and singing from inside the hotel, as well as the Lucky Lady across the street.

Jakob opened the door and pulled Liz into the warm building. They moved quickly inside and closed the door. The large blazing fireplace began warming their frozen faces. Henry Clayton was at the counter and gave them a rousing greeting.

"Liz, I'm glad to see you're back. You look beautiful. I have to tell you, I didn't know what to do with your friend there," he said laughing and pointing at Jakob. "He really missed you." The dining room was filled with guests. There was laughing and loud talking and some were dancing to the musicians playing. Annabelle, who usually waitressed, saw Jakob and came up to greet him. She recognized Liz.

"We're full up, Doc," she said and laughed. "But I got a special place for you and your lady friend." Sure enough, she took them to a quieter spot with a small table.

"Can I get you folks some drinks?" Liz opted not, but then Jakob suggested champagne and Liz smiled and accepted. Annabelle set up the champagne bottle next to the table and poured each a glass. Liz held her glass and noted the bubbles. Jakob touched his glass to Liz's and they both sipped from their glasses. Liz placed her glass on the table, touched Jakob's hand, and smiled a loving smile.

Jakob spoke first. "How could I be so lucky to be with you tonight. When I arrived here from Buffalo I found out you were not here. You just have no idea how lonely I felt. I can't explain it." Liz leaned across the table and kissed Jakob. They silently looked at each other and sipped their champagne. Annabelle came by and asked if they were ready to order, and both nodded. They ordered one of Lukas's special dinners, duck ala orange. And then they talked quietly amidst what was almost bedlam in the dining room. How lucky they were to find themselves in a quieter spot in the dining room. Jozef Ptaszek walked by and played a romantic Chopin waltz on his violin, as Liz hummed the melody. Jozef lived in the Acme mine area before coming to Sheridan. He had a job in the Commercial Bank. His father was a Polish mine worker who migrated to the area. Jozef was an outstanding violinist who would play on special occasions at the hotel. Jakob and Liz talked and were engrossed with each other, in spite of constant interruptions by friends and acquaintances.

"Jakob, you know I almost gave up on you. What happened?"

"I don't know, Liz. I guess I never really thought about a special relationship with anyone. Then all of a sudden when I realized you weren't here, I awoke to the realization I missed you." They had their dinners and kept up their conversation amid the revelry. People would come by and talk with them, wishing them a Happy New Year. They just wished to sit there and be left alone. There was foot-stomping music and drunken singing, but they were oblivious to it all.

Annabelle came by and asked if they might want a small glass of port wine to toast with on the New Year. She winked at Liz, who smiled and accepted. It was just a short while before some yelling started with "Happy New Year," and the band played Auld Lang Syne. There were sounds of shooting, outside somewhere. They got up from their table and Jakob put his arms around Liz. They kissed but didn't part until someone slapped Jakob on the back and wished them a Happy New Year. Laughing and singing, they picked up their glasses and sipped the port wine before kissing again.

Parting, Jakob looked into her eyes. "Happy New Year, Liz."

"Happy New Year, Jakob." They stood together, talking and smiling and punctuated it with kisses.

Suddenly there was a ruckus outside the dining room and someone shouted, "Is Doc Miller here?" People shouted that he was in the dining room. Jakob heard his name called, and several people came to him and told him there was a man looking for him. He left, with Liz following. An older man came up to him excited.

"Are you Doc Miller?"

"Yes, I'm Doc Miller."

"I was in the Lucky Lady watching a card game, and a fight started. The next thing I know someone bumped into the game table and another man came up and hit one of the players on the head with a whiskey bottle. The man fell to the floor bleeding from his head. It was Doc Kelly. I think he might be dead. They said I should find you. Maybe you can help him."

Jakob looked at Liz. "I'm going over to the Lucky Lady." He left running into the cold night, followed by Liz. They crossed the street, slipping and sliding. He pushed the door open and fought his way through the crowd surrounding the fallen Doc Kelly. He was bleeding profusely from his head. Jakob quickly checked his pulse. *Thank God,* he thought, *he isn't dead.* He asked for a towel and started sopping up the blood from his face and head, and discovered a large wound in his scalp and several other cuts. Doc Kelly was unconscious. There was no other doctor in Sheridan; it was left to him, to help the bleeding man. The most bleeding was from a scalp wound. He placed a folded towel over the wound and put considerable pressure on it, and then took a tablecloth and tore it into long strips and wrapped it around Doc's head, to hold the towel in place. The wound had to be sewed, but he had to get the unconscious Doc Kelly where he could do it. Doc Kelly started to moan and regain consciousness.

His eyes opened and he looked up at Jakob and muttered, "Jake, what the hell are you doing here?"

"Hold still Kelly. Someone just opened a whiskey bottle with your head. You got a nasty gash that has to be sutured. We'll put you in Wally Fisk's office. He has a bed there and you can lay on it while I take care of you."

Doc mumbled and moaned, "Okay."

"A couple of you guys help me get him in the office." They gently moved him into the office and placed him on the bed. Liz was right behind him.

"Can I help? What can I do?"

"Stay here with him. I have to go over to his office and get needles and sutures. Just keep pressure on the towel." Someone dropped a coat over Jakob's shoulders as he quickly left to go over to Doc Kelly's office. One of the men had a rig tied up at the Lucky Lady and took Jakob to Kelly's office. Jakob gathered up all he would need and returned to the Lucky Lady and Doc Kelly lying on the bed. Doc's eyes were open and his expression was blank.

"Okay, Kelly, this is going to hurt. No more booze for you. I'm sure you already had plenty." He removed the blood-soaked towel and quickly started picking out pieces of broken glass from the scalp wounds, while sopping up the blood. When he could find no more pieces of glass, he was ready to start suturing. Luckily for Doc Kelly, he was bald in the area of the injury and Jakob didn't have to shave his scalp. There were a number of smaller cuts but one large one that went across his head. Jakob placed the scalp flaps together and holding them in place, he started sewing them. Doc moaned as he pushed the needle through his scalp, but didn't move. With the large flap completely sutured, Jakob tackled the smaller cuts and the one on his forehead. The bleeding lessened to just some oozing.

For a teacher, Liz turned out to be a great nurse as she wiped the blood from the sutured area. She was Jakob's extra hands. One cut still had a piece of glass deep in it and he had to almost dig it out. Doc looked pale from the loss of blood as Jakob finished up. He re-bandaged the area and asked the bartender to get him some ice, which he promptly got from the water barrel outside the Lucky Lady. He wrapped it in a towel and placed it over the wounded area.

Doc was in and out of consciousness and Jakob offered him a sip of whiskey. Doc looked up at Jakob and said, "You know Jake, you did that like you knew what you were doing."

Jakob smiled. "Just a payback for the job you once did on me." Doc closed his eyes and Jakob ushered all the others out of the room and looked at Liz. Her fancy dress was splattered with blood. Her hair was disheveled and dried blood spotted her cheek. Jakob pulled her close to him and kissed her.

"Sorry for all this excitement but I don't know what I would have done without you. Thanks. And by the way, Happy New Year anyway." They sat down, exhausted from the hectic evening. Jakob gave Doc a pain potion he mixed in a spoon with some water, and Doc was soon asleep. In spite of the excitement and the fight, and Sheridan's most revered doctor injured, the partying went on in the next room of the Lucky Lady as Jakob and Liz held vigil over Doc Kelly.

Chapter 9

A New Year

Doc Kelly woke up moaning. He complained of one big headache. The Lucky Lady was quiet. All the partying and noise was over; silence prevailed. Jakob was awakened when he heard the moaning and went over to Doc to see how he was doing. Liz was still asleep in a chair.

"How you doing, Kelly?" Jakob smiled at his bloodied patient.

"My head feels like I've been hit by a beer barrel. What happened to me?" He really didn't remember what had happened. Jakob told him about the incident and how he had been hit with a whiskey bottle. Then the pieces started coming back to him and he remembered how Jakob sewed his scalp together.

"Who did it? I was just minding my own business and playing cards."

"I don't know who did it but there was a fight and somehow you must have been in the way."

Liz heard the talking and got up from her chair and came over to see how Doc was doing. Satisfied he was better, she exclaimed, "Oh my gosh, what time is it?" Jakob looked at his watch.

"Five thirty. You got someplace special you have to go?" He laughed.

"Well, no, but what will I tell Mrs. Howard? What is she going to think of me for being out all night?"

Doc looked up at her and smiled. "Just tell her you were out on an errand of mercy and I'll vouch for you."

She smiled. "That's right. It was an errand of mercy. Oh, that was terrible what happened to you. I feel so badly for you."

Doc grinned slightly, moved his head from left to right slowly and looked around. Meekly, he said, "What you say we find us a cup of coffee? I wonder if they have any around here. I need something to clear this fog in my head."

They opened the office door to the Lucky Lady. It looked like a windstorm had hit it. Everything was catawampus. The place looked closed, but there were still several unconscious bodies lying on the floor. Liz and Jakob made their way out of the Lucky Lady into the bitter cold. There was a light on in the hotel across the street.

"Let's go over to the Sheridan Inn. Maybe Lukas is up and has some coffee made." The restaurant was a mess, but sure enough, Lukas was stirring and had coffee made. "What you folks doing up so early? Doc, what happened to you? I was looking for you and somebody told me you left in a hurry." They explained the incident over a hot cup of coffee. Jakob looked anxiously at Liz.

"We better go back to Doc Kelly. He was the one asking for coffee and saw us leave to come over here. We better take him some coffee too." Lukas gave them some coffee to take over to Doc Kelly. When they arrived back, he had somewhat regained his composure but still didn't look too good. He sipped some coffee slowly but still looked dazed.

"Kelly, you want to go and use my room at the hotel and rest some more? You do need some more rest. How do you feel? Do you feel stable enough to make it over to the hotel? We'll help you. I have to get my lady home, so she can get some good sleep."

"Oh, I can make it. Don't worry about me." Jakob and Liz helped Doc up and out of the Lucky Lady and they slowly crossed over to the hotel and up to Jakob's room. Liz tucked him in bed and Doc closed his eyes. He was out like a light, so Jakob and Liz left for Mrs. Howard's. The gray sky was just starting to lighten and the wind swept the snow into their faces. The cold was biting, in spite of their heavy coats, as they trudged through the snow. Jakob tried to open the door to Mrs. Howard's place but it was frozen shut. It was just a few moments and Mrs Howard was opening the door from the inside.

"My goodness, where have you folks been? I've been worried about you." They related the story about Doc Kelly. "Oh my goodness, that was terrible. I just knew there had to be a good reason for you being out so late. Liz is a good girl." Jakob and Liz smiled and Liz blushed a little.

"Liz, you have to get some sleep. I know it's been a tough night for you but I really appreciate you staying with me watching Doc Kelly." He then asked Mrs. Howard if he could use her couch to rest on because Doc was using his room over in the hotel.

"Oh, land sakes, yes. You folks must have had a terrible night taking care of that poor Doc Kelly. I do hope he will be all right. He is such a nice man. He was lucky to have you nearby." Mrs. Howard placed a pillow under Jakob's head and a blanket over him, as he quickly went back to sleep.

Jakob awakened to the smell of bacon frying. Liz was already up helping Mrs. Howard. As he arose, Liz placed her hands on Jakob's face and tenderly kissed him. Mrs. Howard's eyebrows lifted when she caught them in an embrace. She smiled but said nothing. After the breakfast of eggs and bacon, Jakob excused himself and was off to see Doc Kelly at the hotel. He found him in the dining room having breakfast. Doc grumbled, "I took two of those headache powders and my head still aches. Looks like you might have done a good job sewing up my head. Nothing is sticking out."

The next week Jakob had several people come by his office with bad cuts. "I hear you can really sew people up, Doc." Jakob would smile and tell them his business was teeth, and they should go back over and see Doc Kelly.

Business was really slow for Jakob during the cold and snowy Wyoming weather. Liz was back with her school children and busy. Since he discovered his feelings for Liz, he couldn't spend enough time with her. He would go over to the schoolhouse, have lunch with her, then go back and later take her home from school. He took care of a few patients with their toothaches, but most people wouldn't venture outside with the cold and blowing snow. There wasn't much to do around town either. Stagecoaches were a rarity and even the trains made fewer runs in the winter. There were always some of the guys playing checkers in the general store or just sitting around the stove talking. Most people had something to complain about and the general store was the place people would do it.

It was now Liz who was engrossed in her work. Even though the children would often stay home because of the weather or the sniffles, she gave more of her time individually to those who came to school. Jakob felt left out, but he understood and tried to keep himself busy. Sometimes, he'd stop by the Lucky Lady and shoot the breeze with Andy Meeks or just play a friendly game of cards with some of the boys who hung out there.

Liz and Jakob were now lovebirds, and even though he felt deeply for her, he hadn't gone so far as to propose marriage yet. Over the holidays Jakob got letters from his mother telling him about all that happened in Milwaukee during the Christmas holiday. He got Christmas cards and notes from some of his old friends whenever the train made it to Sheridan. He even got a Christmas card from his old flame, Alice, which he promptly disposed of. His mother was always disturbed that he hadn't written home enough.

Dear Jakob:

I don't understand why you don't write home more often. We miss you so much. Don't you care about us? Daddy tells me you must be very busy, but certainly you should have enough time to write a short letter. Christmas just wasn't the same without you. We went over to Uncle Henry's for the annual Christmas dinner. Aunt Lil was asking about you and wondered if you had taken up with that pretty Alice O'Malley. I told her you were too busy for ladies. But you know, Jakob, Alice can't wait for you forever. I wish you would come back home and sweep her off her feet and marry her.

Jakob became upset by the tone of her letter. His mother still had the idea he was interested in Alice, and she was hoping he would marry her. In his letters home he hadn't mentioned anything about Liz, and now Liz was more than just an acquaintance. He was in love with her and planned to marry her. The word even came out around town he was in love with her and would probably marry her. *Oh my gosh, I better tell mother of my plans.* He realized his mother was overbearing and he just ignored telling her about Liz. If he did, he was sure she would make greater efforts to re-ignite the romance with Alice. He cared for his parents a great deal and didn't want to hurt them. *How am I going to break the news to them?* he thought. He had not yet brought up the subject of marriage to Liz. He was certain she cared for him. *No, I'm sure she loves me but . . . Oh my gosh. Why haven't I told her I love her, because I do? What should I do? If I ask Liz to marry me I should give her a ring. I don't have a ring to give her. There's no real good jewelry store here in Sheridan. There's a store but it doesn't have any real nice rings in it. Then, I do have to ask her father for her hand in marriage. This is getting complicated,* he thought.

He had to first get her a ring. *If I went back to Milwaukee I could buy a ring at Goodman's Jewelry Store or from Harold Pattis. They are friends of the family and would find a nice one for me. This might be a good time for me to go back to Milwaukee. Business is slow and then I could tell my parents of my plans and come back here and propose to Liz.*

Jakob lay awake well into the night. The howling wind and bitter cold outside didn't bother him as he formulated his plans for the future. Then he began to think, *Can I afford to get married? Where would we live? I'm making enough to support Liz but first we would have to have a home. I never thought about that.* He was living in the hotel but they would need more than a single room to live in, so a home was important. He fell asleep formulating plans for his life with Liz

The next day he went to the office to take care of his patients. He worked through the day, with his mind on what plans he had to make. Mrs. Frump remarked that he seemed to have something on his mind, as he prepared to put a filling in her tooth. He fluffed it off and finished the day.

Jakob closed the office and walked over to the schoolhouse. Liz was finishing up the day. The last student left and she was cleaning up.

"Hi, Liz, how would like to go over to the hotel for dinner tonight?"

"Tonight? This is a weekday and you don't usually ask me out during the week. Is there something you want to talk about?"

"Oh, no. I just felt like seeing you tonight," he answered.

"I still have some papers to grade but that won't take too long. Maybe we can go out." She smiled at him. He walked her to Mrs. Howard's and they set the time for dinner. Jakob was so happy that he felt as if he were walking on top of the snow. He stopped by the Lucky Lady and visited with some of the guys.

One of the guys asked Jakob, "How you gettin' on with Liz these days?"

"Oh, fine. Oh, my gosh. I better get going." We're having dinner together tonight."

"Tonight? It's a weekday. What you doin' going out on a weekday?"

"Oh, just thought we'd go out tonight, and Jakob turned around and left. He walked across the street to see Lukas and tell him he was bringing Liz for dinner, and he hoped he'd have something special.

"Don't you worry, Doc. It'll be something special. Hey, how come you going out tonight? It's Wednesday. That's a weekday. You don't generally go out on a weekday."

"Oh, no special reason. I just feel like having one of your special dinners."

Lucas looked at Jakob smiled and shook his head, as he walked out.

Now, why would he go out for dinner when it's just a weekday?

Chapter 10

A Ring For My Lady

Jakob was up early. He couldn't sleep. There was too much on his mind. Lukas had just opened up the dining room when Jakob walked in for his coffee.

"Up early, Doc. What's going on?"

"Not much. I just couldn't sleep. "I guess I just have too many things on my mind and I have some work to do at the office. I sure am looking forward to spring. This winter weather is depressing."

He finished his breakfast, bundled up, and went out in the cold, blustery, gray morn. Some snow had piled up against his office door and he had to sweep it away to get in. He hurriedly started a fire in the stove and waited for the office to warm up before taking off his buffalo-skin coat. Jakob started doing some of his lab work, when his mind drifted off to Liz. An hour must have passed and a weak stream of sun passed through the frosted glass on his window when the door opened, and in walked Doc Kelly.

"I thought you were here. I stopped by the hotel and they told me you had breakfast early. When the hell are you going to take out my stitches? You know, Jake, they just don't fall out. I got a swollen area in the back of my head that hurts like hell when I lay on it. Must be a boil or something. Take a look at it."

"Sit down in my chair, Doctor, and be my guest. I am at your disposal."

"Forget the disposal crap, Jake, and take out the stitches. You dentists always make a big deal out of everything. I would have taken them out a week ago."

"Now, Doctor, you are my patient, and I am in charge here. Sit down and shut up." Doc Kelly took off his coat and head covering, and grumbling, sat down. Jakob surveyed the scalp. "You sure are lucky you're bald. I didn't have to cut your hair to do my embroidery. The wounds are healing well, except for that boil-like area in the back. You're right, it must be a local area of infection. Ten-to one I bet there is some glass still in there I didn't get out. It is time to take out the sutures." The infected area oozed an exudate when he pressed on it. Jakob took one of his dental curettes and probed the wound.

"Ouch! What the hell are you doing? I thought you were supposed to be a painless dentist."

"I am, Doctor, but this isn't a tooth." Doc Kelly grumbled and moaned as Jakob brought up a small piece of glass from the infected site. "Here's the culprit Kelly, a little glass left over from the big party you went to on New Year's Eve."

"I thought you said you got all the glass out. Now, if I was doing the job I would have gotten all the glass out then."

"Well, Kelly, maybe I should have let you do it but you were in no shape to do anything, then or now. Maybe I should have let the bartender do it when you got all bloodied up so you would really have something to gripe about." Doc grinned as Jakob finished cleaning up the area and placing a bandage over the wound. "I shouldn't have to tell you, Doctor, but you better put some hot packs over the area for the next couple days." Doc grumbled as he put on his coat, opened the door and left. Jakob laughed as he was leaving. "Have a good day, Doctor." Picking up his instruments, Jakob was getting them ready to put in the sterilizer, when the door opened. There was Kelly again, with a grin on his face.

"I didn't mean to complain, Jake. I really appreciate the excellent care you gave me. Next time you run into a grizzly, let me know, so I can reciprocate." They looked at each other and both started laughing while looking at the bearskin on the wall of Jakob's office. Kelly left, still laughing, as the door closed.

Jakob finished cleaning up his instruments and his mind started to wander off again to thoughts of Liz. Her lips, her smile, her laugh and how she would tilt her head when she was talking, the twinkle in her eyes, her inquisitive gaze, the way she would hold her hands, her walk—and he smiled. *My God, I sure love that woman,* he thought. *I just got to marry her and have her for my wife.*

Jakob realized he wasn't the only one in town, who had eyes on her, but she didn't pay much attention to the others. But then, Reverend Henderson really took a shine to her, and she was active in his church doing Sunday School and ladies' club. *I got to take her out of circulation before someone else does. I better nail her down for me,* he thought. *I'll give her an engagement ring. That will keep her until I can figure out how I can marry her. That's what I'll do. Except, where will I get the ring? Not here in Sheridan. If I buy a ring here, it will be all over town, before I even give her the ring. I know what I can do. I can get it in Milwaukee and I don't have to go there. I'll write Dad and tell him about Liz and that I plan on marrying her. I'll ask him to find a ring for me. He can go to Anderson's or better still, to Harold Pattis, on 14th Street. He's my old buddy, Dave's dad, and a good old friend. If I get going now I can have a letter on the train out of here in the afternoon. I'm sure I can count on Dad for secrecy in this matter.*

Dear Dad:
    Hope you and Mom had a great holiday. Mine was really terrific. I have some great news to tell you. I have found the girl that I want to marry.
    Her name is Liz Jensen. I've known her for quite-a-while and hadn't said anything to you until I was sure she was the one. She is a mid-westerner just like us. Liz comes from Ames, Iowa, and went to school at Ames Normal. She is teaching school here in Sheridan. I've known her now for a year and a half. She has all the attributes I could desire. We get along real well and we have a lot in common. Needless to say, she is really beautiful. She is sort-of-a

strawberry blonde and quite tall. We go to church together on Sundays. No, she is not a Catholic, but she is a fine Christian woman. I wish you could meet her, Dad. Really, Dad, I just know you would agree she is the girl for me. I know you and Mother had hoped I would marry Alice, but I learned that Alice was not the girl for me. Oh, and by the way, this is just between you and me. I will tell Mother later. I know that she will probably be disappointed at first, but I know she will love Liz when she meets her. The reason I am writing you now is, I have a favor to ask of you. I want to get an engagement ring for Liz and there really is no fine jewelry store here in Sheridan. I thought maybe you could go over to Pattis's store, you know, my friend Dave's dad's store, and pick out a ring for me. I know you will get a good value there and I trust your judgment and your taste. I can afford up to a couple hundred dollars, so you should be able to get me a pretty nice ring. I could go a little more, so I leave it to you and your judgment to buy a really nice ring and something I would be proud to give her. When everything is all set I will bring Liz out to meet you and Mom, but for now I would rather not tell Mom. She might try to talk me out of my decision.

I look forward to hearing from you and hope you will take care of the matter for me. I hope you understand. The winter here has been real cold with lots of snow. I do hope Milwaukee is not as bad. But then, I'm not sure the weather in Milwaukee is any better. My practice is doing quite well, although winter does slow down things. I hope all is well at home.

Your son,
Jakob

Jakob hurried down to the post office so the letter would be on the train going east. Jakob looked at his watch. *Oh, oh, school is out. I think I'll go down to the schoolhouse and see if Liz is still there.* He quickly closed the office and left to see Liz. Sure enough, she was in the schoolhouse cleaning up and correcting papers. She now had thirty students enrolled, with some in each grade. It was really challenging for her to provide an education for those frontier children and to do it in the various grades, but Liz was doing it successfully. Jakob was disrupting, as she continued her correcting. Liz became somewhat irritated with his presence.

"I know what you can do while I finish correcting these papers. Would you please clean the blackboards for me? Please!"

"Okay, I'll do it for you, and then we can go over to the hotel and have a cup of coffee and piece of pie. The kids had you all day. Now I need you to be with me."

"Oh really, did you have such a bad day? Did one of your patients say something nasty to you?" And she laughed. By this time they were facing each other and Jakob couldn't resist putting his arms around her and kissing her tenderly. Liz put her arms around Jakob and looking at him smiled.

"Poor boy. I know you must be hungry. All right, let's go now for coffee and pie so that you don't faint."

Jakob wondered whether his dad would respond to his letter favorably. *What if he confides the contents of the letter to Mother?* he thought. But then Jakob felt his dad wouldn't, because they had a good father and son relationship, and he was sure he would understand and not share his plans with Margaret.

It seemed like forever and the time dragged on. Getting mail from Milwaukee was not an overnight thing. It generally took a couple weeks, sometimes as much as a month, for replies to his letters.

In the meantime Jakob did get a letter from his mother admonishing him for his lack of concern for his family, and going on to telling him of the news in Milwaukee and of course something about the activities of Alice O'Malley. *She still has it in her mind Alice would make me a good wife,* he thought.

It was almost three weeks later when a letter and small package were waiting for Jakob at the post office, both from his dad. Jakob's heart raced because he knew his dad had come through for him. His letter told him he was responsible for breaking the news to his mother. He understood Jakob's feelings and wished him well. He purchased the ring for him within the parameters Jakob had given to him. Mr. Pattis and he selected a very attractive one he could be proud to present to Liz. Dad also said Harold Pattis sends his regards and Mrs. Pattis is excited for you. She wishes her David would find a nice girl to marry.

Jakob quickly took the package to his office and opened it in the dimly lit room. The diamond was larger than he expected and reflected its many facets beautifully. The setting was of shining gold. He carefully examined it from all angles. It was beautiful and yes, he would be proud of it. Now he must find a way to give it to her. Over the last weeks, he thought about Liz and how much he cared for her. Jakob felt he could support her, and knew they just had to get married, because more and more his feelings for her had grown stronger. She was constantly on his mind and he felt she also cared a great deal for him. He just knew she loved him. Jakob felt they must get married, and soon.

The cold winter had slowly moderated and spring was taking over. The snows were melting, and green was starting to show. Wildflowers were popping up in the most unusual places. Occasional birds were flitting about.

Liz and Jakob attended church services on a sunny, but cold Sunday in April. He had rented a horse and buggy at the livery. This was to be the day. The service ended and he told Liz he was going to take her for a ride to view some of the wildflowers along Little Goose Creek, on the way to Big Horn. He helped Liz aboard the buggy and bundled her with blankets, and they started down the rutted, half-frozen trail toward Little Goose Creek. He held her tightly and soon they approached the creek bank. Once completely frozen over, the creek was now patches of water. There were some wildflowers visible in the clear areas of the fields. The bright sun ever so slightly warmed them.

Looking out on the half-frozen landscape, they delighted in the changes spring was giving. Jakob's heart pounded and he held Liz tightly. With a lump in his throat he said, "Liz, I love you. I love you so much I almost find it hard for me to speak. I don't know the words I can use to really tell you of my feelings for you. I almost feel I just can't live without you." He got down on one knee. "Liz, will you marry me?" He already had taken off his glove, and fumbled with the ring box. Removing the glove from her hand he slowly and deliberately placed the ring on her finger. Liz looked down at her hand and gasped. Her eyes opened wide and there was a moment of silence. She started to speak, and then just looked at Jakob for a long moment.

"Jakob, you are serious." She smiled and placed her hands on both sides of his face, then brought her lips up to his and gently kissed him. "Oh, Jakob, I do love you too. I have for a long time. Maybe from the first day I met you. But, I do love you so. This ring is so beautiful. It's much too extravagant. You didn't have to get anything so extravagant to show your love for me. For a long while I wasn't sure just what your feelings were, but I have loved you almost from the very moment I met you." Jakob held her tightly and kissed her passionately.

"I guess I didn't really think about love until I returned from Buffalo and you weren't there. Then all of a sudden it came to me that I truly missed you, and I feared I may have lost you. It was then, at that very moment, I realized how strongly I felt about you." They sat and talked the afternoon away, unaware the sun was slowly slipping away and the chill of night was approaching.

"Hey, I guess we better get back or we'll be caught out here all night." Jakob turned the rig around and they slowly made their way back to town, with Liz snuggled up against him.

The lights and music greeted their arrival back at the Sheridan Inn. Jakob stepped down and tied the horse to the rail. He gave his hand to Liz and helped her down. Arm in arm they entered the Sheridan Inn. Henry Clayton greeted them.

"What are you folks doing out in the cold? It may be April but it's still cold out there." Liz walked up to the fire blazing in the fireplace. The heat accented her rosy cheeks as she sought to warm her body. Jakob answered they had just come back from a ride to Little Goose Creek.

"Goose Creek! What was out there?" They removed their coats and entered the dining room and were greeted by Elsie who was waiting tables. She gave them menus and then asked for their order.

"Lukas has his special elk stew for dinner tonight."

A gentleman at the next table chimed in with, "And it is great."

"Thanks for the recommendation," replied Jakob. "And we'll have a glass of red wine to warm our innards." Jakob smiled to the seated couple. The dining room was busy as Elsie moved quickly from table to table. Liz and Jakob toasted with the wine and spoke quietly.

"Jakob you sly one. You had this all planned, didn't you? No wonder you got the rig. Just to see the wildflowers and Little Goose Creek?" Jakob grinned sheepishly and tightly held her hand.

"You're right. I guess I am. Perhaps that's one side of me you didn't know."

"I am just . . . so completely overwhelmed. So many thoughts have gone through my head as we were coming back." She lifted her wine glass and looked up. "Oh, Jakob, what about you? I love you so much. You make my heart race. This ring is so beautiful. What are you thinking right now?" Jakob smiled and held her hand tightly.

"I'm thinking I want you to marry me. I asked you to marry me Liz, and I meant it. I would say we should do it right now, but I know we have to prepare for the event."

"My heart tells me right now too. We could forget everything but I think we have to act sensibly and plan for the important day. What would you say if we were to set a date in June? That isn't too long for us to wait, is it?"

Jakob smiled. "Then June it will be but I can't wait any longer, knowing I have you to look forward to. You set the date and we will work things out." Elsie came back. She placed their dinner on the table in front of them as they talked.

"You folks better get started on your dinner, or it will be cold and Lukas will be upset." They all laughed and Jakob and Liz started on their dinner. They ate slowly as they continued their plans for the wedding. Elsie asked them if they would like to try the apple pie for dessert but they declined. They left for Mrs. Howard's but were stopped along the way by several of Jakob's patients, who told them that they looked like a couple in love. They climbed the steps to Mrs. Howard's and walked in.

"Land sakes, where have you people been?" beamed Mrs. Howard. Liz smiled, and took off her gloves, and held up her left hand, exposing her ring finger. Mrs. Howard's mouth opened and her eyes grew large. "What is this all about? Liz, that ring. Does it mean you are?"

"That's right. Jakob has asked me to marry him and I have accepted." Mrs. Howard just shook her head, smiled and embraced both of them.

"I'm so happy for both of you. When has the event been scheduled, or has it been scheduled yet?" Liz laughed and excitingly told Mrs. Howard of their tentative plans. They spent the evening talking about the wedding with Mrs. Howard putting in her suggestions about how they should do the grand event. Jakob looked at the clock and made note of the time.

"I'd better leave you as we both have a full day tomorrow. We can continue with the plans tomorrow." He put on his coat and moved toward the door, with Liz following. Mrs. Howard got up and left the room as they embraced. "Tomorrow Liz. Good night my darling. I love you."

"Oh, Jakob I love you too." They kissed and held each other tightly, then slowly parted. Looking back, Jakob slowly closed the door. Liz stood there looking at the door and feeling so very happy.

Chapter 11

A Day in June

The morning sun shone brightly into Jakob's room. His eyes opened to this new day and his first thoughts were of Liz. *She has accepted my proposal to marriage. I just can't believe this is happening to me.* Marriage was always so far from his thoughts, and here he was preparing to give his life to Liz. Then he momentarily thought about Alice O'Malley. *How could I have ever married her? She is attractive and talented, but so self-centered. I can't believe I might have married her. Liz has so many fine attributes, and most of all, she is so loving. I am so lucky to have her love,* he thought.

Oh my gosh, I better get going. I have to go to the office.

He sat in the hotel dining room as Elsie poured a cup of coffee for him. "Nice day, Doc," she said, with a big smile on her face. "Have your breakfast out for you in a jiffy."

Lukas came out with his breakfast quickly. "Good day, Doc. Enjoy." With a big smile on his face he topped off the coffee. Henry Clayton then stopped by and sat across from Jakob.

"I understand some big things are going to happen pretty soon," he said.

"What do you mean, Henry?" answered Jakob.

"Oh, nothing much, except maybe someone is going to get hitched pretty soon."

Jakob blushed and smiled. "Where did you hear something so ridiculous?" Then he started to laugh.

"Oh, I don't know. But you know good news like this gets around."

Jakob smiled. "Yes, this bachelor is going to wed the most beautiful girl in the West, Liz Jensen. News sure gets around fast."

"Got a date set for the big affair?"

"No, not yet, but I'm sure you'll know before I do." Then they both started laughing. Jakob left the dining room shaking his head. *Now how the heck did he find out?* He walked past the general store and got a big wave from Elmer Findley and big hellos from just about everyone he passed. *They all know,* he thought. He opened the door to a cold office and started a fire in the stove. Now, he really was wondering about how all those people could know he was getting married. He just asked Liz yesterday and then brought her home, and they told no one of their plans except . . . except Mrs. Howard. Just then the door opened and in walked Doc Kelly.

"Well, well. Looks like the most eligible bachelor in Sheridan is going to tie the knot." Jakob was now completely flabbergasted.

"How the heck did you find that out, Kelly?"

Doc grinned. "Jake, I know everything that happens in this town and when the most eligible bachelor in Sheridan makes plans to get married, the news travels fast. And ole Doc Kelly will help it along. You sure know how to pick 'em, kid. You're just lucky I'm over the hump or I would have beat you to it. She's one sweet dish." He laughed and walked out the door.

Jakob's day was rather routine but with more patients than usual, and most knew the news of his impending marriage. He cleaned up the office, and closed the door, and headed over to the schoolhouse to see Liz. Classes were over with and she would be grading papers. He opened the schoolhouse door to see his Liz with a desk full of papers and holding up her left hand to show her sparkling ring. Liz quickly got up and they met in an embrace.

"Liz, did you know that this whole town knows about our plans for marriage?"

"I certainly do know."

"Did you spread the word?"

"I did not. I thought you were the one."

"Then who did?" queried Jakob. "The only other ones that knew about this is the horse, who took us to Little Goose Creek, and Mrs. Howard. And horses don't talk."

"Mrs. Howard !" laughed Liz. "You know what? She was up and out of the house before me this morning." Now, they both laughed, and Liz said, "Mrs. Howard was the morning newspaper."

"Liz, pinch me. I can't believe you are going to be my wife." Holding her closely, they embraced again.

"Jakob, please give me just ten minutes more and I'll be finished with my work. And, I won't make you clean the blackboards this time."

"I can't wait that long Liz, but I'll try." It was generally decided Mrs. Howard had spread the good news, and both Liz and Jakob got a lot of attention. Some was friendly joshing and many were words of congratulation.

The next morning Jakob picked up his mail at the post office. It was a letter from his mother. As usual, it started out by scolding him for neglecting to write frequently enough and went on by telling about family news and friends of the family:

> I thought I should tell you that your cousin Albert is getting married to the Johnson's daughter. You know, Jakob, you should be thinking about marriage. I saw Alice O'Malley the other day with her mother. They were at the fashion show at the country-club. Alice is so sweet. She asked about you and how you were doing. I really think you should come back here and marry her. She would make you such a beautiful wife.

Beads of perspiration started to stand out on Jakob's forehead and his heart started to beat faster. *Mother. Oh no I have to break the news to her.* He held his breath and momentarily closed his eyes. *Well, Jakob, whether you like it or not, you are going to have to make a move and bring this out into the open with Mother, and today is the day.* He slowly walked to his office, forming a letter in his mind to his mother, as he walked along. *I'll do it as soon as I get to the office.* As he approached the office there were several people waiting for him, so he had to postpone his task. The day passed quickly but he was busy with patients and he kept mulling over his thoughts on his letter. Finally his last patient left and he sat down to write.

Dear Mother:

I received your letter today and I'm sorry I neglected to write you, but I have been very busy with my practice. Our weather here has started to warm up and it is obvious, spring is approaching. Birds are arriving and trees are starting to bud. The ground is losing frost and the ice is melting. I have some good news to tell you. You mentioned cousin Albert was getting married. Well, he's not the only one. I too am planning to get married. I have asked Elizabeth Jensen, who teaches school here, to marry me. I guess this may come as a surprise to you but I have found the lady of my life, and I love her. She is a beautiful woman, who is kind and generous with her time. I just know you will love her. She helps little children and goes to church. We have a lot in common and I know she will make me a fine wife. There is so much to tell but I will save it for my next letter as I wanted you to be the first to know of my decision. We are planning for a wedding in early June, so please save some time for it because I want you and Dad to come out here for it. Please tell Dad about my decision. I will be writing to him soon.

With all my Love,
Jakob

It was a short letter that took Jakob several hours to write. He had made several starts and three revisions, but it was done. Now to mail it, except it was past six o'clock and the post office was closed. *Oh, my gosh. I bet Liz has left school for home already.*

He stopped by Mrs. Howard's and Liz was having dinner. Mrs. Howard offered Jakob dinner and the talk was about the events of the day. Jakob told Liz about his letter to his mother.

"You know, Jakob, I wondered whether you told your mother about our plans. I'm really looking forward to meeting your family. They will be an important part of our life and I want them to be a part of my family too. I have already written to my family and told them of our plans. I had mentioned to them some time ago,

I found someone I cared for. However, this letter indicated much more than just cared for." Jakob didn't say anything more about his mother who was still hoping for him to marry Alice.

"Jakob, I'm thinking maybe the second Saturday in June would be a good day for our wedding. What do you think?"

"I think that would be a perfect time. You will be through with your school classes and we can make our plans to do whatever we wish."

Jakob sent his dad a letter about his plans for the wedding and told him he would be informing his mother of the date, so they could make plans to attend. Jakob thanked him for finding the ring and taking care of the purchase. He and Liz thought it was beautiful and he hoped his mother would accept his decision to marry Liz and to forget about Alice. Everything seemed to be going well and each day they added to their plans for the wedding. Three weeks had passed and he had not heard from his mother.

Each subsequent day made Jakob a little more nervous. Then he received a letter from his dad. Dad's letter indicated his mother was upset about his upcoming marriage. She still had her mind set on Alice for his wife, and no one else would do. Have patience. She'll come around but I doubt she will attend the wedding. Jakob realized he had more fences to mend.

The weeks slipped by and plans for the wedding were being put into place. It seems like everyone in Sheridan wanted to take part. Both Liz and Jakob were well liked. The wedding was set for the second Saturday in June. Liz would have her younger sister be her bridesmaid and Jakob would have Doc Kelly as his best man. The ceremony would be in the Country Church and Rev. Henderson would tie the knot. The music was going to be provided by the Sheridan Players, who did the music for all the events in town. Harry, the piano player at the Lucky Lady, insisted on playing for the wedding ceremony. Jakob was a little nervous about that. He had never heard him play anything other than honkytonk piano in the Lucky Lady, but Harry insisted and said he could play wedding music. Nobody knew how many people would come because it seemed the whole town was invited. The church ladies were bringing the food. A big tent was to be set up in the churchyard in case it rained. Otherwise, it would be outside. Everybody was excited for Liz and Jakob.

Jakob finally received a letter from his father. He told Jakob they would not be attending the wedding but they would have a wedding party for them in Milwaukee at a later date, so all his friends and family could celebrate with them when they came to Milwaukee. But his mother had resigned herself to the fact he had chosen his own bride. Jakob was deeply disappointed but accepted their decision.

Liz's parents would be attending, as well as several of her aunts who were also happy and excited for her marriage. Mrs. Howard insisted on housing Liz's family. The family came to Sheridan the week before the wedding and met Jakob.

Jakob apologized to her father that he had not asked for permission to marry her. But, he did ask him then. Her father did understand and graciously granted him permission. They all took a liking to Jakob and were pleased Liz had found such a fine potential husband.

June 14th arrived and it was a sunny, warm day. At noon the bell in the church tower started to ring and streams of people came toward the church. It became apparent the church would be filled, and some people would be standing outside. A carriage brought Liz and her party from Mrs. Howard's. Jakob and Doc Kelly came over in a decorated buckboard with a horse that had been fancied up with flowers and a strawhat. Harry was at the piano in the back of the church playing softly. At the right moment he started playing the wedding march, and it sounded as professional as a concert pianist.

Liz's sister, Missy, wore a pretty, long yellow dress with a wide-brimmed hat that had yellow flowers on it. She slowly walked down the aisle and stood across from Jakob.

The people stood up in awe as Liz and her father stood waiting. Jakob first saw her as she stepped inside the church. His eyes misted and his heart pounded as he first viewed his bride. She wore a long white dress. A short veil adorned her head and she carried a small bouquet of daisies. Time stood still for Jakob, as Harry continued playing the wedding march.

Her dad, a tall, lean, blond-haired, distinguished man started walking down the aisle with Liz on his arm. Jakob was a handsome groom: tall, dark-haired with strong features, and dressed in a dark suit with a flower in his lapel. Doc bought a new suit for the occasion, instead of his usual dark green one with a vest and shiny pants, and a coat with a hole in the elbow.

Jakob stepped down to meet his Liz, as her father lifted the veil and kissed his daughter. He turned and shook Jakob's hand, and asked him to care for his daughter. Jakob said he would take care of her as long as he lived, and then Jakob turned to Liz and took her hand. Together they stepped forward and faced the preacher. "Dearly beloved. We are gathered here . . . " and that is all Jakob heard as he looked into Liz's beautiful eyes. The words were imprinted indelibly on his beating heart, then Reverend Henderson asked for the rings. Old Doc started going through all his pockets with a panicked look on his face; he came up empty. Then Jakob reached forward and took the rings out of his right vest pocket and handed them to Doc, who showed a sigh of relief on his face while people in the church chuckled. These rings had a special significance to Jakob, as he made them from gold in his laboratory.

They placed the rings on each other's fingers and made their vows. The Reverend looked at the congregation and spoke. "Is there anyone here who objects to this marriage?"

That's when someone in the back of the church got up and said, "Heck no. Marry them and get it over with."

The church got into an uproar, until the Reverend quieted them down and made the pronouncement they were now man and wife.

"You may now kiss the bride." Jakob looked down at his bride and tenderly kissed her. The church was in a complete uproar as they slowly moved down the aisle with people from both sides wishing them well.

Liz and Jakob were overwhelmed by the well-wishers as they moved out of the church and received their congratulations. It was a perfect June day with a bright, clear sky. The Sheridan Players had set up their instruments outside the tent and soon started the music with some ballads, to set the stage for the bride and groom. The music turned to dancing, as children paired off first, and then their parents started dancing. The church ladies started serving a whole variety of foods on long tables. The merriment was enjoyed by all. They danced and sang and toasted the newlyweds. People came and went. It was a great day for the children who were in awe of their teacher. Several of the ladies from the Lucky Lady came to wish Jakob well, though there were some broken hearts. However, Jakob was the professional man and rarely chose to spend time with any ladies until Liz came into his life. Some of the revelers brought gifts for the newlyweds.

Henry Clayton stopped by and took Jakob aside. "Jakob, it looks like this party could last well into the night. Just between you and me, I have reserved the Presidential Suite for you and Liz. Anytime you see fit, you and the Missus might as well sashay over. No one will know where you are staying, so you won't be bothered. It's been a long day and you two might need some rest." Henry grinned and handed Jakob the key.

Later in the evening Jakob alerted Liz to what Henry had told him. After they had cut the tiered wedding cake one of the church ladies had made, they watched for their moment to leave. It came later when everyone was engrossed in a square dance. The bride and groom just disappeared. Liz and Jakob climbed the stairs to the second floor of the Sheridan Inn. At the end of the hall they turned the key in the large door of what was known as the Presidential Suite. No president had ever stayed there, but when VIPs arrived in town or Senator Billings came to visit, they were given the special Presidential Suite.

Jakob picked up Liz and carried her across the threshold into a large and ornate room. Henry had left refreshments on a table in the middle of the room. It had gotten dark outside but inside, the room's flickering lamps cast shadows on the walls for the newly married couple. The room had a fireplace with a small log burning. They sat at a table together on a small couch, and toasted their marriage with champagne in fancy glasses. It was quiet except for the faint distant sounds from the party they had just left. Both were so much in love and grateful to have each other. They embraced and softly spoke of their love for each other.

Liz excused herself and went into the bedroom as Jakob sipped from his champagne glass, his eyes closed, as he reminisced about the precious moments of the day. The bedroom door opened and then he saw her. Standing in front of him was Liz in a long white lace gown that revealed the seductive beauty of his wife. Her hair was hanging to her shoulders. He arose from his chair and met her. His arms encircled her as she placed her soft hands on his face and tenderly kissed him. They remained locked in each other's arms, lips meeting in a passionate kiss. Jakob reached down and picked up his beauty and slowly carried her into the bedroom and placed her on the large canopied bed. He removed his clothes then laid down in the bed next to her, holding her soft body tightly and passionately kissing. And, they made love.

Jakob awakened to a persistent knock on the door.

"Who's there?" Jakob asked.

"Got some coffee for the newlyweds." He slowly opened the door to find a tray sitting next to the door with coffee, cups, saucers, and small cakes, which he promptly brought in.

Liz awakened and looked up. "Jakob, who was that?" Jakob put the tray on the table and got back in bed and snuggled up to his bride. He looked into her eyes and pushed her hair back and kissed her tenderly .

"It's not important, dear. Someone just brought us some coffee." He continued to hug and kiss her. He looked into her eyes and said, "You know, Liz, today is the first day of the rest of our lives." Liz purred like a kitten as she brought her body close to his, and kissed his neck and cheeks and lips.

Liz looked into his eyes and smiled. "You know what? I think I'll keep you for the rest of my life. Now, let's get up and have some coffee. We still got a lot of lovin' to do." They sat and had their coffee and talked about the wedding, and all the people who were there to celebrate with them. Everything was just so perfect.

There was another knock on the door. Jakob opened it to find Henry Clayton with a special breakfast for them. "No need for you folks to come down for breakfast. Now you just relax. I'll bring you up anything you need. That cord in back of the bed will ring at the front desk when you give a good pull on it, and I'll be right up. You had a long, hard day yesterday, so you just stay put and enjoy each other." He winked and turned around smiling. "No one knows you are even here, and I won't tell them."

He closed the door and Liz looked at Jakob and they both laughed and hugged each other. They sat and talked about the present and their future, and nibbled at their breakfast. Jakob talked about the home he would have for his bride that would be big enough for a family. They would have children, and Liz would give up her job of teaching to care for the family. Liz was radiant as she smiled, engrossed in Jakob's dreams for their future.

Then they heard voices below their window and a rap on the glass. Someone had thrown a pebble.

"Come on down, Jakob and Liz. We know you are up there," they said. Jakob looked at Liz.

"I guess it's no secret where we're at." He looked out the window and a crowd of friends had gathered below. Jakob waved to them and they insisted he and Liz come down.

"Let the party continue!" they all shouted.

Liz looked out and laughing said, "We'll be down shortly. Just wait for us." They clapped and whistled and shouted. Some of the Sheridan Players began with, "Let Me Call You Sweetheart," and they started singing as they waited for Liz and Jakob to come out.

"All right, we'll be down. We'll be right down. They won't take no for an answer, so I guess we better go down and join them," said Jakob. They quickly got dressed and went down the stairs, to be joined by the group who led them into the hotel dining room.

Andy Meeks addressed them. "You should know you can't just up and leave our party. Even if you have your own party." Everyone laughed and shouted. They entered the dining room and started opening bottles and toasting the bride and groom. Even the hotel guests joined in on the fun. The fun and laughter went on well into the day, until one by one, the exhausted group bid them goodbye. Jakob and Liz were once again alone.

Henry Clayton approached them. "Jakob, you and Liz can use the Presidential Suite as long as you wish. We ain't got no one more important than you coming."

"Now that is a real nice offer. I'm sure Mrs. Howard won't mind." Jakob shook Henry's hand and accepted the offer. Arm in arm they ascended the stairs and returned to the Presidential Suite.

Liz smiled and put her arms around Jakob. "Someday I'll tell my children how we once stayed in the Presidential Suite." Jakob lifted Liz up and carried her across the threshold and on to the bed. They passionately kissed and soon made love. "Oh, Jakob I love you so. I am so lucky to have you. You are everything I have ever dreamed of." She looked into his eyes and held him tightly. "I can't believe this is happening to me. Tell me all this is true."

"Liz, it is true. Our love was meant to be. That first day I saw you getting off the train, you caught my eye. Yet, I didn't realize you were the one, until that day I came back from Buffalo and found out you weren't here. I thought I had lost you. It was then I fully realized what a fool I was and I knew I just had to find you again." He tenderly kissed her again and again as they laid still in each other's arms talking softly.

Chapter 12

Honeymoon in Milwaukee

Jakob stopped at the general store to see Elmer Findley. Elmer had a small cottage he offered to rent to Jakob and Liz, just a few streets from the store. The Findleys lived there when they first came to Sheridan. Liz and Jakob made arrangements to rent it until they were able to build a home. There weren't very many places to rent and this would have to do, at least for the time being.

They were still staying in the Sheridan Inn but Liz was anxious to take up housekeeping in her own home. Jakob and Liz hadn't seen Elmer's rental, and they were anxious visit it. The Findleys hadn't lived in it for many years. Elmer told Jakob to just go over and take a look at it. Liz and Jakob walked over to Marion Street to see it. It didn't look like much outside. There was a fence surrounding it, with a gate that needed repair. The yard was full of weeds and the house looked like it needed much repair. Jakob had to lift the gate up to get in the front yard because the top hinge was broken. They followed what seemed to be the path and climbed the stairs to the porch, being careful not to step on a broken board.

The door was shut tight and one of the windows was cracked. At first the door wouldn't open, but when Jakob really pushed hard it did open with a start. They peered inside to see a rather large room with a fireplace across one wall. There was a wooden table and two chairs. Across the other wall was a counter with a small well pump. There were some shelves over the counter top with a small window occupying the middle of the wall. It looked like there might have been a curtain over the window at one time. It was laying on the counter along with some cooking utensils. On the other side of the room was a bed. Over that half of the room was a wood ceiling with a ladder going up to what seem to be another room or loft. The floor was wood with some broken boards.

Liz and Jakob hardly spoke but just looked at each other in complete despair and disappointment. This might have been what could be described as a home on the prairie. Maybe that was what it was when the Findleys first came to Sheridan. They had been in Sheridan a long time.

After staying in the hotel and with Mrs. Howard, this was a real letdown. It was to be their first disappointment. What could they do? There were no other houses for rent that might have been better. Liz was obviously disappointed and distressed, as was Jakob. They walked around the house and tried to visualize how they could make it into a livable home, and slowly retreated out of the house, leaving it to the critters who had inhabited it for years. Tears rolled down Liz's cheeks.

"Oh, Jakob, what are we to do?" They slowly walked back to the hotel and went up to their small suite to discuss their plight. The Findley cottage was really meager. Liz was extremely disappointed. They didn't feel they could afford to build a more suitable home at this time and there were no other homes Jakob knew of for rent that were more suitable. They decided they would not let this keep them from facing the rest of the day with no hope for solving their problem. There just had to be something they could find that was more acceptable.

The next day Jakob went to see Elmer Findley hoping for a solution. Elmer looked at Jakob and knew what was bothering him.

"Are you disappointed in the cottage? I felt you might be. We lived in it when we first came out here back in '85. I built it with my two sons and a carpenter from Ohio. We had been living in a wagon and tent until it was livable. But, I understand, these are different times. You certainly should have something better for you and your lovely wife. George Johnson, the carpenter who helped me, is still in town. I know he can make it very livable for you until you can build the home you really want. There really is no other place in town I know of that is available. Don't worry, I'll fix it up for you. It won't take too long, so just be patient." Jakob felt much better and explained to Liz what Elmer had said. It would be a nice home for them to start their life together.

He later stopped at the post office and received a letter that was waiting for him. It was the first correspondence he had received from his mother since he got married. His mother sent the letter to inform him she had set a date for their wedding reception in Milwaukee, and wanted him and his wife to make plans accordingly. She didn't dwell too much on their wedding in Sheridan, but wrote of her plans for their big party.

Mother decided to have it on the 4th of July and it would be extravagant. Because Jakob hadn't been married in a Catholic Church, she wanted him to be married by a Catholic priest. Jakob was upset his mother would dare carry the party to such an extreme without consulting him. He liked the idea of presenting his wife to his friends and family, but nothing beyond that.

Penning a letter to his mother he objected to her including the second marriage ceremony, and requested only a simple party instead. He agreed to be in Milwaukee for the 4th of July but strongly objected they be married again.

They started making plans for their trip to Milwaukee. Jakob wanted it to be a complete success. He wanted Liz to be accepted by his family, as he had been accepted by the Jensens. His mother's idiosyncrasies were not going to interfere with their trip. In the meantime, he still had his patients to see. Now, more than ever, Jakob had to work hard to support his wife. Liz was excited about the coming trip and meeting Jakob's family and friends. She had never been east of the Mississippi River. Liz was getting everything together to make the best impression possible with Jakob's family. She was, however, a little nervous about the prospect of meeting them, especially Jakob's mother, who seemed to be a bit of a problem.

The day arrived for their leaving to Milwaukee. Their luggage was placed in the baggage car and they boarded the train. Mrs. Howard and some of their friends came to bid them goodbye.

It was a sunny, warm summer day, as the train blew its whistle and slowly chugged out of the station. Soon they would be out of town and the life as they had known it. The train wasn't filled with passengers, but there were many and of all sorts. Most were people going east to see their families. There were salespeople who had come out to sell their wares, as well as railroad contractors going east to meet with their company bosses. The empty Wyoming landscape passed by with hardly any sign of people. The heat of the day was excessive, even with the open windows. Liz brought a basket with a picnic lunch, water and coffee which was no longer hot. There would be no place to stop to eat until later in the day. Some of the passengers passed their time with card games. Others were reading a book or attempted to sleep the time away. The train stops were made to load passengers in various small towns—Gillette, Upton, Newcastle, and Cambria in Wyoming, then Edgemont in South Dakota, and a long distance to Crawford, Nebraska, where they were to change trains. They found a small restaurant where they could rest and have dinner before they boarded the Burlington Missouri at 10:30 p.m. heading for Alliance and points east to Omaha. Fortunately for them, they did have a sleeper car that carried them through the night.

The ride was slow and monotonous. It was a long trip from Omaha to the mighty Mississippi, at Burlington, Iowa. The crossing over the Mississippi on a new bridge showed them the greatness of the river. The heat of the day was more of the same they had experienced. They noticed the differences between Wyoming and the East, after they crossed the Mississippi into Illinois. Corn and wheat fields, along with rolling hills, replaced the mountains and plains. It was a long day that turned into night as they approached Chicago. The darkness was pierced by occasional flickering lights from the towns they passed, until buildings and homes replaced the total darkness.

As they neared the city, they could start to discern big buildings and feel the train slowing down. First the whistle blew, and then the bell rang, as the train made its way into the station. The conductor announced, "Chicago, Chicago, Illinois. Take your luggage. Be sure to take all your luggage." People were moving around in the car before the train made its complete stop.

"It's eight-thirty Liz. Let's get our luggage and head for the hotel." The massive Union Station was crowded with people moving in all directions.

They soon located their luggage and had it taken outside where they found a buggy and driver to take them to the hotel for the night. "Where to, mister?"

"The Palmer House," answered Jakob. The carriage moved along the crowded cobblestone streets. Besides the horse and buggies, there were various wagons and an occasional streetcar sharing the crowded street. They finally stopped in front of a large building, electrically lighted, with a big canopy that extended to the street. There were large doors with people going in and out. With all the passengers and various drivers of the different buggies, it seemed like sheer bedlam. They were greeted by a tall, dark-skinned man with a stove-pipe hat and ornate coat. He had a deep voice.

"Welcome to the Palmer House." He snapped his fingers and a young man took their luggage and led Jakob and Liz to the doors, as another uniformed man opened them so they could enter the hotel. Liz was taken aback by the splendor of the hotel's large and brightly lit entry, dwarfing the Sheridan Inn's, and with all sorts of people milling around. Jakob registered at the large desk inside the reception area. Another uniformed boy led the way to an elevator, which slowly moved up to the fourth floor. Liz was amazed by the noisy contraption that took them up. Carrying their luggage to their room, the young man opened it and turned up the lights. He then checked to see if it was ready to be occupied. Jakob placed a gratuity in his hand as he closed the door. He put his arms around Liz and drew her close to him and tenderly kissed her.

"Welcome to Chicago, Liz. What do you think of it?"

"Oh, Jakob, this is magnificent. I have never seen anything this elegant in my entire life. I mean, the Presidential Suite at the Sheridan Inn. I thought it was really special but this, it's . . . I can't explain it. Do people really live like this?"

Jakob smiled. "Yes, some people do live like this. But you have to understand Chicago is a big business center, and as such it attracts people in business and wealth. Someday Sheridan may approach this splendor, but then again, maybe it won't. However, we can still live happily with a lot less."

Liz held Jakob tightly and kissed him. "We have each other and that is what is really important."

"Freshen up, Liz. It's late, but I bet you're hungry, because I am. Let's go and get a bite to eat." Liz quickly readied herself and they went down in the elevator.

They entered a large dining room and were quickly led to a table by a uniformed maitre d'. On the other side of the large and ornate room with huge crystal chandeliers was an orchestra playing music softly. The floor was crowded with people dancing. At the table, water glasses were filled and a menu was placed in front each of them, as the waiter described special items. It was nearly 10 p.m. and the room was still filled with people eating and dancing. The wine steward brought the wine Jakob had ordered. He poured a small amount in a glass for him to taste. With Jakob's approval, he poured a glass for Liz and finished pouring Jakob's glass. They toasted the event. Jakob got up and asked Liz to dance.

"Oh, Jakob, I don't know if I can dance to this kind of music. Look how fancy those ladies are dressed."

"You are dressed just as nice." Jakob pulled her up gently and led her on to the dance floor. The orchestra was playing a waltz. Jakob held her closely and Liz placed the side of her face on his chest. He noted the fragrance of her hair and felt the closeness of her body, as they moved slowly across the floor to the music.

"Liz, you are the most beautiful lady on the dance floor and your dress is perfect. As a matter of fact, I don't see anyone else on the floor but you and me and the orchestra is playing, just for us." Liz just looked up and smiled. When she smiled like that, she just seemed to radiate. The song ended and Jakob led Liz from the floor. They studied the menu and decided what they would order.

The fancy dressed-waiter looking at Liz asked, "And what may I get for you madam?" Liz made her selections and the waiter looked at Jakob. "Et vous, monsieur?"

When Jakob finished ordering his dinner Liz looked at him and said, "Oh my gosh, Jakob, did you see how much our dinner will be? Are you sure we should eat here?"

"Liz, this is Chicago and the Palmer House, not Sheridan. We will have these moments to remember the rest of our life." They raised their wine glasses, looking into each others eyes.

Liz broke the silence and said, "Jakob, I feel so lucky. I love you so much." A teardrop developed in Jakob's eye.

"Liz, you are so sweet. You are so special. I do love you so." The waiter brought the first course and they began an extraordinary dinner of Coq Au Vin and finished it with Cherries Jubilee for dessert. With the last drop of wine consumed, Jakob took Liz to the dance floor just before the orchestra played its last song. They danced until the last note and stood on the floor holding each other, as the musicians put away their instruments.

"Jakob, the music has stopped. Maybe we should sit down." Jakob smiled and they returned to the table. "It's been a long day. Maybe we should go up to our room."

The maitre d' smiled as they left the dining room. "Au revior."

The sun shone brightly through the shades and Liz awakened from her slumber. She gently brushed Jakob's hair back as he opened his eyes.

"Good morning, Jakob."

Jakob's eyes blinked and he smiled and kissed her. "We have a big day ahead. Best we get dressed and have breakfast." The train was scheduled to leave for Milwaukee at noon, so they had time to eat breakfast which was in another dining room. Liz was amazed at the elegance of the hotel and its various dining rooms; the way they wait on people and treat you, and the finery of the place. Everything was just perfect. After checking out, they walked out of the hotel into the sunshine of Chicago. Looking up, Liz noted the elevated train that rumbled past.

"Jakob did you see that up there?"

Jakob smiled. "This is Chicago, Liz. That's the elevated train; they call it the L." The fancy-dressed greeter led Jakob and Liz to a carriage that would take them to the train station. They made it to the train, with time to spare. Jakob pointed out the various buildings and attractions to Liz and told her about Chicago, as he knew it. He had spent one year there while he went to school, so he got to know the city quite well.

"When we come back to Chicago I want to show you the school I attended." As the train moved along, he told her about the area they were passing through. The train stopped at various cities: Kenosha, Racine, and finally Milwaukee. Jakob hadn't told his parents what time they would arrive. They got a carriage to take them to 2804 West Wisconsin Avenue, his former home.

Milwaukee wasn't nearly as big as Chicago, but it too was big, as Liz saw it. The carriage left the station, and soon they moved along tree-lined streets with big homes. It stopped in front of a large brownstone home on a hill. The home was surrounded by green grass, bushes, colorful flowers, and big trees. They got out of the carriage and walked up the steps to the house. Liz became a little apprehensive, and had been all morning. She was to meet her husband's parents, and she hoped they would like her. *I shouldn't be nervous but I can't help it*, she thought. As they approached the door it opened.

"Mother," Jakob, exclaimed.

"Well, Jakob, I wondered when you would arrive. And, this must be Elizabeth, your wife. I hope you don't mind if I call you Elizabeth. I just don't like nicknames."

"Of course I don't mind you calling me Elizabeth, Mrs. Miller."

"Oh, you dear, why don't you just call me Margaret. I'm not your mother, so it's not appropriate for you to call me Mother. Come on in. I'll bet you folks are starved. I expected you would arrive for lunch and so I have one ready for you, even if you are late. We have so much to talk about." Elizabeth saw an attractive middle-aged woman with nearly black hair and some traces of gray. She was about 5' 7" tall, a little chubby, and with a sharp but charming personality. They were seated at a table that looked out on a large yard. "You will have tea, won't you Elizabeth? Cream and sugar?" As Margaret passed the food she started outlining the schedule she had for their visit. "I'm so glad you arrived when you did, because it will give you time to get ready for tonight. I've invited the relatives to come tonight at six. Uncle Jim and his family, Aunt Mary, the Kramers and of course, Grandfather and Grandmother Miller, Albert and his new wife, and some of the other cousins. You know, Jakob, the rest of the family were also all invited, but some had other plans. They all are anxious to see you, and of course meet Elizabeth. Then, tomorrow, the Fourth of July, at two we'll meet at church. Now, I know you said you didn't want another wedding ceremony, but I had already talked to Monsignor Joseph and he seemed happy to marry you. I didn't want to disappoint him. You do understand, don't you?"

"Mother, I told you I didn't want to go through all that. We were legally married in Sheridan."

"Now Jakob, please bear with me. Elizabeth, you don't mind going through the marriage ceremony again, do you?"

Liz blushed and hesitated. "No, I guess it would be all right, Margaret."

"You know, as Catholics we are supposed to be married in a Catholic Church."

"Yes, I realize all that, Mother, but Jesus was at our wedding in Sheridan. I see this as completely unnecessary."

"Well, enough of that. After the church service we'll go to the country club for the reception. I have all your friends invited, Jakob. You'll be happy to see them all and you can introduce Elizabeth. I also invited the O'Malleys and Alice but they will be in Eagle River for the Fourth, so they won't be there. Oh, this will be a grand event. When it gets dark, there even will be fireworks. Oh my! Daddy has just arrived from the office. Bobby. Bobby, I want you to meet Elizabeth." Liz got up and received Robert Miller.

"I am so happy to meet you."

"I understand Jakob calls you Liz, doesn't he? That's good enough for me. Liz, please call me Bob."

"Dr. Miller, I mean Bob, Jakob has told me so much about you. It is so nice to meet you."

"And Jakob has told me so much about you. He said you are the most beautiful girl in the West and I definitely concur, Jakob. I'll add Milwaukee to that too."

"Dad, you forgot about me, Jakob. I'm here too."

"Jakob! Of course I saw you here," and he embraced him. "I'm so happy you are here son, and you brought me a beautiful daughter."

"Bobby, Jakob brought you a daughter-in-law."

"No, Margaret she will be a daughter for me."

"All right now, Bobby, enough of that. They have to get spruced up for the family party tonight. No more talk. Jakob, your old room is ready for you and Elizabeth." Liz and Jakob moved up the stairs to his old bedroom. They closed the door behind them. Jakob fell back on the bed with a deep sigh.

"Liz, please come here quick, next to me. I need a big hug and a big kiss." Liz smiled and moved, to the bed, and they embraced. "I'm sorry, Liz. I hope my mother hasn't offended you."

"No one can offend me if I have you by my side." They just lay there and closed their eyes relaxing, when soon there was a knock on the door.

"Jakob, Elizabeth. The guests will be arriving at six."

Jakob smiled. "Don't worry, Mother, we will be ready. Kiss me again, Liz."

Liz and Jakob dozed off and were awakened by the sound of voices.

"Oh my gosh, Jakob, the guests are here and we're not ready."

"Don't worry, Liz. Let my mother do the worrying. We'll be ready. We have the whole evening to share with my family."

Then there was a knock on the door. "Jakob, the guests are here."

"Don't worry Mother we'll be down." Liz quickly freshened up and dressed in a light yellow-flowered dress that matched perfectly with her complexion and hair color. Jakob wore brown pants with a white shirt and tie.

"Liz, you look just great. Let's make the grand entrance."

As they moved down the stairs Mother remarked, "Oh, you two, look. Your guests have already arrived and you are late."

"Margaret, they aren't late. We just came early," said Grandfather Miller.

"Hello, everybody." Jakob announced he had brought his wife Liz to meet his family. Grandfather Miller was the first to give Liz a hug and welcome her to the family. Liz looked so fresh and gracious to the group. Each came up to her and welcomed her, almost to a point of ignoring Jakob. But Aunt Jenny put her arms around Jakob and gave him a big kiss, congratulating him for his marriage and his lovely wife. The whole evening went well. The ladies, especially the younger ones, questioned Liz about living in the West. They were excited for her response.

"The Indians, do you have trouble with the Indians?" asked Cousin Nel. Liz handled herself well. They then sat down for a sumptuous dinner with Margaret being the perfect hostess, making sure all were having a good time.

Later, Grandfather Miller engaged Jakob in conversation. "Jakob, when are you coming back to Milwaukee to live and work? Your father could use your help in his office. Wyoming was a good start and experience for you, but certainly you don't mean to stay out there, do you? You could make yourself a very good living here in Milwaukee. Give your wife all the finery she deserves. Raise a family with abundance."

Jakob listened to Grandfather Miller's sales pitch and answered, "Liz and I love our life in Wyoming. I will be successful there and I will be able to give my wife and family all they may need. You should come on a visit to Sheridan. I bet you would love Wyoming, just as we do." Grandfather Miller realized he would be unable to change Jakob's mind and acquiesced to his desires.

The whole evening went well. As time grew late, one-by-one the guests left the party. Jakob's dad congratulated Margaret for the great party she threw for Liz and Jakob, and the event ended on a pleasant note.

Everyone was up bright and early at the Miller household. Liz was trying to sort out yesterday's events as she lay in bed. Liz wasn't exactly upset, but Margaret's insistence of duplicating the wedding ceremony in Jakob's church seemed foolish. She felt Margaret should have taken it up with her in private. But rather than make an issue of it, she would oblige. The party with Jakob's family was successful and she liked them.

They went down for breakfast and Jakob's father was already eating. Liz found him to be very warm and she felt comfortable with him. He was a handsome man and Jakob resembled him a lot, however he was a more quiet and soft-spoken man, while Jakob was more outgoing. He immediately engaged Liz in conversation and wanted to know all about her and her family. He questioned her about her parents and was genuinely interested in them and apologized to Liz for not inviting them to be there for the event. He even said he felt the church ceremony was unnecessary, since they had been through it already, and then asked Liz if she would mind going down the aisle with him in her father's place. Liz said she would be honored to have him do that. Margaret had already asked two of Jakob's friends to act as witnesses. Just then, Margaret came in with their breakfasts. She asked Liz if she had a proper dress to wear in church, because if she didn't, there would be one available. Liz said she had a proper dress and it wouldn't be necessary.

"The monsignor would like to meet with you two before the service, at eleven," announced Margaret.

Jakob's father asked Liz and Jakob if they would like to see his rose garden. Margaret wanted to talk more but Jakob's father declined, and they went out. It was a clear, sunny day and they walked in the soft, green grass to the garden where he proudly displayed his roses. They then sat in the gazebo that overlooked the garden and continued their breakfast conversation. He told Liz he was happy for them and wished them happiness.

"Jakob, you have picked a lovely wife and I know you will be a good husband. I had hoped you would remain in Milwaukee, but I understand your desire to go back to Wyoming. I would like to see Wyoming. You once wrote me about a hunting trip in Wyoming. I would like to come out sometime and maybe we could go hunting together."

"I would like to do that very much, Dad. It would be a grand experience for both of us." Margaret came out to inform them they should get ready to go to the church and meet the monsignor. The church was just a short walk away from their home and Jakob's father volunteered to go with them.

It was a massive structure with high stairs leading to the large entry doors. The pastor's office was in the rectory behind the church. They rang the bell and the door was opened by the housekeeper who invited them in. His dad chose to wait, sitting in the comfortable entry.

The monsignor was a gray-haired man, probably in his sixties. He was cordial but very formal and spoke with a heavy German accent.

"I am soddy you did not vait to get married here in Milwaukee. You know, Jakob, as a Catholic you und your vife should have received instructions by you church. You und your vife have responsibilities to the church. If you have children, how vill they be raised?" He went on to describe the church's attitude on marriage.

"Vill your wife become a Catholic?" Jakob went on to inform the clergyman he could not say whether she would become a Catholic. It was her personal decision and she was a good Christian woman. There was no Catholic Church in Sheridan for them to attend. He was not renouncing his Catholic faith but would attend one of the churches there. The pastor seemed rather irked and said he would marry them. However, it would not be in the sanctuary but rather in the sacristy, because Elizabeth was not Catholic. She could come up the aisle to the altar and then go into the sacristy to be married. The rest of the routine was described, and that was the end of the meeting. They left the monsignor and started for home.

Jakob was somewhat unnerved as he told his father of the meeting. Robert indicated Margaret would be upset that the wedding would not be in the sanctuary because she had invited many of her friends to the church wedding, as well as the reception.

When they returned home, Jakob informed his mother the wedding ceremony would not be performed in the church sanctuary but in the sacristy. Margaret was livid and could not understand why the pastor was so staunch with his *old* church rules and she would be embarrassed if her friends were not part of the ceremony.

"I am going to the church to meet with the monsignor and get this straightened out. After all, we were all brought up in that church." Margaret's meeting with the pastor produced no results. The wedding would go on as he had indicated. This put a damper on Margaret's show.

Margaret hired several carriages to take the wedding party to the church and the reception.

Liz put on the wedding dress she wore in Sheridan, and looked beautiful. Jakob and his father had formal attire he had ordered, as did his best man, Henry Wright. The bridesmaid, Mary Schmidt, a family friend wore a light green gown, and, of course the mother of the groom was elegantly adorned in a blue chiffon dress. The bride and her attendant would carry flowers.

At two, the main section of the church was filled with friends and family. The organist started playing, and the vocalist sang the *Ave Maria*. When she had finished, Jakob came out and stood at the front of the aisle. Margaret came up the aisle to her seat escorted by Henry Wright, who then stood next to Jakob. As the wedding march started, Mary, the bride's maid moved slowly down the aisle and stood to the left side of the altar.

Liz, escorted by her father-in-law now started up the aisle. The people strained and looked back to see the bride. Liz was beautiful in her long, white dress and short veil. She wore a single strand of white pearls Jakob had given her, and held a small bouquet in her hands. She was not pretentious but had an air of refinement. This was not the frontier woman they all expected to see. As Robert and Liz approached Jakob, they turned to face each other. Robert placed a kiss on Liz's cheek and told her she would be the daughter he always wanted. Jakob embraced his father and took the hand of his wife. The monsignor appeared to the side of the altar in his cassock with the marks of his rank and led the wedding party back of the altar, to the sacristy, where the ceremony would take place. In the presence of the attendants, some prayers were said and the vows were again exchanged. He then shook Jakob's and Elizabeth's hand, and wished them well.

"Elizabeth, I pray you vould come back and become a member of the church." He then led them out into the sanctuary and introduced them to the congregation, as man and wife.

Arm-in-arm, and followed by the attendants, Liz and Jakob walked down the altar steps, as their friends applauded and followed them out of the church, to a traditional shower of rice. A receiving line was formed and many friends came up and congratulated and chatted with them.

The wedding party then went down the church steps and got into the waiting carriages, surrounded by the joyous crowd.

The driver honked the big horn on the side of the carriage and slowly moved away from their cheering friends. Their next stop was to have pictures taken. The driver honked his horn all the way with passers-by' cheering and waving to the newlyweds. The streets were decorated with flags and bunting to celebrate the 4th of July. They arrived at the photographer on Michigan Avenue, to have pictures taken, as was traditional for weddings.

Jakob would be seated and Liz was standing next to him, with her hand on his shoulder. The photographer held his flash pan high and squeezed the bulb for the shutter as the flash illuminated the room. All had pictures taken individually, along with a group picture.

With all the pictures taken, the driver took the wedding party on a romp of the streets of Milwaukee. Blowing his big horn to announce the wedding party, they laughed and waved at the crowds in the street. Liz got to see Milwaukee at its very best. Finally, it was back home to rest and freshen up for the reception.

The wedding party and family arrived early at the Milwaukee Country Club so that Margaret could make the inspection of the facilities to be sure they were what she had expected. Everything was just as she had wanted it to be. The staff and waiters were finishing up and the orchestra was setting up their instruments. This was to be a grand event.

The wedding party and family were now ready to receive their guests as they arrived. The many guests congratulated the couple and made small talk or questioned them about Wyoming. Most had little knowledge of Wyoming or their life there. To some it was considered like the end of the world. There was a table where many deposited wedding gifts. Libations were offered to the guests as they filled the reception area. The orchestra began playing.

When all the guests had arrived, they began to play a march, and the bride and groom led the way to the meticulously appointed dining room with white table cloths, napkins, sparkling glassware, dishes and silverware. Wine was poured and Jakob's father led the invocation. Henry Wright proposed the toast to the bride and groom. He knew Jakob quite well and made a humorous presentation. Margaret was in all her glory because this was a perfect wedding reception. The orchestra played soft dinner music, as the guests feasted on special dinner items and chatted with one another.

A four-tiered wedding cake was wheeled into the room and placed in front of the bride and groom. Jakob and Liz came out and made the first cut together. They were cheered. As they sat down, Greg Roberts stood up. He was a childhood friend of Jakob who made a emotional toast to his friend.

The orchestra began a waltz. Jakob looked at Liz, and took her hand, and slowly they moved across the floor. The contrast with the wedding in Sheridan was almost overwhelming. The elegance and pomp prevailed.

Jakob whispered into Liz's ear, "Do you miss Sheridan?"

Liz smiled and kissed his cheek. "Just as long as I'm with you, nothing else really matters." Jakob's father asked to dance with his new daughter and Jakob moved away. Margaret took his arm and danced with her son. The dance floor quickly filled with people. Liz didn't dance with Jakob for most of the evening because everyone wanted to dance with her.

At nine the room was filled with sounds of fireworks exploding out on the golf course. Everyone moved out to view the display of Roman candles, rockets and bright pyrotechnics. The orchestra joined in with Sousa marches, and the guests clapped and sang patriotic songs.

Then it was over. Jakob held Liz tightly and kissed her tenderly. "I bet this is one wedding you will never forget, with fireworks and all." The guests came up to Liz and Jakob and bid them happiness and good fortune. Margaret was happy with the day and the reception was a great success.

Jakob spent a restless night and awoke early. He didn't awaken Liz and decided to get up before the rest of the house. He donned his robe and went into the kitchen to start a pot of coffee. The sun was up and he went out on the porch, which faced the backyard and sat there, thinking about the past days in Milwaukee.

Am I doing the right thing for Liz? We like our Wyoming lifestyle but it is fraught with difficulties. The frontier is not without problems. Am I being fair to her? The home we will be living in is almost austere. If we lived in Milwaukee we would have a completely different life. The past days were very enjoyable. We could live almost a life of luxury if we make our life here in Milwaukee. He thought about his home here and then what he might have to face, when he went back to Wyoming. *How much can Elmer do to the cottage to make it livable for us? It certainly was disappointing when we saw it. Liz and I have to think this over carefully. Maybe Wyoming is just a dream we can put aside for now.* And, then he thought about the friends they had made and the excitement of their life there: Liz and her school children, his practice, the mountains and streams, the sky with no boundaries, the challenges. *Could I really give that up? Would Liz want to move back east?* His thoughts were random. Just then the door opened and his father came out.

"I wondered who made the coffee. What are you doing up so early?"

"Oh, I guess I just couldn't sleep. Maybe it was all the excitement of the last couple days."

"How long are you going to stay with us? You are welcome to stay as long as you wish."

"Oh thanks, Dad. You and Mother have been great. I think we will be going back the first of the week. I need to get back to work. We have to get our house together and get back to a routine. We have lots of planning to do. These past days have been wonderful. I would like to show Liz Milwaukee and see a few of my old friends, and I want to take her down to the beach. She has never seen Lake Michigan."

"I understand and respect your wishes. I do want to take you over to the office and show you what I've been doing here. Lots of changes are going on in dentistry. I want you to know I think you have yourself a fine wife. She is a lovely person, but then I always knew you would find a good wife." The door opened and Liz appeared.

"Jakob, how long have you been out here? You left me sleeping when I could have been out here with you and your dad."

"It's just been man talk and you would probably be bored."

Liz laughed. "What's on the schedule for today?"

The following days were spent visiting with Jakob's friends and seeing Milwaukee. It was a typically hot, sunny July day and Liz packed a lunch to take with them down to the beach to see Lake Michigan. Sitting on a blanket, Jakob brought up his thoughts of that early morning following the wedding reception. Liz looked at Jakob with surprise in her eyes.

"Jakob, I will go along with whatever you wish, but Wyoming is our home now. I like our life there. I really would not want to live here or anywhere other than Sheridan. That's home for us. I'm glad you brought me here to meet your friends and family and it has been a great trip, but I'm ready to go back to Sheridan."

"I thought you'd say that, but I just wanted you to know your wishes are important to me. I've thought about Elmer Findley's cottage and, I want you to know, we will get started on a home of our own just as soon as I can do it."

"That's fine but let's go back to where we belong." The next few days were spent visiting more of Jakob's friends and family. Everyone was interested in their life in Wyoming. Some admired their choice of living a frontier lifestyle and others looked at them as being foolish, when they could have a much easier life living in Milwaukee.

The day had arrived and they were getting ready to leave. Jakob's mother made one more attempt to dissuade them from going back, but to no avail. Jakob's dad talked of visiting Jakob and Liz so he could go elk hunting.

Jakob and Liz climbed aboard the Milwaukee Road heading for Chicago. The wedding gifts they had received were carefully boxed for the trip. They would be added to the others they had received when they moved into their home. The trip to Chicago included another stay at the Palmer House. Jakob extended their stay so he could show Liz some of the sights of the city. He took her to see the school he had graduated from, Chicago College of Dental Surgery. They visited with some of his former teachers and the dean who was interested in Jakob's practice in Wyoming. Then it was off to see some of his classmates who practiced in the city, and Liz saw just how they lived. It seemed Sheridan was a much different world, but it was one she cherished and with her husband, it would be her place in heaven.

The honeymoon to the Midwest was nearing an end, as they boarded the Chicago Burlington and Quincy Railroad headed for Burlington, Iowa, and points west to Sheridan, Wyoming. They had spent more than two weeks on their visit and were anxious to return. They were making their plans for moving into the Findley cottage, not really knowing what to expect. Liz was thinking about the coming school year and whether she would be having more students.

They rode the same trains back to Sheridan and they may have made a few extra stops for cattle that wandered on the tracks, but other than that, it was the same scenery in reverse. As the train slowly pulled into Sheridan they anxiously gathered their belongings. This was the end of the line for them, although the rail line toward the north was already begun. Dusty and weary, they stepped off the train.

Wilbur, from the livery stable, used to meet the train and pick up arrivals, so Jakob hired him to take them and their luggage back to the Sheridan Inn. When they got to the inn, Henry Clayton greeted the now very married Dr. and Mrs. Jakob Miller back to the Sheridan Inn. The porch of the inn was filled with all sorts of people who were auditioning as acts for the Buffalo Bill Cody Wild West Show. There were horses and riders and fancy-dressed ladies vying for a part in his show. At the center was the very prominent Buffalo Bill, who smiled and tipped his large hat to Liz.

Henry Clayton brought Liz and Jakob up to date on the happenings at the Inn. He had rented the presidential suite to Senator Billings who had come to town for the July 4th celebration, and then stayed around to do some politicking.

"Don't you worry Jakob. You and Liz can use your old suite. He won't be around for long and Bill Cody will be leaving in a few days. It will be nice and quiet around here again when he leaves."

With the extra boxes they brought back, there was little room left to move around in. They cleaned up and went down to the dining room for dinner where they were greeted by various friends and acquaintances who questioned them about their trip to the Midwest. It felt good to be back home. The long day came to an end and they entered their room. Jakob picked up Liz, carried her through the door, and placed her on their bed. He took off her hat, as Liz put her arms around Jakob and tenderly kissed him.

"Oh, I like this. It's so good to be back, Honey." Jakob unbuttoned her blouse and looked solemnly at her.

"What does all this mean? What are your intentions, Doctor Miller?" She put her arms around him, Jakob just smiled as they lay down on the bed and he drew her closer to him.

Chapter 13

Starting a Home

Jakob awoke early, at the break of dawn. He began thinking about all he had to do. The trip to Milwaukee had placed him behind in his work schedule. He had a number of patients he had to put off before he left, and was anxious to get back to his patients. Jakob was also concerned about getting into a home of their own so he and Liz could start housekeeping. The fancy hotel suite was all right but it was not like being in their own home. It was also costly and it was small. He and Liz ate in the hotel dining room or some other restaurant in Sheridan, and that made it difficult to save money they would need. His concerns were about the Findley house and he was hoping it could be made livable and comfortable.

Elmer had said he would take care of it before they left for Milwaukee, so Jakob was hoping it might be ready, or almost ready, to move in. Liz was also anxious to get started with her first home. He quietly got dressed, leaving Liz asleep, and went down to the dining room. Lukas had coffee ready and Jakob had his bacon and eggs.

"How was the trip to Milwaukee, Doc?" Lukas, asked.

"It was very nice. But, I'm glad to be back."

"Had some people in here looking for you and asking when you would be back. I told them you would be back soon."

"Well, here I am—I'm back and I'm ready to get to work." Jakob finished his breakfast and left the hotel. He was anxious to see how the Findley house was progressing, so he started walking in that direction. The rest of the town was just starting to awaken and there were people moving around.

It was just a short walk to Marion Street. As he turned the corner, he saw the house ahead. He was pleasantly surprised to see it had been painted, and the fence and gate were fixed. The porch was repaired and there were even some flowers planted in the front yard. Now he was really excited, as he easily opened the front door that had been stuck. The inside looked completely different. The fireplace was cleaned and the kitchen was ready for cooking. There was even a wall separating the bedroom from the rest of the house. The broken window was replaced and a nice curtain over it. It looked like it might be ready to move in. Jakob was excited and pleased. *This will be a fine home for us to get started*, he thought. *Liz will be anxious to see it. I'll go back to get her.* He walked fast, almost running and arrived at the hotel. He waved at some of the people he recognized and greeted Henry Clayton as he entered the hotel, going straight to his room. Liz was awake and moving around the room.

"Hi, Honey. Where have you been?"

"Oh, I couldn't sleep, so I got up and went for some coffee and breakfast and then went over to see the house. I'm really pleased. It looks very nice. I think you will be pleased too."

"That's great. Now I'm excited, Jakob, I really want to get into our own place, even if it is the Findley cottage." She quickly dressed and was ready to leave.

"Let's get you some breakfast first."

"Oh, I don't really care about breakfast. I'm too excited."

"I'm sure it will be fine. I just can't get wait for us to get into our own home. It's small, but we can get by until the day we are ready to build a home." They hurried out of the hotel and moved up the street toward Marion Street. They turned the corner and Liz got her first glimpse of the cottage.

"Jakob, it's painted white. How nice. And look, there are even some flowers in the yard." Jakob opened the door and they walked in. Tears welled in her eyes. "Jakob, it's our first home. It will be fine. I'll make it really homey. I know just what I will do. I can't wait till we get all our gifts in here. I am so excited. Oh, Jakob, I love you so." She put her arms around Jakob and kissed him. She acted like a little girl who got her first doll. The old bed that was there before was gone, and a brass bed occupied the space, along with a chest of drawers. Liz was walking around the house looking at the walls and every aspect of the place. "Perfect, let's get started."

"Not so fast, lady. I have to see Elmer and make sure we can move in now. But you can stop over at Mrs. Howard's place and start getting your things together there. Let's go over and get some coffee at Betty's place and talk about what we will do. We both have lots of work ahead and then I have to go over to the office. I expect there will be some patients in today needing my help." They soon finished their coffee and were ready to start.

"First, I'll stop over at the Findleys, then we'll meet for lunch and I'll let you know what he says." Excited, they both started off going in different directions. Jakob stopped to see Elmer Findley at the general store.

"Jakob, I heard you were back. I knew you would be in this morning. Have you had a chance to see the cottage? It's not quite done, but it should be ready for you to move in within a week."

"Yes, we did go over to see it, and it does look good. Liz is pleased with it and is anxious to move in."

"I've got more furniture coming in. It should be here in a few days. John still has a few things to be done, but it sure looks different. I told you we'd get it fixed up for you. Glad to see you back. This will help tide you over until you are ready to get your own place. Now that it's fixed up, I won't have any trouble renting it. I've had a few people stop by here and say they were looking for you. Looked like they needed you. I told them you would be returning soon."

"I'm back and ready for work. I better get over to the office." As Jakob approached the office he saw some people outside waiting for him.

"Hi, Doc, I shore am glad you got back. I got one cookin' up a fuss. I know you can take care of it. You know Mike the barber can cut hair, but I wouldn't trust him taken out ma tooth." Thus, Jakob's day had started. Liz was spending the morning with Mrs. Howard getting the gifts together for moving. Mrs. Howard set the table and they had some tea and cookies, as Liz took time out to tell her about the Milwaukee trip. Mrs. Howard had some feelings about the second marriage ceremony.

"Land sakes, Liz, the woman had no right to make you go through the marriage ceremony a second time, even if he is a Catholic."

"Oh, I didn't see any reason to make a fuss about it. I did it for Jakob. He was in the middle of the whole thing. Even his dad was upset with her, but it did turn out to be a great party and we did have a nice time." They chatted for some time and Liz related the whole trip to her. Mrs. Howard had become a close friend of Liz and she was truly interested in her life. She had been very kind to her during the time Liz had stayed with her. "Oh my," Liz said, looking at the clock. "It's almost noon and I told Jakob I'd meet him at lunch time. I have to leave now."

Liz got to Jakob's office only to find he had a couple people still waiting for him. He had been busy all morning. She decided to go over to Elmer Findley's general store and look over what he had in stock, and made a list of the things she would need to start housekeeping. She was anxious to make Jakob his first dinner. As she talked to Mrs. Findley, Ella was giving her all kinds of advice on how to start her household. Liz thought she was a sweet lady, but she talked too much and Liz was not much interested in her advice. She had been there long enough and finally excused herself because she had to get back to Jakob's office. Liz arrived just as his last patient was leaving. Jakob quickly left the office and closed the door.

"Let's go over to Grandma's Kitchen and get a bite to eat. I sure had a busy morning. If things keep up like this, we may be able to build the dream house sooner than I thought."

"Jakob, don't worry about that. We'll just do fine in the Findley house."

Grandma's Kitchen was filled with people and most knew Jakob and Liz, so there was plenty of conversation. All were anxious to learn about the trip back to the Midwest. Liz was the center of attention for the ladies who were anxious to learn about happenings in the Midwest. Most had not returned to their former homes back East since moving to Wyoming. The trip to the Midwest was an exercise in contrasts between frontier living and the Midwest lifestyle.

The week passed quickly and Liz and Jakob were ready to move into their home. Jakob got a wagon at the livery stable and Zeke volunteered to help them move in. Liz talked about making Jakob's dinner and had shopped at Elmer's general store to get everything she needed. However, before she started, neighbors and friends kept coming up the walk carrying breads and cakes and cookies, casseroles, vegetables from their gardens, flowers, and other gifts. It was a genuine expression of love frontier style. It seemed like everyone in Sheridan came to wish them well. That was their way of giving them a house warming.

After they had all left, Jakob and Liz were toasting their new home and getting ready to sit down for the dinner their friends had made for them, when Zeke came in breathless.

"Doc Kelly sez he wants ya ta come to his place. They hauled in a ranch hand from da Circle K who been chased over a cliff by a bull. He sez he needs you." Jakob immediately left for Kelly's office. There was a crowd of people in front of the office, as Jakob worked his way in. Doc Kelly looked at Jakob who was now standing next to him.

"This is a bad one, Jake. This guy has some busted bones and his face is pretty mashed up. Looks like maybe a broken jaw and a bunch of teeth. His arm and leg are broken too. Let's get started."

Jakob had not returned from Doc Kelly's office yet, so Liz decided to tidy up their home as she waited for him. The gifts and food items her neighbors and friends brought had to be stored away. It was a real surprise that the neighbors had come by as neither of them expected it. Mrs. Johnson, their new neighbor, brought a buffalo roast that was still warm, and Liz left it out for Jakob to eat when he returned.

The sun was setting and it was getting dark. A silence descended over Sheridan except for an occasional owl hoot or maybe a coyote howl. Liz was becoming concerned Jakob had not returned. He had been gone several hours since Zeke had come for him. She walked out on the porch and was greeted by total darkness. There was some light visible from homes in the distance. The sky was covered with stars but no moon appeared. Liz became gripped with fear and was concerned for Jakob. This was their first night in their new home and she was alone. She thought of going to Doc Kelly's office, but it was so dark and she was confused as to where it might be. *I'm being silly*, she thought. *If someone is badly hurt it might take a while to take care of him.* She remembered when Jakob had been mauled by the bear and how she spent the entire night staying with him. *Maybe the man is badly injured and will need a great deal of care.* Liz slowly turned around and went back into the house. It was so quiet, and the two lamps she had lit created shadows on the wall. She sat down at the table. There was a glow of embers in the fireplace she stirred up, and placed a few pieces of wood to get it started. *I'll just make some tea*, she thought, as she swung the kettle over the fire. Liz found some knitting she had been working on, and sat at the table with the hot tea and continued working on the sweater. It was sometime later when she heard footsteps on the porch. Liz expected it was Jakob until she heard a knock on the door.

"Miz Miller, Miz Miller. It's me, Richard, from the hotel." Liz opened the door. Richard stood in the doorway carrying a lantern. "Miz Miller, I jes came over from Doc Kelly's office. Doc Jakob asked me to tell ya it might be a while fore he gits home. He and Doc Kelly was fixing up some guy that got banged up, and he sas he'd git home jis as soon as they git through."

"Well, thank you, Richard. I do appreciate you coming over to let me know. I was concerned about him."

"Don't you worry, Miz Miller. He be back jis as soon as he can. Evening, now." He tipped his hat and left. Liz closed the door. Her concern allayed, she went back to her knitting. It had been a long and busy day, and her eyes started to close as she laid her head on the table. Liz soon fell asleep, holding her knitting.

Jakob quietly opened the door and saw Liz asleep. He gently kissed her on the cheek. She opened her eyes and saw him next to her.

"Oh, Jakob, you've returned. I didn't mean to fall asleep. I guess I was just tired. I was worried about you, but Richard came by and told me you were still working on that man. I felt better knowing you were all right. What time is it?"

"It's past midnight."

"Jakob. That man, how is he? Will he be all right?"

"He is in pretty rough shape. From what the guys who brought him in said, they were rounding up some cattle and there was a bull in the herd that got pretty ornery. He turned around and headed toward one of the hands and caught his horse with his horn. He spun him around and sent him and the horse over a steep rise. They both went down about ten feet. They had to shoot the horse and they brought the cowhand to Kelly. He was badly banged up and cut up. His left arm and leg were broken. Broke a bunch of his front teeth. We got his arm set and were working on his leg. Then Doc Kelly thought he lost him. The fella's heart stopped and he stopped breathing. Kelly gave him a wallop over his heart and he came around. We waited a while until his heart and breathing seemed okay. I picked a bunch of stones out of his face and sewed up some cuts; some were real gashes. Then I took out some of the broken teeth. I don't think I ever saw such a bloody mess like that. When I left, he was moaning a lot but his heart was beating strong."

"Oh, Jakob. What a terrible experience. Are you all right?"

"Yes, I guess so. They didn't teach me anything like that in dental school. Doc Kelly said he was glad to have me around. That Kelly is one good doctor. He said it reminded him of taking care of soldiers in the war."

"Jakob, you must be exhausted and hungry."

"I guess I'm tired, and you must be too. I'm not hungry though. Put out the lamp and let's go to bed." Jakob carried the other lamp into the bedroom.

"Jakob, do you realize this is our first night in our new home and we are both so tired?" Jakob just smiled.

"There will be other nights." Liz snuggled up to Jakob and kissed him, and they fell asleep in each other's arms.

There was a pounding on the door. They were both aroused from a deep sleep.

"Doc Jakob. Doc Kelly sez he needs you," came the voice from outside. Jakob got up and went to the door.

"Doc Kelly sez the fella's bleeding from his mouth." Jakob put on his clothes and was ready to leave.

"Liz, you stay here and rest. I'll be all right. Where is the tea?"

"It's in the cabinet next to the sink. Wait, I'll fix you some tea."

"Never mind. I'm taking the tea with me." He took the small bag of tea leaves with him and started running out the door. The sun had just come up, and the town was awakening as Jakob opened the door to Doc Kelly's office. Richard was there, as well as some woman he didn't know.

"Jake, this guy is bleeding bad from the mouth where you took out those roots and teeth. I can't stop the bleeding. Got any tricks?"

"Give me some bandage." Jakob cut a piece of bandage and put some of the tea leaves on the bandage to make a poultice. He wet the poultice with water, sopped up the blood, then quickly placed the poultice over the bleeding wound and held it tightly. Kelly looked at him.

"Tea leaves. Where did you get that one, from some old Indian witch doctor?"

"Never mind, just wait. Do you think you could make another one of these up for me?" Kelly made another poultice and smiled.

"He did pretty good through the night, but this morning he woke up swinging and bumped his mouth with his arm. That's when it started bleeding. This guy lost a lot of blood and he can't afford to lose much more." Jakob held the poultice tightly and nodded in agreement.

"Richard, do you think you can make me a cup of coffee? I need some caffeine."

"Never mind, we got coffee. Don't get excited. Richard, pour him a cup of coffee. I don't want the kid to faint." Richard handed Jakob a cup of coffee as Jakob let up on the poultice. The bleeding almost stopped as Jakob changed the poultice. Doc smiled.

"You know, kid, I know about that tea leaf trick. I just didn't think about it. Why don't you go back to your sweety-pie. I think Richard and I can handle this now." The lady sitting quietly in the corner of the room smiled at Jakob.

"My name is Sally. George, whose life you both saved, is my friend. Thank you for all you have done. Thank you." She came up to Jakob and kissed him on the cheek and went over to Kelly and did the same. Kelly raised his eyebrows as he smiled at Jakob. George, lying on the table, moaned and grunted as his eyes opened. Kelly tended to him as Jakob washed his hands. He opened the door to leave.

"I'll be back later to check on you, Kelly." Doc Kelly gave Jakob a disgusted look.

"Don't bother, kid. I have everything under my control." Jakob smiled and closed the office door. He started walking toward home. Herman from the feed store stopped him.

"Hi, Doc. You up kinda early, aren't you?"

"Not really, just another day for me, Herman." He opened the gate in front of his home and stood for a few moments viewing the place. *These last few days have been hectic.* Then he thought about Liz waiting for him inside. *I'm a lucky guy.* He quickly walked up the steps, crossed the porch and opened the door. There was Liz, waiting for him. He put his arms around her and kissed her tenderly.

"I've been waiting for you, Jakob. I'll have breakfast ready for you in just a few minutes. Sit down and have your coffee. Is everything all right with the injured man? You left in such a hurry this morning. I guess you were concerned."

"Yes, I believe he will be fine. He had a rough time of it and was bleeding some, but we got it stopped. Doc Kelly is looking after him. They will probably move him to the hotel for a few days. His lady friend will look after him." With breakfast ready they both sat down to eat. Jakob looked across the table and saw Liz with an apron over her dress, her hair secured with a ribbon and a smile on her face.

"How lucky can a man be to have wife as beautiful as you?" Liz blushed.

"Jakob, this is our home now and we are in this together. But don't expect to get all my attention. I have to start getting ready for school classes, you know. I saw Mayor Burns the other day and he wanted to be sure I would be teaching school in September. I told him I'm planning on it."

"That is fine with me. I know it is something you want to do, and that's great. I guess I realized I'd have to share you with the school kids, but I'll do it just as long as I have all of you when I come home," he said, smiling at Liz.

Chapter 14

Dangerous Undertaking

Jakob picked up his mail from the post office and noticed a letter from Frank Debbs, over in Buffalo. Frank was the owner of The Buffalo General Store. He wrote to Jakob to inform him that a number of people had asked him if Jakob would be returning to Buffalo that summer to do dentistry for the people living there. Because there still was no dentist in Buffalo, Jakob had gone there last fall and stayed till December, and had to return to Sheridan in a snowstorm. Jakob swore he would never do that again. It was a successful trip for him financially, but he came back in a dangerous storm.

Jakob and Liz had just moved into their home, and he hadn't thought of going to Buffalo. But maybe it might be a good idea for him to do so. The expense of the wedding and the Milwaukee trip left his pockets a little empty. His last trip to Buffalo was so successful, financially, and since the people there wanted him to come back, it just might be a good way to get his finances in better shape.

He still had the idea of building his dream home for Liz. However, there was a stumbling block to the idea of going to Buffalo. He didn't want to leave Liz. They were very much in love and the thought of leaving her for even a couple days was impossible, let alone for a longer period of time. He thought of going for perhaps a month, but the idea of leaving her was too much to bear. He kept this thought to himself, and mulled it over for several days. Then, suddenly it occurred to him: maybe he could take Liz with him. She might like the idea of seeing Buffalo. It would be sort of a vacation for her, and she might want to help him in his office. Liz was already planning to teach school in Sheridan, but this would be before school started. That night he brought the idea up to her. She was excited and thought the idea of the Buffalo trip was great. They decided to go there for three or four weeks, and immediately started making plans for the trip.

Jakob told Wilbur Riggs at the livery stable of his need for a horse and wagon. Liz gathered her belongings and needs, and Jakob put his equipment in several trunks, and the date was set. Some of the townspeople grumbled when they heard he was leaving, but he assured them he would be back in a month.

They left early in the morning and started their trek to Buffalo. It wasn't very far and the weather was good. The plan was to camp out one night and make it to Buffalo in two easy days. It was to be a leisurely venture, as Liz was not used to the rigors of traveling by wagon. The sun burned brightly as they lumbered along a trail. Toward the latter part of the afternoon they found a nice stream and a stand of trees that would make a fine place to lay over for the night. Liz wasn't exactly the pioneer type but she had learned to cook over an open fire, and with the help of Jakob they made their supper. They finished their meal and sat watching the sun go down. The sky was clear and filled with stars, and a partial moon rose. They decided to sleep in the open, rather than in the wagon, and lay close together near the open fire and watched the celestial display. Jakob assured Liz it was safe and explained the sounds of the night to her. They snuggled closely and soon were fast asleep.

Jakob was up before sunrise and started making breakfast. Liz awoke to the smells of fresh coffee and bacon frying. He encouraged Liz to hurry because he wanted to get an early start for the rest of the trip. Actually, Jakob had some concerns. During the night the horse was unsettled and some of the night noises were unusual. They quickly packed and hitched the horse and soon were on their way. The wagon moved as fast as it could go, which is not very fast, and the day was clear. The sun rose brightly over the eastern sky.

Jakob turned around and noticed what appeared to be a number of riders in the distance, on the bluff above them. The riders were too far away for him to discern who they were, but the riders appeared to be going the same direction they were going. He kept looking back and saw them gaining on them. It was then he decided they might be Indians. Jakob became a little concerned, although he had never experienced problems with Indians and had even taken care of some in his office. More recently, there had been no problems with Indians in the vicinity of Sheridan, but then anything was possible. Why would they be following them? He kept checking back and now became even more concerned, as the distance between them rapidly closed. He counted eight riders. Liz noticed Jakob was looking back and she also turned around.

"Jakob, are those riders following us?" He answered that he didn't think so, but he was really concerned. As they closed in, they started firing into the air and were soon surrounding them, shooting into the air and yelping. He could now see their painted faces. They rode back and forth, in front of and around the wagon, as if to harass them. Liz now became terribly frightened and tears ran down her cheeks. Jakob also became frightened and confused by their actions. Nothing like this had ever happened to him and he was concerned for Liz. He knew the Indians could be unpredictable, and it didn't take too much for them to become aggressive.

Jakob had a carbine next to him, but if he fired it, he might kill one or two and the others would certainly kill them. He held up his hand in a peaceful sign but it seemed to no avail. They just continued to menace them. Suddenly, one of them turned his horse and headed straight toward the wagon, slapping it with his crop. He then went back to the others. They appeared to be talking among themselves until he came back again, approaching Jakob's side of the wagon. His fearful painted face was frightening until he broke out in a smile, and Jakob saw he seemed to be lacking his front teeth. He said something to Jakob in Indian but

Jakob did not understand. Then he pointed to his open mouth, without front teeth and continued talking to Jakob. It was then Jakob realized this was the young Indian who was brought to his office after he had been kicked by a horse. He evidently recognized Jakob. Jakob made gestures and spoke to the Indian, and he smiled.

The young brave gave the peace sign and the others yelped. He then motioned Jakob to follow him as the others raced ahead. Jakob still wasn't sure what he should do but he felt there was no imminent danger, so he continued following as the Indian rode back and forth for a couple hours. Before long they saw signs ahead of an Indian village. The other riders came back, as well as a bunch of barking dogs until one of the riders made a swat at the dogs with his crop and they went off yelping.

They entered the Indian village. Everyone was outside their tepees and seemed to be waiting for them. The chief approached the wagon and in very difficult English showed the peace sign and said *welcome*. The others danced and showed their favor. Liz was still trembling as she sat close to Jakob. Jakob tried to allay her fears, as he realized the Indians were really friendly. The chief had evidently learned some English but was hard to understand.

He asked them to come down from the wagon and sit with him by the fire. Holding a peace pipe, he passed it to Jakob. Others came and sat in a circle by the fire. Food was soon brought out. Liz clung to Jakob as they sat with the chief. The large fire was in the middle of a field, with tepees surrounding it. Squaws with their papooses on their backs stood behind the men. The young brave who brought them to the village came up to Jakob and Liz with his squaw and papoose. He wanted to show off his family. Liz started losing her fears when she saw the women and children of the village. There was a lot of activity and dancing and drumming. Jakob passed the peace pipe to the Indian next to him who tried to engage him in conversation, but Jakob didn't understand. The chief tried to make known he was pleased Jakob had helped the brave who had been injured by one of the ponies.

He then took Liz and Jakob to a tepee that had been prepared for them. Several of the squaws were dispatched to help them. They gave Liz special attention. Later, they prepared for the evening. Liz wondered what the different foods were. Jakob wasn't sure himself but didn't tell Liz she might have dined on roasted dog which they often ate. The dancing and drums went on far into the night. When they had their fill of food and entertainment they entered their tepee. Jakob was concerned about their belongings but found them already inside the tepee. Liz was interested in the children and questioned Jakob about their education.

"Do they go to school? Do they have someone to teach them to read and write?" Jakob laughed and assured her they did not attend any school, as she would think of it. She then realized they would not have gotten any formal education, and immediately started thinking about how she might be able to teach them to read and write.

In the morning they were awakened by the barking of dogs and activity in the village. The children were attracted to Liz and soon she was teaching them, using fingers and toes. The squaws were also attracted to her. Liz looked on them as people not too different from her and Jakob, except they didn't have an education as she knew it.

They just have not had any opportunity as our children have. I wonder if there would be something I could do for them, she thought. This was the first time she had any real contact with Indians and she saw a need she felt should be met. Jakob realized that this visit was detracting from his original mission to Buffalo and decided to leave, but not before he treated several of the Indians for their dental problems. Though he never mentioned fees, the Indians gave what they had in return for services rendered. They were genuinely grateful for him helping them.

Jakob thanked the chief and told him he had to leave. He then encouraged the young brave, who had brought them there, to visit him in Sheridan, and told him he could make him some new teeth to replace the ones he had to take out. He wasn't sure he understood him but he tried. The chief ordered the braves to escort them back to where they had been on the trail to Buffalo. What had been a frightening moment in their lives turned out to be a lesson in relationships with the Indians.

When they reached the trail to Buffalo the Indians left them. They moved along at the pace of the wagon and quietly mulled the experience with the Indians. Liz was the first to speak. "Jakob, I would like to do something to help the Indian children. Maybe I could spend a day at the reservation holding classes for them. They seem to be intelligent but need regular lessons. I have extra books I could use. What do you think?"

Jakob thought a while and answered her query. "Your idea is a good one, Liz, but there is the problem of distance. It would take the better part of a day to get to the village so your idea of spending a day at the village would mean at least a three-day trip. You have your students in Sheridan you are committed to. I doubt you could get the Indians to bring the children to Sheridan and even if they did, you might find the townspeople would look unfavorably at what you want to do. Maybe you could spend a week at the reservation next summer; that might be a start. The Indians have their own culture and I'm afraid what you are suggesting might be very difficult."

"Jakob, a week would be hardly enough time to do much, but it would be a start. Then maybe we can figure something out. I really want to do something for those people." They continued with their conversation about the Indians. Liz was impressed by what she had seen of tribal life and now had another view of the Indian population, other than what she had learned from the people in Sheridan.

"They are not savages, they are people. They are just a different culture from us and we have to learn to live with them."

The day passed quickly and Buffalo appeared ahead. Jakob saw what appeared to be substantial growth in Buffalo since he left there last December. But it lacked the kind of growth and infrastructure of Sheridan. The railroad had made all the difference in Sheridan's success. They stopped at Frank Debb's General Store and Frank was glad to see them. Jakob had some notices printed that could be posted in his store, as well as other places in town. They went to the Occidental Hotel where they rented a room. Jakob was able to rent the same storage shed for his office he had the previous year. His next stop was to get an article in the local paper, *The Buffalo Echo*. He met with Harry Johnson who gave him a half-page ad. Most of the people in Buffalo read the *Echo*, so this was the best way to let everyone know Jakob was there and open for business.

He left Liz to rest in the hotel room while he made stops in the various drinking establishments. He even found a few more than they had the previous year. Jakob didn't exactly take a count, but he felt there were more in Buffalo than in Sheridan. Buffalo was located in Johnson County. Sheridan had split off from Johnson County, and there was some enmity between the two cities, but Jakob was careful not to get involved in the local politics. He was invited there to help take care of the people.

Jakob had hardly enough time to get his office together before he had people waiting for him to open up. He managed to get a barber chair to use from John Rodgers, whose shop was not far from the hotel. John needed a crown on a tooth that had a broken cusp when he was chewing on ribs, so Jakob promised to do it for him if he could use one of his chairs.

Liz came down to the office with Jakob and spruced up the place. She found a few chairs at Frank's store and a couple nice cushions for his patients to sit on. He also had a little table she bought and placed a couple magazines and a newspaper on it for the patients to read. Liz could also register their name in his work ledger and collect Jakob's fees.

All of a sudden the drab little office took on a home-like atmosphere. The men were mostly enthralled with Liz who would often speak to them. The ladies felt more comfortable with her presence. The weeks flew by and Jakob's time in Buffalo paid off. In fact, he did so well he was concerned with taking the money back to Sheridan with him. He decided to put most of the money in the Bank of Buffalo for safekeeping. The trail to Sheridan was well traveled but highwaymen also traveled it so he left most of his poke there.

Liz was due to start her classes in a week, so Jakob dismantled his office and started for home. The weather held and the trip was made in one long day on the trail. It was a good experience for Liz. She had the opportunity see Jakob at work and also to work with him. It gave her a new insight into frontier living. Soon she would be back doing what she liked most, teaching the children in Sheridan, and Jakob would be back in his office with his patients. The Indian experience was something that gave her a lot to think and talk about.

Chapter 15

Life in Sheridan

Jakob and Liz were living in the home Elmer Findley had readied for them. Liz had used her homemaking skills to make it livable and pleasant. She had received many gifts from friends in Sheridan, as well as the gifts they had received from their trip to Milwaukee, from Jakob's friends and family. Some of those were not exactly suited for the frontier home, but she put them away to be used later. Their house was warm and friendly.

She was preparing to get ready for classes. The number of students increased significantly, which would take more of her time, but it would also give her more money to use for her home. Sheridan was growing and there was now another school that was organized under the auspices of a Methodist Church.

The railroad was building another line which would go north toward Billings. They had brought in an influx of new people to help build the new line. The population was definitely increasing in Sheridan and there were many new people needing services. There was also a new drug store and two more general stores.

A new doctor also set up practice and that was good. Doc Kelly was so busy he could not take time off for any hobbies or personal interests. He also was getting a bit cranky, probably from being overworked. Dr. Frederic Ross came from the Jefferson School of Medicine in Philadelphia. He was young but seemed well qualified. Many of the old-timers in Sheridan still didn't want to go to him because they had loyalty to Doc Kelly or maybe because they sometimes didn't pay Doc Kelly for services. They would be expected to pay Doctor Ross. Dr. Ross was finding his practice flourishing. Many of the younger ladies in town found him to be more attractive, understanding and of course unmarried, so he became the most prominent eligible bachelor.

The Army personnel from nearby Fort Phil Kearny were always in and out of town. The young officers were invited for special events and dances. They made a nice pool of potential mates for the young unmarried ladies. There were more social events now than there were when Jakob had first arrived in town. Another newspaper, *The Sheridan Enterprise*, opened for business and there were two newspapers vying for the local business. There was also a growing population of Chinese immigrants. They had laundries and had even opened restaurants which were frequented by townspeople who liked that style of cooking.

Weekends in Sheridan were generally quite busy. Cowboys from the various nearby ranches came in to let off steam on weekends, and of course they would find themselves in all kinds of trouble. The sheriff kept his establishment filled to capacity. The two doctors were also kept busy because the mixture of gambling and whiskey always led to disagreements, and disagreements were all too often settled with fists or guns which led to busted teeth or busted bodies, so Jakob was always on call. The only problem was when his patients had spent too much time at the poker or faro table, they might be unable to pay for his services. Or if they had spent too much money with the ladies at the Frontier and Cowboy saloons, Jakob would often have to wait to get paid for his services—that is, if he ever got paid. Doing business on the frontier was filled with problems and shortcomings, but then, it also had its rewards.

Liz was at a meeting of the church ladies so Jakob decided to stop over at the Lucky Lady to see his friend Andy Meeks. The place was its usual busy self with loud music and card playing. At the big corner table there was an unusually large group of people gathered. The crowd there was rather quiet.

"What's going on over there?' asked Jakob.

"Oh, haven't you heard? Diamond Lil is in town." Diamond Lil would periodically visit the Lucky Lady and challenge some of the better local poker players. She generally would leave town with significant winnings. Her trademark was a show of diamonds on her fingers, as well as other visible parts of her body. She was rather attractive but shunned relationships with local available men. Lil had a sweet voice but could share expletives with the best of them. She moved from town to town, and poker was her game. On several occasions foolish predators attempted to separate her from her poke or jewelry, but Diamond Lil was known to have notches on her revolvers, which she located in strategic places on her body. Of late, no one had been foolish enough to challenge her.

After he finished his whiskey and conversation with Andy Meeks, Jakob decided to look in on the game. Most of the crowd was standing close to Diamond Lil. There was space on the side opposite her, so Jakob pushed in and observed the skilled lady. She looked up from her hand, saw Jakob and smiled at him.

"Hey there, big boy. Want to join in on the game? There's room for you."

The crowd chuckled and Jakob blushed and remarked, "You're a little too good for me. Besides, poker isn't really my game."

Lil winked at Jakob and replied, "Oh, I know your game. You and I have to get together for some business."

The crowd broke out in whistles and laughter and remarks, like, "Hey, Doc, wait till Liz hears about this."

When the crowd started to settle down, Lil said, "Okay boys, that's between me and him. Settle down and let's get back to the game." She threw out a trump and started to pick up her winnings. Jakob observed the skillful Lil for a while and then decided to leave. As he turned and started out, Lil looked up. "See you later, big boy." Again, the crowd started laughing and making remarks, and Lil chastised the group. "Now, boys, remember that's between me and him. Pay attention to the cards."

Jakob was a little embarrassed by the display and Andy Meeks yelled over at him, he better watch his step. As he walked through the swinging doors he could still hear the laughing and the piano player's choice of songs.

Jakob decided to meet Liz over at the church and walked the short distance, but was stopped several times by some of the townspeople for short chats. He certainly knew a lot of people in Sheridan but he also saw a lot of new faces these past months. The railroad had its good effect on the town but it also brought in some undesirables. Fortunately the sheriff usually took care of them. It was known that occasionally some of the Hole in the Wall Gang came by without the knowledge of the sheriff. But they would do their business and slip out.

The ladies church group was outside the church chatting after their meeting when Liz looked up to see Jakob approaching. She said her goodbyes and approached Jakob, and the two walked off toward home. Liz gave Jakob all the gossip she had heard, as well as the news about the church social that was being planned.

"Jakob, you aren't too active with our church. I wish you would be. There are some very nice people I wish we could be better friends with."

Jakob looked at Liz and smiled. "Oh, we could become friends with lots of people here in town. We already have lots of friends but it has nothing to do with my being in the church men's club. I don't shun the group but I do have other friends I like to associate with too. We go to church services and I take part in them. I still remember how gracious they were when we got married, but I also enjoy some of my friends who aren't part of the church."

Liz looked a little exasperated but smiled. "Yes, I know, that bunch at the Lucky Lady. Oh, I'm sure some of them are your friends but there is another element there you don't belong with. I know you don't associate with them, but they are still there. Oh, let's drop it, but I do wish you would consider being a little more active in the church. Now, let's see . . . what are we going to have for dinner?" Jakob thought a while as they walked along.

"You know we could go out for dinner tonight. We haven't done that for a while. I saw Lukas, from the hotel, and he mentioned he hadn't seen us recently. Or, we could try that new Chinese restaurant over on Coffen Avenue. I heard it was pretty good. I think it is called Lee Wong. What do you say? We'll celebrate something."

"Oh, I know, Jakob! We can celebrate us! Let's go home and I'll change into that new dress you bought for me."

Jakob looked at Liz with a quizzical look and said, "I don't remember buying you a dress."

Liz smiled coyly and said, "Oh, yes you did. I was in the New York Store on South Main Street when I saw it, and I just knew you would want me to have it. So I bought it for you."

Jakob burst out laughing. "Okay, you win. I did buy the dress for you. I should at least see it on you so we can celebrate my good fortune for having such a conniving wife." They laughed until they arrived at the gate in front of their home. They walked up the steps and Liz opened the door.

"Wait!" Jakob scooped Liz up from the porch and carried her in, then sat her on the bed. "Now, I want to see that new dress." Liz found the dress and proceeded to take off her school dress. Jakob put his arms around her and kissed her softly.

"Don't you want me to put on my new dress?" Jakob smiled and drew her close to him.

"Not just yet, Liz, not just yet. I can wait a while," he said as he nudged her on to the bed and began to kiss her.

Later Liz did put on her new dress, and they entered the dining room of the Sheridan Inn. It was Saturday night and the dining room was almost filled to capacity with hotel guests. Annabelle, the hostess that night, found a table for them in a quiet section of the room. Liz looked radiant and Jakob commended her for the dress he had bought her. Annabelle brought them a bottle of champagne that Lukas had sent out. They toasted to their good fortune and marriage, reminiscing about their lives together. Jakob held Liz's hands and repeated his vows to her that he would always care for her and love her, and would build a home they would raise their family in. Their little home on Marion Street was just temporary and he wanted so much more for her. It was obvious they cared much for each other. Some of the diners noted their expressions and smiled at the couple. Lukas had prepared a special dinner for them of roast elk with a wild mushroom sauce. It was the perfect evening. Lukas later came out of the kitchen to chat with them. He asked them how they liked the roast.

They agreed that it was very good, and Jakob's thoughts broke into a smile as he said, "You know, Liz, it was an elk that brought us together." Liz and Lukas quizzically looked at Jakob.

"Whatever do you mean, Jakob? I don't understand."

"Well, Elizabeth, if I hadn't gone on that hunting trip with Zeke, and I hadn't shot that elk and then gotten bashed by that bear, and didn't have you mopping my brow in Doc Kelly's office all night, I might never have seen those beautiful eyes looking down on me that made my heart beat faster."

"Jakob you are impossible." They all laughed as they spoke of that horrible moment in time. The dining room was now almost empty when they decided to call it a day. They thanked Lukas for the champagne and bid him good-night.

Monday morning can be a busy time for Jakob. Toward the end of the morning, he saw a very attractive lady in the waiting room dressed as if she were going to a ball. She wore a long, dark skirt and a ruffled pink blouse with long sleeves. Coupled with light-colored, high button shoes, she wore a large brimmed hat adorned with an array of feathers. Her slender fingers with polished nails carried a variety of diamond rings.

"Hello, big boy. I told you I would be seeing you. I've come to do business with you." It was Diamond Lil. Jakob was flabbergasted and smiled.

"I told you I don't play cards." And he laughed.

"Well, big boy I didn't come here to play cards. I came here for some of your excellent services. I was told you are the best dentist in town."

Jakob laughed. "Well, Lady, I happen to be the only dentist in town." And now Lil laughed.

"All my life I have had problems with my ivories. My teeth were always full of holes, but I found tooth carpenters to fill them. I've had nightmares about losing them and then having to take out my false teeth at night and put them in a cup. Really, that is one thing I fear the most. That's why I'm here to see you."

Jakob sobered and answered, "And that, my dear lady, is the reason I am here to serve you."

"I haven't seen one of you guys for a while. The last guy I saw was in Saint Louie. I didn't feel comfortable with him as a dentist or as a, well . . . , as a doctor, if you know what I mean. He was too interested in my diamonds and ah . . . ."

"Well, I can tell you I'm only interested in your teeth. However, you'll have to take off that hat, before I can look at those teeth." Jakob did a cursory examination and told Lil she did have some teeth that needed work done on them.

Out of character and serious, Lil explained she was a singer and wanted to leave the gambling world to be an entertainer. She had done some singing in Saint Louie and Memphis, and thoroughly enjoyed it. "I got a good voice, Doc. Honest. And I'm not too bad to look at for my age. And please don't ask me my age, because I will have to lie to you and I want to be honest with you." Jakob was smiling as she continued. "So here is what I am proposing to you, and it's not marriage because I hear you got yourself a humdinger of a gal. I was told when I am on stage and singing and smiling, my teeth look like hell. Well, they do. All that gold. I know you got to fill those holes with something, but I like to smile and laugh. I've never had a guy tell me I have a nice smile. They compliment the rest of me or my rocks but not my smile. And I like to smile a lot."

Jakob studied her face as she talked and realized that her smile wasn't pleasant, but it was overcome by the rest of her and her personality.

"Doc, could you replace some of that gold with diamonds? When I'm on stage and the lights hit me, they would sparkle. I could smile more." Jakob listened as she continued to tell him about herself and her dreams. All of a sudden he was feeling like some father confessor. "So, Doc, what can you do for me? Can you put some diamonds in my teeth so my teeth will sparkle? I got plenty of diamonds of all sizes. What we got to lose? What do you say?"

Jakob continued to study her face and her teeth. "Lil, you have provided me with a real challenge. I have some ideas, but let me think more about it. We can get together tomorrow and maybe I can help you out."

Lil picked up her hat, got up out of the chair and gently tapped Jakob on the cheek with her fingertips. "Thanks big boy. I knew I could talk to you." She opened the door to the office and slithered away. Jakob stood silent and looked into the distance, thinking about the event and what he thought he could do for her.

He finished the day and walked over to the schoolhouse to meet Liz. She was at her desk with papers she was grading. A few students were still there; several were at their desks, and one was cleaning the blackboards, and another putting books on the shelf. Liz acknowledged Jakob's presence and told him she would be busy for a while. There were two boys sitting at their desks looking glum. Evidently there was a problem, as they were busy writing on their tablets, but Liz didn't want to discuss it. Jakob realizing she would be busy for a while, left the schoolhouse and waited outside.

There were several children outside talking, and he approached them and started a conservation. He asked them various questions. They seemed somewhat reluctant to answer, excused themselves and went home. Jakob then saw the girls leave the schoolhouse, followed by the two boys chasing after them and yelling. Jakob assumed Liz was finished and went into the schoolhouse. Liz was putting her desk in order and got her things together. She seemed troubled.

"I'm ready to leave now, Honey." She closed and locked the door, and they headed for home. They didn't talk as they usually do, and walked some distance in silence.

Finally Jakob said, "Liz, you are so quiet. You seem engrossed in your thoughts. Is there something wrong?"

Liz looked up at Jakob. "Well, you aren't very talkative either. Is there something wrong with you?"

Jakob laughed. "No, there isn't anything wrong, but I do have a problem I have to solve and I'm considering a solution." Then he related the story of Diamond Lil and what she wanted him to do. He had the solution but he wasn't sure it was the right thing. "I can make crowns for some of her teeth and I could put diamonds into them, but I would have to take the nerves out of those teeth. Even though they have large, unsightly fillings in them, it would be a rather radical way to do it. It seems somewhat wrong for me to do it that way, yet her desire for a more pleasant appearance seems like the right thing to do for her."

Liz smiled. "I'm sure you will treat her correctly and it will be the right thing to do for her." Then Liz looked at him seriously.

"I have two boys in my school who are posing a problem for me. I haven't ever had a serious discipline problem but these boys are disrupting my class. They are new to the school. Their father moved to Sheridan this summer. His wife died and the boys are motherless and unruly. I feel sorry for them but they are making it difficult for me to take care of the other children. He works for the railroad and the boys are left alone to fend for themselves most of the time."

"Well, Liz, if they are a problem for you maybe you should refuse to school them. You shouldn't have to put up with their shenanigans."

"Yes, I know, but they really need schooling. I don't think they've had much education and they are way behind for their age. One is twelve and the other is thirteen. If I let them go they may never catch up and they could end up in real trouble later in life." Jakob could see she was really concerned.

"Maybe you could talk with the father and he could do the disciplining."

"I have questioned them but they say their father can't come in because he works all the time."

"Maybe you could ask the lady in Mayor Burns's office to talk to the father. That would sort of take things out of your hands. You know, bring in a little authority."

"That just might be a good idea. Yes, I will do that." They had arrived at home and went in. Liz put her arms around Jakob and tenderly kissed him. "I do need you, Jakob, to help me. I don't know what I would do without you." Jakob was moved by her words and held her tightly.

"That's what it means to be married. We are there to help each other. We are one. I plan on being here with you whenever you are in need, and pray you will likewise be here with me. We will always live our lives that way."

Jakob left for his office early the next morning. As usual, he anticipated meeting people on the way and would be stopping to chat with them before continuing to the office. As he was approaching his office he saw Diamond Lil coming from the hotel. She wore a long denim skirt with dark-colored, high-button shoes, and a perfectly tailored denim shirt. She had a brimmed denim hat with a feather in it. There were diamond and gold bracelets on her wrists and diamond rings on several fingers, as well as long diamond earrings. She muffled her smile to hide her teeth.

"Good morning, big boy. I see you are here bright and early."

"I didn't expect you here so early. Thought you would be sleeping in after a big night of cards."

"No, I wanted to beat the crowd here. But I did have a good night of cards. I had to, so I could afford your fees."

Jakob smiled and answered, "I believe I have a treatment plan that will satisfy you." He told her he planned to devitalize—take the nerves out of two teeth and place crowns on them along with diamonds. The teeth had big fillings in them so he would not be using sound teeth. He also told her he would place other fillings, of a new tooth-colored material, in the other teeth, so that she would have an attractive smile. Lil was thrilled with what he had planned and agreed to the terms. She handed him some diamonds he could select and use for her teeth. Jakob told her the treatment would take quite a bit of time, so she would have to stay in Sheridan for about a month.

"No problem, Doc. I have plenty of card players here to keep me entertained, and I'll make enough to pay you." They started with treatment that day. Lil was a good patient, although the work was somewhat uncomfortable. Her treatment required a high degree of skill. Actually, he was challenged; normally this type of work was done in the big cities out east. Each night Lil was in the Lucky Lady plying her trade. When she talked, it would be with her mouth partially closed or covered by her hand. The players at the Lucky Lady tried to get a look at her but she was too wily to let them see her teeth with her dental work in progress.

When Jakob finally completed Lil's dentistry, she looked into a mirror to see the result. The tough gal broke down and sobbed.

"Doc you made me a happy gal. I am so pleased." That night she went to the Lucky Lady to play cards and bought drinks for the house, as she showed off her smile and the sparkling diamond inlayed teeth. Lil got up and sat on a stool next to Harry at the piano and sang a few numbers for the crowd. All agreed she had a beautiful voice and she got standing ovations.

The next day she stopped at Jakob's office to settle up with him. She tipped him heavily, even after Jakob told her it was not customary to tip a professional man. She insisted what he had done for her would change her life. She put her arms around him and gave him a kiss on his cheek. Lil left the following week, and was headed for Memphis.

Liz came home from school that afternoon and complained about the two boys who had given her problems of discipline. They had disrupted her class, as on numerous other occasions, and she was upset. Mrs. Robbins, in the mayor's office, had tried to contact the father but was never able to find him at home. She finally talked to the sheriff who said he would try to find the father. The boys' names were Jeb and Jud Wilkins. The next day, just before class was dismissed, a large unshaven and disheveled man entered the schoolroom.

"I'm Harold Wilkins. Them there are my two boys that are sitting there. I hear they causing you trouble, ma'am." Liz was startled at the man's presence and his demeanor, and stammered when she responded

"Yes, as a matter of fact they have been problems in the classroom. They have been disrupting my class and intimidating the other children."

The other children in the class room slowly moved out of the room, looking back at the large, overbearing man who was frightening to them.

In a moment Harold Wilkins swiftly moved across the room toward the boys' desks and pulled Jeb out of the seat. Holding the terrified boy by his shirt with one hand, he slapped him across the face with the other hand. Then letting him go, the child fell to the floor, whimpering. "That'll teach ya to cause that woman trouble, you little worm."

Liz, horrified, screamed, "Stop. Don't do that."

She rushed from behind her desk to the startled young boy and kneeled down, taking his head into her arms and pulling him to her bosom. "How could you do that to a child? That's no way to handle the problem, you brute."

She held the sobbing boy tightly as tears came to her eyes. "Please don't cry. You'll be all right. We'll get this taken care of. Come on, Jeb, get up and sit down at your desk." Liz looked sharply at the startled man who was taken aback by her outcry.

"I'm sorry, lady, but I don't want my kid causin' any trouble fer youze. He ain't really a bad boy, he jest don't have a mom. I jest can't be with them all the time, so they's home or out somewhere by they selves. I jest don't know what to do. I gotta work. I should be at work now but the sheriff come and git me. They me kids. I don't mean no harm. I don't know what to do."

Liz was bewildered with the circumstances. She saw Harold as an abusive man, but he was also in a situation that was difficult for him to control.

"Mr. Wilkins, I want you to sit here," she said as she pointed to the chair next to her desk, "so we can discuss the problem. You boys pull your desks up here. I want you to realize I am a teacher and I am here to help you gain an education. Mine is no easy task. I have thirty-eight children in this room and I am trying to help all of them, but you are making it hard for me to help them. Teaching is serious work, and you are being selfish. I don't *have* to teach you. I can refuse to have you in my classroom. But I want to help you learn to read and to write and to do arithmetic, but you have to help me by being cooperative. Isn't that right, Mr. Wilkins?"

"Yes ma'am. Do you hear dat, boys? I kent teach you cuz I have to work. You listen to the lady."

The boys, had their heads down. "Yeah, Pa. We'ze promise to listen to the lady," Jeb answered. "We'en not goin' to give her any trouble."

Liz looked firmly at each of them. "I guess we all understand each other then. I expect you two boys to behave in and out of class. No chasing the girls. Understand? And, I want you to do your schoolwork and homework every day. I will give you as much attention as I can so you can catch up with the other students your age. This means you may have to stay after school so I can give you more work to do. Do we understand each other?"

The boys nodded. "Yes, ma'am."

Liz looked at the big bewildered man. "Your part, Mr. Wilkins, will be to see to it they live up to our agreement. I definitely don't want you to hit these boys if there is a problem. Understand? That doesn't solve the problem, it only makes it worse. We can work it out with your help. Do you understand, Mr. Wilkins?"

Harold nodded.

"Thank you. You may all leave now." Harold got up and motioned to the boys to come along.

"I thank ya, ma'am fer your help. I'll see to it they be good in school."

Liz watched them leave the school, putting up her hands to hold her head. She sighed deeply in relief and just sat still, looking ahead. Tears welled in her eyes. *My God I hope I never have to go through that again,* she said quietly to herself.

Jakob entered the room and looked at the distraught Liz. "Liz, what's the matter? Who was the big man with the two boys who just left the school?" Liz smiled.

"Oh, those boys were my students and that was their father. I just had an unnerving parent teacher-conference. Let me get my things together and we can go home."

Jakob quizzically looked at Liz. "Are you sure everything is all right?"

Liz nodded with a controlled smile. "Yes, everything is just fine."

Chapter 16

Their First Christmas

It was Jakob and Liz's first Christmas since they got married. The cottage they lived in was small but they were happy. They finally had their own home. Elmer Findley had a stove delivered to the cottage which now enabled Liz to cook or bake anything she wanted. It had an oven to bake her pies and cakes and it would also help to heat the cottage. He also delivered a couch, a rug and several more chairs to complete the furnishings he had promised them. The cottage was furnished. It was small but comfy.

Liz has spent a lot of time with her school children trying to make their Christmas at school festive and memorable. She knew several of the children would not have much of a Christmas because of the loss of parents, so she took it upon herself to make arrangement with some of the mothers to provide gifts for those children. The two Wilkins boys who had been such a problem for her had no mother, but would receive anonymous gifts from two sources. One of Liz's fifth-grade students, a ten-year-old girl, was living with her grandparents and had lost both her mother and father. She received two anonymous gifts. Little Mary Jenkins, a third grader whose mother just disappeared, received several gifts. Mary was being taken care of by a neighbor.

On the last day of classes before the Christmas break, Liz had a Christmas party for her thirty-eight students. She brought cookies she had baked and served them with hot chocolate. Harry from the Lucky Lady brought his concertina to the school and the kids sang Christmas carols.

Liz was available to assist with the church celebration of Christmas, and had enlisted children to put on the Christmas narrative for the congregation. It was done well and the church members were grateful for what she had done. This was something new for the church, and they were delighted with Liz for initiating it.

Jakob brought home gifts of cakes, breads and various other Christmas delights his patients would leave at his office. It was their way of spreading Christmas cheer to Jakob and Liz. They were both nostalgic and missed being with their families back East but their home was now Sheridan and now they had each other.

This was Liz's first Christmas as a married woman, and she worked hard to make her home as festive as she could. She had made Christmas decorations for the house and Jakob brought in a small tree that Liz decorated for the Christmas holiday. She had hidden gifts for Jakob in various parts of their small house. Jakob was seen making stops at various stores and shops in town. The New York Store had opened and provided fine clothing from the Eastern markets. Jakob and Liz looked forward to the holiday. Packages were sent to Milwaukee and Ames, Iowa, and packages from their homes were received along with cards and letters.

Liz and Jakob would exchange their gifts on the eve of Christmas, opening them while sitting near the tree. Jakob had made Liz a special gift of two hearts from gold, which hung from a gold necklace chain; she would wear them to the party at the Findleys. Liz bought Jakob a heavy winter coat he could wear during the cold Wyoming days. She also bought Jakob fishing equipment he would use in the Wyoming streams. Jakob shopped The New York Store for sweaters and boots which Liz needed. Both were thrilled with their gifts.

An invitation from Elmer and Ella Findley to their Christmas party was happily received. They looked forward to the party, Jakob having attended it the previous year. Liz wanted to participate and baked bread and rolls she would bring. Most of the other ladies would also bring something for Ella's table. The winter was typical of Wyoming. The first snows started in late November and the temperatures hovered in the below-freezing range, but added to that, were the winds, which blew the snows into drifts. Jakob was not seeing the usual number of patients now. It was rare that people from outside Sheridan would come in.

Christmas day, the Schroeders stopped by to pick up Liz and Jakob with their horse-drawn sleigh. To add to the Christmas cheer, Frank had sleigh bells that jingled as the horses moved along. The walkway and porch of the Findley home had been cleared of snow.

A group of hardy, red cheeked carolers met them as they arrived, and they listened to their voices singing their favorite carols before going in. Elmer welcomed them. Liz and Jakob were now identified as the newlyweds. Liz presented her baked goods to Ella who graciously accepted them. Her table was filled to overflowing. They received their traditional cups of brandy-spiked eggnog and were toasted by the group.

Harry, from the Lucky Lady, was there with his concertina and caroling was part of the fare.

It was Elle Burns who first noticed the gold hearts Liz wore on the chain hanging from her slender neck. "Where did you get that beautiful necklace?" she exclaimed.

All eyes turned to Liz as she blushed, then responded. "It's my Christmas gift from my husband. He made it for me." The ladies looked with envy at her hearts. One of them looked at her husband and chided him.

"Maybe I should have married a dentist instead of a rancher."

He returned the remark with a look of disgust and said to Jakob, "You keep doing things like that, and all our wives will revolt." Jakob laughed with the other men, and suggested they all must have treated their lovely wives with special gifts at Christmas, from how nice they looked.

When the newly arrived guest Colonel Bill Cody stepped into the room, the tenor of the party changed. He immediately saw Liz and approached her.

"Well now, I haven't met this lovely young lady yet."

Liz blushed and answered, "I'm Mrs. Elizabeth Miller, but you may call me Liz. This is my husband Doctor Jakob Miller. I'm sure you know him."

Cody's eyes shifted to Jakob. "I certainly do know him, and he is a very lucky man." The attention of the guests then shifted to Colonel Cody who was well known to all. The Findleys and their friends represented an important part of Sheridan's society; they were the movers and shakers. Liz and Jakob were fondly received and became part of the group.

Ella invited all to the table for the sumptuous dinner. Elmer must have built his own table to accommodate all the guests present. A large goose and turkey were placed in the middle of the table to be served and the group hushed, as an invocation was given.

Several of the friends asked Liz and Jakob when they would be having a family. Liz blushed and explained that she already had thirty-eight children.

That remark brought a lot of laughs until Ella said, "Those don't count Liz," which created more laughter.

The evening brought everyone there a bounty of fun and fellowship. Later in the evening, Mandy Schroeder asked Liz if they were interested in leaving because her husband had exceeded his limit in spirits and she would have to be the driver. Liz laughed and agreed it was time to leave as there were others going. They bundled up, gave thanks to the host and hostess for the grand day and opened the door to a cold winter night. The snow had stopped but the piercing cold remained. They felt lucky they had the Schroeders to take them home in their sleigh.

They thanked the Schroeders for the ride and entered their cold home. The fire in the fireplace in the cottage was low and their humble abode had chilled down some, but it didn't take too long and their home was warm again. They sat before the fireplace and Liz snuggled up to Jakob and they talked about the evening spent with their friends.

"Did you notice the look on the faces of the ladies when they saw my beautiful necklace? You are so talented, Jakob. Who would have thought you would be able to make such a beautiful necklace?" The room had warmed and they were ready to go to bed. Liz looked at Jakob and took his face in her hands.

"Jakob, this is our first married Christmas together. Do you think we could have had as grand a day if we stayed in Milwaukee?"

"I would have had a good time with you anywhere Liz, but those people we spent the Christmas day with were really a special group. Now, we have another special day to look forward to. New Year's Eve is just around the corner."

"You are my Christmas present. How lucky we are to have each other." She lay back and tucked her face against his arm.

"Oh, New Year's Eve is six days away but I can wait. I have a very special dress my mother sent me with some of my other things I had. It will just be perfect for the party. We can go dancing just as we did at the Palmer house, remember?"

It was New Year's Eve morning and Jakob was awakened to a pounding on his front door. He quickly got up, and put his robe on, and answered the door.

"Hey, Doc. You gonna be at the office today? I gotta hurtin' tooth that's driving me crazy." Jakob answered he would be there later in the morning, and to stop by after nine. "Thanks, Doc, I'll be there."

"Jakob, who was that, and why did he have to come here and wake us up? What time is it?"

"Just a hurtin' patient, Liz." Jakob looked at the clock as he lit a lamp. "It's early, so why don't you just go back to sleep," he replied, as he added wood to the fireplace and moved the embers around. He filled the coffee pot with water and coffee and put it on the stove, and turned around to see Liz next to him.

"I can't sleep now," she said, as she put her arms around him and kissed him. "Why must people bother us so early?"

"I guess it is because they want to let me know they are hurtin'."

They sat at the table and Jakob poured a cup of coffee for Liz, who remarked he always made the best coffee.

"Liz, you only say that because you like to have me make the coffee. Isn't that right?" She smiled coyly and shook her head in the affirmative.

Jakob and Liz got ready for the New Year's Eve party. Liz was dressed in a beautiful beige velvet gown. It had long sleeves that were puffed on top. The neck was rounded and she wore the gold hearts Jakob had made for her. Her blonde hair she set in an up-sweep. The high-button shoes were also beige. Liz looked beautiful. She wore her long fur coat and had a scarf covering her hair, tied under her chin. Little Henry came by with a sleigh to take them to the Sheridan Inn. You could hear the music from outside as they entered the Inn. Henry Clayton greeted them with a cheery "Happy New Year." They checked in their outer clothes and entered the dining room. As she entered the dining room all eyes were turned toward Liz and people smiled and greeted her.

Annabelle had their table ready for them. After they sat she brought out the champagne and they ordered their favorite roast duck after Lukas came out to greet them.

The Sheridan Players played a variety of music but they liked the slow numbers and Liz would dance holding Jakob close to her. They met with many of their friends on the dance floor and those who stopped by their table. While they were eating, Jozef came by and played their favorites for them. In the more quiet moments they spoke of their dreams and wishes for the coming year.

"Jakob, at the Christmas party some of the people asked me if we were planning a family. Some kidded me. Do you ever think about having children?"

"I guess I have. When it happens Liz, we'll face it together." The time for the countdown to the new year was under way. They stood on the floor holding each other and kissed as Happy New Year was announced and they sang "Auld Lang Syne," welcoming in 1898.

The happy holidays were now in the past and Liz was busy with her pupils. On some colder days fewer were present but she was always there. Jakob found his patient load much diminished.

He stopped in the Lucky Lady to visit with his friend Andy Meeks. The place was crowded as usual. Even though Liz didn't feel the Lucky Lady was the sort of place Jakob should frequent, it was also a social place many of the businessmen would come to visit, learn what was going on in town, and relax with friends. The weekly *Sheridan Post* or *Enterprise* normally didn't print the kind of news Jakob gathered in the Lucky Lady.

Mayor Burns walked in and stood next to Jakob. He was an older man, somewhat dignified, but typical of the type involved in frontier politics. He did have a way of making the town run efficiently. He had been the sheriff in the early days of Sheridan. Then Frank Walters came to town and got a job as his deputy. John Burns kept the peace, but he didn't really like or fit the job of sheriff, personality-wise. He really wasn't hard or tough enough for the job.

The mayor then was Bill Williams, a friendly old gentleman. Bill was in his sixties and was responsible for some positive changes in early Sheridan. In the winter of 1892 he came down with influenza. Doc Kelly did all he could for him. He lasted through the whole winter but just got weaker and weaker, and then died. They had a big funeral for him and buried Bill with honors in Mt. Hope Cemetery.

There was a special election and John Burns was elected mayor, after he resigned as sheriff. Frank Walters wanted to be sheriff, so he was elected sheriff. John Burns liked to talk about the old times in Sheridan and related that story often.

Mayor Burns looked at Jakob and said, "Doc, you've been around town awhile and have a lot of friends. I'm thinking you should get involved in the workings of our community. People respect you and you have a good head on your shoulders. We need a commissioner to take over Phil O'Neal's place. Not much work to do, but it would help out the town. What do you say?" Jakob was taken aback by the mayor's remarks. He never thought of doing anything but his dental practice and now he was married and he felt his life was complete. He didn't want any other responsibilities. He would go with his friends fishing in the streams and hunting birds, but never go after big game since his tussle with the grizzly. He had a reminder of that event hanging on the office wall, and the scars on his arm. But he certainly never, ever thought in terms of politics.

"Mayor, I'm not sure politics are for me. I've got a thin skin and I'm not much for controversy. Maybe we should pass on that one."

"Now, Doc, don't just give up on it. Give it some thought. You just might enjoy a little change of pace in your life."

"Well, John, let me sleep on it. I'll pass it by Liz and see what she thinks."

"Good enough for me, Doc. Think about it, but remember, you'll be giving back to your town some of what they gave you. Here now, let me buy you a drink to solidify our friendship." Andy poured them both a drink and they toasted their friendship. Jakob excused himself and left to meet Liz at the schoolhouse. Mayor Burns waved.

"Remember our discussion, Doc." Jakob nodded and left the Lucky Lady. The distance to the schoolhouse was a fairly long walk and Jakob mulled over his talk with the mayor. He thought about the notion of *friendship* the mayor referred to. Actually, he was hardly a real friend, up until the conversation today. He had an acquaintance and patient relationship with him, but saw him very rarely. *But, so be it. I'll bring it up with Liz and see what she thinks about it. I suppose it wouldn't hurt being a commissioner, if it didn't take too much time.* As he walked up to the schoolhouse Liz was coming out. She usually carried a small briefcase with school papers. Jakob was still some distance away. His thoughts of Liz took over. *God, she's beautiful. Since our marriage, she has really blossomed out, from being that sweet young thing I married to being a gorgeous, intelligent woman, and to think she is my wife.* They met and he encircled her with his arms and held her tightly, kissing her.

Breaking away from him, Liz exclaimed, "Jakob, we are in the middle of Sheridan. What do you think you are doing?" Jakob laughed.

"Oh, just kissing my wife, the woman I love. Nothing wrong in that, is there?"

"But what will people think?"

Looking around Jakob answered, "I don't see anybody watching. If there is, maybe they will think that man sure loves his wife, and I do love you. Is that so bad?" Liz started to laugh.

"Oh, you nut. You are incorrigible. It's much too cold to stand out here. Let's go home. I have a surprise for you."

Jakob's eyes opened wide. "What is the surprise? Tell me, Please."

Liz laughed and answered, "You'll see." They walked hand in hand to their home and up the stairs. Jakob opened the door and swept her off her feet, taking her into the house. He carried her into the bedroom and placed her on the bed.

"Jakob, what do you think you're doing?"

"Well, you did say surprise."

"Okay, I'll tell you. I baked the chocolate cake you like so much. We'll have it after dinner." She giggled. Jakob pouted. "Now please get the fire going, it's cold in here."

"Is that all my surprise will be? Is there something more?"

"Now, Jakob, take care of the fire and come help me get dinner together." Liz made a buffalo stew that had simmered all day over the glowing embers of the fire. After finishing their dinner, Liz served Jakob the cake she had baked as Jakob told her about his meeting with Mayor Burns. She listened intently and smiled.

"Jakob, is this what you want to do? If it is, I am all for it. But if you would rather not, I suggest you stand your ground with the mayor. Actually, I think it is a good idea. You have much to say about Sheridan and I am sure you would be effective, but it is your decision to do what you want." Jakob listened to her carefully. He thought Liz had a good head on her shoulders and he would continue to give it thought.

They cleaned up the dishes and decided to sit near the fireplace on the couch. The lamps glowed, casting strange shadows. They sat silently. Liz snuggled close to Jakob, feeling the warmth of his body, as she laid her head on his shoulders. She felt secure being so close to him. Liz broke the silence.

"Jakob, are you happy? I mean really happy. Sometimes I just can't make myself believe I could be so happy being married, and with you." Jakob listened as Liz continued. "When I was a child I would often look up at the sky to watch the stars and wonder if there was someone I would one day be able to look up into the sky with, who would inspire me and love me." He picked up Liz's head and kissed her.

"Of course I'm happy. You have made my life complete."

"Would you like it as much if we had someone living with us?"

"What do you mean?"

"I mean, if we had someone else living with us, in this home, like . . . what if we had a baby?"

"Of course I would like it if we had a baby. You know that. Don't you remember when I told you that?"

"Jakob?"

"Yes?"

"Jakob, we are going to have a baby."

Jakob's mouth opened and, his breathing stopped. "A baby. A baby? You mean it? You are, we are, having a baby. You mean it? Oh, my gosh. Oh, Liz, we are going to have a baby." He held her tightly and lovingly kissed her. "Oh, Liz I love you so. We are going to have a baby. Are you sure?" They just sat there, in each other's arms as Jakob's thoughts raced.

"I'm sure now, Jakob." Liz then got up and put the tea kettle on the stove to warm some water for tea. "You get another piece of chocolate cake," she said.

Jakob lifted her chin and said,"The cake really wasn't the surprise you had for me, was it?"

Liz smiled. "No Jakob, I can make you a chocolate cake any old day, but the baby, well, that is a special effort."

Jakob finished his chocolate cake and they went to bed. Jakob just lay there with his eyes open. His mind was racing. He listened to Liz breathing and lifted his head up to see her closed eyes. Lying back, his thoughts were of the many tender moments with Liz, and then thoughts of a baby entered his mind and with the soft sound of wind. It helped him go to sleep, until he awoke to the sound of a neighbor's rooster.

Jakob looked at his sleeping beauty, still sound asleep. It was time for him to get up. He quietly got up and dressed. He stirred the fire adding some wood and filled the coffee pot. The sound of Liz's voice calling him sent Jakob to her bed.

"Jakob, do I have to get up too? Why don't we just stop the world and lay here just listening to the wind? But then, I know we can't stop the world, so I guess I'll just have to get up too. Also, if I don't get up there will be thirty-eight freezing cold kids on the school steps."

They walked together to the school. Jakob would go with Liz and then to his office. Sometimes, he would stop at the Sheridan Inn and have coffee with Lukas. He was anxious to spread the news of becoming a father with his special friends but then thought he better wait to spread the word; Liz should be the first to make the announcement. He was about ready to explode. The thought that Liz was having a baby totally engrossed all his thoughts. He was like a coffee pot ready to boil over, but he had to control and contain his joy. He talked with Lukas about the weather and how cold it was and how he was looking forward to spring.

"Lukas, you know we haven't had your famous roast duck for a long time." Lukas told him he would have one for him on Saturday if he and Liz came in.

"Good enough for me. We'll be in." He then left for his office.

The dining room was open for dinner. Liz and Jakob were ready for that special roast duck, along with the harvest vegetables prepared as only Lukas could do them. There were only a few people in the dining room when a tall, well-dressed gentlemen entered the room. He was more lavishly dressed than the townsfolk, and wore a derby. Elsie was the waitress, and she approached him. "I have a table for you," she said.

He answered with a heavy English accent. "I'm looking for Dr. Miller, the dentist. Do you know where I can find him?"

"Oh, yes, he is sitting right over there. Do you want me to tell him you want to speak with him?" Elsie came over to Jakob and told him there was a gentleman who wished to talk with him. Jakob got up from the table and approached the man. He introduced himself as James Widicker, and said that he had a dental problem. Jakob noticed the swelling on the left side of his face.

"I see your problem. Do you have pain?"

"Yes, I do. Can you see me in your surgery?" Jakob told him his office was a short distance from the hotel and they could go there.

"Why don't you finish your dinner. I can wait for you. I'll just sit at one of the tables and have some tea. Don't hurry. I'll be all right." Jakob thanked him and told him he would see him after he finished his dinner.

After finishing their dinner Jakob waved goodbye to Lukas, and he and Liz and the gentleman went outside, where there was a fancy covered wagon tied to the post. A young man in cowboy attire stepped up on the rig, followed by James Widicker, Jakob and Liz. Jakob directed the driver to his office. The gentleman followed Jakob and Liz in. It was obvious he was a stranger, just by his dress. In his heavy English accent he informed Jakob he was visiting his father's good friend, Oliver Henry, who had a ranch some distance away, toward the Bighorn Mountains.

"Oh, I know Oliver Henry."

"Well, yes, he is the one who told me to see you. This tooth has been bothering me since I left England and now it has become almost unbearable."

"I can understand that," said Jakob as he examined the area. He felt the man's forehead and thought he might have a raised temperature. A large area of swelling surrounded one of his molars. "You have an abscess over an infected tooth. Fortunately for you, we can drain it and take out the tooth on another day."

"Well, please do what you can because I have terrible pain." Jakob prepared to open up the tooth and drain the abscess. Mr. Widicker had almost instant relief from the pain. Jakob gave him instructions for care, and suggested he stay in town for a few days because of the distance to the ranch. He also suggested he stay at the Sheridan Inn, so that Jakob could follow his progress. Jakob would see him the next day.

The Oliver Henry Ranch had been in existence for many years. A number of Englishmen came to Wyoming and settled in ranching. Some had come in through Canada and others through the eastern United States. Many were there to raise horses, which they shipped back to England. During the Crimean War they shipped many horses which were used for the English cavalry. They also did cattle ranching. These were interesting people and some were the offspring of titled English parents. Jakob was always happy to care for them, as they offered him the opportunity to help people with a different culture. They made good patients. Jakob directed him back to the Sheridan Inn where James Widicker registered. Liz and Jakob then went home and Liz finished her school work before they both prepared for bed.

Thoughts of Liz and the baby raced through Jakob's mind, all through the day. He now knew they had to have a bigger home. The Findley cottage was fine for the two of them, but with the baby coming they would need a bigger place, but could they afford one? His business was definitely successful and he now had a good savings account. Maybe, they just might be able to find a bigger home or even build a home. The question was where? *It would be nice to be in town near the office and school. The school? Oh, my gosh, Liz will have to give up teaching. That's going to create a problem. Who will take her place? She won't be able to teach for too long. What was a moment of elation and joy has suddenly become a time for planning.* Jakob left his office to meet Liz at school. Her rambunctious Jeb and Jud had started to behave and showed signs of improvement in their class work. They saw in Liz, what might have been their mother and now respected her, as she challenged their learning process. They left the schoolhouse as Jakob approached, whooping and hollering. Liz was cleaning her desk as Jakob came to her.

"How are the delinquents doing?" he asked.

"Oh Jakob, they are not delinquents. They are just boys that need special attention. I am seeing improvement in both their conduct, and they are doing better with their class work. I do believe they are really quite intelligent and if I can motivate them, they could improve sufficiently. There's a real problem in that family. The father is having a hard time being a mother and father to those two boys."

"If anyone can help them, it will be you," countered Jakob. Liz closed the door of the school and they walked toward their home on Marion Street. The conversation was about Liz's pregnancy. Jakob reminded her their house would be too small and they had to think about something bigger. Liz would eventually have to leave her job as school teacher, and it would put a strain on their finances.

"Liz, we are going to either build a home for our family to be, or I am going to have to find a suitable new home for us. Right now there is nothing available to rent that would be suitable. I'll have to talk to Elmer Findley. He may have some ideas. When should we announce about our family to be?"

Liz smiled. "Oh, Jakob, I guess our happiness is going to be coupled by some changes in our life we never really thought about, but we can work them out. I should be able to continue working for quite a while. I've thought about the need to find someone to take over my teaching. I know just the person. She graduated with me from teachers' college. I will write her and see if she would be interested. Anne White would be perfect.

"I wasn't going to make any special announcement just yet, but we have much to do in preparation for our baby, so maybe I will mention it at the church group meeting. Jakob, I am so happy."

Jakob's mind was filled with thoughts about Liz and the baby, the need for a bigger home, the Mayor's request he fill a spot on the town council and his ever expanding practice. How would he put them all together and handle them successfully?

He stopped by the post office for his mail. There was a letter for Liz, as well as a letter from his mother in Milwaukee. He chatted with Elmer who was also there getting his mail.

"Jakob, you must know about us building a new home. Ella and I want something bigger as our family has grown. Business has been good and I felt now was the time for us to build the home of our dreams. It's over there on Clarendon Avenue with the big homes. We're getting close to having it ready to move in. I have been thinking, maybe you and Liz might be interested in our Loucks Street home. You know, you've been in it for our Christmas party. It's a good sized place but I'm sure you would grow into it. The cottage you're living in isn't really for you and Liz. It was a good start because nothing was available but my place on Loucks Street would be a good buy. I can always rent the cottage now that it's fixed up. Talk it over with Liz."

"Well . . . maybe." *Did Elmer know about Liz? But how could he. We haven't told anyone yet. This may be the opportunity we need. I'll bring it up with Liz,* he thought.

The letter from home was typical of Mother's newsy letters, and it ended as usual with her admonition to Jakob to write more frequently. Jakob, still recovering from the news he was going to be a father, decided he would share that with his parents. He went to his office to write a letter to them. As he started his letter, he was interrupted, when his first patient of the day arrived.

James Widicker was looking much improved. Jakob had taken him out of pain and the abscess had drained, and now a decision had to be made whether the offending tooth would be removed. He asked Jakob if there was a chance of saving the tooth. Jakob agreed to treat the tooth and to do a root canal filling and a crown. Mr. Widicker was in favor of him doing the treatment. Jakob got started and set up future appointments for treatments.

Jakob learned more from James Widicker about the Oliver Henry Ranch raising horses for shipment back to England. Mr. Widicker and his wife were staying at the ranch indefinitely to learn about the business. He informed Jakob his father was a titled baron in England. They were interested in the breed of horses that were being raised and they also were into raising cattle. He invited Jakob and his wife to visit the Oliver Henry Ranch for Oliver's seventieth birthday, which would be July 1st. There would be a grand birthday party, with more visitors from England coming. Jakob's interest perked. *Liz would be delighted to meet these people*, he thought.

There were several people waiting to see Jakob and another visit was planned for Mr. Widicker. It was a busy day for Jakob and the letter he started was put aside.

Liz stopped by Jakob's office after her class was finished but Jakob was still hard at work. She moved on to their home to begin dinner. Jakob would follow when he was finished. It had been a long day for Jakob when he arrived home for dinner. Each discussed their day and Jakob told of his letter from home. He felt he must answer when they finished dinner and the table was cleared. He set about finishing the letter he began in the office.

Dear Mother and Father:
    Your letter came today and I wanted to answer it a soon as I could.
    I have wonderful news for you. The other day Liz announced to me she will be having a baby. She seemed quite certain, so this is why I am telling you. We are both very happy about it. I wanted you to be the first to know because you will share in this and become grandparents. I don't know whether you thought about it, when we were there for that great wedding reception that you gave us. We are making all kinds of plans for our future. Liz is teaching at the Sheridan Elementary School and is very busy. She has thirty-eight students that depend on her for their education. I guess the day will come when she has to leave that job for an even bigger one, Motherhood. I'm thinking that we may have to find a bigger home for us to live in. Dad my practice here is really growing. I am seeing many new patients almost daily. The people here are very friendly and are almost like old friends to me. I was hoping maybe you and Mother would come out to see us for a visit although, the cold weather makes it too difficult to travel at this time. I was also hoping you would be out for some hunting as you once mentioned. We have good bird hunting as well as big game. Many things are happening here and I would hope we could share them with you and Mother. Maybe one day you will be able to make the trip. Liz is feeling quite well and sends her regards and love to both of you.

Respectfully yours,
Jakob

Chapter 17

A New Home on Loucks Street

Jakob went to talk with Elmer Findley about buying his home on Loucks Street. Elmer's new home was well underway and it looked like it would be lavish. He spoke with Jakob about selling his current home and was now aware Liz would be having a baby. Jakob made it known to him they would need a bigger home as Elmer's cottage was small and was originally intended to be just a temporary home for them.

He asked Elmer about his asking price for his present home, which was very nice and quite large. Elmer had a price tag on it beyond what Jakob was comfortable with. It really was beyond his means. He mentioned it to Elmer and said he would give it some consideration. Elmer was a fine man and a good friend of Jakob's, but he was also a successful businessman. Selling his current home was just a business deal to him, but Elmer left the door open for negotiation. During the short time he had been in Sheridan, Jakob became somewhat successful and had a bright future, but he felt Elmer's home could extend his finances beyond their means. He stopped by the bank and spoke with Mr. Randolph about borrowing some money. Jakob had known Mr. Randolph since he came to Sheridan and was also banking at the First National Bank. The first meeting they had was exploratory and Jakob did not exactly set any amount he might need. However, Jakob felt the Findley house would be a good investment for them.

Jakob noticed Liz had a restless night. He woke up earlier than usual and got up to make the coffee. Liz slept on but moaned in her sleep. He drank his coffee while thinking about Liz's pregnancy and starting a family. *This will certainly change our lifestyle. The Findley house would really be fine. It is considerably bigger than we need, but there could be more children in our future. But, can I afford to buy the Findley house?* he thought.

He could hear Liz stirring and then she started to feel ill. She was sitting on the edge of the bed with a chamber pot, retching and vomiting. Poor Liz was obviously sick.

"What's the matter, Liz?"

"I just feel terrible. I haven't felt well for the last couple days. Today I just feel very sick, something like indigestion, but worse. I guess this must be what the ladies call morning sickness."

Jakob looked quizzically at Liz. "I don't understand. What is that?"

"Well, it happens to women who are with child, in the early days of pregnancy." Jakob didn't seem to understand but suggested he make some tea for Liz. It was something which often helped indigestion and maybe it might make her feel better. He took a cool towel and wiped her forehead and gave her some hot tea. At first the tea didn't seem to help, but then she said she felt a little better.

"I don't feel I can teach today. Even if I feel better later, I don't think I will feel well enough to face a classroom full of children."

"I'll place a notice on the schoolhouse door for the children to see, and then they can go back home," said Jakob. He tried to make Liz as comfortable as possible and made a sign to place on the schoolhouse door. Jakob left for his office but first placed the notice. He told one of the mothers who had arrived early with her daughter Liz was sick and would not be in. She agreed to wait and tell the other children.

Jakob saw his patients but was concerned with Liz at home. He looked in on her at noon and found her up but not completely recovered. He tried to make her as comfortable as he could before returning to his office. His day dragged on but he finished early and went back to look in on Liz, who was only slightly recovered. Jakob suggested making some supper but Liz was not enthusiastic about eating anything. He wondered if the next few days would be more of the same for Liz.

Liz awoke the next day with the same problem. She was unable to have classes for her students. Several of the mothers got together and tried to hold classes for the students, but it was obvious the time had come to make better arrangements. Liz was sick enough that she couldn't continue teaching, and the school was closed, at least for the time being.

Jakob was busy with his practice and did the best he could to take care of his wife but her teaching was out of the question. Neighbors and friends looked in on her and brought meals for them, while Liz put up with her morning discomfort. It was some weeks later when she seemed to do better and even talked about returning to her school classes.

Efforts were already being made to get someone to substitute for her. Liz wrote to her classmate friend in Iowa but she was not available. Then one day, the train brought in George Mortimer who was, by his credentials, a professor from an Eastern school. He was a middle-aged man who was recently widowed and wished to start a new life, and he chose Sheridan because of an old friend with whom he had been corresponding. She too had been widowed. Her late husband, William Thompson, had owned the grain mill.

Mr. Mortimer was readily accepted and Liz was definitely free from her teaching. She had been meeting with Mr. Mortimer and felt he could handle the position. Her students loved her and were not too happy to see her leave, but she encouraged them to accept Mr. Mortimer as their teacher. Liz now became a full-time housewife. She felt better and life for them took on a new meaning.

Jakob met with the banker and Elmer Findley several times, and it was now definite: he would buy Elmer's present home when the Findleys moved into their new home. Their new home would be ready in a couple months and Elmer was happy to have his present home sold, and Jakob was looking forward to moving in. They had worked out the details of the sale and both would benefit from the arrangement.

The day finally arrived and Elmer stopped by Jakob's office to talk with him. "Jakob, I thought I'd stop by to let you know my new place is nearly done, and we will start moving in within a few weeks. Ella is real anxious to move in and I'm sure your wife feels the same. Ladies aren't as patient as we men, but we have to satisfy them or they will make our lives miserable."

Jakob laughed. "Anyhow, you can start making plans for your move. I'll keep you informed as we progress. I'm happy you will take over my place. I know the cottage isn't really appropriate for people like you and Liz."

This was really good news for Jakob because he and Liz were anxious to make the move into Elmer's home and had already been making plans for their new home. Elmer's new home would be on Clarendon Avenue, where there were big homes being built for the wealthier residents of Sheridan. Elmer was very successful with his general store on Main Street, as well as his other land investments.

Liz and Jakob's new home was much bigger than they really needed or even wanted, but it turned out to be a good investment for them. They were happy to get it. It was a larger, two-story home with four bedrooms—three large ones on the second floor. The big living-dining room would be ideal for large groups of friends such as the Findleys used to have at their big Christmas parties, and the large kitchen with its big stove would make big parties possible.

This house already had electricity and water was piped in. The fireplace was made from local stone and occupied much of one wall in the living room. The dining room had a big bay window with a seat in it and faced the yard. The master bedroom was on the first floor, and another room would be for Liz's sewing and crafts. Jakob had already planned to use one of the second-floor bedrooms for his library and office. The big porch surrounding two sides of the home had a swing suspended from the ceiling. On the other side of the house was a small greenhouse for Liz's plants. Next to the door leading from the kitchen, was the outside entrance to a cold cellar for storing fruits and vegetables from their garden. The home was built of wood with a generous use of gingerbread trimming. The second floor had dormers on both sides and the bedrooms were large. It was painted white with contrasting green shutters. The entrance from the street to the backyard went to a barn for horses and a wagon. There was a small attached workshop. The yard was spacious with an area Ella used for a big garden. There were fruit trees and bushes, and a big old maple tree with a swing attached. This was truly a family home and Liz and Jakob would be a family very soon.

Jakob couldn't wait until he got home to tell Liz the good news. He had a busy day which kept him in the office until late in the afternoon, so he had to patiently finish his day. He hurried home and picked up Liz and danced her around.

"Liz, I have good news for you. The Findleys are getting ready to move. Their home is nearly finished." Liz embraced Jakob, holding him tightly and kissing him.

"Oh, Jakob, I'm so happy. We have been waiting so patiently these last months. I can't wait until we can move in. It will be so good to be in such a big house."

"Oh! Guess what? For this special occasion we can celebrate the event. I've baked you an apple pie. I used the last of the apples we had stored from our tree."

"Liz, I knew you had baked a pie because when I walked in I could smell it baking. How did you know I was bringing good news?"

"When you come in, you are my good news." Jakob brushed her hair back, held her and kissed her. They were excited and talked more about their new home. Liz was now four months pregnant and was showing it. They were a happy couple and anxious for the baby to arrive. And, now they would soon be getting into their new home. Their furnishings were rather meager for the big house but they would be getting more as time went on. Both still had items they left back East which could now be shipped to them.

The weather was finally getting warmer and they would be in their new home in a short time. Sheridan had many new residents arriving; the city was growing fast. With the arrival of the railroad real progress had taken place. The coal mines were producing much-needed coal for the trains as well as home use.

The mining industry was expanding. They had their own communities just a short distance from Sheridan. The miners were arrivals from the eastern European countries seeking a better life. There was also a community of Japanese and Chinese people who came looking for work and settled in the outskirts of Sheridan. Some of these people were now part of Jakob's expanding practice. They were happy-go-lucky folks and family oriented; some had large families. Liz still couldn't stop being the teacher, even with her pregnancy. She and some of her lady friends had adult classes on Saturdays at the schoolhouse and would even be getting groups of children from the Acme mining community to start language and reading. Her helpers made it possible for a good number of men and women, as well as their children, to learn to read and write.

Jakob, in spite of some language barriers, managed to communicate, and the people loved him. Their means were not great but they would always bring with them those things that were part of their lifestyles, whether it was a loaf of bread, or some ethnic delicacy, vegetable or meat or something that they made in their home or grew in their garden. They were always grateful for what he did for them.

With the help from friends who brought their wagons to move their belongings to Loucks Street, Liz and Jakob were finally in their new home. They were extremely happy with their spacious home, even if it was going to be more work for them to take care of it.

Once again, their friends and new neighbors welcomed them with housewarming gifts and there was a reason for a party. Some of the Sheridan Players, who had played at their wedding, came by to lend music to the festivities. It was a grand show of love and fellowship among the people of Sheridan. Liz had given much to her community with her teaching and now the reading programs. The people gratefully reciprocated.

Jakob wrote a letter to his parents in Milwaukee to tell them about his move and invited them to visit.

Dear Mother and Father:

There is much good news in our life I want to share with you. We have finally moved into our new home. Oh, it isn't real new. It belonged to the Findleys, who own a big general store here. They have built a new home and theirs was available, so we bought it. It will be perfect when the baby arrives. There is so much room now for all our needs and we can afford it. Maybe you can see fit to send me those items I left behind in Milwaukee. I now have plenty room for everything. Transportation out here is much improved since I came here. Little by little Sheridan will become a modern city like Milwaukee. We even have electricity in our home. We also have room to keep horses and a wagon and I am looking for the right kind of horses for my use. Some of the streets here will be soon be paved. Much is happening here. Our weather is now warming and spring flowers are in bloom. I am still hoping you both will come to visit us and see what beautiful country this is. I look out of the window of my office and can see the beautiful Bighorn Mountains in the distance. And just a few hundred yards from here is Little Goose Creek. We also now have plenty of room for you to stay with us. Liz is doing well and anxiously awaiting our baby, who will be your grandchild.

Love and best wishes,
Jakob

His parents still had not been to Sheridan. Jakob was always hoping he could get his family to visit Sheridan and see what a beautiful place it was to live in.

The walk from their new Loucks Street home to his office was longer than from the Marion Street home, and Jakob was making plans to get some horses but he thought he might see his friend Oliver Henry for them because he raised such beautiful animals. In the meantime, he walked the distance to the office.

He stopped at the post office to get his mail and there was a usual wordy letter from his mother about all the happenings in Milwaukee. He also got an official letter from Mayor Burns about a meeting in City Hall next week. Jakob was appointed a commissioner by the mayor, and up to now was not required to do anything official. He wasn't looking forward to any such extracurricular activities, but realized he did have some responsibility to the community. After all, he was a professional business man and an owner of property, his home.

Liz's pregnancy was undoubtedly something they had to consider in their current lifestyle. The morning sickness she had experienced didn't bother her too much anymore. Liz was starting to show her motherhood. While Liz was teaching, her housework was secondary, but now she started to focus more on housework and making their new home more livable. Even though she came to Sheridan shortly after graduating from teacher's college, Liz had already learned much about housekeeping from her mother, when she was a little girl. Living on a farm required the whole family to pitch in. Her mother had already taught her how to sew, which would enable her to make curtains and other household items.

Her cooking showed much expertise, and Jakob was pleased with the special cookies or cakes she made for him. Her teaching position had kept her from doing all the things housewives spend time on, but now she was a full-time housewife.

They were still the love-birds they were before they got married. Jakob put aside special days when he would take her out for dinner and romance her. Sheridan was growing and more eateries became available. But a favorite was Lukas at the hotel, who always gave them special attention.

Liz was also becoming more active in the community. She spent time with the church ladies' group, especially with some of the younger ladies. They respected her for her teaching experience and dealing with children.

Jakob was usually busy in his dental office. His practice was flourishing. He had the personality that inspired confidence, and above-average skill in his profession. He always made himself available to his patients and was dedicated to his patients' care.

Both looked forward to the baby, and together began making preparations for the birth. Liz would ask him if he wanted a baby boy or girl. His thoughts of having a son came first in his mind, but he would always say either a boy or a girl would be loved. Liz, in pregnancy, was as radiant and beautiful as ever, but with more maturity.

Liz stopped by Elmer Findley's store to pick up some items she needed. Ella Findley was there, and of course Ella liked to talk. She would give advice on any subject of which she was knowledgeable, and that was almost everything. She had all sorts of suggestions for Liz, which she was not really anxious to receive, but Liz respected her. Ella did have six children, so she was experienced with motherhood, and so Liz patiently listened to her.

There were constantly rumors around town about problems with Indians, even though the Indians did nothing provocative. Jakob was busy with patients one day when a group of Indians came into his office. Several of his patients looked nervously at them. Jakob recognized one of the Indians as the young brave he had helped when he was kicked by a pony sometime ago. He was part of the group who rode up to their wagon when he and Liz were going to Buffalo.

He had his squaw and papoose with him. With a combination of sign language and pidgin English, Jakob found out she had a broken tooth that caused her much pain; it had to be removed. Their medicine men were not capable of handling a situation such as this, so they came to see Jakob. Strong as Indians are in tolerating pain, it had become unbearable for her. The brave had experienced Jakob's healing powers and developed a trust in this white man.

Normally, Jakob would use some whiskey to sedate a patient, while someone else held them still. He would then quickly remove the offending tooth. However, his father recently had sent him something he said would control the pain. He took the little white pill, put it in a spoon with water and heated it to dissolve the pill in the water. Using a syringe, he withdrew the solution and prepared to inject the cocaine solution to obtund the pain. With the Indians looking on, he injected the solution around the tooth he would remove. He waited a short time and then proceeded to remove the broken tooth. The frightened but brave squaw had the tooth removed with no pain. She smiled, surprised. Jakob placed a gauze compress over the wound and had her wait in his outer room while he prepared for his next patient. The Indians were amazed at the treatment, and spoke with one another. As best he could, he gave her instructions on the care of the wound and dismissed them. They left happy and animated over what had happened.

Jakob then faced his next patient, who told him he should have refused to treat the savage. Jakob was taken aback by his attitude, and told him the woman was in pain and needed treatment, and he felt he was obliged to treat the Indians with the same degree of compassion and dignity he gave everyone else.

Some weeks later the Indian squaw came by and left a pair of buckskin moccasins with Jakob. On those occasions when Jakob treated the Indians, he felt they appreciated his kindness, as they would usually bring something to him in return as their way of thanking him for what he had done for them. They had little or no money so they usually bartered. Jakob enjoyed a good relationship with the Indians. His visit to their village was remembered by those Indians, who saw Jakob as their friend.

Liz and Jakob had finished their dinner and were sitting near the fireplace. Liz laid her head on Jakob's shoulder, snuggling next to him.

"Jakob, I have an idea. I have been thinking about this for a long time and I want to discuss it with you. You know, I have a lot of spare time since I stopped teaching school. I have caught up on my housework and I could be putting that spare time to good use."

"So what are you suggesting, Liz?"

"Remember that Mr. Wilkins who had those two boys who were giving me trouble in school? I'm sure he didn't have much education. I bet he can't read or write, and he couldn't help his boys with schoolwork because he didn't have any education himself." Jakob nodded in agreement. "I have been thinking we could extend our class in teaching adults the very basics of reading and writing. I'm sure there are a lot of people in town who can't read and write. I would even like to teach the Indians, but of course it might be hard because they are so far out of town. What do you think?" Jakob shook his head and smiled.

"Liz, you amaze me. Here you are going to have a baby soon and you want to commit yourself to a difficult task. You are already doing some teaching."

"Oh, it won't be too hard. I would only do it maybe one or two times a week. I'm sure I could get the pastor to let me use the church, or maybe we could even use the schoolhouse, on Saturday mornings for regular classes."

"If I said I didn't think you should do this, what would you say? Would you do it anyway?"

"Of course I wouldn't do it. We are in this marriage together. I would be disappointed, but I feel you would eventually see the value of providing, what I would call adult education. I'm sure you realize how important the effort would be. In fact, I would think you might even want to help me. I am sure there would be others in town who would join in on the idea if I asked them, like some more of the ladies in the church."

"Liz, I'm going to say it again. You are an amazing woman. No, I wouldn't forbid you or stand in your way. Go ahead with your idea, if you think you can get enough help to do it. Yes, I will do whatever I can to help you. In fact, I will bring it up with the mayor. It would be nice to have him on your side. After all, he said I have civic duties I should pursue. I would rather help you than be a judge at the county fair. But, I want you to be aware that your health and the baby are to always come first."

"Oh, I just knew you would agree with me. Of course my baby and my health come first. Your idea of enlisting the help of the mayor is a good idea. Why don't you take it up with him, or maybe we both should? I'll put together some ideas and we can take it from there."

The next weeks found Liz spending her afternoons finalizing her plans for adult education in Sheridan. Jakob was still experiencing the winter doldrums in his dental practice. Spring had arrived but it was still cold. It seemed like the only business that didn't suffer was the saloons; they flourished. The card games, gambling, drinking and the ladies were as busy as ever.

Both Liz and Jakob got letters from home and both expressed concern that Liz would take care of herself. Jakob's mother had plenty advice for Liz, and his father was certain he was going to have a grandson. Jakob researched all the material he could about pregnancy. He had Liz in his dental chair monthly to be sure her teeth were free of cavities and her gums were healthy. He talked with Doc Kelly, who was not too helpful, but insisted Liz make arrangements with Agnes Johnson, who was a midwife of prominence in Sheridan. Doc Kelly felt she was probably as capable as he was in delivering the baby, but if there was a problem he would take over. Jakob even spoke with Dr. Ross, the new physician in town, with reference to Liz's pregnancy, and he agreed that Agnes Johnson was perfectly capable. He insisted proper diet was important for Liz and made suggestions for her diet. He also indicated postpartum was something to be concerned with. Everything necessary for Liz and her baby was being done. Dr. Ross also insisted she get sufficient rest, so Liz would often nap in the afternoon.

Her clothes were starting to get tight and her friend Annie had some looser fitting clothes available, so she gave them to Liz to wear. Liz had her strange moods and desires but Jakob was aware of these things and helped her through this period in time.

They went to see the mayor about Liz's thoughts on a more formal adult education class. He wasn't too enthusiastic about her idea but went along with it, and even said Liz could use the schoolhouse on Saturdays. Liz started to spread the word about her adult education classes. She had talked to her ladies group at church and asked for volunteers to help her. She found some who were just as enthusiastic as she was. They felt the program would evolve into a one-on-one program. *The Sheridan Post* ran a story on the adult education class.

On the first day of the program it rained hard. Liz went to the schoolhouse with Jakob and only one man showed up. Liz was not discouraged and prepared lessons for him. In future weeks more showed up, and Liz assigned them to her volunteers. As she had thought it was not easy and the numbers interested were not many. But it was a start.

As the weeks past, cold days moderated into a warm spring. Some of her students persisted and some fell by the wayside. Liz was satisfied her idea was accepted and more new people began showing up for the class. *The Sheridan Post* gave Liz some kudos and encouraged people to attend her class. One day Mr. Mortimer showed up and said he would help with her class. This gave her adult education class a real boost. Liz's waistline was starting to expand considerably but she was not going to let it stop her from teaching her class.

One day Lee Wong, who owned a restaurant, showed up. He had his wife with him and managed to communicate they both wanted to learn to read and write English. This would be a real challenge for Liz because their language skills were very limited. Mr. Wong could barely speak any English. His restaurant served good food, but no one could understand him when he spoke. Hence, his business was affected. Mrs. Wong just grinned and shook her head when anyone talked to her. But Liz took them aside and started to teach them, as if they were little children just learning to speak.

On another occasion, the squaw Jakob had taken care of some months before came to the schoolhouse. She looked around, and was about to leave, when Liz saw her. She took the woman by the arm, led her to a desk and motioned her to sit down. This presented another challenge for Liz because she, too, had no English language skills, and with the papoose on her back, Liz had to make special arrangements for her. There was some concern with the other pupils about having an Indian in the class, but Liz allayed their apprehensions. The biggest problem Liz had with her was pronouncing her name, so she just called her Moon Song. She became one of her best students and learned rapidly.

Chapter 18

Jakob's New Job

Mayor Burns was the typical frontier politician: short on stature but long on words. He always had a chaw of tobacco in his cheek which he moved from side to side as he talked, and occasionally took time to use the cuspidor. Jakob arrived at the City Hall on time. He was surprised to see a number of other people in the Sheridan business community there: Harold Stevens from the First National Bank, Edgar Wright from *The Sheridan Post*, Ernest Johnson from the Johnson's Drug Store and Herman Banister from the Sheridan Drug Store. The mayor welcomed each one for coming to the meeting.

"I suppose you wonder why I have chosen you for this meeting," said the mayor. "I picked you because I felt each of you has some talent you can lend to our fair city. You men are the potential shakers and movers of our city, and Sheridan needs you for your abilities." Jakob looked at the others as they had moved their eyes to catch a glimpse of each other. "Sheridan needs your talent to make it even greater than it already is. We are growing and you can help us take advantage of the growth. We have to plan and direct the growth and you will help do that." Jakob listened as the mayor went on and on but spoke in generalities. *What does he want and what does he expect us to do?* he thought. "One of the important items in our future agenda is the county fair. It is just a few months away and it brings to our city many people from all over Wyoming. This is an event everybody here looks forward to. The fair has to be carefully planned in advance so it will be even better and more successful than it has been in the past and you gentlemen are going to make it so." Harold Stevens, the banker, raised his hand.

"Mister Mayor, don't you have a committee to take care of putting the fair together? We can help but we are not men who build grandstands and stalls for animals. We are business people."

"That's right Harold. I'm thinking about more important jobs, like judging various contests such as horse races, livestock and home baking, things that bring people to the fair."

The group snickered and one of them asked, "Do you want me to judge the homemade jelly?"

"How about the pigs, Mister Mayor?"

"That's not exactly what I mean. The fair is big and you are important citizens who will lend prestige to it."

Harold Stevens smiled and answered, "Mister Mayor, I'm sure those in the group will do all they can to help in the fair, even judging some of the contests. Is there anything else you need our expertise for?"

"This fair will need your input, as well as other areas we will discuss in the near future. Right now I just want to alert you to the great needs of the fair. We will also need to meet on planning for the extension of the city water supply, as well as the further electrification of Sheridan. The telephone will be here and someday everyone will own one. There is much to do to keep this city going forward. I'm sure you understand. Gentlemen, I will need your help." With that, the mayor expectorated into the cuspidor.

Jakob left the meeting a little chagrined. The mayor was just recruiting judges for the fair, but Jakob was primarily interested in the need for a better supply of water. Having water hauled into Sheridan in barrels on a wagon was downright unsanitary, even if it came from a clean stream. In some areas this was still being done. Main Street needed to be paved. It had ruts that were challenging, especially after a rain or during the winter when the ground was frozen. He wasn't too excited about being a judge at the fair. He left the meeting somewhat disappointed as he walked toward his office.

A group of Indians stood in front of his office waiting for him, and they followed him in when he opened the door. One of the squaws appeared to be in pain and was holding the right side of her face. Moon Song, who Jakob had taken care of some months ago, was present and was trying to interpret for the squaw who held her hand over the side of her face. Moon Song had become a regular member of the Saturday reading class Liz was running and she did a fair job of explaining the problem to Jakob.

The teeth of the Indians were generally not good. Their diet and lack of care led to many dental problems for them, but the barrier of language and culture made it difficult to provide them with information on care of their teeth. They generally looked for help only in emergencies, when nothing could be done other than extract the tooth. Jakob thought he would seek Liz's advice on how he might present the Indians with information on proper care of their teeth. Maybe something could be done for them.

In the meantime, all he could do was remove the two offending teeth the squaw came in with and take her out of pain. As usual, they would leave with him several items of Indian ware, but this time they also brought in a brown and white ball of fur—a puppy dog—and gave it to him. Jakob didn't want to refuse it but he also didn't want it. What would he do with a puppy? After he accepted the puppy he wondered how he would get rid of it. He placed the puppy in a box in his laboratory, thinking he would deal with it later. The moccasins she gave him, Liz could probably use.

His day was filled with the usual problems dentists see, but he still hadn't solved the problem of what to do with the puppy. He couldn't leave it in the office so he decided to take it home; maybe Liz would have an idea of what to do with it. Jakob placed the puppy in a large cloth bag and carried it home. He walked into the house holding the bag behind him, as he was greeted by Liz.

"What are you holding behind you, Jakob? Is it a surprise for me?"

"Well . . . ah . . . no, but yes, it is a special surprise for you." He reached down into the bag and brought out the ball of fur.

"Jakob, you brought me a puppy. Oh, how sweet of you. Oh, it's so cute. You darling, how did you know I always wanted a puppy?" Jakob breathed a sigh of relief and smiled.

"You know Liz, I just thought you would love to have this little puppy." Liz oohed and aahed as she held the pup up looking it over.

"What kind of dog is this and where did you get it? Oh, how sweet of you to think of me." Jakob worked out of what was a problem to him and made it a joy in Liz's life.

"Jakob, what kind of a dog is this? Do you know?"

"Well, Liz, it's . . . an Indian dog. Yes, an Indian dog. You know Indians have lots of dogs." Jakob explained to Liz about the Indian coming in to see him and how the squaw gave him the puppy, but he left out his thoughts about not wanting to keep the dog. "Where are you going to keep the dog, Liz? You know they need special care."

"Oh, don't worry, I've taken care of dogs since I was a little girl." She got a bowl of milk and put it on the floor, and the dog happily started lapping it up. "Oh, the poor thing was thirsty." She left the dog and started putting dinner on the table. Liz was thrilled to get the dog and much of dinner talk was about the cute dog. The gift from Jakob.

Liz then told Jakob about the garden she would be starting. She already had some sprouting seeds in her greenhouse and was excited about that. Liz finally got around to asking Jakob about the mayor's meeting and the rest of his day. He covered all aspects of his day.

Liz then told him about her trip to the new fabric store at the far end of Main Street where she had bought curtain materials for the bedroom windows. Liz's was excited about making their new house into a home. They were both happy with the home they bought and set about making it the way they wanted it to be.

Oliver Henry came into Sheridan to buy supplies and stopped by to see Jakob. He had heard Jakob and Liz bought Elmer Findley's place and wanted to see it. Liz invited him for dinner. Jakob said he wanted to buy a couple of horses, and asked whether he had any available. He told him what he wanted and asked Oliver if he had a horse that he could use with a buggy as well as for riding. He wasn't looking for any particular breed of horse. When the baby came it would be nice to have a buckboard or buggy to get around town and family outings. Oliver indicated he would find something for Jakob.

It was several weeks later Oliver again came to Sheridan. This time he brought a couple of chestnut-colored horses for Jakob to see. He stopped by the house and put them in the barn Jakob had prepared for them. Jakob and Liz were thrilled with them. He looked them over carefully, petting and talking to them and just getting acquainted with them. He loved horses and would occasionally get one from Wilbur Riggs at the livery when he needed to use a rig or wanted to ride. But now these would be his and he was thrilled to have them. He was satisfied they would be fine, but Oliver said he should make sure they would be all right for him, before letting him purchase them. One would be for Liz, though she would not be ready to ride for some time. He bought a buggy from Wilbur that he had available and was anxious to try one out. They were beautiful animals and seemed friendly, gentle and even-tempered.

The following Sunday, after church Jakob took Liz and the buggy for a visit to Big Horn. It was a beautiful day and it was not too long of a ride. Big Horn was a community which at one time was destined for great growth but was squelched by Sheridan and the arrival of the railroad. He thought this ride was a good way for them to become acquainted with one of the horses and to better enjoy the countryside. It was late May and the fields were covered with wildflowers of all sorts and many of the trees already adorned in their green splendor, as they rode slowly along Little Goose Creek. Many birds and wild fowl were flying in and out of the brush.

They stopped at Emma's Cafe for an early supper of fried chicken. Emma was a patient of Jakob's and was happy to see him. Having their own horse and buggy made this a special treat. They even brought home some cookies baked by Emma, who invited them to come back again. Having the rig available meant Jakob could use it to make the rounds of the various communities with his dental equipment. Often he was asked to go to some outlying places since some people had difficulty making the trip to Sheridan. In the past he would generally get a rig from Wilbur Riggs but now he had his own. They arrived home after their pleasant day. Jakob took care of the horse and later they sat together recounting the beauty of Wyoming's spring landscape before getting ready for bed.

"Jakob would you come over here please? I have something I want to show you." Liz was getting ready for bed, and had most of her clothes off, sitting on the bed. Jakob came over to her.

"What is it you want to show me?" Liz took his hand and placed it on her enlarging abdomen.

"Do you feel that?"

"Feel what?"

"The baby, our baby. Can't you feel it kicking and moving?" Jakob's eyes opened wide and he smiled.

"Oh my gosh. I do. I do . . . I can feel the baby. I can feel it moving. Oh my gosh. How long has he been, I mean she, I mean our baby? How long have you felt our baby?"

"It has been a while but it has recently been more pronounced. I thought maybe you felt it when we were close but then you don't have it inside of you."

"How long will it be before we can hold it in our arms? Do you wonder what it will be, like maybe a boy or a girl?" said Jakob.

"I guess sometimes I do, and then again I don't know what I wish for. I just think what it will be like to have a baby," said Liz. "I think about how it would be if we have a boy. You would be able to do so many things with him. But then I think if we have a girl and what it would be like to have someone who I could dress pretty and would be in the kitchen when I was cooking and baking. Then I think about how you would hug and kiss her and take her with you when you went shopping or when you bought her a pony. It doesn't matter what it will be. It will be what God has ordained for us to have." They lay on the bed holding each other and softly talking about what it will be like to have the baby Liz is carrying. Each day Jakob found another reason why he loved Liz.

Liz kept herself busy with her new home. She worked each day at doing something to make it more homey. Her garden needed attention and she would find time to work in it. Skippy was always present whatever she did. The ball of fur Jakob almost rejected became their constant companion. Jakob was busy as ever in his office and he too found time to add to the house. He had his horses who needed a lot of attention, and he enjoyed riding them. They were gentle animals and made fine companions. He was looking forward to when Liz could ride with him but the best advice was not until after the baby arrived.

Chapter 19

First Anniversary

It didn't take too long for the ball of fur to become a ball of fire. Skippy had become a member of the Miller household and held a prominent place. He kept the household in permanent laughter from his antics. No one was really sure what his breed was, but he had the marking of a sheep dog and had grown considerably. He was Liz's charge and followed her wherever she went but also shared his love for Jakob.

Jakob took to horseback riding, now that he had his own horses and Skippy would like to follow along. The dentist who had exited a stagecoach just a few years before in his black and white hounds-tooth suit with a wing-collared shirt and a black derby was now dressing appropriately for Sheridan, Wyoming, in Levi's and blue shirt, with a red bandana, a ten-gallon hat and riding boots. The transformation of the city slicker from Milwaukee, Wisconsin, to a Wyoming resident was not too difficult. His riding became quite good. However, Liz did not think it was good enough to let him enter in the various competitions at the upcoming Sheridan County Fair.

Jakob was in his office when one of his patients remarked that his wedding anniversary was coming up. That surprised Jakob who had almost forgotten about the date.

"How did you happen to remember that?" asked Jakob.

"Hey, Doc, don't you remember? I played drums with the band at the reception." Jakob apologized for having forgotten he was there and in the band.

"Do you think maybe you might be having a party to celebrate? If you do, we'd be available to play. Jes let me know." Jakob said he had not made any plans yet and would take it up with Liz.

Jakob's life had been very busy since the day in June when they got married. He thought about their marriage and all that happened during those ensuing months, and he had never been happier. He and Liz had grown closer than ever. Jakob never thought such a thing could have been possible, and he felt they had been blessed with so much in the short time they have been married. He remembered promising to build Liz a home. Well, it didn't exactly happen but the home they now had would have taken them many years to build. It was more than they had ever dreamed was possible. And now Liz was going to have a baby.

I have to give her something special as an anniversary present, he thought. *What can it be? It has to be something really special.* For the next few days Jakob walked in and out of various stores in Sheridan, and finally he saw something in the jewelry store that gave him an idea. Jakob went into his laboratory and with wax he created a heart ring to match the two hearts he gave her for Christmas. He then made it out of gold, polishing it to a brilliant shine. He stored it for that special day.

Even though Liz was pregnant, she had been a very busy housewife with her new house. She had made curtains for their bedroom and started others for the living room. They had received their personal furnishings from their Eastern home, as well as gifts from their families, and the empty rooms started to become livable. After dinner Liz and Jakob walked around their yard to see their garden growth. The seeds germinated in Liz's greenhouse were starting to produce sprouts and blooms. They sat on the front porch swing and waved to their neighbors who might pass by, with Skippy laying at their feet.

Jakob spoke. "Liz, you know our wedding anniversary is next week." Liz snuggled up close to him.

"Jakob, you remembered. I knew you would. You have made me so happy. We have so much and we are so lucky. I never thought we'd have such a nice house, and our love for each other grows stronger." She placed her hands on the sides of his face and kissed him gently. "Aren't you glad we came back here to Sheridan? When you asked me back in Milwaukee if I was sure I wanted to return here, I wondered if you really wanted to come back, or whether the lure of the East would change your mind."

"Funny, I thought the same of you. I wondered whether the glamor of the big Eastern cities might tempt you to change your mind about Sheridan."

"Jakob, we are truly one, as our vows professed. We have begun to think the same." Jakob kissed Liz and held her tightly.

"Should we do something special?"

"Every day is something special, Jakob. Just take me out for dinner to the Sheridan Inn and then maybe we can dance to the music of Jozef's violin. You know, since that night in the Palmer House in Chicago I have come to like dancing with you, especially when you hold me tight. I feel like I melt into you."

The week passed slowly and then Saturday arrived. Jakob told Lukas of his wishes for their anniversary dinner. The day came and they were welcomed at the Sheridan Inn. Liz was dressed in her yellow flowered dress with her white lace gloves that went to her elbows. She wore a white flower Jakob had bought her on her left wrist. They sat at their favorite table sipping champagne and reminiscing about their wedding day until their dinner arrived. It was Lukas's special duck, with yams, spiced apples and all the trimmings. People stopped by their table to congratulate them on their anniversary. Then, Jozef came by to play his violin and they got up and slowly danced by their table. When he stopped, Jakob took out the heart ring and placed it on her finger. Liz wore the hearts on the chain around her neck.

"Jakob, the hearts: you made them and now this ring. It is so beautiful."

"So are you Liz. You are so beautiful. You make my heart race. These two hearts represent yours and mine and they are next to each other on the chain as they shall always be." Tears welled in Liz's eyes and he kissed her while Jozef played, "I Love You Truly." They stood there holding each other until they were interrupted by Elsie who placed the desert on their table.

"Jakob, maybe we should sit down. Jozef is now playing on the other side of the room and our dessert is on the table." They sat and had their desert and soon left for home, so deeply in love. Jakob picked up Liz and carried her inside and placed her on their bed. The glow of that anniversary date lived in their hearts in the coming weeks.

The middle of June was court week in Sheridan. As the county seat of Sheridan County, the county courthouse was in Sheridan. Court week brought in a whole variety of individuals from the northern part of Sheridan County and beyond. At times, it almost seemed like a Roman circus. Lawyers and their clients assembled for the administration of justice in Sheridan. It was fun to watch the lawyers practice their presentations in the local barber shops with the men watching.

The cases were both civil and criminal. In the criminal area the trials could be for murder, manslaughter, bodily injury or stolen property. Stolen property such as horses and livestock, and wholesale cattle rustling, with changing or disfigurement of brands, were especially held in contempt. With the influx of population there was a burst of potential patients for Jakob. Besides the participants in the trials, there were those who would have jury duty and the onlookers who came to see justice performed.

Jakob often wondered whether he liked taking care of some of those unsavory individuals who came from places unknown. It was difficult to discern which were the recipients of criminal justice from those who were in town for the social atmosphere, except when the sheriff brought them in wearing handcuffs. Occasionally some very respectable citizens came for business and pleasure, and they were gladly accepted by Jakob as patients. One such person was a lady by the name of Martha Cannary, best known as Calamity Jane. She would often stop in Sheridan to visit old friends, but she also had need for Jakob's services. Jakob found her to be very civil and didn't really know how much to believe of her exploits.

Court week brought a lot of money into Sheridan, but much of it was left in the various saloons along Main Street and the houses of ill repute. The city jail was filled and emptied almost daily. Jakob sometimes wondered whether he welcomed or abhorred court week. But, it was part of life in Sheridan.

Chapter 20

Oliver Henry's Birthday

Jakob was at the Sheridan Inn having dinner with Liz. As they were finishing dinner, James Widicker, the Englishman, stopped by their table. Jakob invited him to sit with them. Mr. Widicker said he was just stopping to see him for just a few moments.

"When I was having my dental work done, I told you about the birthday party being planned for Oliver Henry at his ranch, and he wanted me to make sure you and your wife would be attending."

The Oliver Henry Ranch was a full day's ride from Sheridan. Jakob looked at Liz and asked her if she thought she would be able to make the trip. Liz was now feeling much better and was excited to go. She had heard about the lavish Oliver Henry Ranch, and was thrilled they were invited. Widicker told them Oliver had said they would have a room in the ranch house, all to themselves. The ranch house was supposed to be very big. He even said one of Oliver Henry's men would come in and get them in their wagon. Jakob agreed to the date and said they would be ready. Widicker assured them everything would be taken care of for their comfort and Oliver was looking forward to them being there.

Jakob talked with Doc Kelly and told him what he was planning on doing and whether he felt it would be all right for Liz to make the trip. Kelly thought Liz could make the trip safely but she should get enough rest. Jakob made arrangements for the animals to be taken care of by his neighbor. He felt they would be gone maybe four or five days.

It was Friday, June 30, at four in the morning when Oliver Henry's driver stopped by Jakob's house. Liz and Jakob were excited and ready. They put their luggage in the back of the covered wagon. It was a chilly morning and Liz was bundled up with a buffalo skin to cover her until the sun came up and warmed the air. She sat comfortably in the back of the wagon while Jakob was seated next to the driver. It would be a couple hours before sunup. The trail was not smooth but Liz was comfortable. The hot coffee they brought was now lukewarm, but it was acceptable. At sunup it started to get warmer and the sky was clear. They brought stored apples from the tree behind their house to snack on. It was midday when they stopped to have a lunch of cold meats and bread Liz had packed, and then they were on their way to the ranch.

Later in the afternoon they saw wisps of smoke far ahead and then some buildings appeared. A large herd of cattle with riders working them appeared to the right some distance away. Passing through the gateway to the Oliver Henry Ranch, they were soon approaching a group of buildings with a prominent large, two-story log house. They passed wagons and horses with riders and a large corral. The log house had a big veranda, and as they approached people soon appeared on it. The wagon stopped in front of the house and Jakob helped Liz down. People with smiling faces began welcoming Liz and Jakob and some introduced themselves. Oliver Henry came out with his wife and introduced her. She was a handsome lady, tall and slender, light-skinned and dark haired with a warm smile.

"Doctor and Mrs. Miller, we're so happy you could come. I want you to meet my wife Abigail. We all call her Abby." Others came forward and also introduced themselves. It was obvious they were English by their accents and dress. Oliver invited them into the house and a trail of people followed them in.

The main building of the ranch was built of cottonwood logs, with five rooms on the first floor and seven on the second. A huge fireplace adorned one of the walls with a small fire in it. Liz felt chilled by the ride and moved close to it to warm herself. Abby came over to Liz and placed a brightly colored shawl around her, and gave Liz a hug. All the windows in the ranch were open and a comfortable cool breeze was felt. The driver took their luggage up to the second-floor bedroom. Couches and chairs were placed near the fireplace and a young woman brought out trays of china with cups and saucers. Tea was poured into them for the group. Trays of cheeses and breads and small pieces of meats and fish were also passed around. The furniture was an interesting mixture of ranch style in the large drawing room to one side, and English style in the dining area on the other side. Liz was amazed by what she saw. The ornate stairway to the second floor started in the middle of the great room and had stairs of rosewood and railings of walnut that had been imported from England. The floors were hardwood, with oriental rugs in various places.

James Widicker came up to Liz and Jakob and welcomed them. He introduced his wife, Geraldine, an attractive English lady who showed her breeding. She was considerably younger than her husband, probably the same age as Liz. Others crowded around and anxiously introduced themselves to Liz and Jakob. It was a jolly crowd of people, quite different from what Liz was used to in Sheridan. Oliver Henry was a tall handsome man, with brown hair that contained liberal traces of gray and a trimmed beard. He had a deep-sounding laugh as he moved through the room with a decanter of Scotch whiskey, suggesting to the group they have some in their tea. The ladies generally refused and preferred milk with their tea.

Abby came over to Liz and suggested she take a short nap before dinner which would be at seven. It was still bright and sunny. Jakob and Liz excused themselves and walked up the staircase to their second-floor room that was designated as their bedroom. It was quite large and was furnished in English-style furniture. The bed was a four-poster with a canopy over it. Liz was thrilled with the furnishings and said she felt like she was residing in an English castle, until she looked out the window and saw the corral with horses in it. Tired from the long ride in the wagon and excited by the grand welcoming of the crowd, she quickly fell asleep. Jakob lay in bed with thoughts of the trip and the friendly people. He too soon fell asleep.

He swore he had just closed his eyes when he heard melodious chimes that had awakened them. Liz was startled awake.

"Jakob, where are we?"

"We're at the Oliver Henry Ranch, Liz."

Liz sat up. "Oh my gosh, we are. And you are my knight in shining armor. I'm so glad you took it off before you laid down with me."

"It's six-thirty, so we have a half hour to get ready for dinner. The English always dress special for dinner." Jakob dressed in his Sunday suit. Liz brought the gown she had worn in Milwaukee. It was tight but she still looked terrific. And because it had cooled off some, she wore the shawl Abby had given her over her shoulders but later she would take it off. The chimes played again.

"I guess it's time we go down for dinner." Coming out of their room they heard voices and laughter, and the crowd could be seen as they went down the stairs. They were greeted warmly by their newfound friends, as they stepped off the stairway. For the most part, the men were dressed in English dinner jackets and the ladies in gowns. Liz fit in perfectly. The table was in the large dining room and could easily seat all the people present. Oliver Henry was dressed in Levis and a western shirt with a narrow black tie—his typical daily dress. And Abby, likewise, wore a skirt and a puffed-sleeve blouse. They didn't mind the fancy dinner dress of the others. Liz and Jakob were probably the youngest in the crowd. The table had white linens and napkins, with splendid silver and shining glass. Two large candelabra with burning candles adorned the table. The butler was in typical English attire, as were the other servers. Name cards were placed, and when all were seated, the wine was poured.

Oliver Henry led the toast. It seemed there was a toast with each course. They toasted the Queen and the President of the United States, as well as others who were present, including Jakob and Liz. They had a dinner of roast beef, roast duck and pheasant, and were served by ladies in white blouses and black skirts with white caps. The conversation was animated. Most wanted to know about how Liz and Jakob came to Wyoming. The others were visitors from England. Some were titled or heirs of the titled. Others were adventuresome, and some had been dealing in horses the Oliver Henry Ranch was breeding especially for sending back to England.

As was common in England, after dinner the men slipped off to have their cigars and port, while the women had their tea, or port, if they chose. Liz was in awe of the experience she was having, and the ladies were charmed by her presence.

She told them of her pregnancy and one of them said, "I wondered if I detected a bit of a bump there." To which all the ladies laughed.

The evening went by fast, with lots of interesting conversation. Soon one by one they paired off and sat by the fireplace talking. Jakob and Liz learned much about England and the customs of the people. It really was an exciting experience for them. Liz sat cuddled up to Jakob warming before the large fireplace because the night air cooled the ranch. Soon their eyelids grew heavy and they excused themselves and moved to their room. The room had a wood-stove to take the chill out of the air, but it had not been readied for them. The bed had been turned back and had a blanket on it to keep them warm. Some of the guests stayed in another building that was used as a guest house.

The sun entered their bedroom through a small opening in the drapes and Jakob awakened. He heard the Henrys moving about in the hallway, outside their room. Liz was still sleeping. Jakob's thoughts were of Liz and the baby she carried. His life had now entered a new phase and he was excited about the family he would be having. His job was now to prepare for a family. He thought, *What will it be, a boy or a girl?* The thought of a son he would raise to be a companion he could take fishing or hunting excited him, but then he envisioned a curly-haired, lovable girl who would emulate his Liz and grow to be a loving beauty, which gave him a feeling of warmth. *How can I possibly pick the one I want most, when my Liz will present it to me? Either will make us happy.*

He quietly dressed and left Liz sleeping, while he walked down the stairs to meet with some of the other men who were standing and drinking coffee. Oliver had planned to take the men to do some bird hunting in the morning. The afternoon would be spent seeing the workings of the ranch, and the evening would be Oliver Henry's seventieth birthday party. Abby had her own plans for the women.

Breakfast would soon be served, so Jakob went to awaken Liz. She was already up, and soon they joined the others for a ranch breakfast of pancakes, eggs, bacon and scones. Liz still had an uneasy stomach, and ate lightly.

After breakfast the men met down at the corral for their horses. They rode to a nearby stream that passed through a wooded area. Then they dismounted and slowly walked toward the stream. Many ducks flew in and out of the area and soon the hunters had their limit of ducks. The dogs picked up the fallen birds and brought them to the hunters. There were enough for a sumptuous dinner.

The group made their way back to the ranch for lunch. The afternoon was spent with Oliver showing off the workings of the ranch. His men showed their skills of horsemanship and handling of the cows. The Oliver Henry ranch was a big one, and it was successful. It was a treat for the English who watched excitedly. The day had been filled with the activities. The ladies had shared "high tea" with Abby and her staff.

Abby was as much a part of the working ranch as her husband, something that amazed the English ladies, whose days back in England were more of social contacts and leisure. People from the other ranches started moving in for what was going to be a great party for Oliver. Tables of food were put up and the musicians arrived with their instruments. Jakob and Liz moved through the gathered revelers. Some of the ranchers were patients of Jakob who came to Sheridan to see him. There was plenty to eat and drink. The ducks that were shot in the morning were dressed and roasted on a spit to perfection. Beef, pork and sausages were also part of the fare, with various vegetables and breads.

They dined with various wines that the Henrys imported from France, Spain and Portugal. The whiskeys were largely locally made, but some arrived from Kentucky. The Englishmen sipped their Scotch whiskey but the hard drinkers took them down straight, as they would in a Sheridan saloon. They drank and ate to their hearts' content and some may have had too much of both. The band played music to please them all. The fiddle, the piano, guitars, accordion and drums satisfied the dancers. It was a group of contrasts, with the English in their formal-attire and the locals with boots and denim and even a couple of city slickers.

The good band encouraged all to dance. Liz made a big hit with the party folk. She wore the dress she purchased in Milwaukee and attracted all the men. She was so beautiful, young and pure. The men would curb their language, lest they offend her. She was the lady who gained respect. The English were especially impressed with her teaching background and queried her about her experiences and admired her for her accomplishments. The men were all anxious to dance with her. Poor Jakob felt let out as Liz waltzed across the floor with a Lord or a cattle baron.

The baker had baked Oliver a six-tiered cake with sugar frosting and fruit. Oliver cut his birthday cake and the pieces were distributed to the guests. The band played the birthday song as they all sang "happy birthday" in various degrees of ability, but Oliver didn't mind. It was his night to celebrate and he did. The night carried on and some of the revelers were falling by the wayside. The wives prodded their men to decline more refreshments, while some had already overdone it. Some of his closer neighbors started leaving for home earlier, with the wives taking the reins for their impaired husbands. Jakob didn't know where Oliver put all the guests, but many stayed overnight. Some brought sleeping rolls that were put down in the large living area. Some chose to talk late into the night and fell asleep in the large chairs. Liz and Jakob, exhausted from the activities of the day, went to their room and were soon asleep.

Jakob awakened with the first crack of light that came through the bedroom drapes. The room was cool. He went back to bed and just lay thinking about the events of the past few days. Liz remained fast asleep. They had a great time with the people at the Oliver Henry Ranch, but the time had come for them to return home. He had concerns about returning to work, and of course Liz remained dominant in his mind. She was pregnant and he didn't want to subject her to too much activity. *The party was maybe too much*, he thought, but she had such a good time. Everyone wished to dance with her and she enjoyed being with the people. It was a long ride back to Sheridan. It would be wise if they left as early as possible. Liz was starting to awaken, so Jakob thought he would hurry it along and kissed her on the lips.

"Is it time to get up already?" she asked.

"It's early, but I think we should get going and return home. How are you feeling today after that big night?"

"Hmmm . . . I guess I'm all right. I believe we had enough partying to last for a long time. How are you doing?"

"Like you, I've had enough partying to last me for a long time too. I hear people moving around in the hall, so we might as well get up. Maybe we can get an early start home." They dressed and left their room to go to the dining room. Many of the guests were up and about and already having their coffee. Oliver invited all to come to breakfast, which was now being served.

"I know you are anxious to return to Sheridan, Jakob, so I have alerted my driver to be ready to leave at your request. I am truly happy you made it here to celebrate my big day. I always wanted to get to know you better than just being your patient, and we enjoyed having your lovely wife with us. Abby has become quite fond of her."

Jakob and Liz had breakfast with the group. The other Wyoming guests were starting to leave. The English continued their conversation with Jakob and Liz, and promised to visit when they came to Sheridan. Geraldine Widicker came to see them off and gave Liz a hug. She and Liz became fast friends. The driver put their belongings into the wagon along with a basket of food for their lunch. Liz was bedded down on a bunch of buffalo skins and the wagon moved out amongst a lot of cheerios and goodbyes.

It was a cool day with a clouded sky. A distinct possibility of rain concerned Jakob. The wagon moved along as best as it could on the trail. They didn't stop for lunch because they wanted to get as far as possible before dark. Jakob and Liz just ate in the wagon. The driver did as well, and still held the reins. There was some light rain now and then.

They entered Sheridan at dark. Other than the activities in the saloons, the town was quiet. They opened the door to their Loucks Street home. The lunch basket from the Henrys was enough to serve for a light-late night snack. They were tired from the long ride and glad to be home.

Chapter 21

The County Fair

The party at the Oliver Henry Ranch was a great experience. Jakob and Liz had a very good time, but Liz came home exhausted. The wagon ride to and from the ranch was not easy. That, plus all the activity at the ranch, was just too much for her. Jakob wondered if they should have gone. Liz was pregnant now, and even though she felt good, she should not have overly exerted herself. But with a few days' rest, she was up and about.

Her pregnancy was undoubtedly something they had to consider every day. The morning sickness she had experienced didn't bother her too much anymore. Liz was definitely showing her motherhood. As the English lady at the party had said, "There's a bit of a bump there." And the bump was becoming more prominent. Liz was back in the home she loved and taking up where she left off. Her ever-present companion was Skippy who followed her wherever she went.

The time for the Sheridan County Fair arrived and Jakob would soon be assuming his duties as a judge. Some of the visitors arrived on horseback and families usually came by wagon. Distant visitors arrived by train or stagecoach and the hotels started filling up. Indians put up their tepees on the outskirts of town. They were Cheyenne and Crows who dressed in full regalia. Ranch hands from all over the area came to participate in the riding events. The aristocratic English families came and Oliver Henry brought some of his horses and cattle for the show, along with a few of his ranch hands. The county fair was held at the old grounds and race track near the sugar factory so there was plenty of room.

Jakob was informed of his expected duties. He had conferred with former judges and of course became familiar with all the rules because the contestants were quite serious about the events. There were monetary prizes, so each entrant had reason to want to win.

Jakob was to judge the various horse-related contests. There were several horse races followed by the wagon races. These were always exciting.

One of the races that really excited the grandstands was the bed race. They would use several judges to make sure everything was done correctly. The contestants, and there were many, would roll out their bedroll. They would then take their boots off and place them at the head of the bed for a pillow, and then crawl under the bed roll. Their packhorse, saddle-horse, and the saddle would be nearby. At the sound of the gun, each entrant would jump up, put his boots on, roll up the bedroll and rope it on the packhorse, place the saddle on their horse, mount the saddled horse and lead the packhorse around the track. The first one under the wire with everything in place won. That was the funniest of all the races.

Jakob had told the mayor that he didn't want to do any of the various woman-related contests such as bakery or preserves or household contests, since his wife would probably be entering some of those contests. That might put him in jeopardy with either his wife or the other ladies of the community. But the mayor was a wily one and without notifying him, scheduled Jakob to judge livestock, something Jakob knew very little about. When he got into a confrontation with the mayor about it, Doc Kelly was standing next to him and took Jakob's side.

"Mayor, you have made a bad choice in using Jakob to judge livestock," said Kelly.

"How's that, Doc?"

"He don't know a shank from a sirloin. All he can do is look at their teeth, and there's more to judging cattle than just their teeth." The crowd around the three broke out in laughter, including the incensed Jakob.

The mayor looked at the two and said, "Maybe you're right, Doc," as he moved the quid in his mouth to the other side and let it drop in a pile of hay, just missing one of the bystanders. "You got a point there. He probably doesn't know much about cattle. But you do, Kelly. Didn't you once deliver a breech calf for Abe Hunter? You can take Doc Jake's place." Doc Kelly's face got red.

"No, no, not me, Mayor. You gotta go get someone else. I'm too busy. I won't do it."

"Now, Doc, everyone one in town respects you. Do it for the community that loves you so much. You ain't never been one to take part in the fair. You'll find out you like doing it. Ain't that right, Jake?"

"You're absolutely right, Mr. Mayor. Kelly, you've got to do it. You have special ability and we all know you to be a fair man who wouldn't cheat anybody. Kelly, you are a natural. You have good judgment."

Kelly stared at Jakob with a mean look, then looked at the mayor. "All right, I'll do it. But just this time. Don't expect me to ever do it again. You understand?" The crowd cheered as Jakob turned aside and laughed. Kelly walked away in a huff, grumbling.

The fair was a great success for Sheridan and Jakob discovered he really enjoyed being out with the community, and made many friends.

In his time between judging the different events, he was busy at the office. Besides the new people who came to town, there was the usual emergency work from fights in the streets and bars and the injuries received by participants in the contests.

Liz entered a number of the baking contests and won a blue ribbon for her apple pie and honorable mention on her bread. The thing that made her most gratified was the number of students from the reading and writing classes who stopped by to thank her for starting it. She was grateful to the ladies who helped her and thanked them accordingly for their help.

Jakob's work at the county fair did open up a new avenue for him. More people became aware he was not just Doc Jakob, the dentist; he was also a respected member of the community. Jakob's relationship with the mayor hit new highs and he was invited to come to the city meetings to voice his views on various projects before the city.

There was, however, one problem Jakob had with the mayor, and it was as a patient. His chewing of tobacco, besides being unhealthy, was an unsightly dental problem. Jakob would give him his professional advice about the dangers of chewing tobacco. The mayor would patiently listen to him and agree. However, on leaving his office Jakob could see him walk ten steps and stop before biting off a chaw of tobacco, and then moving on. As time went on, they did develop a better relationship, but the mayor never did give up his chaw of tobacco.

Chapter 22

Sultry Lady of Song

Jakob received a letter from a former patient of his, Lillian Massey, who told him she was coming to Sheridan and wanted to be seen for dental work. At first Jakob couldn't figure out who it was. The letter came in a pink, scented envelope with fancy writing. Then he remembered. The letter was from a patient he knew as Diamond Lil. He had restored her front teeth, and at her request he even placed diamonds in a couple of them. She had left for Memphis to seek fame as a singer. In the letter she told him she would be giving a performance at the Cady Opera House.

The Cady Opera House was Sheridan's cultural center. It was being built when Jakob first arrived in Sheridan, at the north end of Main Street. At first, many of the old timers snickered at the idea of an opera house in a wild west city, but they were wrong. It soon became a center of entertainment, especially for those who seldom went to saloons for their entertainment. Opera was introduced to Sheridan, at the Cady. Other kinds of entertainment like vaudeville, dramatic theater, lectures and various homegrown productions were also enjoyed there. Culture had arrived in Sheridan early, and was there to stay and now the lady who was known to the gamblers as Diamond Lil was coming to Sheridan as the "Sultry Lady of Song," Lillian Massey. Jakob brought the news home to Liz who tipped her head and smiled.

"Well, Jakob, it looks like you'll be seeing your lady friend and patient again. Isn't she the one who referred to you as *big boy*?" And she laughed.

"Liz, I see a little of a green eyed monster in that remark."

Liz continued laughing and answered, "No Jakob, I was just kidding you. I know she was fond of you for transforming her very unattractive smile to one that was beautiful, and she was grateful for what you did. It will be interesting to see her performance. You said she has a good voice."

"Yes, she does have a good voice and is an attractive lady for her age. Although, I don't have the slightest idea of her age, but she is pretty well preserved. I hope her reason for coming here is to entertain and not because her dental work failed." Jakob laughed and Liz joined in.

"Oh no, Jakob, you have to be kidding. Anyhow, I'm looking forward to seeing her perform and maybe you'll even introduce her to me."

During the next weeks, there were advertisements in *The Sheridan Post* and the *Enterprise* about the "Sultry Lady of Song" who would be performing on September 18th, at the Cady Opera House. It told all about her fame at theaters in Memphis, St. Louis, and even Chicago. There was excitement in Sheridan about the performance, except no one knew she was Diamond Lil. It was only Jakob who knew. Lillian Massey arrived in Sheridan on the Burlington Missouri Wednesday Special at 3 p.m., and was staying at the Sheridan Inn.

Thursday morning she was waiting for Jakob, adorned in her fancy dress with a big brimmed hat and carrying a parasol. This was a new Lil who had come to Sheridan. She had lost a few pounds and really filled out her dress, like an hourglass. Jakob could instantly see the change. Actually, she was almost unrecognizable to Jakob. Lil said she wanted Jakob to see if she was in need of more dental work and if so, to do it.

"Hey, big boy, polish them up for me." Jakob carefully looked over his "masterpiece," as she had referred to the work he had done on her. Her teeth were without any need for further care, for which she was grateful. He did a cleaning and polishing of her teeth and remarked how well she had taken care of them, since he saw her last.

"I have to take care of my smile. It's part of my business, and my business has been good since you fixed them up for me, big boy." Since the last time Jakob had seen her, her hair took on a new blonde color and her speech became sultry. Lil had really changed her image. She talked about her life in Saint Louie and Memphis and how it had been successful, but she wanted to come back to her "old hunting grounds," as she put it. Lil said she still liked a good card game every now and then, but it was not her primary source of income. She gave Jakob two passes to her performance on Saturday night and said she was looking forward to seeing him and his *Sweetie pie* there. Lil left Jakob's office and walked back to the Sheridan Inn, amid the glances and stares of people she encountered along the way.

That afternoon, Jakob stopped at the Lucky Lady after office hours. Andy Meeks put a glass in front of him and poured a drink.

"Well, look who's here—Doctor Miller, the celebrity dentist. I understand the Sultry Lady of Song was in your office today, getting her ivories all shined up for her performance this weekend."

"Now how did you find that out?"

"Jake. Sorry, I mean Doctor Miller, things like that get around." Doc Kelly was standing next to Jakob on one side and Mayor Burns walked up and stood on the other side of him.

"What's going on kid? I don't get any fancy patients like you do."

"Doc, who was in to see you at your office today? Share the news," said Mayor Burns.

"Now where did you guys find out about the Sultry Lady of Song coming to see me?"

"Hey, when a gal like that is in town and walks out of your office, people notice," said Kelly. Jakob just smiled like the Cheshire Cat and answered their queries.

"You gentlemen don't seem to realize amongst you here in Sheridan is the most famous dentist of the West." That started howls of laughter and brought the house down.

"Cut it out, Jake. Remember, we knew you when you got off the stage in that hounds-tooth suit and derby, looking for a place to yank teeth. So don't pull that 'famous dentist' stuff on your old buddies here." Doc Kelly went on, "Andy, give him another drink, on me. Maybe that'll loosen up his tongue." The Lucky Lady was in an uproar of laughter.

"Now I know you guys want me to tell all, but as a professional man I have to respect the privacy of my patients. All I can tell you is go to her performance on Saturday at the Cady and maybe, just maybe, I will introduce you to her." It became apparent no one who saw her recognized her as Diamond Lil, so Jakob decided to keep it as is. That perked up their imaginations and interest, and with that said, Jakob excused himself to go home for dinner.

Saturday came and everyone was going to see the performance of the Sultry Lady of Song. Lil kept everything low key and stayed in the hotel. Had her meals sent up to her room and also made arrangements with Harry, the piano player at the Lucky Lady to accompany her. Harry would sneak over to the hotel and had rehearsals with her on their piano. On the billboard of the Cady was a picture of Lil, and it indicated Oscar Morgan would accompany her on the piano. Jakob realized no one at the Lucky Lady knew that Oscar Morgan was really Harry, the piano player's real name. The Cady was a sellout. Liz and Jakob went over to the Cady early. Poor Liz, who was now pregnant and close to delivery, walked slowly up to the third floor and they took seats in the front row.

At seven o'clock sharp, the manager of the Cady came out and stood in front of the curtain to welcome everybody and to tell more about the performer, who had successfully toured in many Eastern cities. When finished he disappeared behind the curtain.

The curtain slowly opened and on the stage, front and center, was the black grand piano with a vase of red roses on a table next to it. Oscar Morgan, in a tuxedo, walked to the piano, bowed to the audience and sat down. At first the crowd didn't recognize Harry in his tuxedo, all fancied up but when they did, the crowd started clapping. Harry got up and took another bow before sitting down. When the crowd quieted down, slowly, but deliberately, Lil walked on stage. She received strong applause and deeply bowed. Lil was wearing a long, green gown that followed all the contours of her well-endowed body and white gloves covered her hands and arms above her elbows. She was adorned with long diamond earnings that hung from her ears and her fingers had diamond rings. A diamond bracelet encircled her left wrist and a white boa was draped loosely over her shoulders. She had a dazzlingly smile and bowed deeply to the audience, who again gave applause as she walked up to the piano and addressed the crowd.

"Hello folks. It's just so nice to be with you, back here in Wyoming. Sheridan has always been one of my favorite places and Oscar is one of my favorite accompanists." Oscar played a few notes as she hummed, and Lil started her first rendition. The crowd was quiet as she softly and in a sultry low voice sang a love song. The crowd broke into applause as Lil smiled and threw them a kiss and then broke into another love song. The footlights danced off her sparkling teeth. No one in the audience realized the sparkle came from the diamonds inlayed in her teeth.

Lil sang and talked to the audience, reciting love poems. The crowd loved her performance. In the middle of it a young man dressed in black pants and a white shirt, with a black bow tie, and carrying a tray brought Lil a full Champagne glass that she toasted the audience with. She slowly sipped from it, then placed it back on the tray. The young man bowed and left the stage. Toward the end of the performance Jozef, the violinist from the Sheridan Inn, came out playing a Chopin melody. Lil introduced him, as he continued playing and then she added words to the melody. "I will always love you," as she slowly waltzed across the stage, "and you will be with me in my dreams." She bowed deeply to the audience. The crowd loudly applauded and gave her a standing ovation. Lil smiled and her teeth sparkled as the curtain closed. It opened and closed three times.

As the crowd started to leave, Lil walked through the curtain and down the stairs at the side of the stage, over to Liz and Jakob, who she kissed on the cheek. Jakob introduced her to Liz and to those around them. Doc Kelly came up to meet her. Jakob introduced her to Kelly as Lillian Massey. Doc looked carefully at her, as if he knew her. Up to now, no one seemed to recognize her.

"You know, Miss Massey, you sure look like someone I once knew who used to play one helluva game of poker." Lil smiled a coquettish smile.

"Now I wonder who that could have been, Doctor?"

"After all that singing, I bet you could use some nourishment. Why don't you join me at the Sheridan Inn for some thing to eat, and maybe a drink?"

"Well Doctor, I just might do that." Turning to the group, she smiled and said, "It has just been so nice being with you all." Adjusting her boa, she blew a kiss to the group; then Lil gave her arm to Kelly and the two went off talking. Liz glanced at Jakob with a bewildered look on her face, took his arm and they walked off leaving the rest behind.

"We can do the same, Jakob." Liz slowly descended the stairs of the Cady holding on to the railing. Harley Robinson, the owner of the Bighorn Drug Store saw Jakob.

"That was some show, Doc. Is she really one of your patients? She sure can sing, and what a smile." Jakob just grinned as he walked on. Jakob helped Liz get in the buggy and they moved along to the Sheridan Inn.

"You know, Jakob, I sure hope I can have this baby soon. It's getting harder and harder for me to get up into this buggy." The Cady was just a short distance from the Inn and they were soon there. Jakob tied up the rig and helped Liz down. They were greeted by Henry Clayton as they walked into the hotel.

"I heard the show Miss Massey put on was great. I just knew it would be because I heard her rehearsal. She sure is one pretty woman. What a beautiful smile! Glad you came, Doc. We haven't seen you for a while." Jakob nodded and smiled, and Liz remarked Henry looked well.

"Well, thank you, Liz. Lukas will be happy you folks came by." They went into the dining room and Elsie met them at the door with a big smile.

"I have a good table for you. I'd take you over near Doc Kelly but he said he didn't want to be disturbed. He said something about celebrating Miss Massey's performance."

"This table will be fine. Liz and I will be perfectly comfortable here. I'll have a whiskey and Liz would rather have a cup of tea." Lukas came by and they talked, as they partook of his buffalo roast. After they finished, Liz looked at Jakob.

"You know, Jakob, I feel tired. Maybe we should go on home now." Jakob could see Liz was uncomfortable so they decided to go home. As they were leaving, he caught Doc Kelly's eye and waved to him. Kelly nodded and smiled. When they arrived home, Liz said she was even more tired. It had been a big day for her so she went to bed. Jakob decided to stay up for awhile to read a book. He was concerned for Liz and wondered if her time for delivery had arrived.

Sunday was usually Liz and Jakob's day for church. After breakfast Jakob got the rig out and drove Liz to church. The Reverend Henderson, who married Liz and Jakob, led the service. Afterwards, many of the people attending came up to Liz and Jakob to tell them they enjoyed the show at the Cady. Most wondered where Lil was from and how she had become a patient of Jakob, but he did not reveal Lillian Massey's background. Later, they stopped at the Sheridan Inn for a light lunch and the topic of conversation was the previous night's show. Liz was not herself, and asked if they could leave because she felt very uncomfortable.

When they arrived home Liz went to bed and asked Jakob if he could find Agnes Johnson, the midwife, because she felt maybe her time had come for the delivery of the baby. Jakob made sure Liz was comfortable and in bed. He became nervous and quickly left the house. *I hope I can find her home. What if she's on another call? Then what will I do?* His heart was pounding as he thought of Liz going through labor. He pressed the horse to go faster. Agnes Johnson lived on West Fifth Street, near Florence Avenue. He stopped at a house on Fifth and no one was in. Then he went to another house and they pointed out the Johnson house farther down the street. Jakob became apprehensive as he approached the house. He knocked on the door and there was no answer. He tried several times before he went around to the back of the house and found Agnes working in her garden.

"Agnes, Liz is having some difficulty and asked me to get you. Will you come over now and see her?"

"Of course I will. Let me get my things together." She quickly took off her apron and went into her bedroom and soon came out with a clean change of dress. She carried a black bag and another larger cloth bag with her. "Let's go," she said, as they hurried to the buggy. While they were on their way, Agnes questioned Jakob about Liz and said she believed there was plenty of time.

"That climb up the stairs at the Cady could have started things going. Don't you worry, she will be all right." Jakob thought, *Yes, don't worry, huh. It's not your wife.* It wasn't too long and Agnes was at Liz's bedside with Jakob next to her.

She looked up at Jakob. "Why don't you just go somewhere. I'll take care of things here and let you know what's happening."

All of a sudden Jakob, who was always in charge, was no longer necessary. He was in the way. *I'm not sure I like her,* he thought. *I want to know what's going on. She's my wife.* Leaving the bedroom he went out to the porch and sat on the swing for a while, but it was windy and cool, so he went back inside to his chair. Skippy, who had been looking for attention when Jakob and Agnes Johnson arrived, sat by Jakob's chair and looking up at him, made a low moan and placed a paw on his lap.

Jakob sat silently thinking of Liz. *What can I do for her? I've never been this helpless in my entire life. Why hasn't Agnes come out here and let me know what's going on?* His emotions went from anger to fear, and then after what felt like eternity, Agnes came out of the bedroom and was there next to him.

"Doc, she is going to have her baby. Her water just broke and she is starting to have some contractions. Don't worry. If you want to go in with her now, go ahead. It will still be a while. I'm going to get things ready."

"Then it's all right if I go in now, right?"

"Yes, go right ahead. It would be nice if I had some help. I'm going to see if Anne Long down the street will come over and help me. She has helped me before, and I like to have her with me, if possible. Can I take your rig? I can handle it. Liz will be fine."

"Yes, go ahead. I'm going in to be with her." He got out off his chair and went to the bedroom followed by Skippy. Jakob opened the door. Liz was propped up with pillows and smiled as Jakob walked in.

"Liz, how are you doing?" Liz smiled.

"Everything is fine, Jakob. Please don't worry about me. Agnes is just fine. I feel comfortable having her here." Just then, Liz started to grimace in pain and moaned, "Oh, oh, hmm," and the pain let up and she smiled weakly. "It's starting to hurt more but this is normal. That womb has to contract and bring our baby out. Oh, oh, hmm . . . hold my hand, honey." Jakob held her hand, and stroked her forehead, and kissed it. Liz looked up at him and weakly smiled. "Oh, I'm so sorry, but when those contractions come it just hurts so. I'll try to be brave."

"Honey, don't worry. I know it must hurt. Just squeeze my hand as hard as you can." It seemed like an eternity since Agnes had left. *When is she coming back?* he thought. It seemed like the contractions were coming faster and stronger. *Oh, my God, what if she doesn't get back in time and the baby comes? What should I do?* Jakob took a cold towel and wiped Liz's perspiring forehead as she wrenched with pain.

"I'm here with you, honey. Everything will be all right." Skippy paced back and forth and moaned. Jakob heard the door open and the two ladies walked into the room. Agnes, with her stethoscope around her neck, pushed her way past Jakob and attended to Liz. Anne Long was on the other side of the bed.

"Okay, I'll take over now." Jakob moved aside.

"But—"

"Never mind now. Annie and I will handle this. Why don't you go back on the porch or wherever? She will be fine. Go ahead. There's nothing for you to do here."

Jakob was almost dumb-struck as he slowly moved out of the room with Skippy following him. Liz was now moaning louder, and as he left he heard Agnes giving her instruction on how to push. He went back and sat in his chair with the dog pacing around him. The screams grew louder. He walked outside, down the stairs and up to the horse that was tied to a post. Jakob petted the horse and held its head. The sky was darkening. He looked up at the stars and remembered the limerick Liz had recited that night on the swing as she looked at the stars. Tears came to his eyes as he remembered his prayer to God he made once, asking for help, and the vows he made to Liz that he would be with her always. Shivering, he walked back inside, with all these thoughts racing through his mind.

Minutes turned to hours. Time seemed to stand still. He walked through the house. Had some coffee. Went back to his chair and sat for what seemed like eternity. Suddenly, the door opened behind him and he turned around to find Annie standing there.

"Well, Doctor, it's over. You have a daughter now, and your wife is doing fine. Give us a couple minutes and you can come in." He heard the baby screaming. Annie left and Jakob turned around, looking through the window at the stars.

"Thank you, God." He walked through the house with Skippy following and entered the bedroom. Liz was propped up holding the baby in her arms and smiling at her most prized possession.

"Jakob, come take a look what God has given us. I hope you are all right because I am." Jakob moved to the bed and bent down to see his daughter. Smiling, he kissed Liz's forehead and touched the little form in Liz's arms.

"She's beautiful, Liz. She's just beautiful. Just as you are." Tears came down his cheeks as he held Liz's face in his hands and kissed her ever so tenderly.

Liz, trying to hold back her tears said, "Remember that night on the swing when I looked up to the stars and recited that children's verse of 'Star light, star bright, first star I see tonight'? My wish came true. I hope you don't mind but I have a name for our doll, if it's all right with you. She will be Elizabeth Ann and we will call her BethAnn." Jakob kissed Liz and smiled.

"I think I will put you in charge of all the wishes in this family. The name is perfect. It's the greatest gift you could ever give me." Agnes smiled at Jakob.

"All right, enough of that stuff. You can now go back to your chair and let me get things put together here. I'm not through yet." Jakob shrugged his shoulders, left the room and went back to his chair with Skippy lying next to him.

"Well, Skip, this has been one tough night, but we got through it." The dog looked up at Jakob and gave a muffled *woof*.

Jakob heard the bedroom door open and both ladies came out. Agnes Johnson spoke to Jakob.

"Your wife is doing just fine. She went thorough the delivery better than I had expected. She was physically in good condition and it was important. She is sleeping right now and the baby is also sleeping in the basket, next to the bed. BethAnn had her first meal and Liz was thrilled.

"Annie is going to stay here with you tonight and she will take care of Liz and the baby. Tomorrow, she will teach Liz all she needs to know about taking care of the baby as well as herself. She'll teach her how to feed BethAnn and to take care of her breasts. Annie will also give you instruction so you can take over, if necessary. It would be nice if you could find someone to help Liz at least for a few days. Do you know of anyone you can get? Maybe a friend or a neighbor? Annie will be around for a few days if you want her. Things are going to change drastically around this house, but you and Liz will learn what to do. Liz is a smart gal and she will be a good mother. Any questions?" Jakob looked somewhat shocked and stammered a few questions. Agnes laughed.

"Don't worry, you aren't the first father. After you have a half-dozen, you'll know how to do everything. Just make sure Liz gets enough rest and eats well. I will continue to look in on her, but I hope you can get some help. Maybe a squaw, if you know of one. Do you know someone in your practice? How about one of those ladies from over at Acme? One of those Polish or Italian ladies must know how to care of babies and mothers. They have plenty of their own. It's kind of far for them to travel but maybe one can stay over.

"Now, if you can take me back to my place, maybe I can get some sleep." The ride back to Agnes's house was slow because of the darkness; the moon was almost gone. They made it safely and Jakob turned around and headed back. Even the saloons along Main Street were closed. The town was dark. He got the horse bedded for the night and went back into the house.

Annie was lying on the couch and Jakob went up the stairs to a bedroom. He had never slept there, but the bed was comfortable. He was tired but couldn't fall asleep. He thought about Liz and what she had been through, and he thought about the baby. She was so small, with such a little face and she had dark hair—a little girl for him to shower his attention on. Just then he heard the baby cry. Skippy got up, went to the door and looked down the stairs. He couldn't understand what was going on. Then she really let loose and screamed as if to say, "Hey, listen to me. I want your attention. Do you hear me?" *I wonder if I should go down there, but maybe I'd just be in the way. Besides, Annie is there. She will take care of things.* And then there was complete silence. The crying stopped and everything was quiet again. *I guess things will be different around here,* he thought, and then fell asleep.

It seemed like he had just fallen asleep, when the crying started again. She really got his attention and he lay awake listening. It was still dark. The crying stopped. Now, he couldn't fall asleep. Thoughts of Liz, the baby, and his office filled his mind for a long time. He tossed and turned, but finally fell asleep.

Once again Jakob was awakened by BethAnn's crying. His eyes opened wide as the gray light of dawn came through the windows. He could barely see the clock but it looked like 5:30. *Oh, no, I wish I could get at least an hour more of sleep,* he thought, and he dozed off. Then he had a strange feeling and awoke to Skippy licking his face.

"Oh no, Skippy, let me alone." The dog moaned and groaned. "All right, I'll let you out." Jakob got up and put on his robe then stumbled down the stairs and opened the door to let Skippy out. It was quiet in the house but Jakob was fully awake. He filled the coffee pot with water and coffee, putting it on the stove to boil. He looked out the window as the sun started to shine. The sound of Skippy scratching on the door broke the quiet of the early morning. Skippy was wide awake and looking for attention, but Jakob had to wait for the coffee to finish boiling before he could really give it to him.

Annie sauntered into the kitchen rubbing her eyes as Jakob poured them coffee. Annie smiled at Jakob. "Good morning. How does it feel to be a full-fledged father?"

Jakob smiled. "I think I can handle it." He got up and went to the bedroom door and slowly opened it, and looked inside.

"Hi, Honey. I smell coffee. Can you help me get up? I feel like I've been kicked in the stomach by a mule." Jakob entered the room quietly and lay on the bed next to Liz, kissing her tenderly. He held her face and kissed her again.

"Come on, Liz. I'll help you. Swing your legs over the side of the bed." She moaned a little while getting up, then they moved to the kitchen. Liz smacked her lips as she sipped the hot coffee. Sitting down, she looked at Annie.

"To think that wee little thing could make me feel so sore." They all laughed, and as they laughed BethAnn made it known she wanted to join the party. Annie went in and changed her and brought her out to Liz who fondled and kissed her. That didn't help her disposition, so Liz opened her gown and placed BethAnn's mouth to her breast. Except for the soft sound of her suckling, all was quiet again.

Chapter 23

A Happy Father

Jakob found himself not really knowing what to do. Annie was with Liz, filling her in with all she needed to know about caring for a baby. BethAnn was now asleep after her feeding. There just wasn't anything for Jakob to do, so he excused himself and headed for his office. He stopped first at Elmer Findley's general store. It was customary in Sheridan for the father of a newborn baby to get a box of cigars and give a cigar to each of his friends. Elmer greeted Jakob as he came into the store.

"Well, Elmer, you can congratulate me. Liz had her baby last night."

"She did? Well, congratulations, Doc. What was it a boy or a girl?"

"It is a girl and we have named her BethAnn."

"That's great. I bet you're happy. How's the mother doing? Did she have a tough time with the delivery? Ella always had a hard time with her deliveries and when they were over she would look at me and angrily say, Never again, Elmer. Never again." Elmer started laughing. "We've had six kids, you know."

"Well, I guess I don't exactly know whether she had a very hard time with the delivery. It seemed like it may have been, but then Agnes kicked me out of the room and all I heard was a lot of commotion and some screaming. Liz was pretty weak when it was over, and I felt pretty bad for her. Agnes said we had a perfect baby, weighing in at six pounds, six ounces. She sure is a beauty and has lots of hair. Liz is very happy. She's with Annie now, going over the routines and care of a baby with her and I was just in the way, so I decided to get out and go to the office. So here I am. I decided to stop here first."

"And . . . you came here to get a box of cigars for the boys, and I'll be the first to get one. Well, Doc, congratulations." Elmer took the first cigar and lit it up. "You're now on your way to filling the house I sold you. I'm happy for you, and Ella will be too when I tell her. She will be out to see Liz with all kinds of her own suggestions and advice on caring for the baby. You can tell Liz to just let it go in one ear and out the other, but then again, Ella has had six and ought to know something about babies. You know, Doc, that's the way Sheridan grows—one kid at a time." Elmer laughed and slapped Jakob on the back. "Give my regards to the Missus."

Jakob left and headed for the office. He opened up and went in. No one was waiting for him so he just straightened things up and sat down thinking about the baby. He was happy the delivery was over, and was anxious to spread the word about his new daughter to his friends. He closed the door of his office and went to the bank, next door, to tell to Harold Stevens about his new daughter and give him a cigar. There were several others in the bank he knew; they congratulated him and he gave them each a cigar. The conversation went on about Liz and the baby. Harold remarked Jakob might one day be opening an account for the baby. Jozef, the teller, was fond of Jakob and Liz. He too congratulated Jakob and received a cigar. Jakob engaged Jozef in quiet conversation and asked him to stop over at the office, because he wanted to discuss something with him and that was not the best time or place. He then went over to the Lucky Lady to see his friend Andy Meeks.

"What you doing over here at his time of the day, Doc? You should be over at the office yanking teeth."

"Good news, Andy. Liz had her baby. It's a girl. Six pounds, six ounces. Got lots of hair and is just too beautiful for words."

"Well, that's just great, Doc. How's Liz doing? I bet she's glad to have it over with." Jakob gave Andy a cigar, which he immediately lit up. "What say we have a drink on the house?"

"Nope, it's a little early for that. I'll take a rain check on the offer. I still have to go over to the office. I have another mouth to feed, so I have work to do." Andy agreed and Jakob headed back to his office. When he arrived, there were a couple patients waiting for him.

"I heard the news, Doc. I hear you got a baby girl. Do you think you can take care of this tooth that has been bothering me, or are you too shook up over the event? See, this here snag has been killin' me for the whole week. I guess we better get it taken out." Jakob agreed and took care of him. There were a couple other patients who came in and he promptly helped them. The rest of his morning gave him time to think about his baby. It was noon and Jozef from the bank came to see him on his lunch hour.

"You asked me to come over, Doc, so here I am. What is it you want to talk about?" Jakob explained to Jozef Liz would probably need some help with the baby for awhile, and wondered if he knew of someone over in Acme who might be able to help her. He asked Jakob for details of what kind of help she might need. Acme people were generally Eastern Europeans and were hard-working people. The men worked the mines and their women were homemakers, often anxious to make extra money doing odd jobs. Jozef thought for a few moments and then came up with an idea.

"You know, I just might have the person that could help you. It's *Chucha*."

"Who?"

"It's *Chucha*, that means aunt in Polish. She's my mother's sister and her name is Lokadia Grabowski. We call her Lottie or Chucha. She's been widowed many years and had a bunch of kids, and now grandkids. Chucha knows about babies and how to take care of them. She is an experienced lady and she loves babies. I don't know for sure if she would do it, but I bet I could convince her to help you.

It would also get her out of my mother's hair as they are constantly arguing.

"The problem is she doesn't speak much English, but I bet your wife could help with that. Liz is a teacher and the one who has taught a lot of people. Those people out in Acme came from the old country for a better life here, but lots of people don't take to them. They don't speak English well enough, so they just stick together speaking in their native language, and don't get out amongst others very much. They have their own Polish or Italian or Slovac-speaking community, even though they live in this country. They never learn English. Chucha lost my uncle Wojciech quite a few years ago and raised her kids by herself. And, what a cook she is! Doc, she would be perfect for you and the Missus and your baby. I'm going back home this weekend and I'll see if I can bring her here, so you can meet her. She likes me, so I think she will come if I ask her. You do have room for her to stay at your place, don't you, because she can't be traveling back and forth every day?"

"Certainly. She would have her own bedroom. She sounds interesting and I would like to meet her, and yes, Liz could help her learn some English." Jozef left and Jakob closed the office and headed home for lunch.

As he walked in, he saw several neighbors there oohing and aahing over BethAnn. There were also dishes of food to last for the week which the ladies had brought over. Liz looked better but tired from all the visitors who came to see the baby.

"Jakob, you'll never guess all the people who have come by to see me and BethAnn. Our baby is just so cute." Liz was excited about all the visitors she had in the morning and talked about all she learned from Annie. Annie was still there fussing around the house. She said she thought she should stay at least another day to help Liz get things going and hoped we could find some help. Jakob told Liz of his talk with Jozef and about his aunt. Liz wondered if it really would be necessary to get help for her. Jakob told her Jozef would bring his aunt out and then they could decide what they wanted to do.

"I really believe you should have some help, at least for now." The baby was starting to cry and Liz went in to get her. Liz rocked her a little and she stopped crying. Liz felt that BethAnn was really more alert now. "Let me have her, Liz. I can hold her for awhile." Liz handed her to Jakob, as he carefully fondled the baby. "Look, Liz, she's smiling to me."

"Jakob, babies don't react and smile at this early age."

"Well, she is. Look at her." Liz looked, but was certain she was not smiling at him. But then she did appear to be smiling . . . until she started to cry.

"What do I do now, Liz?" Jakob cradled the baby, talked to her and she stopped crying. "See, Liz, she isn't crying anymore." Liz smiled.

"I can see you are going to be the perfect father and I am going to have to put up with your perfection. But then, I just knew you would be, so I am going to have to live with it." She laughed and kissed him on the cheek.

"Don't you think that our little angel is simply adorable?"

"Of course she is, and that's because you are her mother." The next days Liz and Jakob became more acquainted with their baby and found more things to love about her.

The following Sunday Jozef stopped by the Miller house. He had brought his aunt Lokadia to meet Liz and Jakob. Both were a little apprehensive about the visit. Jozef introduced her as Aunt Lottie; she was a sweet little lady. Her height must have been a little over five feet and she was large of girth. Her generous smile was loving and her head was covered with a scarf which Jozef said was a *babushka*. Later she would remove it, revealing long gray hair rolled into a bun. Her eyes were brown. When introduced she said, *"Dzien dobry Pan e Pani"* (Good day, Mister and Missus.) She laughed and blushed. "I no *reusmi* (understand) English." and then she laughed some more. "I vant sp-ek English. I learn better. I try." She seemed nervous and somewhat embarrassed. Liz sensed her discomfort and went up to her and hugged her. She smiled and embraced Liz. Her smile showed a loss of teeth, which Jakob immediately noticed. That was not usual, for these Europeans were plagued with dental problems. Liz asked them to sit down. "You baby. I vant *vigi*."

Jozef broke in and said, "She wants to see your baby." Liz went into the bedroom and came out holding BethAnn in her arms. Lottie spoke to Jozef, who interpreted what she said to him. "She would like to hold the baby. Would you let her?"

"Oh, of course she can hold her." Liz took BethAnn to her and placed her in her arms. The lady gently placed her close to her bosom then kissed her on the forehead. A tear flowed down her cheek as she gazed reverently at the child. She slowly shook her head and smiled.

"Wadney, bardsa wadney." Jozef said that she thinks the baby is beautiful, very beautiful. Jozef acted as interpreter between his aunt and Liz. The meeting was somewhat awkward but Liz was pleased with her.

"She sort of reminds me of my Aunt Jenny." Jozef asked if there was anything else they wanted to know. Liz was satisfied they would be able to make a decision in the next few days. Chucha hugged both Liz and Jakob and they parted company.

Later Jakob asked, "What do you think Liz?"

"I think she will be fine. We may have a bit of trouble in communicating but I feel in a very short time we will understand each other. She is a beautiful and sweet little old lady. She is kinda chunky, but loving. We too may end up learning a new language. Let's just sleep on it."

The next few days were not easy for Liz. The baby was up a good portion of the night. She had to be fed and her diaper changed regularly. The feeding was Liz's department and Jakob soon became proficient in changing the diapers. The Miller household was living on BethAnn's schedule. Jakob still had to take care of his patients, and both he and Liz were deprived of sleep. They decided to hire Chucha. She could help Liz catch up with her sleep and care of the baby, as well as the house.

Jakob told Jozef they would gladly hire his aunt. Chucha arrived the following Sunday with her baggage, which consisted of a couple suitcases and several cloth bags. She also brought some baskets with groceries and foodstuffs. Liz and Jakob were treated to a variety of new aromas from the sausages and food she had brought with her.

Chucha took over the kitchen, which had been neglected since the arrival of BethAnn and it didn't take long before it was in perfect order. Chucha wore a white apron over her colorful house dress. She was meticulous with her housekeeping, and she hummed and sang while she went about her work. For a women of her age she was a bundle of energy. Liz would interrupt her work to point out different things with their English pronunciations, and Chucha would repeat and remember them. Her bedroom was efficiently organized and had a cross placed near her bed. She made prayer a part of her daily routine and asked *Boza* (God) and *Matka Boska* (Virgin Mary) for assistance and made the sign of the cross over various tasks. It wasn't too long before she used English words to describe things in the houses. She also introduced the family to a delicious dark bread that she called *chleb*.

Liz began complaining she couldn't do anything in her kitchen. Chucha had already done it. BethAnn was recognizing both Liz and Jakob and was smiling and making cooing noises. Liz was enthralled with her and Jakob would occasionally have his special time with BethAnn. Chucha would go back to Acme with Jozef when he went to visit his family, then return with him. It was during those times, Liz and Jakob realized how much she really did. Even Skippy accepted Chucha, who would save table scraps for him. They came to look forward to some of the Polish dishes that she would prepare for them. Her pot of chicken soup was almost a staple in the kitchen and was medicine for most aches and pains. The cold cellar was filled with various root vegetables that she used in her cooking. Liz was pleased with her use of English, even if it sounded fractured.

BethAnn was introduced to various foods Chucha made especially for her, even as she continued with her mother's milk. The baby was developing her own personality and was moving on all fours. She loved Chucha, who always found time to play with her and sing little Polish ditties. She would bless the baby as well as the household.

Jakob and Liz realized they could manage their life without Chucha but couldn't see fit to let her go. She made herself indispensable. Chucha made it possible for Liz to give time to her adult education program. She also joined the Women's Club of Sheridan and took part in their activities.

The seasons had changed since BethAnn arrived and winter had begun. Sheridan was preparing for Christmas and snow dusted the landscape. This would be BethAnn's first Christmas and Liz was preparing the home with decorations. Much had changed in Sheridan since they first arrived. There were more stores and services available. The population had expanded considerably. The railroads brought new businesses to care for the expanded populations. The mayor called on his new commissioners for advice and suggestions to improve the community. More electricity was introduced to Sheridan and the much-needed water system was expanded. New Main Street stores were being built of brick and stone, gradually replacing the old wooden store fronts.

Liz and Jakob went Christmas shopping for BethAnn. In The New York store they found several cute dresses for her. Liz liked to dress BethAnn in dresses and bonnets. They also found a teddy bear with a music box that played *Rockaby Baby*. They couldn't wait to give the teddy bear to BethAnn, even though it was supposed to be a Christmas present. They were thrilled to hear her laugh as she listened to the music. Jakob also brought home a small pine tree for decorating. Liz made a variety of ornaments she would hang on the tree. BethAnn was attracted to the variety of colors and shapes she saw. Liz was excited with the Christmas preparations and tried to make it special for her baby and Jakob. She remembered the traditions she grew up with and together they would celebrate the day as a family.

Chucha was experiencing mixed emotions. She wanted to spend Christmas with her new family, and yet her family in Acme wanted her to be with them. Liz insisted she spend the holiday with her family in Acme, so she left with Jozef on the Eve of Christmas.

Chucha had insisted she prepare the Polish Christmas Eve supper for Liz and Jakob; she called the dinner *Wigelia*. She had adopted the Millers as her family. The supper was a Polish tradition. It would have thirteen courses to depict Christ and his twelve Apostles. She prepared them ahead of time and instructed Liz how to serve them. The dinner consisted of pickled herring, trout from a local stream, mushroom soup, sauerkraut, pickled beets, *pierogi* (dumplings made with a filling of potato), red cabbage, homemade noodles, honey, fruit, poppyseed rolls, cookies, and a honey liqueur she called *Krupnic*, that she made.

She left thin wafers called *opl'atki*. Liz and Jakob were to break off a piece of each other's wafer and ask forgiveness for any transgressions they may have committed in the past year. This was to be done before the dinner. It was a Polish custom to show forgiveness, peace and love. Liz was thrilled by Chucha's love and concern for them. They had never experienced such kindness and love. Liz and Jakob had the traditional Polish Christmas Eve supper and afterwords exchanged gifts. They sat by the blazing fireplace with BethAnn. Both were overcome with nostalgia of Christmas memories of their childhood and of love for their lovely baby. The sound of wind and blowing snow was proof of a Wyoming winter.

They lay under a warm feather bed, snuggling and recounting the blessings they had. Just as they were about asleep, BethAnn made it known she desired their attention and a late night snack. BethAnn had a routine that had to be followed, and it could be demanding.

Christmas day arrived, bright and cold. Jakob was grateful they were in their new house. In spite of the severe weather, they remained comfortable. Jakob had prepared a breakfast with hot coffee and on the stove he would be frying eggs and bacon accompanied with Chucha's poppyseed rolls. Liz had BethAnn diapered and fed, and together they sat for breakfast. Skippy, who liked to romp in the snow, came in quickly out of the cold.

There was a church service later in the morning which they had planned to attend. The horse and buggy were ready and BethAnn was bundled up and in Liz's arms, before she went into the cold. The service was short and led by Reverend Henderson. The church was filled to capacity but the stove was unable to warm the sanctuary. It was cold inside. The homily was on the meaning of the birth of Christ. Liz held BethAnn closely and wondered if the mother of Jesus felt the same love for the Christ child she felt for BethAnn. There were quick Christmas greetings exchanged among the congregation as all were anxious to return to their warm homes.

Liz and Jakob had been invited to the Findleys' extravagant Christmas party in their new home, but debated going because of the cold weather. They were concerned with taking BethAnn out into the cold as the Findley house was farther away than the church. They decided to bundle up BethAnn and place her under a buffalo skin cover. Liz and Jakob were anxious to see the Findleys' new home which was supposed to be quite elaborate. Fortunately, the snow was not too deep and was only blowing around, but it still took a half hour to get there. Elmer made it possible for Jakob to put their horse in his barn and not face the severe cold and wind while they attended the party.

The home was decorated on the outside with garlands and a large wreath. Elmer welcomed them as he opened the big door. A fireplace was blazing inside the entry and the guests were having a good time. They welcomed Liz and Jakob and wanted to see BethAnn as soon as she was unwrapped. A hot toddy awaited them. Jakob and Liz were well-known to the crowd and were quickly absorbed in the merriment. As with past parties, Colonel Cody entertained his friends with stories of the Indian Wars. He warmly greeted Liz and Jakob but paid special attention to Liz. She was as beautiful as ever. Her childbearing had given her a radiance beyond her charm. She was loved by all, and several of the ladies at the party were members of her adult education group.

Ella Findley had one of her extravagant dinners. Christmas goose was a specialty, along with turkey and duck. The elk and beef roasts filled out the entrees. She was a great hostess and the Christmas party was a fabulous success. Spirits flowed freely. Sheridan was blessed with the railroad. It seemed like anything was possible, and food items previously unheard of were now available in Sheridan. The party was in full swing but it was apparent BethAnn had her fill of partying and wanted to go home, so the Millers left early.

BethAnn felt better in the quiet of her home. The lack of commotion made her happy, and BethAnn was soon asleep in her crib. Jakob and Liz sat by the fireplace discussing the evening. They both agreed taking BethAnn to the party was not in the best interest of the baby. They agreed she wasn't ready to do things like that.

Christmas was over and life would soon return to normal activities. Jakob brought up the letter his mother had sent to them. She and Jakob's father had not been to Sheridan yet to see the baby. Jakob had hoped they might have visited when the baby was first born. He realized it was a long, hard trip to make, but thought they would have come anyway. However, they had invited Jakob and Liz to bring the baby to Milwaukee. But such a trip would have been impossible for the newborn, so they were not being reasonable. Jakob's mother wondered when BethAnn would be baptized. This was something Liz and Jakob had briefly discussed but had not gone further with any plans.

"Liz, BethAnn is more than four months old. In the Catholic Church we believe she should be baptized. Have you thought anything about this?"

Liz reflected on what Jakob said. "I guess I have thought a little about it, but that's all. In my church, we believe in baptism, but it is generally done later in the child's life. What are you suggesting? Are you considering doing it in a Catholic Church? I understand there is now a Catholic Church in Sheridan. I remember the priest in Milwaukee saying our children should be brought up as Catholic. I didn't think much about it at the time. How do you feel, Jakob?"

"This is part of my faith and I would like to do just that. The church we go to is fine but it seems to lack something my church offers. How do you feel? Would you consider joining my church? We have never discussed this. What are your feelings?"

"Jakob. We are one in everything and this is something we have not discussed before. It's not that I don't pray. I did a whole lot before and during BethAnn's birth. Before I could make any decision, I would have to learn more about your faith. Maybe then I could make a informed decision. As far as I am concerned, I feel we could make that decision for her, and I would not object to having her baptized in the Catholic Church." Jakob took Liz into his arms, held her and kissed her.

"Then I think we should proceed with the baptism of BethAnn. We'll make contact with the Pastor of the church and find out what we need to do."

"And I'll try to learn something about the Catholic faith before I make my decision."

In the meantime Skippy, ever patient, came up to Jakob and nosed him. He wanted to be let outside and Jakob led him to the door. But he wasn't outside very long and was soon ready to come in and lay by the fireplace.

It was a long, full day and Liz and Jakob were ready to retire. Liz entered the bed wearing a long and revealing nightgown Jakob had bought her for Christmas. They snuggled under the warm feather bed in each other's arms kissing and eventually succumbing to sleep.

Their sleep was interrupted with BethAnn crying, followed by her coughing. Liz got out of bed and picked her up. She was wet and needed to be changed, but Liz noticed she seemed warm and she continued to cough. Liz fed her and she continued to cough and cry. Liz placed her close to her body and rocked her gently. BethAnn coughed intermittently and cried. Liz softly hummed and sang to her until BethAnn was asleep, then she placed her in her crib. BethAnn slept for a while, then intermittently awoke coughing and crying. Liz again rocked her until she fell asleep. That continued for the rest of the night. BethAnn had a cold and a fever.

Jakob felt helpless with Liz caring for the baby. The light of day entered the room and he was already awake. He took the sleeping baby from the arms of Liz, and gave her the opportunity to get some rest. As he looked down at the helpless infant in his arms, he realized she was a beautiful part of his wife and himself he was holding. He was swept with emotion as he closely held his daughter. BethAnn continued to sleep in his arms and coughed intermittently. He dosed off, only to awaken to the cold nose of Skippy against his leg. Skippy was wanting to go out. He carefully laid BethAnn in the crib and covered her, as Skippy anxiously waited for Jakob to let him out.

There was nothing else to do but make a pot of coffee and stay up. Sipping his morning coffee, Jakob reviewed the past days. They should never have taken BethAnn out. Being among all those people with her sensitive immune system was not good for her. Now she was sick. What could they do for the poor little thing? Liz slept soundly until BethAnn started to cough and cry. Jakob picked up the baby and carried her into the kitchen, with Liz following.

"Let me have her, Jakob. I'll take care of her now."

"That's all right Liz, I can handle her for now."

"No, she needs me, and I'll take care of her." With that, Jakob handed the baby to her mother and smiled.

"You win."

"Of course," Liz giggled, and she moved back into the bedroom with her baby. The rest of the day was one of caring for a sick BethAnn. Jakob went to see the pharmacist who gave him some things to give to BethAnn. They even rubbed an ointment on her chest. Liz and Jakob were concerned for their baby and took turns trying to make her comfortable.

Later in the day, Jakob went to his office to take care of a patient who had stopped by the house asking to be helped. Jozef later stopped by with Chucha who was ready to take over. She came in with bags of foodstuffs she had made for Christmas with her relatives. She was elated to be back with her new family and gave them hugs and kisses before she even removed her babushka. Happy to be back, she immediately took over where she had left off. She talked about her visit home, with Jozef interpreting for her.

Before he left, Jozef sat down with Jakob and told him how much her job with them meant. She was an entirely different person from before. Jozef's mother and she had bickered with one another, but now they were once again happy sisters. Chucha had elected herself to be the mother of the Miller family and made herself indispensable. She had found a reason to live and be happy.

During the week following Christmas, they spent most of the time taking care of BethAnn. Chucha had rubbed some kind of concoction on BethAnn's chest and it seemed to help. The cough subsided and she was more comfortable. Her temperature left her and she was a happy baby again.

Henry Clayton stopped by Jakob's office to inform him of the New Year's Eve party at the Sheridan Inn, and to invite him and Liz to come. Jakob told him he would ask Liz if she thought they should come, as BethAnn was still sick. Henry then suggested bringing BethAnn and putting her in one of the rooms with someone to take care of her. Jakob brought up the idea with Liz, who thought they should not take the baby out of the house. But maybe Chucha would take care of BethAnn. Liz was good at communicating with Chucha. She was gaining an English vocabulary and Liz was gaining a Polish vocabulary. Together they were able to communicate.

They would be going to the New Year's Eve celebration. The last day of 1898 would be celebrated. Liz dressed in the beautiful green dress she wore the first time they went to the Sheridan Inn New Year's Eve celebration. She wore her wide-brimmed hat with white feathers and high-laced light-brown shoes. Liz was adorned with the gold necklace with two gold hearts Jakob had given her last Christmas, and the gold heart ring he gave her on their anniversary. She looked ravishing as they walked into the dining room. Many of the hotel guests looked admiringly at this glamorous young mother walking through the dining room as Elsie was leading them to their special table. The orchestra was playing.

"This is your table. I saved it for you when Henry told me you were coming.

Lukas has prepared your favorite roast duck dinner and I have a bottle of Champagne chilled for you."

"How nice of you, Elsie, to think of us," said Liz.

"Oh, you people are special and we haven't seen you for a long time."

"We are parents now and haven't been out very much these days," said Jakob.

"Oh, we understand. We just miss you and are happy you were able to come out this night. I'll have your Champagne up in just a few minutes." She left and Jakob and Liz sat looking at each other. Liz held Jakob's hand.

"Jakob, take me to the dance floor. I want you to dance with me like we did that night in the Empire Room of the Palmer House. Remember?" They went to the dance floor and danced with Jozef looking on, playing his violin and smiling at the two lovers.

The music stopped and Jakob said, "Let's sit down and have our Champagne." They toasted and sipped their Champagne and talked about the past year and the good things that happened to them. BethAnn was the center of their conversation and the center of their lives.

"Oh Jakob, I hope I left enough milk for her."

"Of course you did. Don't worry. Chucha will take care of her. Everything will be all right. Their sumptuous dinner of roasted duck with mushrooms and a cherry sauce arrived and Jozef came by to play a favorite Chopin melody for them. This was a night to remember. Friends stopped by their table to chat and they renewed their vows of eternal love. As midnight approached they waltzed to the music and gaiety of the evening. At midnight they held each other tightly and their lips met in a kiss that didn't part until a friend boldly interrupted them. They sang the traditional "Auld Lang Syne" and swayed together on the dance floor.

It was now 1899 and they wondered what that year would bring for them. The music tempo changed and they decided to go to their table. Guests of the Inn came by to wish them a happy new year, as did many old friends. They finally sat down with laughter and joy and kissed. Jakob looked at Liz.

"Do you remember that New Year's Eve we spent over in the Lucky Lady sewing up Doc Kelly's scalp?"

"Oh my gosh, Jakob. That was terrible. I'll never forget that night."

"I know it's getting late, but let's stop over at the Lucky Lady to see if old Kelly is there before we go back home."

"Jakob, do you think we should? Okay, let's go." They left the Sheridan Inn and crossed Broadway to the Lucky Lady. The place was filled with revelers and Harry was at the piano playing up a storm. Jakob and Liz made their way to the bar and Andy Meeks, seeing them, shouted out.

"Doc! Liz! Happy New Year!" He put two glasses in front of them and poured each a whiskey. "This is the one I owe you, Doc." Jakob picked up his glass and drank down the whiskey. Liz looked at her glass and put it up to her lips and tasted it, then had a horrible look on her face. Andy Meeks laughed. "Liz, that's not for you. You are a special lady. Let me give you something you can handle." He took a bottle from the back of the bar and poured her a glass of port. Some of the crowd came up to them and wished them a happy new year. The table in the corner of the room with the card players was surrounded by onlookers. Jakob could see Doc Kelly, so he and Liz went over to the table. Kelly looked up and saw Jakob with Liz standing next to him.

"Kid, what are you doing here, and with your wife too?"

Jakob laughed. "Just came here to make sure everything was going well with you. I remember a couple years ago when Liz and I spent the night with you here."

"Don't you worry about me, Kid. You notice I'm sitting with my back to the wall now. You're welcome to join the game. I'm sure these other gents here wouldn't mind."

"No thanks, Kelly. If I sat down with you guys I might go home with the biggest pot, and you wouldn't like that." The table broke up in laughter.

"Your play, Jake. Hey Liz, why don't you take your boyfriend home and put him to bed. This is kinda late for him to be up." The crowd laughed.

"Okay, Kelly. If you have any problems just call on me. Good luck and a happy new year to you all." They worked their way out of the crowd and left the Lucky Lady for home.

As they walked in, Chucha was curled up in a chair with Skippy at her feet. Liz approached Chucha and gave her a hug.

She looked at Liz with a smile that developed on her face, and laughed. Liz said, *"Dabranitz* Chucha. *Ya ch koham mu Pani.* (Goodnight. I love you my lady)." Chucha, surprised by Liz's Polish, laughed, and gave her a hug.

"Goodnight Liz, *mu Pan* Doctor." She picked up the throw she used for a cover, and left laughing.

Jakob sat down on the couch in front of the fireplace and Liz curled up next to him, mesmerized by the fire. Jakob looked down at Liz.

"You amaze me, Liz. How could I be so lucky to have you for my wife?"

Chapter 24

BethAnn Meets Her Grandparents

This Wyoming winter was particularly cold and snowy. Jakob's practice was now limited to mainly emergency work. Jakob decided to cut his hours in the office. He stayed home or used his time for special things he needed to do. If patients really needed him they would stop by his house, and he would then go to his office and take care of them.

It was a particularly bitter cold day and the stove in the office could barely keep up with the cold. Father John Binotti stopped at Jakob's office. He was in pain and had waited too long to seek treatment for an abscessed tooth. John Binotti introduced himself as the pastor at the newly formed Catholic church in Sheridan. Jakob treated his tooth and relieved his pain. He had heard a Catholic church had been recently been organized in Sheridan, but this was the first time he met the pastor.

After he had completed the treatment, Jakob spoke to him about BethAnn and their desire to have her baptized. Jakob told him he was a Catholic but Liz wasn't, but they agreed BethAnn should be baptized in the Catholic church. Father John was a very personable young man, probably the same age as Jakob. They spoke at length about the baby being baptized. He told Jakob the church services were being held in an empty store until they found a suitable building to convert into a church, as the number of parishioners was rapidly increasing. The church was called St. Ignatius. Father John was a member of the Jesuit Order and he came from Chicago.

"I would like to meet with Liz to discuss the matter," he said.

Jakob told Liz about his meeting with the Reverend. Liz was interested and suggested maybe Jakob could invite him over for dinner so she could meet him. At his next appointment, Jakob extended the invitation to John Binotti for dinner the following Sunday.

Chucha made one of her special dinners of chicken soup, her perogi, baked chicken with vegetables, and chleb. She was excited to meet him too, as she was raised a Catholic in her home village of Skulsk, in Poland.

Father John arrived and they chatted with him. He was a very learned man, with a warm personality and a good sense of humor. They learned of his background in Chicago as the son of Italian immigrants, and one of nine children. He told them he had joined the Jesuit Order because they were teachers and missionaries. Sheridan was to be a mission for him and he hoped one day to build a school there. They continued their conversation at the table, dining on

Chucha's culinary art. She served a special cookie for dessert, and the after-dinner drink called *Krupnic*.

Liz and Jakob were enthralled with the conversation. It was something philosophical and he had a remarkable sense of humor. This was something they lacked in Sheridan with their friends. They also spoke about BethAnn, as she was particularly charming to Father John who freely expressed his love for children. The evening ended and he invited them to come to a service at St. Ignatius the next Sunday. It was located on the northern end of Main Street.

Chucha was really impressed with Father John. He lavishly complimented her on the meal and finished everything on his plate, which satisfied her. Liz and Jakob were beginning to understand some of her Polish vocabulary and coupled with her English pronunciations she was doing well communicating. Father John expressed his gratitude for the dinner and left.

BethAnn, the main subject of conversation, indicated she too was hungry. Liz and Jakob sat by the blazing fireplace, with Liz nursing BethAnn. As they recounted the visit, Jakob said he would like to visit his church the next Sunday.

"I think I would like to attend services there. He speaks like a teacher and has such a interesting background." Liz agreed and thought they should attend to learn more about the church.

The next Sunday, Jakob and Liz attended church services at St. Ignatius Church. It was an old building that was once a general store. There were benches for seats and the altar was a plain old wooden table at the front of the room. The room was stark but the church was filled to capacity with worshipers. A coal stove provided some heat on this very cold winter day.

The ceremony was called the Mass and was something Liz had never attended. There were two young altar boys who assisted Father John. He gave the sermon from behind a speaker's stand, at the left side of the altar. The sermon was on the true meaning of love. He delivered it with animation, enthusiasm and sincerity. Members of the congregation came forward and knelt in front of the priest, to receive Communion. Most of the people, including Jakob, received the Communion. There were some announcements at the end and a few committee meetings were scheduled for the week.

Father John also announced he would be having a service in Acme later in the afternoon. There were many Catholics in Acme among the ethnic population. Prayers were asked for a number of people who were sick and one who had died. He welcomed all newcomers and invited them to return. The service ended and the participants passed by Father John, and shook his hand, then continued walking out the door. He recognized Jakob and Liz, thanked them again for the dinner and for coming to Mass, and asked them to return. Outside the church, some of the people congregated and talked with one another. Several recognized Jakob and Liz and welcomed them. There wasn't too much talk, as it was too cold and everyone was anxious to leave for home.

They returned to their warm home and sat before the fireplace with hot coffee. BethAnn was asleep. Liz spoke. "Jakob, I guess I don't understand all that was going on . . . the things Father John was doing and saying. He was saying things in Latin, but it has been a long time since I took Latin and I only understood some of the words. However, I did appreciate his sermon on love. He held my attention. I remember hearing something similar to what he said, at my church in Ames. I did feel more comfortable here, in this poor building, than in your magnificent church in Milwaukee."

Jakob smiled and answered, "Latin is the universal language of the church and is used all over the world. Maybe someday they will pray in the language of the congregation. Yes, I too felt better here than in Milwaukee. If you're in agreement we can set a tentative date for BethAnn to be baptized. I'll invite my parents to come. You can do likewise with your family. I hope all will come. It will give our parents a chance to see how we live here in Sheridan and also to meet our BethAnn. It is too cold now but I'll try to set it up sometime in April, when the weather is better. Do you agree?"

"I agree, and I hope they will all come so they can meet each other and see spring beginning in Wyoming." Jakob proceeded to write home and invited his parents to come out sometime in April for the baptism of BethAnn; Liz did likewise with her family. They were excited about the possibility of their families coming to Sheridan.

Liz soon received a letter back from her mother saying it would be possible for them to come in the latter part of April. They were anxious to meet their granddaughter. Jakob's mother wrote back that it would be difficult for them to come in April because of several commitments, and hoped they could do it in May or June. She was also concerned with the long train ride. Jakob was disappointed and upset his mother could not come in April, although Liz thought the first week of May would be just fine. Jakob wrote back and suggested they should arrive on May 7th, with the baptism on May 10th. Jakob's father added he now had a telephone and could be reached by phone. There were some telephones in Sheridan, and Elmer Findley had one in his store. Margaret Miller agreed to the May dates to visit and be present at the baptism of BethAnn.

BethAnn was growing so fast and was a great joy to both Liz and Jakob. She recognized a few words and made sounds, as well as moved about on all fours. Each day was something new with BethAnn. The severe weather was easing and spring had arrived. Jakob was getting busier in his practice. Mayor Burns was calling on his commissioners for planning the summer fair and for various improvements in the city, so Jakob had his meetings at the city hall. Liz and the adult education group were having their classes, but the number of volunteer teachers was insufficient for the number of potential students. She had her own private student in Chucha who was slowly learning English.

Each day BethAnn delighted the Millers with something new. Jakob looked forward to coming home from his office to spend time with BethAnn and play with her.

He had talked to his father via the new telephone, making the call at Elmer Findley's general store. Everything was all set for their arrival by train on May 7th. Liz's parents, her sister and her aunt would arrive on May 8th. They were both excited the parents would be coming. If they all stayed at their home on Loukes Street, it would have been pretty crowded, so they made arrangements at the Sheridan Inn for their stay. Chucha was preparing for the arrival of the families and was baking all kinds of treats. She was excited to be a part of the event.

BethAnn was too young to realize the event was for her but Liz and Jakob were certain she would do her best to entertain the guests. The dark hair she was born with had changed to a blonde color, and with her blue eyes she was a real beauty. Liz always dressed her in frilly dresses and bonnets. Her personality was a reflection of the love she received. She was a happy baby and babbled at the slightest event that took place.

May 7th arrived and there was excitement in the house. Jakob took the day off from the office. As he was getting ready to pick up his parents from the train station, someone arrived at their house in pain and needed emergency treatment. This added to the stress of his day. Jakob left for his office but stopped at the train station first, to find out if the train would be on time. Lloyd, the train stationmaster, told Jakob the train would probably be a little late, which gave Jakob some time to see his patient and get back in time to pick up his parents. Unfortunately, Jakob needed extra time for his emergency patient.

He finally left his office and could hear the whistle of the train in the distance. When he arrived at the depot, the bell was ringing and the train was coming to a stop. He tied up the rig and arrived just in time to see his parents step off the passenger car platform. His father was beaming, and shook his hand, and embraced him; mother followed with words to the effect she was happy to see him, but the long train ride was very tiring. Jakob helped his dad put their luggage in the carriage.

"My, Jakob, I never realized you were so far away. I thought we would never get here. I didn't realize Wyoming was so barren. I didn't see hardly any trees until we were almost here. Being from Wisconsin, I'm used to seeing lots of trees. But I did see mountains in the distance."

"Well, Mother, you have just arrived in Sheridan. I will show you plenty of trees and you'll see the beauty of Wyoming. I'm going to take you to the house now so you have a chance to see BethAnn and Liz. Then later we'll come back to the Sheridan Inn where you will be staying."

"Oh, I thought we would be staying with you. Don't you have enough room?"

"We thought it might be too crowded for your comfort. Liz's family will be coming too and they will also stay at the Inn. You will have the opportunity to meet them for the first time." Jakob turned the wagon into his driveway.

"Oh, is this your home? Well, it certainly does look very nice. Are you sure it's not big enough for us to stay here—but I'm sure you know better. Your streets aren't paved yet, are they?"

"Look, Mother. Liz and BethAnn are on the porch waving to you."

"Oh yes, how nice." Jakob helped his mother and dad from the carriage and they were soon on the porch exchanging greetings.

"Oh, what a beautiful baby. My granddaughter! Elizabeth, can I hold her?" Liz passed the baby to Margaret who smiled adoringly at BethAnn and whispered something to her. BethAnn looked intently at her grandmother and smiled, giving Margaret a reason to place a kiss on her forehead. Margaret looked at Jakob. "Jakob, why didn't you tell me I have such a beautiful granddaughter?"

"Mother, I did inform you she is gorgeous. You just didn't listen. I guess it is hard to describe someone who is so beautiful. You have to see her yourself." Jakob's dad asked Margaret if he could hold the baby, and reluctantly she gave her to him.

"You can hold her for just a little bit, Bobby, then I want her back." Liz invited them into the house, with Grandfather Bob tightly holding Beth Ann who was now cooing and smiling to him.

"Just because you are the grandmother doesn't mean you get to hold her all the time, Margaret."

Margaret looked around the house and saw Chucha, who was quietly observing the gathering. "Now, who is that, Jakob?"

"I guess I haven't told you, Mother. That is Chucha. She is helping Liz with the baby and the housework. She is a Polish lady and Chucha means aunt, in Polish. So that's what we call her. She is widowed and lives in Acme. I know you will love her when you get to know her. She doesn't speak much English yet, but she is learning."

Margaret approached Chucha, who in turn gave her a hug and kissed her on the cheek, and laughing, said a distinct "Hello" to her. Liz filled Margaret in on Chucha's duties and Margaret understood. She gave high marks to Liz for the decorating of the home and asked to see the entire house.

Jakob's dad was thoroughly impressed with their home and congratulated him for buying it. "You know, Jakob, I do want to see your office while we're here. I'm sure it will please me because I know you have great ability, just by what I can see here."

Jakob's mother was pleased with everything she saw, and gave praise to Liz. She just couldn't take her eyes off of BethAnn. Jakob didn't think his mother was the warm grandmother type, but little BethAnn struck deep inside her heart.

The Jensen family arrived the next day and had their turn to meet BethAnn. All felt BethAnn was the most beautiful baby in the West. It was also a first for the Millers and Jensens to be together and a pleasant visit was in the making. Wyoming weather couldn't have been better. The last of winter was replaced with sunshine and mild temperatures. Tulips and dogwood were in bloom with lilacs not far behind. Sheridan people were sure spring was early that year.

The day for BethAnn to become a Christian arrived. A Godfather and Godmother had been picked. Mary Rodgers, one of Liz's volunteer teachers, was to be the Godmother and Elmer Findley, Jakob's good friend, was to be the Godfather. Both, were members of St. Ignatius Church. The ceremony was held before the church service on Sunday. The general-store-made-church was filled to overflowing for the service. Father John proceeded to pour the holy water from a vessel over the back of BethAnn's head to signify the washing away of her original sins. BethAnn didn't take it very kindly and issued her protest. She was quickly dried and a beautiful Baptismal dress was placed on her for the rest of the ceremony. The prayer of rejection of Satan was said by the congregation, and BethAnn was now one of the congregation. She received applause, which she accepted graciously.

Liz had announced an open house at their home for all their friends to see the newly baptized Christian. Chucha had put out a spread of her finest foods for the visitors. Most of the arrivals brought gifts for BethAnn, who was on her best behavior. She looked angelic in her Baptismal dress, however, it hampered her from scooting around on all fours. Father John Binotti arrived as the honored guest and gave the affair his blessing. He truly had a gift for being with people. His sense of humor made all feel at ease in his presence.

Jozef arrived with his violin and did his finest with Chopin and Beethoven. He was followed by Harry, the piano player from the Lucky Lady who broke out his concertina, and Ralph Smith from the Sheridan Players who took out his guitar. The music then changed tempo. BethAnn was serenaded, and when the players moved to the porch, the dancing started, even though it was still a chilly day.

BethAnn had one big party, as one of their neighbors said. Mrs. Howard, Liz's first friend in Sheridan, came to the open house. She insisted on holding and becoming acquainted with BethAnn. The Jensens and the Millers had seen Sheridan hospitality at its very best, and Jakob and Liz were thrilled with the event. One by one the guests left, each thanking Liz and Jakob for the wonderful time they had. The families later sat around the large dining table enjoying Chucha's cookies and sipping her Krupnic, the honey liquor. They recounted the event and praised BethAnn for bringing them all together.

The next day, Jakob's father wanted to see his office, so Jakob made arrangements to take him there. As it turned out, Margaret also wanted to go along. The Jensens decided to spend the morning with Liz and BethAnn and asked to see Jakob's office the following day.

They arrived at the office and as Jakob opened the door, Margaret gasped as she viewed the bearskin and head on one wall, and the elk antlers on the other.

"Jakob, where did you get them? That bear, it looks so vicious. My God, do you have them out here in Wyoming?"

Jakob blushed and chuckled a bit. "Yes, Mother, I shot that elk on a hunting trip. Oh, and . . . the bear, it . . . it was shot by my guide. His name is Zeke. He's really a great shot."

"You were there when it happened? Oh, my God, Jakob!"

"Oh, yes, Mother, that Zeke . . . he's a great hunter." Jakob had not told his mother about his brush with death. She had not seen his scarred arm as he always kept it covered with his shirt sleeve. He quickly opened the door to his inner office. "Dad, this is my operatory. I know it's not as fancy as yours, but I get to do a lot of work here." He showed him his laboratory where he made false teeth and did his gold work.

His father looked over everything and put his arm around Jakob. "Son, you do me proud. I knew you had potential but this is way beyond my expectations. Now, I really wish I had you in my office. You could do well anywhere, and Sheridan is lucky to have you." Jakob blushed and thanked his father for the compliment. "Jakob, I'm going to send you some of my equipment so you'll have a more modern office. I'm cutting back and don't need it. That chair—I don't see how you can work with it. And you do already have electricity here in Sheridan. I'm sure you can get it here in your office. Oh, what you couldn't do with an electric unit and motor!" Margaret looked proudly at her son and smiled.

"Lunch is on me, son. Where do you want to go?" Just then, the door to the office opened and an older gentleman stood in front of Jakob.

"Doc, I got a lot of pain. My face is so swollen. I can hardly open my eye. Can you help me please?"

"Sure I will. These folks here will wait for me. They are my parents. Come into my office and sit down here. You don't mind if my dad comes in, do you? He's a dentist too, and maybe he will help me."

"No problem, Doc. Just help me. I didn't sleep all night with this pain." The two dentists looked into his mouth to see the basis of the problem. It didn't take long and they were tending to their patient. Jakob saw the nature of the infection and took care of it. He had his patient more comfortable and gave him instructions as to what do until he would see him the next day.

"It was Wilbur Riggs, at the livery, that told me to see you. He said you would take care of me and he was right. Thanks. See you tomorrow, Doc." He left with a smile on his still-swollen face.

"It's still not too late for lunch, son. You did your good deed for the day." They left for the Sheridan Inn dining room where Lukas came out to greet them.

"I've got a good elk stew with mashed potatoes, gravy and string beans for you folks. For dessert I have a bread pudding and good, hot coffee. I guess you folks must be his mother and father. You got one helluva great kid. Take it from me."

Jakob blushed and laughed as Margaret answered, "Oh, we know that. Did you see our granddaughter? She has to be the most beautiful baby I have ever seen, and she is so sweet."

"I've seen her and you are so right, Grandmother. Funny thing though, I have never heard a grandmother say otherwise." They all laughed. "I'll have your lunch out just as soon as I can." There were others who came by, anxious to meet Jakob's parents as they ate one of Lukas's best lunches.

Jakob acted as a guide and took his visitors to see as much as he could of Sheridan and the Wyoming countryside. Liz and Jakob wanted them to understand what their life was like in the West. The long-awaited visit was over for the Millers and the Jensens as they boarded their trains that would take them east to their homes.

Chapter 25

The Convention

Jakob received a letter from his dental school graduating class inviting him to the school's homecoming in Chicago. He had missed other homecomings over the past years but decided to try to make this one. It was to be on June 20th, and was to be held in conjunction with the convention of the Chicago Dental Society. This was an opportunity for Jakob to see his classmates for the first time since he graduated and it was also an opportunity to take part in a convention of the Chicago Dental Society. It was to be an educational program of what is new in dental care and treatment. There was much to be learned in his profession since he graduated from dental school, and they offered lectures on all aspects of dentistry.

Since graduation, he had no contact with any dentists, other than his father. He didn't look forward to the long train ride to Chicago but felt it was important he go and expand his education since he graduated from dental school. However, he would have to leave Liz and BethAnn for ten days, which was difficult for him. It would be the first time he left them for any length of time. He planned on meeting his father who would also be going to the convention. They would stay together at the Congress Hotel, where the convention was being held.

The long trip by train brought him into Union Station, Chicago. The buggy ride to the Congress Hotel was not too far, but in Chicago traffic it took almost an hour. He registered for the hotel room with his father, although he hadn't arrived as yet. After cleaning up from the long, dusty train ride and changing clothes, he decided to go down to the exhibition hall of the Chicago Dental Society and register for the convention. The room was filled with people milling around. He had to stand in a long line, then finally he stood ready to register. His registration from Sheridan, Wyoming, caused a bit of a stir. The lady who registered him said she thought he probably had come the greatest distance of anyone she had registered for the convention. Several of the dentists overheard the conversation and came up to him. They asked him what it was like to practice dentistry out on the western frontier. It wasn't too long before there was a circle of dentists surrounding Jakob, asking him questions about Wyoming. One, an older, distinguished gentleman with a ribbon on his lapel asked Jakob to meet with him at a table nearby, because he wanted to talk with him further.

He introduced himself as Doctor James Furlong who practiced in a prestigious downtown Chicago office building. He was pleasantly surprised to learn Jakob had graduated from the Chicago College of Dental Surgery, and would also be at the homecoming.

"Why, that's the school I graduated from. It was a number of years ago and the school was in another location, but it was still a very fine school. I heard you mention you were from Wyoming, on our country's western frontier. That would make an interesting talk many would like to hear. I would like you to give a talk to this society about your experiences and frontier dentistry. Most of us dentists here practice in a large city. Did you see how they were anxious to have you answer their questions about Wyoming? I am on the speaker's committee and would like you to give a talk about your experiences."

"Doctor, I wish I had known this before I came here, then maybe I could have put together a talk, but—"

"I realize this is very short notice, but I'm sure you can do it. These dentists here will understand. As a start, I can give you some questions you could answer. You can do it I'm sure. I'll introduce you and make them understand what short notice I have given to you. What do you say?"

"Furlong, what are you doing here with my son?" They both looked up from the table where they were talking.

"Bob Miller! Is this your son? I should have realized it. A good-looking young man like this, had to be your son." They shook hands heartily and Dr. Furlong said, "I didn't realize you had a dentist son. I'm trying to talk him into giving a talk before the society on his experiences with frontier dentistry. Please help me, he seems reluctant."

"I tell you what, Furlong. Tell him you'll buy him and me dinner tonight and I bet he'll do it. He'll probably also tell you all about his beautiful daughter—my granddaughter."

Looking at Jakob he asked, "You will, won't you, son?"

"You both sure know how to put me on the spot. Don't expect any oratory from me."

"All right," smiled the doctor. "We'll have dinner tonight up in the main dining room at seven-thirty, if that will get you to do it. If it's all right with you, I'll put together some questions for you to help you get started. You can do as you please and you can keep it informal, fair enough? Those dentists will give you their attention, I promise you. We're all city guys here. This will be an interesting treat for us. I'll let you know where we will fit you into the program tonight. Bob it's really good seeing you. I still can't believe I met your son. We'll be together later."

Dr. Furlong left and Jakob's dad looked at him. "Well, that's a surprise. I haven't seen him in ages. He's a big figure with the dental society and a fine man. Are you nervous about facing this scholastic group? You don't have to be. You can do it. You know your subject. Just make some notes. Talk from the heart. You may find you enjoy doing it. Let's go down to the coffee shop and get a coffee."

After cleaning up and dressing for the occasion, Jakob and his dad went to the main dining room, known as the Michigan Boulevard Room, to have dinner with Dr. Furlong. They met the maitre d', who led them to their table. The Michigan Boulevard Room was large and ornate, with its high ceilings and majestic chandeliers. The walls had panels of mirrors with brightly lit sconces. At the middle of the room was a dance floor, and playing was a string ensemble. The tables were set with white tablecloths and napkins. Silverware and wine glasses adorned the table. Large upholstered chairs were neatly placed at the tables.

"Hey, Dad I get into a place like this and I almost feel like I'm out of place. It is sure elegant. The Sheridan Inn is pretty fancy but this place is—I mean, like a king's palace."

"Jakob, don't you ever feel you are beneath this kind of lavishness. You are a professional man and have dignity, doing an important service to those you treat."

Just then Dr. Furlong came to the table. "Bob, Jakob, glad to see you two again. I'm happy we are able to get together. This dinner idea you had is great. I want to get to know your son better. I figured out just where I will put him in the Society's schedule. Tuesday afternoon we will have our business meeting at two o'clock. His talk will be right after the general business meeting, the day after tomorrow. After that dull meeting, he can brighten things up. I brought some good questions you can incorporate in your presentation. Now, let's forget about shop talk and get on with our dinner."

"I'll do the best I can. You know, I graduated in '95, so I don't have the kind of experience you and Dad have."

"It makes no difference, Jakob. You have a story to tell, we want to hear. Bob, how come you didn't get this guy to work in your office? He would be great in your fancy practice."

"Jim, I wish I could have, but he had other ideas . . . big ones. I'm proud of his accomplishments. I had an opportunity to see him work in his office and he is very capable. Well, enough of that. We'll not spend the entire evening talking shop." The evening went fine, with good food and wine in an atmosphere of splendor.

The following days were spent with Jakob taking in various lectures and seeing some of his former classmates at his homecoming. All were amazed Jakob had taken his dental practice to Sheridan, Wyoming, as the others stayed in Chicago or other nearby cities. Some admired Jakob for his challenge, but others felt they would never consider his type of practice.

Jakob was now very busy. He found enough time to work on his talk and decided to do it as a presentation followed with questions and answers. Jakob gained some confidence, but in quiet moments he felt a queasy stomach and wished he had never agreed to do it.

The day came, and as he sat on the platform listening to others speak, deep down he wished they would change their mind and forget all about him. Dr. Furlong stood before the assembly and confidently introduced Jakob. He mentioned his friendship with Jakob's father, and gave the seated dentists Jakob's credentials and how he wanted to hear Jakob's story on frontier dentistry. He then invited Jakob to step up to the podium and tell them his story. Jakob stood up, forced his legs to take him to the speaker's stand. His heart was pounding and he forced a smile, as he stood in front of the large group. He placed his notes in front of him and looked down at them. Then, before speaking, he looked up at the assembled group in front of him. He remembered Dr Furlong's advice: "Just get up there and tell them your story, as you know it."

"Thank you, Dr. Furlong, for the generous introduction." All of a sudden he forgot the audience as being the adversary, but were people who wanted to hear his story about Sheridan, Wyoming. He spoke with knowledge of his subject and answered their questions. They gave him a good round of applause, which he humbly received. Jakob walked away from the podium and sat down. Dr. Furlong got up to the podium and thanked Jakob for his interesting presentation, made additional comments, then he adjourned the meeting.

"Doctor, that was very good and I thank you. We all now have an idea of what it's like to live and practice dentistry under conditions on the frontier," said one of the dentists in the audience. "Incidentally, I don't think I would go hunting to get elk antlers for my office. I'd just put pictures on the wall." Jakob just smiled at that remark and then laughed about the reference to his trophies, as did the others listening to the conversation. He did mention the story of the charging bear. His dad and others came up to congratulate him on his talk. Jakob was a success.

The following days were busy, with Jakob attending more lectures. He met other classmates and dentists who remarked on his presentation. It was getting near to the end of his stay and Jakob was getting homesick and thinking about Liz and his baby.

"Dad, I want to get some gifts for Liz and BethAnn to take back with me. Where do you think I should go?"

His dad thought a bit and then he said, "There are some stores just down Michigan Boulevard, not far from the hotel but over on State Street there is a special department store that recently opened called Marshall Field's, and from what I have heard, it is supposed to be extra special. It's a long walk, but we can get a driver to take us there." They took a driver and carriage and got out in front of a large, stately department store. It did look special. The people working there were dressed uniformly and were very polite. Displays of various items were done with care and showed a degree of special attention. One whole section of the store was for children's clothes and he found several special things he bought for BethAnn.

The woman's floor was lavish, with clothes of all sorts. He visualized Liz in so many different things. One mannequin wore a dress he just knew she should have and he bought it, as well as a white-lace nightgown to reveal her bodily curves. He really missed Liz. In their toy department he found a toy to amuse

BethAnn. His shopping list was now complete. This was certainly different form Elmer Findley's general store and even the newer New York Store on Main Street. But then, this was the big city, Chicago. Jakob's dad suggested they finish the day by having dinner at the Burgoff Restaurant to enjoy some of their specialty meals and beer.

The next day Jakob and his dad took the carriage to the Union Station to get their respective trains, the Chicago Burlington and Quincy for Jakob, and the Milwaukee Road for his dad.

Jakob looked at his dad and embraced him. "Dad, this has been a great time for me. Coming here to spend time with you and sharing the time at the convention with you has been special. We have something in common besides being father and son. I want you to know I have really enjoyed being here with you. I hope you realize my going to Wyoming was not because I didn't want to be with you in your office. I have, at times, had some regrets I didn't team up with you, but I have fulfilled my dreams by going to Wyoming and doing what I am now doing. So, thanks for being with me and understanding."

His father looked at him and shook his head slowly, while smiling. "I'm happy you pursued your dream, and yes, we do have much in common. We'll do this again." They embraced and went in different directions to find their trains. Jakob boarded the CB&Q and found his compartment. Sitting and looking out the window as other passengers boarded the train, he felt nostalgic as he thought of his father. He noted the gray hair and the wrinkles on his face and realized he was getting on in years. *Funny, how I never noticed that before. I hope he is happy. He and Mother seem to have a good relationship but they do have different personalities. I know he loves her very much as well as his profession. He does have many friends and has accomplished much. Why has it taken me so long to discover the relationship that we now seem to have?*

"ALL ABOARD . . . ALL ABOARD . . . ALL ABOARD." Some people were running to get on the train and there were others embracing and saying their farewells, and then there was a jerk, as the train started to slowly move. People walking alongside the slowly moving train were waving their last goodbyes. The train started to pick up speed and moved out of the covered station into the sunlight. Jerking as it passed switches, Jakob could now see the tall buildings of the city. He sat back in his seat and closed his eyes. The sounds of people moving and talking as they passed his door continued for some time, then he dozed off.

"Aurora, Aurora, Illinois." The train was going through a small city. The train bell was clanging as the train pulled into the station. There was some activity with people waiting to get aboard. A wagon filled with suitcases and boxes was pulled past his window to be loaded in the baggage car and again it was, "ALL ABOARD." The train gave a strong jerk, then a steady pull as it picked up speed. Soon, it was moving rapidly out of the city and through farmland. Corn stalks and cows feeding added to the landscape, with an occasional horse pulling a wagon. Long fences stretched across fields. Jakob thought of the long train ride ahead and he became anxious as he thought about Liz and BethAnn. He missed them so much. All through the meeting his thoughts would go back to his Liz and BethAnn.

This was the first time they had been separated and it really bothered him, in spite of the fact his time was taken up by the events of the convention and the homecoming at his school. He thought about the meetings held at his school, in the fourth floor amphitheater. It was the first time he had returned in four years. His teachers were anxious for him to relate his experiences since graduation. He was glad he went because he saw some of his good friends. Doctor Johnson chided Jakob for having gone so far from the school, but was happy he was enjoying his profession. His mind was abuzz with thoughts of the lectures he had heard and how he would use the information he had gotten. Then he realized he was getting hungry. *My gosh, look at the time,* he thought. *It's almost 8:00.*

He left his compartment and sought the conductor, who told him where the dining car was. Not all the trains on this trip had a dining car, but the Chicago Burlington and Quincy did. He was seated at a table with a salesmen going to Omaha, and they engaged in small talk. When he arrived back at his compartment, his seat had been made into a bed. It had gotten dark outside, except for the occasional light in the distance. He closed the drape and laid back, with only the small reading lamp lighting his compartment. His random thoughts were of his father and the great visit they had. They had never done this before. He revisited the experience of the talk to the assembled dentists and he couldn't believe he had done it. *I have never done anything like this before. I didn't think I could do it,* he thought. He was actually amazed he had the courage to do it. He was anxious to see his BethAnn, who learned something new each day. The clickety-clack of the train passing over the tracks lulled him to sleep. He awoke several times as the train made stops. Then, there was light creeping into his compartment. He opened his eyes and heard the conductor announce they would be arriving in Burlington, Iowa.

He left the CB&Q and waited in the station for the Burlington and Missouri. Jakob had coffee and a roll in the station house while he waited. Yesterday's newspaper was on the counter and he looked through it.

The Burlington Missouri was late leaving, and it didn't have the luxuries of the previous train. Jakob didn't have a compartment, but he did have the Pullman car for sleeping. The longest part of the trip was ahead. He would have an opportunity to get off the train at Omaha and Crawford to get something to eat. The trip was exhausting, with many stops. The days were hot, even with the open windows. When that final call of "Sheridan, Sheridan, Wyoming," came, he was more than ready to get off the train.

He gathered his belongings and waited for his baggage on the depot platform. Wilbur Riggs had a wagon at the station which Jakob promptly hired to take him home. It wasn't too long before he was parked next to the house. Liz was waiting for him, sitting on the porch, in the swing. She quickly left the porch when she saw the rig turn in toward the house, and was there to shower him with hugs and kisses as he stepped to the ground. They stood, locked in an embrace.

"Oh, Jakob, you're finally home. It's been so long being here without you. I missed you so."

Skippy was bouncing up and down and moaning his greetings. He also was happy Jakob was home. Chucha, hearing the commotion, came out carrying BethAnn in her arms, and greeted Jakob. BethAnn seeing Jakob began smiling and sounding "Da Da" with her arms spread out for Jakob to take her, which he immediately did. It was the homecoming Jakob had wanted since the beginning of the trip.

They were all talking at once, as Jakob tightly held his baby, smothering her with kisses. They moved onto the porch and into the house. Liz had decorated the house with signs and paper cutouts. "Welcome Home, Jakob, and Welcome Home, Daddy" were hung from the doorways and the table was set with the finest. The candles would be lit for the planned sumptuous dinner.

They all sat in the living area awaiting Jakob's report on the trip. Liz snuggled close to him on the couch. BethAnn placed her hands on Jakob's face and placed a kiss on his cheek. This was something new she had learned. Chucha brought out glasses of wine to celebrate his arrival. All talked randomly, even Chucha. Her grasp of English was coming along fine. She was now able to put several words together and was proud of her accomplishment. After finishing their wine, all sat down together. Jakob invited Chucha to eat with them. This was considered a special occasion and she was generally considered one of the family. As they ate, Jakob related his experiences on the trip. He spoke at length about the time he spent with his father. Then he told Liz about his experience with Dr. Furlong and his talk at the dental society.

"Jakob, you have never done anything like that before, but I bet you did a good job. I have often thought you would be good speaking before groups. I bet you could do well in politics." Jakob laughed.

"You have no idea of the agony I went through prior to getting up before the group. No, politics is not for me." After dinner Jakob grabbed Liz and held her tightly, then kissed her tenderly.

"I missed you so much. If I ever have to go anywhere, you will have to go with me. I can't be without you." He went into his suitcase and removed the gifts he had bought. He gave BethAnn the Raggedy Ann Doll, which she immediately hugged. Then he gave Liz a box which Marshall Field's had ornately wrapped for him. Liz started to carefully unwrap it.

"Jakob, this box is almost too pretty to unwrap." She carefully opened the box, and gasping in delight she removed the dress he had bought her. Her eyes flashed as she held it up. "This is beautiful. You are a dear. I don't think I have ever had such a pretty dress. Oh, where can I wear it? It has to be special. Oh, thank you." And she proceeded to place a kiss on his lips.

"That's not all. I want you to open this box too." Liz opened the second box carefully so as not to damage the wrapping paper. From it, she lifted the lace nightgown. Looking at Jakob and smiling coyly, she encircled him with her arms and kissed him passionately.

"I will have a lot of use for this gift. In fact I may just try it out tonight. Come to think of it, maybe you should take more trips. You bring such nice things back with you when you return." And she giggled. Chucha was watching all the goings-on and smiling, so Jakob took her a box of special candies from Marshall Field's, which really thrilled her. BethAnn was engrossed with her doll, while all this was going on and was not interested in the dress Jakob brought her. Liz took her gifts to the bedroom and prepared to get BethAnn ready for sleep. She sat in her rocker and nursed her. Chucha finished up the dishes and went up to her room.

Jakob sat in his chair thinking about how happy he was to be home, as Liz slithered into the room in her nightgown and sat on his lap. Putting her arms around him, she kissed him tenderly. They sat that way softly speaking to one another until Liz got up and took Jakob's hand, leading him into the bedroom.

Chapter 26

A Satisfied Patient

Jakob's alarm was the cold nose of Skippy against his back. He hadn't planned on getting up this early, but he was going to the office anyway, even though the sign he left telling his patients when he was coming back was set for tomorrow. BethAnn was now sleeping through the nights and usually got up when Jakob and Liz got up, but Skippy was adamant. He nosed Jakob a second time, so he finally got up, let Skippy out and decided to make the coffee. Skippy was chasing birds or squirrels as Jakob watched him from the window. The pot came to a boil and it wasn't too long before Liz was sitting on his lap kissing him and telling how much she had missed him.

The sound of footsteps coming down the stairs meant Chucha would be arriving to join them. Liz giggled, looked at Jakob, and quickly got up taking another seat next to the table.

"Good morning Pan e missus Liz." Chucha tried some of her English but always managed to use some Polish. She had a great disposition and waking up was always on a positive note for her. She had the cups out and was pouring the brew for Jakob and Liz. Yesterday, she had baked her special breakfast cake and was cutting slices for both of them when BethAnn made it known she wanted to join the crowd.

Chucha motioned she would pick up BethAnn and tend to her so Liz could stay with Jakob and have their coffee together. Neither Liz nor Jakob had expected to keep her with them this long, but she had made herself indispensable and they couldn't get up the courage to let her go. She was almost like one of the family now, and though keeping her was an added household expense, she made things easier for Liz. It gave her time to do other things she enjoyed doing. And her frugality with groceries saved them money on household expenses. At least, that's how they justified keeping her.

Chucha brought out BethAnn who, seeing Jakob, had her arms out so Jakob could take her.

Liz complained, "I want you, BethAnn." She laughed to Liz, but took Jakob's arms. She really missed Jakob when he was gone and it was apparent. Jakob gave her a piece of the breakfast cake, which she relished. She was getting her deciduous teeth now and could handle the soft cake. Jakob noted the time and said he wanted to go to the office. Even though he didn't expect patients, he had other things he could do. Liz wanted him to stay home so they could go on a picnic together. Jakob acquiesced and said he would return early so they could maybe go out. Liz reluctantly agreed.

As he approached his office he noticed several people sitting on the bench in front who appeared to be waiting for him.

"Hi, Doc, I figured ya be in, even though you got the sign that says you'll be in tomorra. But I heard you got back in town and I got this ache." Thus Jakob's day began. Later, Mayor Burns stopped by to remind Jakob of a meeting they would be having on Friday for the Sheridan County Fair. To fill out his morning, Andy Meeks stopped by at lunch time.

"What you say we go to that new Chinese restaurant on Root Street?" Jakob agreed and quickly closed the door to the office before anyone else came in. Jakob didn't stop by the Lucky Lady very often anymore, but he and Andy Meeks, being good friends, would find time to go to lunch once in a while. Andy would generally fill in Jakob on the news around town. After lunch, Jakob did go home and took Liz and BethAnn for a picnic at their favorite spot near, Little Goose Creek, even though he had already eaten lunch. They spent an enjoyable day together.

Jakob was getting ready to take Liz to church Sunday morning when Doc Kelly presented himself at their front door.

"Jake, you got to help me. Look at me. See this swelling under my eye. I've got unbearable throbbing pain. You got to do something for me." Jakob examined the area and then looked into his mouth to see an offending tooth.

"Kelly, you got an abscessed tooth that's causing the swelling and pain."

"Well do something, dammit. I can't have this happening to me. I got people to take care of. Do something!"

"All right Kelly, don't worry. I'll take care of it but I can't do it here. Let's go down to my office."

"This damn thing is killing me. Do you understand?"

"Of course I understand. If you let me get my coat and hat we can get in your rig and drive over to the office and believe me, I will do my very best for you." They got into Doc Kelly's buggy and at breakneck speed went to Jakob's office. Doc Kelly took his coat off and threw it in the corner, then quickly sat in the old barber chair with his mouth open. He pointed to the tooth that bothered him.

"You can see it. This is the tooth." Jakob placed his finger on the tooth to check its mobility and Kelly jumped up. "Ouch, yes, that's the tooth. Now do something!"

"Now Doctor, please be patient and I will take care of it." Jakob was becoming irritated. He got ready with a syringe to numb the pain.

"What are you going to do with that?"

"I'm going to numb the area so it won't hurt you, otherwise you won't be able to take the pain."

"Just take the damn thing out. I can take it. Forget it, I can take pain. What do you think, I'm a pansy?"

"All right Doctor, I will do exactly as you wish." Jakob took the proper forceps, placed it over the tooth and squeezed tightly. Kelly jumped up screaming. Jakob calmly removed the forceps out of his mouth and placed it on the instrument tray. Kelly was holding his face and moaning. Jakob then took the syringe and injected the area surrounding the tooth.

Kelly looked up at Jakob, and with a hurt look explained to Jakob. "Jake, you know it really hurt. I guess I should have listened to you."

Jakob just smiled. "No problem Kelly." While waiting for the effect of the cocaine, they chatted about the weather and other nondescript things.

Soon Kelly looked up at Jakob and touched his tooth. "Hey, that tooth doesn't hurt any more." Jakob picked up the forceps and proceeded to remove the tooth, which he placed on his instrument tray. "You know, Jake, I have to admit, it didn't hurt at all. Not bad, kid, not bad. Sorry I was so demanding but that damn thing really hurt. Come on, let's go to the Lady. I'll buy you a drink. They're open."

"We'll wait just a while to make sure you don't have any bleeding before leaving." Jakob placed a piece of gauze over the wound and instructed Kelly to bite on it. He cleaned up after the surgery and they left for the Lucky Lady.

Andy Meeks was behind the bar and with a surprised look on his face. "What are you two gents up to this early morning? This is the first time I've ever seen you together on a Sunday morning." Doc Kelly grinned at Andy Meeks.

"Never you mind. Just pour us a drink." He started talking holding the gauze in place and frustrated said, "Can I take this damm thing out of my mouth now?"

Jakob laughed. "Sure go ahead. If you start bleeding again, we can always find something to stuff in your mouth."

They talked to Andy a while, and Kelly, with a strange look on his face said, "Hey, I thought you said this wouldn't hurt anymore?"

"Sorry, Kelly, I didn't say that. The numbing has worn off. Why don't you take one of those powders you hand out and go home and put some ice on your face. You'll be all right. And while you're at it, you can take me home to my family."

"Good idea, Jake!" They bid Andy Meeks good-bye and Doc Kelly took Jakob home. Getting out of the buggy, Kelly looked at Jakob.

"Thanks a lot, kid. I hope I don't have to see you again, professionally I mean, for a long time. Not that I didn't appreciate your help." And he rode off laughing. Jakob smiled and went up the stairs and into the house. Liz was there to greet him.

"Jakob, is everything all right? You've been gone a long time. Is Doc Kelly okay?" Jakob laughed and picked up BethAnn who was holding his leg.

"Yes, he's fine. Everything is just fine."

Chapter 27

1900

Jakob was taking down the Christmas tree because the holiday season was over. BethAnn was disappointed and wanted him to leave it up, but he convinced her it was time to take it down. This was her second Christmas and it really made an impression on her. BethAnn was walking and was getting into everything. She had to be watched closely, so as not to get into trouble. BethAnn was starting to put words together and Liz was helping her with talking. It was exciting just to see her grow. Liz dressed her in feminine clothes and she was the perfect little lady. Chucha would make special foods, especially for her. She was getting teeth but hardly enough for her to chew most foods. Liz had stopped nursing and BethAnn was getting nourishment from essentially the same foods Jakob and Liz ate. Life was back to a normal pace, except the house was cluttered with BethAnn's Christmas toys.

The holidays were officially over and the new century had just begun. Jakob's practice was going through the typical winter doldrums. He spent more time at home. Sometimes he would spend time in his workshop, building something he needed for the office or at home. He built furnishings for BethAnn's room, and even a new bed because she no longer used her baby bed. During the coldest weather, he needed a fire in the stove to heat the shop while working on a cabinet, bookcase or table. His skill was almost professional quality.

The bitter cold Wyoming weather kept most folks indoors. He now had a sleigh which could be pulled by the horses, and was able to take Liz and BethAnn for sleigh rides or even to church, after a heavy snow. They attended Fr. John Binotti's St. Ignatius Church regularly. Liz still had not decided to become a Catholic, although she was actively studying about Catholicism and was regularly participating in church services. She and Jakob would sometimes attend the Congregational Church they were married in. They had many friends there and didn't want to lose contact with them. Her adult education program was still active and many of the ladies from the church were helping Liz with the program. Liz also planned a program especially for the local Indians later in the summer.

"If we can teach them to read and write, they will become citizens and will be an important part of the community." She had made some attempts to promote better relationships with the Indians, during the Sheridan County Fair.

Winters were frequently times for social events. There was always a Fireman's Ball held at the Sheridan Inn, and Jakob and Liz would definitely attend. It was usually a very big event and many in town attended.

Neighbors would often get together for pot-lucks. It was a way to get to know each other better. This led to helping each other in time of need. Liz took part in a number of woman's groups, as her interests were many, but BethAnn took a lot of her time. Being a mother, she felt BethAnn was her primary responsibility.

Jakob was often asked by Doc Kelly to assist him in taking care of people who were injured in accidents of various sorts. Working in the mines at Acme or Monarch was dangerous, and head injuries were not uncommon. Those injuries that involved the mouth were handled by Jakob. Doc Kelly would stop by Jakob's office to get him and they would ride to the accident site. If the injuries were such that it would be better not to move the injured, they would be treated on site Otherwise they were taken care of in his office.

Jakob sat in his big chair facing the warm fireplace, with BethAnn in his arms. He held her and talked to her as she faced him. She patted his face and kissed him. They were having a father daughter talk. Chucha came into the room and invited them to the table for Sunday dinner. Liz was in the bedroom lying down on the bed and Jakob came in to get her.

"Chucha has dinner on the table, hon. Come, sit down with us." Liz looked up at Jakob.

"Jakob, I don't feel good." And she started to cough. "My throat hurts and my head aches." Jakob had noticed she had been coughing recently, but didn't do more than to take notice.

"Liz, you have been coughing some. Do you feel like you are getting a cold?"

"Yes, I have been coughing and my throat is sore, but my head aches too and I feel warm. I also have been having the chills."

"Don't you feel like eating? Chucha made some soup." Liz shook her head. "Would you like a cup of tea? Maybe tea would soothe your throat. I could even put some honey in it."

"Maybe that would make my throat feel better." Jakob bent down and kissed Liz on the forehead.

"You do feel warm. I'll get you some tea and maybe you can get some more rest. We did get up early this morning." Jakob came back in awhile with the cup of tea and a piece of the breakfast cake. "Why don't you sit up and I'll help you with the tea. I also have a piece of cake you can dip in it." Jakob helped Liz with her tea and she had some of the cake, but refused to finish it. She looked tired and generally sick as she laid on the pillow and closed her eyes. Jakob pulled up the cover and kissed her on the forehead. Liz coughed a little and seemed to doze off. He stood next to the bed and watched as she slept and was concerned. Soon he left her and sat down for dinner. Chucha was already feeding BethAnn as she babbled and talked, asking for Liz. Chucha questioned Jakob about Liz, and he tried to allay her concerns. "She doesn't feel well and is now resting."

They finished dinner and Chucha cleaned up while Jakob took BethAnn into the living room. BethAnn took up with some of her toys and Jakob found a book to read. Tired of her toys, BethAnn put them aside and climbed up on Jakob's lap.

"Well, so much for the book, BethAnn," and he softly began to sing to her. She laid her head on his chest, closed her eyes, and was soon asleep. Jakob took her to her bed and laid her down. He pulled a cover over her and watched her sleep. Jakob noticed he could hear Liz breathing and went to the bed and gently placed his hand on her forehead. It seemed quite warm. He lifted the cover up to her neck and tucked it in. Jakob watched her for awhile and slowly turned away, leaving the room. He went back to his chair and sat down, thinking about Liz. His eyes closed and he fell asleep.

It was some time later when he was awakened by Liz's hard coughing. He got up and went to Liz, who was now sitting up in bed and coughing, almost uncontrollably. Jakob sat next to her and held her as she continued coughing. He placed his lips on her forehead and noted it felt warmer than before.

"Liz, can I get you some more tea to soothe your throat?" Liz nodded, and he left the room to make some tea. He brought back the tea and helped her with it.

"Jakob, my head really aches and my chest hurts, especially when I breathe." Jakob noticed her chest sounded congested and put his ear to her chest to listen more closely.

"Let me get you a willow bark powder. It will help with the pain and you'll feel better." He mixed the powder with some water on a spoon, and gave it to her. "I'm going to the drug store to see if George Williams has something I can give you for your cough." Liz lay back and Jakob kissed her tenderly on her forehead, which now seemed quite warm. "I'll be back as soon as I can. You just close your eyes and rest."

Jakob walked into George Williams's drug store. He was sitting at one of the tables in the back of the store playing checkers with one of his friends.

"Doc, what brings you out on this cold Sunday afternoon? Expect you'd be sitting by the fireplace reading a book. How's that little girl of yours?"

"She's fine, George, but I have a sick wife. I thought maybe you could help me out." He went on to describe her symptoms.

"Hmm . . . don't sound good. There's a lot of grippe and pneumonia around here. Some are mighty sick people. She got a fever?" Jakob nodded. "How 'bout the congestion?"

"She has a wheeze when she breathes. She is quite weak."

"Has she seen Doc yet?"

"No, she actually just got sicker earlier this morning. She had been coughing a little the last couple days, but around noon today she started complaining of the sore throat, headache, and the rest."

"Well, let me make you some of my cough mixture and I'll give you some ointment you can rub on her chest. It will make her feel better. You got some pain powders, don't you?" Jakob nodded in the affirmative. "Keep her warm and have the lady who works for you make some chicken soup. I don't know why, but it does help. If her throat is bothering her, you can have her gargle with warm salt water. A little honey is okay. If she has trouble sleeping, you can make her some chamomile tea. Let her breathe in some steam from the tea kettle. It may help her with the congestion. That's about all we can do for now. See how she does through the night and you can let me know. Better still, get ahold of Kelly."

"I'll see about Kelly, or if I can't find him, I'll get ahold of Doctor Ross."

"Yes, he's a good doctor. If you can get him to come in, he would be fine. Well good luck and take good care of that lady. We have to keep her well, so she can take care of the baby." Jakob left with George's prescriptions and advice but also with a greater concern for Liz. He didn't want to hear the words grippe, and pneumonia. There was a lot of it in Sheridan and they were deadly. Terror gripped Jakob.

Jakob arrived home and went into the bedroom. Liz appeared to be resting, but her eyes opened. "I have some prescriptions for you. George Williams wants you to take this cough mixture every four hours, and I have some salve to rub on your chest which should make it feel better." He rubbed the salve on her chest. It had an odor but it was soothing. He put a flannel shirt over her, covering her chest, and another flannel nightgown over her to keep her warm. Then he gave her the cough medicine. Liz did complain of chills, but seemed more comfortable and fell asleep.

Jakob went back to his chair. BethAnn was playing with Skippy, who liked her attention. The terror that struck his heart after he left the drug store came back and it stayed with him. He silently prayed. He couldn't bear the thought he could lose Liz. He just closed his eyes and continued praying. Chucha came up to Jakob and saw the pain in his face.

"What matter, Pan?" Jakob looked at her, shook his head and looked away. And she knew what was in his heart.

"BethAnn shouldn't be in our room. We don't want her to get sick. You can put her in her bedroom and you can look after her. Liz is very sick." Chucha nodded she understood and said she would make the supper. Jakob told her some chicken soup would be good for Liz. George's cough mixture seemed to help her coughing, but the fever remained. She had a little soup for supper but wasn't really hungry. BethAnn asked for her mommy but Jakob just told her she was sleeping. The evening went slowly, with Jakob in his chair. It was now time for BethAnn to go to sleep and Chucha put her in her bedroom. Jakob read from his book but couldn't concentrate on anything. He took his pillow and blanket and sat in her rocker, watching Liz and listening to her breathing. He was awakened later by her sudden coughing. He sat on the bed next to her and held her up, while she continued to cough. She finally stopped and he gently placed her head back on the pillow.

"My throat is so sore. Can I have something to drink?" Jakob gave her some warm water with honey in it, and then gave her some of the cough mixture. It probably had some codeine in it and would suppress the coughing. He wiped her brow and kissed it, and Liz closed her eyes and went back asleep. He tried to fall back asleep but couldn't so he went into the living room and sat in his chair looking at the fire in the fireplace. The dancing flames mesmerized him and he was soon asleep, until the clock chimed four. He woke up and heard Liz moaning. He went back into her bedroom and sat on the bed. *She must have been dreaming*, he thought, and he sat back in the rocker and feel asleep.

Skippy, who had been lying next to him, nosed Jakob, who ignored him several times before he got Jakob up. He let Skippy out and then went back to the rocker. Once again he was unable to fall asleep. Light now entered the room and he heard the clock chime six o'clock. His night was over. He gave up and went back to the kitchen and made coffee. Sitting and sipping his coffee, he was thinking about what he would do today. He had to go to the office because he would have patients there. Jakob thought he would have Chucha look after Liz in the morning and he would close the office after noon and come back to look after Liz himself. *First, I should go see Kelly and have him come and see Liz.* Just then he heard Chucha coming down the stairs with BethAnn. BethAnn went to him and he told Chucha what he planned on doing. He looked in on Liz who was now awake.

"How you feeling, Liz? Any better?"

"I feel sore all over. Everything hurts me." Jakob thought she definitely had influenza but felt he should see Doc Kelly and ask him to look at Liz right away. He stopped at Kelly's office and he was in.

"Hey, Kid, what brings you in to see ole Doc Kelly? Got a problem you need a real doctor for?"

"Yes I do Kelly. I'm here because of Liz. She's pretty sick." And he went on to relate her symptoms.

"Doesn't sound good, Jake. Sounds like she may have influenza, but we have to be concerned with pneumonia. What are you doing for her?" Jakob related what he had done. "Did you take her temperature?"

"No, I don't have a thermometer at home, but she feels real hot."

"I better take a look at her. There's a lot of this stuff around. Let's go over to your place." On the way over to Jakob's house, Kelly questioned Jakob further about her condition. He seemed genuinely concerned.

"I'm scared, Kelly. I'm really scared."

"Well, let's not jump to conclusions. Here we are, at your place." Kelly carried his bag followed by Jakob, into the house and into the bedroom. Liz was awake and weakly smiled at Doc Kelly. "Come on Liz, let's have a look at you." He placed a thermometer under her tongue and his stethoscope on her chest and moved it from place to place, not saying anything. He ran it across her back and then removed the thermometer and looked at it. "One hundred four." He looked seriously at Liz. "Liz, you are a sick lady." He listened to her heart, and turning to Jakob he sighed. "I can't say for sure there is fluid in the lungs, but . . . " Then he shook his head. "The stuff that George gave you is okay, but I've got something I think will be better. Give her lots of fluids and fruit juices and keep her warm. Use the ointment on her chest.

"Liz you are going to be all right. Jakob will get a couple of new prescriptions for you. I'll be back to see you tonight." He walked into the living room. "Stay with her. Pray. We need all the help we can get. Now take me back to my office." Jakob walked out of his home, followed by Doc Kelly. Neither spoke. They got to his office and Kelly got out of the carriage.

"Kelly . . . "

"She's a very sick lady. It's probably the same influenza that's been around here for awhile. I don't think it's pneumonia yet. If she doesn't have it by tonight, we have a good chance she can get through it. I'll stop by tonight. In the meantime you take care of her. Sorry, Jake, I wish I knew better but don't give up, she's young and has a strong heart." Doc Kelly went into his office. Jakob just sat there, looking off into the distance before he slapped the reins and moved on.

He stopped at George Williams's drug store to get Kelly's prescriptions filled. George agreed they might be better for her than what he had given Jakob. Jakob then stopped at his office and made a sign saying, he would not be in until further notice. Recognizing the seriousness of Liz's condition, he thought of notifying his parents and Liz's parents. He stopped at Findley's store and made the call home. He explained the seriousness of Liz's condition to his dad. Liz's parents did not have a telephone available, so he stopped by the telegraph office and put together a telegram, and then he went on to take care of Liz.

Liz was resting when Jakob arrived. He took BethAnn into the living room and sat in his chair with her. She asked for Liz and Jakob answered her that mommy was sleeping. It seemed to satisfy her and he placed her on the floor to play with her toys. She sat holding her Raggedy Ann doll and talking to her. Jakob picked up his book and started to read. He heard Liz moaning and got up to look in on her. She awakened and he went to her.

"How are you doing, Liz? Is there anything I can get for you? How about some soup? You must be hungry." Liz just shook her head. She now seemed to be delirious. "I have some new medicine for you Kelly prescribed. I'll get it for you." He helped her sit up and put some in a teaspoon and gave it to her. She was very weak and her temperature was obviously high. He brought home a thermometer and placed it under her tongue and waited for it to register. The temperature had increased to 105 degrees. In spite of the medicine her temperature was higher. He took a cool cloth and wiped her forehead, trying to make her comfortable. Liz seemed to fall back asleep.

BethAnn called Jakob and he went to see her. Skippy was now laying next to her. He picked up BethAnn and held her close to him, as tears ran down his cheeks. BethAnn placed her hands on his face and kissed him. His fears came back to him, and he held her close to his heart before placing her back on the floor with Skippy. Chucha was in the kitchen getting dinner ready, as Jakob listened to sounds of Liz in the bedroom. The house seemed deathly quiet except for BethAnn's voice. Then Liz started to cough, almost uncontrollably and Jakob went to her and helped her sit up, giving her some water. He placed a couple pillows behind her back so she could sit up. She weakly smiled at him.

"Can I see my baby, please?"

"Of course you can. I'll get her." He left the room and came back with BethAnn in his arms.

BethAnn shouted, "Mommy, Mommy," and stretched to reach her. Jakob was holding her back and telling her mommy can't hold her because she is sick. Tears flowed down BethAnn's cheeks as Jakob tried to console her. Liz weakly smiled and softly told her not to cry.

"I love you, BethAnn." As tears flowed down Liz's cheeks, she continued talking. "Don't cry baby. Mommy will be all right."

Liz closed her eyes and Jakob told BethAnn, "Mommy, has to sleep now." And he took her out of the room.

Chucha announced dinner was on the table and took BethAnn to feed her. Jakob went back to make sure Liz was comfortable when she opened her eyes.

"Jakob take care of my baby."

"Of course I will. You don't have to worry honey. We just have to make you well."

"I know. I know you love her. Jakob . . . I love you so much. Will you do me a favor?"

"Of course. What do you want me to do?"

"I'd like to see Father John Binotti. I want to talk with him."

"Sure. Okay, I'll go see him tomorrow. Now let me get you something to eat." Liz shook her head no. "But, you need some nourishment. I'll get you some soup." He came back carrying a cup with soup in it and began to feed her.

"That's enough. I can't eat any more." Jakob backed off. She had about a half cup. "Let me rest now." Jakob found himself completely unnerved. Liz was looking for John Binotti's counsel.

She just can't give up, he thought. *She must feel she can't make it*. And he sat down and silently prayed. Chucha came into the room and motioned for him to come and eat. He sat down but didn't feel much like eating, so he talked to BethAnn. Later, when Liz woke up, he gave her some more soup.

Doc Kelly came by and examined Liz. Her temperature was still running high and the coughing seemed to increase. He listened to her chest and looked up at Jakob and slowly shook his head.

"Liz, you have to eat some and drink the juices. I'll be back tomorrow to see you." He left the room and looked at Jakob seriously. "Her lungs are filling up. I don't know what more we can do." He left Jakob standing alone. Then Jakob slowly moved into the bedroom.

"Liz, I'm going to rub some of this ointment on your chest." He pulled down her gown and applied the ointment liberally and gently spread it across her chest. He placed the flannel over it and brought up her gown. *Her skin is so white,* he thought, as he pulled up her blanket. He tenderly placed a kiss on her cheek and looked away, fearing she might see the tear that rolled down his face. He sat in the rocker and watched as she slept, then left the room to be with BethAnn and tried to entertain her, before it was time for her to go to sleep. It was a long night for Jakob who spent it in the rocker across from Liz's bed.

The light filtered in the window through the shades and Skippy was in to get Jakob, who then let him outside. He started the coffee and sat looking out on a dismal, overcast day. Liz was moaning and moving around in bed, and Jakob went in to see her.

She was awake, and putting on his best bravado, he said, "Hi Honey. You slept pretty good. Can I get you something to drink? I have some coffee made, or I can get you some milk or juice?" Liz weakly answered she would like some coffee and Jakob quickly got a cup for her. "Let me make you some oatmeal. You can handle that." Liz was not too enthusiastic about the oatmeal but accepted the idea. Jakob went to the kitchen and made it for her. He helped her by feeding it to her, and when she indicated she didn't want anymore, he withdrew it. He gave her the medicines and prepared to give her a sponge bath. Liz just lay back hardly moving as he carefully cleaned her body. He added perfume to the water to give it a slight flagrance. Then he changed the bed sheets and pillow cases, as they had a perspiration odor. He propped her up some and said, "There now, that should make you feel better. You even look better. I'm going to see if I can find John Binotti. Maybe he will be able to see you today." He heard BethAnn with Chucha in the kitchen. "I'll bring BethAnn in to see you, okay?" Liz nodded and weakly smiled.

Chucha was about to give BethAnn her breakfast when Jakob came in. BethAnn was ready to be hugged so Jakob picked her up and carried her into the bedroom. She squealed, "Mommy, Mommy." Jakob held her as she tugged to go to Liz and touched her.

"Not right now BethAnn, mommy has to go to sleep." BethAnn didn't seem to understand and she started to cry. Jakob had to pacify her until she finally calmed down. Liz spoke to her and threw her kisses, which BethAnn did likewise. The ordeal tired Liz and she closed her eyes as Jakob took BethAnn back to Chucha for her breakfast

Jakob left to find John Binotti who lived in a small house near the makeshift church. A new church was being prepared, one that would be more suitable for the increase in church membership. It would have a bell and even a short steeple. John Binotti was having breakfast when Jakob knocked on the door. He explained the nature of the call and Father John could see Jakob was very upset. He spoke with Jakob and tried to allay his fears.

"Of course I will see her. I want to be there with her. You go back home to her and I will be there just as soon as I can." Jakob left and mulled over what Father John had said to him. He came home to find Liz was resting, and was satisfied. He sat in his chair with BethAnn awaiting the priest. It wasn't too long before he was at the door and Jakob was letting him in.

"She's sleeping now. Shall I wake her?" John shook his head.

"No, just let her sleep. I'll wait for her. Maybe I can have a cup of coffee with you." They sat down together and talked. Though they knew each other from previous contacts, John Binotti asked about Jakob's and Liz's life together. He had a way of making Jakob feel like he was deeply concerned. Jakob then heard Liz fussing and then coughing, and went into her room with the priest following. He propped Liz up on pillows and gave her some medicine.

"Liz, Father John is here to see you. Would you like to talk with him?"

Liz weakly smiled. "Oh yes, I would. Hello, Father." He came to her bed, took her hand and sat down next to her.

"I'm so sorry you're sick." He looked at Jakob momentarily, who turned around and left the room. Jakob sat in his chair by the fire and Chucha brought BethAnn to him. He put her on his lap and started to sing softly to her. The thoughts in his mind spun as he as held his beloved baby.

It seemed like it had been an hour, and BethAnn had dozed off, when Father John left the bedroom and approached Jakob.

He looked at Jakob and said, " She's ready." Jakob looked at him; his mouth opened but he didn't speak. "You have a beautiful wife. She is a worthy mother. It is in God's hands. I think she is still awake if you want to go in with her. I'll drop by tomorrow to see her." BethAnn put her arms up to Father John and he took her from Jakob. He placed his hand on her head and blessed her. Jakob went into the room but Liz was asleep, so he came back out. He took BethAnn in his arms and the priest left.

The rest of the afternoon Liz slept on and off. Doc Kelly came by to see her late in the afternoon. He listened to her chest and heart. There was no apparent progress. She definitely had pneumonia. Jakob was now monitoring her fluids. Her coughing was severe and her chest pained her whenever she coughed. It seemed they could do no more. He could see her slipping; she seemed weaker. He stayed at her bedside doing whatever she needed. Sometimes she mumbled in her sleep.

It was the first day the sun had appeared for several weeks and crept through the shades. Jakob awoke to let the dog out and came back to Liz. She was awake. He wiped her brow with a cool cloth and she looked up at him and weakly smiled. He held her head and kissed her.

"I love you Jakob. Thank you for being so good to me. I love you." He helped her sit up and placed pillows in back of her, then put his arms around her and spoke softly.

"I love you too." She smiled and closed her eyes He continued speaking softly to her for awhile and waited for her answer. But she didn't answer.

"Liz . . . Liz." Her eyes were closed and she was breathing but she didn't answer. He thought she had fallen asleep, and he took his arms away and then just sat next to her. Her breathing was labored and then it stopped. "Liz. Liz." She didn't respond. He placed his hands on her face. "Liz, oh my God, Liz! Please don't leave me." She wasn't breathing. He tried her neck pulse. "Oh, Liz, don't leave me," and he burst into tears and buried his face in the pillow next to her. Chucha heard him and came into the room as he sobbed uncontrollably. Tears streamed down his face. Jakob kissed the motionless Liz. "Oh, Liz, what am going to do without you." He held her and caressed her and just lay next to her until he felt a tug on his shoulder. Kelly was standing there.

"Come on, Jake. Let me check her." Jakob got up and sat in the rocker with his hands over his face. He was devastated. Doc Kelley listened for her vitals and then said, "She is gone." Kelly led Jakob out of the room and sat him in his chair. With red eyes Chucha handed Jakob a cup of coffee. He placed it to his lips and took a sip. Kelly stood over him. "Jake, we did the best we could. I know what you feel because I went through this myself. It's horrible but we have to go on. You have a baby to raise." Jakob just looked silently, completely distraught.

"Yes, I know." There was a knock on the front door and Chucha opened it to let Father John in. He knew what had happened and entered the bedroom. Jakob nursed the coffee until Father John came out of the bedroom and approached Jakob. He sat with him and comforted him as best as he could.

"I'll be back at noon and we'll talk." And he left.

Then Kelly added, "Jakob, I'll stop and see Herbert O'Brian and he'll be here to take over for you with Liz. In the meantime, take one of these with some water and lie down and rest. I know you have been up with Liz nights. I'll be back later."

Chucha was feeding BethAnn. As Jakob looked at her, he wondered, *What will I tell my baby?* And he started to sob. It took a while for him to gain his composure. Jakob went into the kitchen and picked up BethAnn. He spoke with her but was unable to say anything more about Liz, but he told her he was laying down for awhile because he was tired.

Jakob had not slept long when Chucha woke him up. Herb O'Brian had come to make arrangements for Liz's funeral. He asked Jakob whether he wanted an open casket and if so, did he have a special dress for her. He thought a while and agreed to have her seen. Jakob decided he wanted her to be clad in the dress he brought her from Chicago, when he went to Marshall Field's. Liz was saving it for a special occasion. He found it and sobbed. This wasn't the special occasion he had bought it for and his eyes filled with tears. He knew she would be beautiful in it. It was lavender, a color she looked well in. Herb took Liz away, as Jakob broke down.

BethAnn had been sleeping and Chucha brought her to Jakob. He still hadn't told her about Liz, and he was agonizing over how to do it. He held her, and kissed her and talked to her but was unable to find the words.

There was a knock on the door and Chucha answered, then brought in Jakob's mother and father. They stood before him, and before he even spoke they knew Liz had passed away. He stood up and faced them, but could not contain his sorrow as they embraced him. They said they had prepared to leave Milwaukee immediately after he had called them. Both were deeply grieved. They sat and Jakob related the circumstances of Liz's death. Jakob had not yet notified Liz's parents, so he and his father decided to go to the Western Union office. However, just before leaving, Western Union delivered a telegram indicating they had left for Sheridan.

Chucha invited all to sit for dinner. As they sat down, BethAnn asked for her mother. No one knew what to say, but Jakob, holding the baby, explained as best as he could what had happened. At first she said nothing, but then, realized her mother was not there. She began to cry, as Jakob held her and tried to soothe her. Margaret looked soulfully at Jakob.

"Jakob, the next days are going to be very difficult for all of us. I'm sure many of your friends will come by to express their sorrow and we will have to be able to receive them, no matter how much we grieve. Let me and Dad help you. They can't know how you truly feel—no one can. But they will try to share your grief. We'll do our best for you."

No one really felt like eating but they did share their thoughts as they tried to eat. John Binotti stopped to see Jakob and spoke with him privately. He offered to do the service at Liz's burial. Jakob seemed numb. He spoke little when talked to. Later in the evening, Doc Kelly stopped by to see Jakob. Instead of his general normal bravado, he too was short on words and didn't stay long. Jakob went to bed that night emotionally broken and physically exhausted.

He slept sporadically and awoke to face another difficult day. Liz's parents would arrive that morning and Herb O'Brian would return Liz to her home. It was a deeply emotional moment for Jakob to see his Liz, as she lay in a plain wood casket dressed in the lavender dress Jakob had bought for her. Her beautiful lifeless body brought everyone to tears.

Jakob was emotionally broken, numb, as he received mourners. A constant stream of people came to express their grief. They brought something to express their sorrow. The kitchen was filled with cakes and cookies, casseroles, and items to express their feelings for Jakob and Liz. Some brought flowers from the only floral shop in Sheridan. The floral shop brought three white gardenias which he placed on Liz. The days drew on with friends and some who they really didn't know passed through the house. Some were people Liz had in her education classes as well as children she taught. Her close friend, Mrs. Howard, Margaret and Liz's mother, Rosemary, helped Jakob through those trying days. Liz had touched many peoples lives.

A procession of hundreds entered the Mt. Hope Cemetery and Liz was laid to final rest. Father John officiated the ceremony as Jakob and all looked on. And then . . . everything became so final.

Jakob was feeling pain inside himself he could not describe. Many later stopped by the house for coffee and cakes, speaking quietly and reflecting on the memories they had of Liz. Jakob moved about and thanked them for their expressions of love and support.

The home was now empty, except for the immediate family. Jakob thanked them for being there and for being supportive and helping him in his greatest hour of need.

In a quiet moment Margaret talked with Jakob.

"I know how difficult this has been for you. I'm thinking of the days ahead. BethAnn has lost her mother and you are facing the job of raising her. It's not going to be easy. I talked this over with Daddy. Why don't you let me take her home with me? I have the time and love to give her. She would have the best of everything I could give her." Jakob looked at her almost incredulously.

"Oh no! No, I couldn't do that. I know you mean well, but I couldn't do that. I just lost my wife. I couldn't lose my baby too. You have no idea how much I love her. She needs me more than ever now. No Mother, I couldn't do that. I would have nothing to live for."

"She needs special care to raise her properly. I know you have Chucha and she is a good lady, but I could do so much better. She hardly speaks any English."

"No, Mother, BethAnn will live with her father. She needs me and I need her. Chucha may not be perfect but she will do all right. No, Mother, please, I thank you for your concern and I know you mean well. I gave my promise to Liz that I would care for her baby. I won't give her up." Margaret recognized Jakob's agony.

"I understand your feelings. I want you to understand I will always be there for you." Jakob put his arms around his mother and kissed her holding her tightly.

"I know, I'm still your little boy Mom, and I realize now that I am not completely alone. I still have you and Dad and my adorable baby." BethAnn was playing with her Raggedy Ann doll with Skippy next to her. Jakob picked her up and held her tightly. She placed her hands on his face and kissed him, and he held her close to his heart.

Chapter 28

The Healing

A heavyhearted Jakob saw his parents leave Sheridan on the 10 a.m. train headed for Milwaukee.

The Jensens were scheduled to leave the next day. Jakob's great loss was shared by them, too. Tragedy had struck deeply into their lives; Liz was their first child. She was everything a daughter could be to them. They saw her leave her home in Iowa a grown young woman, ready to take up her life in Sheridan, Wyoming, not knowing whether she would ever return. With their blessing, they had accepted her decision. Then they saw her marry Jakob, the man of her dreams, who they learned to respect and love. Now they wanted to spend another day with him and BethAnn.

BethAnn took to her grandparents and enjoyed being with them. Ralph and Rosemary Jensen were plain people, but they were hard-working and good, God-fearing individuals. They saw BethAnn as the mirror image of their Liz. Her blonde hair, facial features and eyes were all Liz. In the days they spent with Jakob, they understood why Liz had loved him so much. Just as Bob Miller had accepted Liz as a daughter, so did the Jensens accept Jakob as their son. They parted company grieving, but knowing they had Jakob's and BethAnn's love.

Jakob left the train station for home, with BethAnn sitting next to him. The home was warm and comfortable, but remnants of the past days remained. The fireplace burned brightly. Jakob put BethAnn on the couch and removed her heavy winter clothing. She stood silently, until he picked her up and sat down with her. Lovingly, she put her arms around his neck and kissed him. He held her tightly and sang softly to her. Jakob and Liz use to make up tunes with melodies and sing them to her, and she would quietly listen to them. Some tunes were funny and caused her to laugh, while others were love songs. Liz would do this for BethAnn and she loved it. They would laugh as BethAnn would try to imitate them. The warm room with the flickering fire, plus the pain and stress of the recent days had left Jakob weary, and they both dozed off.

Soon Chucha came in to tell them she had lunch ready. Chucha had been incredibly helpful. She was always there and helped the guests, as well as those who came to offer their condolences. There was no way to measure what she had done for Liz and Jakob. She loved them both, and she grieved for Liz, as if she were her own. She tried to take as much of the burden off of Jakob as she could. Jozef, who brought Chucha to Liz and Jakob, felt he lost a good friend in Liz. The days passed slowly as life without Liz continued.

Hardly a day passed that Jakob didn't think of Liz. He woke up at night thinking he heard Liz call to him. BethAnn would spontaneously begin to cry and say "I want my Mommy." Hearing this was like having a spear pierce his soul. But, as time passed, they slowly healed and could once again laugh.

Jakob went back to work sooner than he might have wanted, but his patients needed him. He had to put aside the past and face his future. The mayor called a meeting of his committee and he joined in and participated. Jakob attended his church and was called on to help with the building of the new St. Ignatius Church.

There were times Jakob had feelings that God left him when he needed him most, and felt angry he no longer had his Liz. BethAnn was deprived of her mother when she needed her. *How could this possibly happen to him? It wasn't fair. Why? Why?* he thought. But there could be no possible answers. Then he realized his anger brought no relief or help, and slowly he rejected those thoughts. He realized they did nothing, but only deepened his resentment and extended the grief. Jakob had to continue living. After all, he had BethAnn, and the attitude he had assumed was not helpful to either of them.

John Binotti was instrumental in his recovery. They became good friends. Father Binotti was his listener and supported him spiritually during that terrible period. Jakob often went to the cemetery to visit Liz's gravesite. She meant so much to him and he still couldn't get over she was gone. He wanted so much to talk things over with her.

The long winter slowly turned into spring. Jakob frequently took BethAnn with him for a ride in the buggy, which many times ended at Little Goose Creek where he had proposed to Liz. He and BethAnn walked along the creek and watched the birds or picked wildflowers to take to the gravesite or home. He tried to spend as much time as he could with BethAnn. She was so observant and excited about the things she saw.

Jakob tried hard to be both a father and mother to BethAnn. He was fortunate to have Chucha to care for her when he wasn't home. She was very kind to BethAnn and looked after her as if she were her own granddaughter. When Chucha was in the garden BethAnn was with her placing seeds in the ground. Surprisingly, Chucha was doing well with English, and spoke increasingly more fluently. There were other children in the area and their mothers would often invite BethAnn to play with them.

BethAnn would sometimes bring up Liz and ask, "When will I see Mommy again?" She still couldn't comprehend her demise. It was difficult for Jakob to try to explain away some of her questions. He would often refer to Liz as an angel that was looking after BethAnn and Liz was always with her, even though BethAnn couldn't see her.

Jakob found solace in riding off into the foothills of the Bighorns on his favorite chestnut, Jenny. She was a good, gentle riding horse and they sometimes spent a day together. Occasionally, Jakob put BethAnn in the saddle with him, which was a thrill for her. He couldn't wait until she was old enough for him to get her a pony. Sometimes, he put her in the saddle alone and he would lead Jenny. Skippy became a constant companion of BethAnn. He followed her wherever she went, and was very protective of her. Anyone who approached her knew he was there.

Fortunately for Jakob, he had many friends who were supportive of him and he was often invited to dinners or other events. Liz had many friends who went out of their way to help him and BethAnn. She was invited to play with their children and even attended their birthday parties. It was unexpected support, but living on the frontier produced special people, who were used to helping one another.

Jakob frequently received letters from the Jensens as well as his parents, and they often sent gifts to BethAnn so she might better remember them. Time seemed to fly by as Jakob was busy with his dental practice.

The time arrived for him to make his summer trip to Buffalo. He agonized over what he should do. He didn't want to leave BethAnn behind with Chucha, yet he didn't think he should take her. However, he had developed friends in Buffalo and they indicated he could stay with them. They had a big house and said that they would be delighted to take care of BethAnn while he was taking care of patients. The people in Buffalo looked forward to him coming as they still had no resident dentist. Chucha agreed to stay in his house and take care of the home and animals while they were gone.

He loaded his wagon with his equipment, and with BethAnn alongside, he headed for Buffalo. It was summer and the trail was in reasonably good condition. With an early start, he was able to make it in one day. Chucha packed them a lunch and they picnicked on the way. There were other riders on the trail but fortunately they didn't experience any problems.

They arrived in Buffalo and stopped at the Hillmans', an elderly couple from Racine, Wisconsin. When they had learned Jakob came from Milwaukee, they immediately became friends. George Hillman was a carpenter who came to Buffalo to ply his trade. Jakob had helped him with a serious dental problem. They had rooms ready for Jakob and BethAnn. Mary Hillman was a typical grandmother and had cookies ready for BethAnn when they arrived. Jakob sat and talked with the Hillmans, and they were invited to have supper with them. BethAnn got along fine with Mary, who immediately took over.

The next morning Jakob went over to the Occidental Hotel to set up shop. Harold Peters had the storeroom cleared out for his office. He was glad to see Jakob and they talked about the latest news in Buffalo. Jakob learned they had a new sawbones who took over for Jeremy Jones. Apparently Jeremy couldn't take the rigors of a frontier Doc at his advanced age.

"Doc Fredericks came from St. Louis and is a much younger man. He's probably older than you Doc, but a lot younger than Doc Jeremy, who went back to Louisville where he came from. He just took over Doc Jeremy's place on South Main Street. Ya oughta go see him so he knows you're in town. One thing about Doc Fredericks, is he don't mind gettin' in his buggy and traveling out of town for a sick patient. That's something Jeremy jes wouldn't do." Jakob mentioned he had to get a barber chair.

"No problem Doc. I saw Harley and told him you was comin', and he said he'd have a couple of the guys deliver it jes as soon as you got here."

"Then I'll stop by his shop and tell him I'm here. I'll also put up one of my posters in his shop, like I did last time." He stopped at the *Buffalo Horn* and put the announcement in the newspaper. Jakob had a lot of groundwork to cover before he was ready for business. He had already met a couple of potential patients in the Occidental bar who asked him when he'd be ready.

After finalizing his advertisement in the *Buffalo Horn*, Jakob went to see the new doctor. He stopped at his office, but it was filled with patients. Jakob just introduced himself and was ready to leave when Doc Fredericks suggested they meet for a drink at the Occidental bar at six. Jakob agreed and left for Harley's Barber Shop. Harley was cutting hair but stopped to shake Jakob's hand. He went outside and got a couple guys to take his extra chair over to Jakob's office, then came back and continued cutting hair.

Jakob put up a poster in the shop and began to leave when Harley said, "I'll be over to see you, Doc." Jakob finished posting his announcements and stopped by the Occidental Hotel to meet with Doc Fredericks. Jim Fredericks was a tall, skinny man with a black mustache and graying hair. He was friendly enough and asked Jakob if he would help him with some of the people who got banged up.

"I heard you can fix broken jaws. With all the fights we have on Saturdays, I always expect to see a broken jaw. But I never fixed one."

"That's not exactly my thing Jim. But I'll be glad to give you an assist if you ever need me." They talked about Buffalo and the problems Doc Fredericks was having. Then Jakob showed him where his temporary office would be.

"You know, I might just come by to see you, while you're around." Jakob said he'd be glad to help him out. They shook hands and Jakob left to see the Hillmans and BethAnn. Mary Hillman greeted Jakob.

"I figured you'd be late for dinner, with you getting everything ready to start your business. We usually eat at five, but I saved you a supper. So why don't you sit down as soon as you're ready." BethAnn was all over Jakob, telling him about her day with Aunt Mary. That's what Mary Hillman wanted to be called. Jakob was happy to be able to take BethAnn with him and having someone like Mary Hillman take care of her was just great.

He set up his office the next day, and it wasn't too soon because he had people come in for treatment that day. The people of Buffalo were happy he was there to provide them with the services they needed.

The following weekend Mary Hillman was going to have a birthday party for George. He would be sixty years old and a big party was set for Saturday. George was a popular man so there would be a lot of people there. She even planned to bring in some musicians. George smoked cigars, so Jakob brought him a box of cigars for a present.

Everyone was anxious to meet Jakob; he even saw some of his previous patients. Mary Hillman's neighbor was there, so Jakob was introduced to Martha Johnson, a widow lady who paid a lot of attention to him. She made it a point to bring Jakob some of the birthday cake and to be near him. She was attractive but Jakob did not feel comfortable being alone with her, so he made sure there was always someone else with them. He danced with BethAnn but avoided doing so with any of the ladies. During the following weeks Martha as well as Eleanor Foster, another lady friend of the Hillmans', visited quite often. But Jakob was not interested in any relationships.

Jakob's patient load diminished considerably and he had been away from Sheridan for five weeks so he thought it was time for him to return home. He was sure there would be patients waiting for him to return, and so he closed his office in Buffalo. It was September and he could anticipate the weather getting cooler. He certainly didn't want to wait too long, like he did the first year, when he had to return in a snow storm. Mary Hillman was sorry to see BethAnn leave. Jakob thought it was a good experience for Mary, having BethAnn to take care of. BethAnn also benefited by being with Mary who was so kind to her.

Harold Peters had a bunch of people over to the Occidental Hotel for a farewell party for Jakob. Attending were some of his new friends, as well as many old ones. Jakob was sorry he had to leave because he found the people in Buffalo very genuine, and enjoyed working there. His wagon was loaded for the return trip. The Hillmans were sorry to see them leave. Aunt Mary broke down and cried when she kissed and hugged BethAnn. She gave her a doll that she had saved since when she was a little girl. They took their basket filled with treats and lunch fixings. There were a couple riders who planned to go with them, as they had business to do in Sheridan. Jakob was happy to have them ride along. He would be traveling with a sizable amount of money—his profits from the trip—and it was something to be concerned about.

The trip going back home was without any problems, although just before they got to Sheridan it started to rain hard. Jakob put BethAnn inside the wagon and she kept pretty dry.

Chucha was happy to see them. She hugged both Jakob and BethAnn and immediately started making them something to eat. Skippy welcomed them in his own way and stayed close to BethAnn. Chucha then filled Jakob in on the happenings since he had left. When the rain stopped, they all went on the porch. Some of the neighbors stopped by to welcome them back. Chucha took over when it was time for BethAnn to go to sleep.

Jakob remained outside thinking about his trip to Buffalo. He had done well financially and enjoyed being there. The Hillmans were kind to him. He chuckled when he thought about the young widows he met. *I have no interest in any lady. I will never find another Liz.*

PART II
A NEW BEGINNING

Chapter 29

A Newfound Friend

Five Years Later

Jakob's Monday luncheon group was ending their weekly meeting. Harold Stevens confronted Jakob.

"Jake, don't forget the mayor's meeting. He's expecting us Wednesday to fill us in on the plans for the fair."

"Yes, I'll be there. I have to get back to the office. See you later, Harold."

Jakob started walking out of the Sheridan Inn dining room when he recognized an attractive lady at one of the tables having lunch. *Oh my gosh. That's Geraldine Widicker, James's wife.*

"Mrs. Widicker! Hello there. I haven't seen you for a long time. How are you?"

"Doctor Miller. Oh, I'm so sorry but I didn't recognize you. It has been a long time. I remember now . . . the Oliver Henry birthday party. You and your wife were there at the ranch. How nice to see you. Would you care to sit down?"

"Yes, I would, but for just for a few minutes. I'm on my way to my office. What are you doing here in Sheridan?"

"I'm here on business. I have to see my banker to take care of a few things. And, as long as we're talking, I really should also come in to see you. It's been a long time since I was in your office. I could be having some dental problems because I haven't seen a dentist for several years."

"Well I'm available. Just stop by my office. It's still in the same place."

"I've just put off doing a lot of things these past years." She paused and looked distressed. "I don't know whether you know it, but I lost my James three years ago. He had a cancer that took his life. We had gone back to England to see his family when it was discovered. The doctors there treated him, but it was too late. It's been very difficult these past years without him. I returned here a little more than a year ago. We bought the Oliver Henry Ranch four and a half years ago, just before Oliver went back to England to take over his late father's earldom, Hereford. We had barely started operating the ranch when we went back to England. James left his two nephews in charge of the ranch, along with the ranch foreman. I returned to the ranch when I became aware it was having financial problems."

"I am so sorry for all your problems. I guess I remember hearing you had gone back to England, but I didn't realize what had happened. Please accept my condolences for the loss of your husband. I remember James. He was a fine person. I'm sure all of this must be difficult for you.

"I'm sorry, but I really must go to my office. Maybe we can talk later. We could get together and talk further tonight. At dinner? Will you be staying here overnight?"

Mrs. Widicker nodded. "Yes, I will be staying overnight. I may be here for several days."

"Well good, then we can have dinner together tonight and talk more. I would like to hear more about your problems. Maybe I can be of some assistance."

"Oh yes, it would be nice. I plan on being here as long as necessary. I'd like that. What time do you suggest?"

"Would seven be all right?" Missus Widicker agreed and Jakob left for his office thinking about the Widickers. *That's too bad about him passing on. They were nice people and just getting into ranching. I wonder if she is also one of those with a title?*

Jakob had a busy day and finished later than usual. He went home to be greeted by BethAnn and Chucha, who had dinner ready for him. He told Chucha he wouldn't be eating because he was having dinner at the Inn with a friend. But he sat with them for awhile as BethAnn related all the things she had done that day.

"I even picked some strawberries from the garden," she said. BethAnn was a delight at seven years and was always doing something interesting. Chucha kept track of her and they would often take long walks or stop to see neighbors. BethAnn also had a number of friends nearby she would visit.

Jakob went to his room to get ready for his dinner engagement. He then kissed BethAnn goodbye and told her he would be back before her bedtime.

He met Geraldine Widicker in the Sheridan Inn dining room. Annabelle was now waiting tables, and she warmly greeted Jakob.

"Doc, I haven't seen you for awhile. This lady said she was waiting for you, so I found a nice table for you. Lukas has some good specials tonight. I'll be back soon for your drink order."

"Geraldine, I'm so glad we could have dinner together."

"Well, it's nice to be invited, Doctor. Thank you."

Jakob smiled. "If I may call you Geraldine, you can certainly drop the formality and the 'Doctor' and call me Jakob. I still remember the great party we went to at Oliver Henry's. You were Geraldine then, so you must still be Geraldine now. Oliver sure knew how to have a party. It was his seventieth birthday; wasn't it?"

"Yes it was a great party. I had heard from Oliver that you lost your wife." Jakob nodded and looked down. "She was such a lovely lady. I'm truly sorry. That must be hard for you. She did have the baby, didn't she? And it was a girl?"

Jakob nodded and answered. "It's been awhile now. Time has a way of slipping by and healing. BethAnn is going to be eight. She is a real beauty, just like her mother. I don't know what I would have done without her. We have so much fun together. She will be having a birthday soon and I want to get her a pony. She just loves horses and riding with me." Annabelle came back and asked if they wanted wine or a cocktail.

Jakob looked at Geraldine. "What would you like to have?"

Geraldine smiled and looked up at Jakob shyly. "You know what I really would like to have?"

"Well?"

"I would like to have a martini, Jakob."

"A martini! I don't believe I've had one of those more than once or twice. Very interesting. Then that's what we shall both have Annabelle. A martini." He smiled. "Now I remember, you English do like your gin don't you?"

Geraldine laughed. "I guess we do." They talked in generalities as they sipped their cocktails. Annabelle came back and told them of the special menu items. Soon Lukas came and welcomed Jakob, who then introduced him to Geraldine.

"I haven't seen you at dinner for awhile, Doc. I'm glad to have you back. I have a couple of your favorites today: duck ala orange and my elk stew. You can take your time ordering. I just wanted to stop by and say hello. Oh, I also have the regular items on the menu, if you should want one of them. Enjoy your dinner. Nice to meet you, ma'am."

Annabelle came back and took their order. It was a warm summer day and the big ceiling fan cooled the dining room as they sipped their cocktails. Jakob noticed that Geraldine was a very attractive lady, maybe a little younger than Jakob. Her hair was dark, almost black, and she had big brown eyes and long lashes and a pleasant smile. Interesting? She had a slight English accent as she spoke, but not so much that she might be difficult to understand. Her colloquialisms and mannerisms were interesting.

William, the bartender, came over. "How do you folks like the martinis?"

Geraldine smiled. "It is just perfect. Why, it is just like Robert used to make them back at Landry Manor." And she picked up her glass and sipped.

Jakob queried her. "And who is Robert, may I ask?"

"Oh, he is a footman who makes the drinks back at Landry Manor in England." And she smiled. "He has been there for ages. Why, he is definitely part of the establishment. It was my grand-papa who hired him first, years and years ago."

"You are going to have to tell me more about your family and your life in England sometime, and how you happened to come to Sheridan."

"Oh, that will take a long time and you probably wouldn't be interested."

"No, I really would be." And they continued chatting. Jakob looked down at his glass.

"My glass is empty and that tasted very good! Would you care for another?"

Geraldine looked at Jakob, then smiled and cocked her head slightly. "Well just maybe, if you will be having one. That would be just jolly."

Jakob signaled Annabelle for another drink and William made them another. They kept their conversation light and enjoyed each other's company. Dinner came and they kept the conversation going. Jakob found her easy to talk to. They finished their dinner and were offered dessert, but each said they were filled and declined it.

Coffee was served when Jakob posed a question. "You said you were having problems with your ranch. What might they be? Do you want to talk about them?"

"Yes, I do, if you would care to listen. While I was in England with James and his medical problems, I became aware of some losses of income at the ranch. We were always able to make a reasonable profit, but the longer I was in England the more those profits disappeared and became losses. I was so caught up with James and his problems, I overlooked them. The bank made me aware of the situation, when we neglected some payments. I didn't understand because we bought and sold the same number of cattle and horses, but our expenses increased drastically. Roger and Steven, my husband's nephews, can't seem to explain why those losses occurred. That is why I must confer with the banker."

"Well, there must be some logical explanation. The bank should be able to figure it out. You must have your books of sales and expenses."

"I do, but I fear Roger and Steven have not been honest in their handling of funds, and it would put me in a most uncomfortable position."

Jakob looked disturbed and tried to abate her fears. "You might be fearing the worst. I'm sure it can all be explained. Who will you be talking to?"

"I will be meeting with Harold Stevens at the First National Bank."

"Oh, I know Harold Stevens. He is on the mayor's committee for Sheridan's development with me. Have you met him yet?" Geraldine indicated she had not. "He is a fine person and has a good business head. You could mention you have talked with me and he might take a more personal interest in your problem. It might just help. Oh-oh, the time is getting late and I told BethAnn I would be back before she went to bed. I'm sorry. We were just getting to know each other, and now I have to leave. I know what we can do. We can continue this talk again tomorrow, and have dinner, after you meet Harold. Hopefully, we can get some constructive answers. How about it, will that work for you?"

"That would be fine with me. I'm so happy I ran into you. Really, I feel so much better after talking with you. At least now I know someone here in Sheridan. May I stop by your office if I have time tomorrow, because I do need to see you professionally and this would be an ideal time for me while I'm here? I think I might have some dental problems you could take care of. That is, if you have available time for me?"

"No problem. I'm sure I can work you into my schedule. And, tomorrow night, we can continue with our chat and have dinner together again."

Jakob left for home and arrived later than he had thought he would. BethAnn came up to him as he entered the kitchen and hugged him.

"Chucha and I made some cookies. Want to try some?" Jakob tried the cookie and smacked his lips, then told her he thought they were just great. They went out on the porch and sat on the swing. Skippy was sitting on the floor next to them and BethAnn snuck him a cookie, which he relished.

"Look, Daddy, Skippy likes my cookies too." They sat and talked, when BethAnn then seriously quizzed Jakob. "Daddy, I was sitting here this afternoon with Skippy when I noticed a lot of butterflies going from flower to flower. What do butterflies do, Daddy?" Jakob smiled. "Do you know why Daddy?"

"Well . . . Maybe they were delivering butter to the flowers."

BethAnn looked suspiciously at Jakob.

"Daddy, you are kidding me." Jakob grabbed her and kissed her as she tried to wiggle away. Then it struck him. He thought of Liz, and a tear slid down his cheek as he held BethAnn closely and rocked the swing. She would keep his memories of Liz alive. It had gotten dark with no moon. The sky was full of stars.

"Well, Honey, I guess the time has come for you to go to bed." BethAnn pouted and sorrowfully looked at Jakob.

"Do I really have to?" Jakob nodded and they got up and went into the house. BethAnn led the way up the stairs to her room, with Jakob following. She started to remove her clothes as Jakob reminded her to be sure to brush her teeth.

"I'll be back to tuck you in." He went downstairs and sat in his chair thinking about dinner with Geraldine until he heard BethAnn call him. He quickly went back to her. "There now, you are officially, safely tucked in." He kissed her. "Your guardian angel can now take over. Good night, my love."

"Night, Daddy." Jakob went down to his favorite chair. He sat silently with an empty mind, until he again thought of Geraldine. Then he realized it was the first time he had eaten dinner with a lady since Liz had passed away. He had a strange feeling, almost like he cheated on Liz, and he started to feel guilty. *Oh no. I shouldn't feel this way. I haven't cheated on Liz. I wouldn't do that to her. But it feels good to be with a nice lady,* and he mulled it over. There were many thoughts about Liz and Geraldine in his mind as he sat.

Chucha came down from her room and asked Jakob if there was anything he wanted, before she went to bed. He thanked her and bid her good night. Then he reflected on Chucha and how fortunate he was to have her with him. *I don't know how I could ever manage taking care of BethAnn without her. I guess God was looking after us when he sent her into our lives. Chucha was not a young woman but she just took over. I don't have to tell her what to do. How could she possibly know what I need? It's almost uncanny.* Her English was now acceptable, even though she would sometimes slip into a Polish word or two. The sound of the grandfather clock noted it was eleven and Jakob was starting to doze off.

It was in the afternoon of a busy day for Jakob when Geraldine came into his office. She waited for awhile before Jakob was able to see her. He found a few things she needed to have taken care of and was able to do them for her. They spoke only briefly, but he made arrangements to have dinner together that evening.

Jakob went home after his office hours and spent some time with BethAnn. They went on a short ride with Jenny. BethAnn just loved being on the horse; she always petted her and talked to her. They rode out of town toward Big Horn. It was a nice, warm day, and the area where they rode was pleasant. They saw people along the way whom they knew and stopped at a creek to watch the birds before turning around and going back home. Chucha would have dinner for BethAnn and he had to get ready to have dinner at the Sheridan Inn with Geraldine. Jakob had found himself looking forward to seeing her. He spruced himself up for the dinner.

Jakob came into the Inn just before seven and went into the dining room. Annabelle had already seated Geraldine. She wore a yellow, flowered sheer dress and a necklace made with small multicolored flowers and typical of English ladies, wore gloves. Her dark hair had an upsweep to it. Jakob noticed she really looked quite attractive, more so than he first realized. He noted the way she held her hands.

"Well, fancy meeting you here Mrs. Widicker. I seem to remember seeing you somewhere else today."

"Oh, Doctor, have you forgotten our appointment already?" She laughed.

"Of course, I remember now. You are the lady who drinks martinis, Lady Geraldine."

"I haven't heard anyone call me that since I came to this country. You are very proper, sir. Thank you." Jakob shook her hand and sat down. "Where have you learned manners like that?" Jakob smiled and was about to answer when Annabelle came to their table.

"You folks gonna have the same as yesterday? Martinis?" Jakob nodded.

"Of course. We English do like our martinis, don't we, my Lady?"

"But of course." Annabelle shook her head, not understanding the act, and went to the bar.

"Am I being proper? Would I pass as an English gentleman?"

Geraldine laughed. "Everything would be perfect, but you don't have the proper attire. An English gentleman would come to dinner with the proper dinner jacket, but then, this isn't Lord Henry's Hereford Manor. This is the Sheridan Inn in the U.S. of A. Thank you for the dinner invitation and you may call me Geraldine."

Annabelle arrived with the martinis and placed them in front of them, then said she would return with the menus shortly. They toasted with their drinks and slowly sipped them.

"We didn't get a chance to talk about your problem yet. Did you see Harold Stevens?"

"Yes, I saw him. We went over my profit and loss statement and found a number of discrepancies. It seems as though James's nephews have taken advantage of their responsibilities and used what wasn't theirs. They absconded with a sizable amount of money. Mr. Stevens did some checking and it appears they had large gambling losses which have contributed to my losses."

"Oh-oh. That doesn't sound good to me. How are you going to handle that? Are you going to prosecute?"

Geraldine thought a moment and shook her head. "I am in a complete quandary. I am not sure what I should do. I hate to make a scandal of this unsavory situation. They have actually stolen from me. I'm thinking I will confer with their father, James's brother Roger, to see if we can work this thing out between us. I just feel terrible about all of this. I plan on sending him a wire and will wait to hear from him. Does that seem like a good possible solution?"

Jakob agreed and felt it was the best way to handle the problem. "It would be for the father to make good on the losses, even if the nephews should be responsible themselves."

They had finished their drinks and Annabelle was ready to take their dinner order. Jakob looked at Geraldine and suggested another martini.

Geraldine looked as if in a quandary and declined.

"I don't ordinarily have a second." They talked continuously. Jakob found her to be serious, but with a pleasant sense of humor. He learned about the operation of the ranch. She told him it had been difficult and the current problem hadn't made it any easier for her. She liked Wyoming but was lonesome for her family and home. "I want this to be my success. I am sure James would have been a success. We have invested much. When Oliver Henry left, he was fair to us in the terms of the sale."

They ate their dinner and Jakob recommended the apple pie, so Geraldine tried it.

"Jakob, if I continue eating like this I will need a new wardrobe."

Jakob just laughed and said he was sure no such thing would happen.

"I have been doing all the talking, but I haven't heard much about you."

Jakob just smiled. "Now tell me about Jakob. There is more to him than just a dentist . . . not that a dentist isn't a lot."

"You saw that bear on the wall of my office, didn't you?"

"Yes, I did. How dangerous it must have been."

"That's right. How big and dangerous he was. He was nearly the end of me when I left my office and went hunting. So now, I stay close to the office and I'm safe there."

"Oh, you silly. You can't mean that you were attacked by the bear?"

"Well, that could have been the end of Jakob, but there's been more than that to the story. I love my profession and the people I take care of. Life in Sheridan has been interesting. I have my little BethAnn and I love her so. You are going to have to meet her. I know you will love her too. Like you, I have a loss too. It is sometimes insurmountable, but we have to go on. I'm finding my way in the people around me—the new people I meet, like you. It's just nice to be able to have dinner together and to talk with you."

"Well, thank you, Jakob. It so nice for you to say that. I guess I pretty much feel the same as you do. It is so nice to have become reacquainted with you. I'm going back to the ranch tomorrow. I have much at stake there and I feel I should go back and try to put things together."

"You didn't tell me about the foreman. Is he capable of handling things? Can he be trusted?"

"George Roberts has been around for many years. He was Oliver Henry's foreman and I am sure he is capable, and I believe he can be trusted. I want to thank you, Jakob, for your help. You have no idea how good I feel knowing there is someone around I can talk with. I'll be back in town, but I'm not sure just when. Maybe I can buy you dinner next time with a martini, since I know you like them. The Oliver Henry Ranch is not that far. Maybe you'll find your way out there. That's an open invitation. You could even bring BethAnn with you and we could show her an operating ranch. I want to meet her. I'm also going to keep my eye out for a pony."

"I just might take you up on the invitation. I better get going, now." Jakob got up, followed by Geraldine. They got as far as the door when Jakob turned to face her; Geraldine moved close to him and placed a kiss on his cheek.

"Thank you, Jakob, for everything, especially for being the friend I really needed." She turned and went up the stairs to her room, and Jakob left for home.

Chapter 30

Sheridan County Fair

BethAnn stopped before a squaw who had beaded dresses displayed on the ground before her tepee.

"Daddy, I would like to have one of these dresses. I have some money from a Christmas gift I got from Grandmother Jensen. I'd like to buy it. Do you like it?" The squaw recognized BethAnn liked the dress and held it up for them to view, turning it from back to front and saying something that sounded like "two dollar."

Jakob smiled: "You don't have anything like that. Do you think you would like it? Would it fit you?"

"Oh, yes. I really would like it. I could try it on and see if it fits me."

"Go ahead, try it on and see how it fits." He spoke in his best Indian, but mainly in sign language, as BethAnn tried on the dress. It was too small so the Indian immediately gave her a bigger one to try.

"This one is bigger and I can fit into it. It's even a little loose on me and I like it more than the other one. See, this one has a deer on it."

"If that's the one you want, show her the two dollars and see if she will take it." The woman seemed satisfied and BethAnn had her dress.

The Sheridan County Fair was ready to open. Jakob had been working on it since Mayor Burns asked him to serve on the committee some years ago. At first he was not interested in doing it, but he had done the job for eight years and actually enjoyed it. He had recruited enough people to help him judge the various contests and races. It gave him an opportunity to work with many different people. Each year the fair had gotten bigger, and this year was expected to be the biggest. The fair was an opportunity for old friends and families to gather for a good time.

The various Indian tribes would usually come and participate. The Crow and Cheyenne would come in their wagons and set up their tepees along the Big and Little Goose Creeks. They would also enter the various contests, but they especially liked the horse races. The Indians were very competitive and skilled riders. Jakob felt they, at times, were treated unfairly if it was a close race. All too often the white man was considered first. When Jakob judged the races, he would not let his opinion be swayed by racial difference. The fair was also an opportunity for the squaws to sell or barter off their wares of fancy buckskins, bead-work and moccasins.

Jakob had taken BethAnn with him to the tribal areas to visit some of his Indian friends, when they stopped and bought her the dress. He had always taken care of them when they were in need and was trusted by them, so they considered him their friend. During the fair, they put on their special dress and entertained the interested white people who came by. They usually invited Jakob to their powwows where he would be seated with the Chiefs.

"Daddy, tonight when we go to the powwow I'll wear my dress. Will I be with Moon Song and her girls?"

"I would think so. She usually wants you to be with her." Moon Song had been one of Liz's pupils and had learned to read and write English.

The fair was always a very busy time for Jakob, mainly because of the many visitors who came. There were those who also tried to get their dental needs taken care of. Some were very serious and required a lot of his time. The various contests sometimes produced injuries as a result of accidents to the participants. Doctors Kelly and Ross, as well as the other new doctors who had come to Sheridan, had their share of injuries to care for. Sheridan was no longer the small Western town Jakob had first experienced; it had grown considerably to over three thousand people.

BethAnn had raised rabbits and was prepared to enter them for judging with the other small farm animals. She and some of her friends were excited to participate. It was her first time to compete in the Fair. They had been encouraged by her teacher to enter her rabbits which she had raised from little bunnies.

Jakob was at the racetrack grounds helping to register the various cowboys who would enter the horse races, when he noticed several cowboys from the Oliver Henry Ranch. In the background and in saddle was a tall, slender lady in Western attire whom he immediately recognized. It was Geraldine Widicker, who then dismounted and waved her hat to Jakob. There were also some girls registering to enter the races, but this lady was in a class of her own. Jakob made his way to her and they met.

"Geraldine! What a pleasant surprise!" They embraced. They both seemed to realize what they had done and suddenly let their arms down, and then almost embarrassed just looked at each other, smiling.

"Geraldine, when did you arrive?"

"I got here yesterday with some of my cowboys. I wondered where I'd find you. I stopped by your office and found the sign saying you would be at the fair."

"Oh, I've been here and there and everywhere around here. I always work at the fair. I wear many hats here and judging the horse races is one of them. I'm so glad to see you. How about dinner tonight?"

"That would be just fine. Remember now, Jakob. I owe you this one."

"No, you don't. You're still my guest, remember? And besides, I asked you first." Geraldine shook her head.

"Don't shake your head at me Lady Geraldine or I won't let you ride in the races."

"You don't have to worry about that. I wasn't planning to ride in the races. But my men will be showing off my best horses and I know a couple of them will also be racing. I'm sure you wouldn't interfere in that, would you?"

Jakob laughed. "No, I wouldn't do that. We'll worry about who pays later."

"Doctor, you can be very difficult. Is your daughter BethAnn here? I really want to meet her."

"Yes, she's here. And I want you to meet her. BethAnn is over at the small farm animals barn. She has raised and entered her rabbits for judging and is really excited. We can go over to see her. They are probably doing the judging right now."

Geraldine was leading her horse as they started walking toward the small farm animals barn. Jakob looked at her in her attractive Western dress and commented. "You shore look mighty pretty in dat outfit. Bet the folks back in Hereford wouldn't recognize you."

"Silly. You think all we do is wear long dresses and big hats at Hereford and Landry Manor? Well, sometimes we wear other outfits like top hats, shirts with ties, coats and riding britches . . . and . . . " She burst out laughing. "You like to make fun of me, don't you? Just because I'm English."

Jakob smiled. "No, I don't make fun of you. But I do like to tease you. Here we are, let's go inside." Geraldine tied her horse to a fence and they walked into a large building with foul smells and noises. People were milling around. There was noise, loud talk and children were running around everywhere. Some were holding ducks and chickens and others were leading goats and sheep.

"Oh, there she is! What do you know, it looks like she has a ribbon." They pushed and shoved their way through the crowd, until they reached the caged small animals. BethAnn saw Jakob.

"Daddy! Daddy. Look, I have a ribbon. I won a ribbon for my Dilly." And she took Jakob's arm and pulled him over to the cage where she proudly displayed the ribbon.

"BethAnn, that is so nice. I am so proud of you. You raised that rabbit from a tiny little bunny. You took such very good care of it, and look, it won you a ribbon." He took her up in his arms and kissed her as she hugged him.

"I have someone with me I want you to meet, and she wants to meet you. She is a special friend." BethAnn faced Geraldine and at first cautiously, and then smiled.

"Hello, I'm BethAnn. What is your name?" Geraldine saw a beautiful little girl with a smile that made you immediately fall in love with her.

"My name is Geraldine and I'm so happy to meet you. How wonderful. You won a ribbon for your rabbit. You should be proud for the achievement. I'm proud to know someone who won a ribbon. Your daddy told me a lot about you, and now I know why he loves you so much."

BethAnn blushed a little, smiling. "Thank you for saying that to me. My daddy and I are friends and I know he loves me. Do you live in Sheridan?"

"No, I don't live in Sheridan. I live on a ranch near the Bighorn Mountains. I raise horses and cows. I brought some horses to show the people here in Sheridan. They are special horses. Some of them will be sent back to the country I came from. I was born in England. Do you know where that is?"

"England? Oh, England is far away from here."

"Yes, it is far away. Would you like to see some of my horses? I would like to show them to you." BethAnn was excited and asked Jakob if they could go see her horses. At first thought he had other things to do and wanted to get back to them, but he acquiesced to BethAnn and agreed to see the horses. They walked some distance to where Geraldine had set up her horses and wagons for their stay at the fair. She had brought a number of very fine animals for showing. She pointed out several which would be raced. The men were proud of the animals and led them in front of Jakob and BethAnn.

BethAnn reached up and touched and petted several of the horses. Then she noticed one they had not brought to her. It looked smaller then the rest.

"What kind of a horse is that?" she asked.

Geraldine smiled. "Oh, that one. I wondered when you would ask about her." She gestured to one of the men. "George, BethAnn would like to see Nelly. Would you bring her here?" When he arrived with the horse, he handed the reins to Geraldine. BethAnn went up to the horse and pet it. The horse moved its head down and BethAnn put her hands on both sides of its head, then put her arm around its neck and petted her.

"Oh, she's so beautiful and not so big as the others, so I can hug her. I like her color. She is mostly brown."

"They call that color sorrel."

"Did you say her name is Nelly?" Geraldine smiled and nodded. "Oh, you're so pretty, Nelly." Nelly snorted as BethAnn continued to pet her.

"Do you like her?"

"Oh, yes I do. She is so nice."

"Would you like to have her?" BethAnn's eyes widened.

"Oh! Yes, I would." Jakob looked at Geraldine and his mouth opened to speak.

"I brought her here for you, BethAnn. I want you to own her. She will be yours." Both BethAnn and Jakob were momentarily unable to speak.

"I don't have a little girl to give a pony to. Actually, she is a mustang. I know you, and I want you to have her. She needs to have you to take care of her." BethAnn was speechless as she held the pony, slowly stroking it.

"Geraldine, this is wonderful but we have to talk about this."

"What's there to talk about, Jakob? I just gave your daughter a pony. You said you wanted her to have a pony, didn't you?"

"Yes, but . . ."

"There are no buts. BethAnn has a pony." BethAnn left the pony and went to Geraldine, put her arms around her and thanked her. Geraldine stooped down and kissed her as BethAnn returned the kiss, thanking her again. "I know you will love and take care of Nelly and you will enjoy having her. Your daddy will buy a saddle so you can ride her. She is gentle and you will enjoy her." Jakob, shaking his head, looked at Geraldine questioningly.

"Geraldine, what can I say? You certainly made my little girl very happy, and me too. What can I say but thank you. I still can't believe your generosity and kindness. There are a couple of saddle makers here at the fair. I will see if one of them might have a saddle for Nelly."

"I'll keep Nelly here and tomorrow we'll bring her over to your place. Is that all right, BethAnn? As long as she is here maybe the saddle maker can take a look at her, in case he has to make a saddle."

"Oh, yes, whatever is the best thing to do." BethAnn petted and hugged the horse. "Daddy, she is mine. I just can't believe I have this beautiful horse. We can go riding together and I'll have my own horse." BethAnn was in ecstasy.

"We have a lot to do to get ready for Nelly. So maybe we better go back and get your rabbit and take it home. And we have to stop by and see the saddle makers. Say your goodbyes now." BethAnn went back to Geraldine. She thanked her again and hugged her.

"Good-bye Nelly. I'll see you tomorrow and then you can come home with me." They left, with BethAnn looking back as they led the horse back to the corral.

When they arrived home from the fair, BethAnn ran into the house to find Chucha and the news of the pony exploded from her. She was so thrilled, almost beyond words and Chucha listened as she described the pony. The news of her ribbon for the rabbit now took low priority. Jakob told Chucha he would be having dinner with a friend at the Inn.

"Are you going to have dinner with Geraldine, Daddy? She is so nice. I just can't believe she gave me the horse. I love it. I will take care of it. I really will." Jakob picked up BethAnn and hugged her and kissed her.

"That was very nice of Geraldine to give you the horse. She is a nice lady and I am glad she gave it to you. We will have lots of fun together riding. Maybe sometime we can ride out to her ranch to see her. Okay now get yourself washed up for dinner. I am going to meet Geraldine for dinner and I will tell her again how happy she made you." BethAnn left the room skipping and up the stairs to her room.

Jakob could now clean up and dress. He checked carefully which shirt he should wear with what pants, whether he should wear a coat. *Oh my gosh, I have to hurry or I'll be late.* Looking into the mirror he sobered up. *What's the matter with me?*

Taking the stairs to the Sheridan Inn two at a time, he was quickly inside. Henry Clayton was at the desk.

"Jakob, what are you doing here? I thought you'd still be at the fair tending the races."

"Well, Henry, I just thought maybe the dining room needed some business, so I came for dinner."

"Oh-oh, now I get it. Well, she's in there waiting for you." Jakob grinned and went into the dining room and Annabelle directed him to the table where Geraldine sat. A lady wearing a powder blue light dress with matching hat and gloves, and a long string of pearls, was waiting for him.

"Lady Geraldine, I presume," he said and he picked up her hand and kissed it. She looked up at him and smiled, then shook her head a little.

"Well, Sir Jakob, I didn't think you liked my other outfit so I put on something a little more appropriate, but I just can't win, can I?"

"Oh my Lady, you have won. You look ravishing." He turned to Annabelle. "Annabelle, would you bring this lady and me a martini. A William special for a special evening."

"Jakob, you are something else. Saying things like that makes me feel young again."

"What do you mean by young again? You *are* young and you're beautiful."

"Jakob, stop it. You are going to make me blush." Jakob smiled and took her hand.

"I do mean what I said. You are beautiful and you do beautiful things. That was very nice, what you did for BethAnn. I can't ever repay you. You just made that sweet child very happy. Oops, our martini is here." They lifted their drinks. "Here's to a very sweet lady."

"Jakob, when I heard about BethAnn, I just knew I had to give her the pony. You are so fortunate to have her. We didn't have children and I really wanted them. But . . . I . . . I'm really happy BethAnn likes Nelly. She will be a good breed for her."

"I really didn't expect to see you so soon. I had completely forgotten about the fair. Otherwise, I might have realized that you would be back. Hooray for the fair! I missed you."

"Really." Geraldine smiled, looking at Jakob. "Hmm . . . it's nice to know I've been missed, because I missed you too." Lukas came up to the table and sat down.

"Doc, I didn't expect to see you with all the goings on at the Fair, but I'm glad you're here with this lovely lady. My pleasure to see you again Ma'am. I jes wanted to stop by and say hello and tell you about a couple things I got for specials. I got a special wild duck with a chokecherry sauce, and I got a spring lamb rack. I know you'd like it, Doc. It's my pleasure to see you, Geraldine. You folks can finish your drinks. Bon appetite." And Lukas went back to his kitchen.

"He's really fond of you, Jakob."

"Oh, we've been friends since I came to Sheridan. Another martini?"

"No. One was just perfect."

"Okay, we'll just have one tonight. I've been wanting to ask you about the problem with the nephews. What's happening?"

"I took it up with their dad, as I said I would. As of now, the issue is not resolved. I have sent them back to England. Their father should know enough to do the honorable thing. The issue is closed for now."

"And you don't want to talk about it any more, right?" Geraldine nodded in the affirmative. They each enjoyed their dinner and Jakob ordered a port wine. They spoke like they had known each other for ages.

"It's still light out, and will be for another hour. Let's go for a ride and I'll show you some things you may not have seen in Sheridan." Jakob helped Geraldine into the buggy and they slowly went through town and on to the trail to Big Horn. Jakob pointed out landmarks along the way, then they stopped alongside a stream. It was silent except for the sounds of the moving water. They watched birds circling in the sky, and heard the rustle of them, in the brush. Jakob looked at Geraldine.

"Pleasant here, isn't it? I sometimes come here, when I want to be alone. It gives me a chance to, I don't know , sort of meditate, to think about my life and where it's taking me. Do you ever feel that way?"

Geraldine was silent. She looked into Jakob's eyes and shook her head back and forth slowly. "I'm seeing a different side of Jakob Miller— a serious side, I had not seen. I like it and can understand it. Where is your life taking you?"

"I'm not sure. I know what I must do. I have a beautiful daughter and I must do my best for her. I love her so much. Do you understand?"

"Yes, I do understand. And what about Jakob? Where is he going?"

"I . . . I don't exactly know. I do know one thing," he said looking seriously at Geraldine. "I know I could care about you." Geraldine was silent and groping for what to say. Then she answered slowly.

"And I could care about you. But we hardly know each other."

"That's right, we hardly know each other. But we can learn about each other. I want to learn everything I can about Geraldine, and we'll start tomorrow at dinner."

And she laughed. "Oh, Jakob, you take a melodramatic moment and you make me laugh. Dinner tomorrow it will be. I do have to leave for the ranch Friday, so we'll have one more day. We also have to get Nelly to your place tomorrow. So please take me back to the Inn."

"Okay, I'll take you back, but only if you give me a kiss when we get there." Geraldine started to laugh and shook her head.

"Why are you laughing?"

"You don't have to coerce me."

Chapter 31

Lady Geraldine

Jakob and BethAnn brought Nelly home. BethAnn was in a seventh heaven. One of the saddle makers at the fair had a saddle she could use on Nelly. He also said he would make one especially for her, and it would even have her name engraved on it. She couldn't wait to put the saddle on Nelly. Geraldine came with them and instructed BethAnn. Jakob hadn't realized Geraldine was an expert horsewoman. She had a horse as a youngster and had taken part in many equestrian events in England. Geraldine spent several hours with BethAnn teaching her what she needed to know to own a horse. BethAnn was eager and learned fast. Before leaving, Geraldine invited Jakob and BethAnn to her ranch so she could give her more lessons in horsemanship. Geraldine even suggested BethAnn could stay several weeks with her. BethAnn was thrilled with the idea. She couldn't wait until she and Jakob could go for a ride in the nearby countryside, but Jakob had to go back to his office to see some patients and Geraldine had to return to the fair to finish her business there. But before leaving she and Jakob made plans to meet for dinner at the Sheridan Inn.

Jakob saw some patients who had come from Buffalo. They couldn't wait until he made his yearly trek there. His day seemed to drag on, as he was anxious to get back to the fair to make sure everything was taken care of. However, there were moments throughout the day when thoughts of Geraldine came to him.

He finally got back to the fair in time to be able to judge two races. His clock was ticking and he hurriedly left for home. When he arrived, BethAnn was ready to go riding with him; she had Nelly saddled up. He had to find enough time for them to spend at least an hour together. She was so thrilled with this new adventure. BethAnn wore her Indian outfit over her Levi's. She mounted Nelly and proudly rode her mustang alongside Jakob and would wave at people they knew. They stopped to see several of her friends to show Nelly to them and BethAnn promised to let them ride her sometime. The ride ended all too soon for BethAnn and she led her pride and joy into the barn. She had already learned how to water and feed the horse and to groom it. Chucha called her for supper and the young horsewoman was almost too excited to eat. But she washed up and sat down with Chucha because Jakob would be meeting Geraldine for dinner.

Jakob tied his rig in front of the Sheridan Inn with a number of others already there. The Inn was busy and there was a lot of activity. The veranda was filled with young men and women, and he noticed Bill Cody was among them. With the fair on, it was a good time for him to audition new people for his traveling show. Jakob stopped to watch for a few minutes but was anxious to see Geraldine. Henry Clayton greeted him as he entered the Inn.

"I normally don't see you very often and now, I see you three days in a row. Glad to see you, Doc. There's a beautiful lady in the dining room and I think she might be waiting for you."

"Thanks Henry. If she's beautiful, you can be sure I will see her." Jakob and Henry both laughed. The dining room was crowded with guests but Geraldine stood out in her multicolored organdy dress. A jade necklace adorned her slender neck, and her hair was perfectly styled. She saw Jakob enter the room and gave him a most seductive smile.

"Jakob, dinner is on me tonight. You do understand that, don't you." He smiled and kissed her cheek as he sat down."

"You win, my Lady. I'm at your disposal. I hope you didn't have too wait long. I took BethAnn for a short ride. She is just beside herself. I just had to go out with her. She and the horse were waiting and ready for me. I am so happy for her. You have no idea how happy you have made her."

"I do know how happy she is, because I've been there. I remember when my papa gave me my first horse. I was seven and happy beyond words. It was my birthday. My papa was so good to me—he did spoil me. I was his first girl, and he did like girls . . . something like you, Jakob." Jakob was smiling at Geraldine when he became aware Annabelle was waiting to take their drink order.

"You folks want to order the usual, a martini?"

"That's right, Annabelle. Tell William to make one of his specials." Looking back at Geraldine, Jakob smiled. "What makes you think I like girls? Well, maybe I do. There's nothing wrong in that, is there? I also like ladies—special ones like the one sitting across the table from me."

"I also think you are a bit of a flirt, Sir Jakob." Jakob took on a hurt appearance.

"Do you really feel I flirt? Well, maybe with you. But then just a little." Annabelle brought the martinis, Jakob picked up his glass, followed by Geraldine, and they touched them together to toast the evening.

"You're leaving tomorrow, aren't you? You know I will miss you."

"And I'll miss you too. But we have things we must do. You with your patients and me with my ranch. I do want you to come and visit me and to bring BethAnn with you. I haven't seen very much of her and I can't help but love her. I never realized how much I miss not having children. Do you understand?" Annabelle came with the menu for the evening and suggested the fresh brook trout. They both agreed to the fish and Annabelle left. Jakob continued with the discussion.

"Yes, I do understand. We both have losses in our lives and having BethAnn takes up part of the loss for me. It gives me something to live for. I also have something to look forward to when I go home. Maybe someday you will be able to fill the void you have in your life. You are a very nice person and you deserve better. We both have things to sort out."

"Thank you, Jakob. You give me hope. I like to talk with you. Sometimes it is hard to express my feeling with people, but you are so easy to talk to. I feel you have compassion and empathy. I will miss you. Sometimes I feel I just must talk with someone who understands me. I think you understand me." Looking soulfully into Jakob's eyes, she looked almost fearful or lonely, then she suddenly smiled. "Oh, don't bother with me. I'm just being silly." Jakob took her hands and squeezed them.

"No, you're not. Somehow I feel we can work things out."

Annabelle was setting the dinners down on the table. "Would you like a glass of wine with dinner?"

Geraldine answered No, I don't think so. The martini was just fine. The dinner looks delicious."

Then Jakob looked at Geraldine and said, "You know, I really do like talking with you." As they ate, they had light conversation about the events at the fair. One of her cowboys had won a race and the showing of her horses proved to be successful. Someone there had an interest in buying some, so Geraldine felt her display of her horses was worthwhile. They finished their dinner and Jakob ordered a dessert wine for them to sip. Jakob took her hand.

"We've seen each over these last couple months more than just a few times. I remember you from the party at Oliver Henry's ranch and I knew your husband, but we never did get to talk about each other's lives. I think you know something about me, but I have learned very little about you. I know you came from England and I know you're beautiful." Geraldine smiled. "I know I care about you. England is a big and important country. But where in England are you from? I know your father loved you, or loves you, and you are Lady Geraldine. Does that mean you are a daughter of an English Lord? Did I put too big of load on you?" Jakob smiled and looked rather quizzically at Geraldine.

"You have given me a big task to explain my existence, but I'll try to fill your request. My father was the third son of an earl, so he didn't inherit the title and properties. And I am the first daughter of the Baron of Landry Manor. It's in Suffolk, a train ride from London. My home is not exactly an English castle but it is pretty fancy. I have a younger brother who will inherit the titles and all that goes with them. Also, I have two younger sisters. So when I said my father spoiled me, he also spoiled the others. It's just I was first. His name is Gerald Randolph Landry the Third, and because I was the first child they named me after him. My mother's name was Mary Sarah, so that name was given to my first sister. I think Mama wanted me named after her, but my papa wasn't taking any chances his name wouldn't be perpetuated. My brother was then named Randolph Edward Landry the Third after my grandfather and great-grandfather.

And, last of all, my other sister is Eleanor Jane. So that takes care of my family. Are you following me?"

"Of course I'm following you, and it sounds exciting." Geraldine lifted her eyebrows and smiled.

"My mother had a difficult delivery, so when I arrived there was much joy. Consequently, my middle name is Joy and Papa always said I was his joy. Sometimes he called me Joy instead of Geraldine, to a point. Papa did treat me special but my mama did give me her special attention too. I think both could have given more attention to the others, and I sometimes felt resentment among them. Maybe it's just me, because I do have a fine relationship with my siblings. When I became of age they were concerned I was not yet wed. There were some who pursued me, but I couldn't accept. When I turned twenty-one there became more concern I might end up an old maid. I guess I had turned down too many but I liked my life as it was. The birthday horse was my first. Soon I was riding other and better trained horses and was going to various events and shows, which added to my independence.

"James Widicker's family were old friends of my family and soon he was coming to parties at my father's home. There were some business ties between the families as well, and James had some nobility. They liked him and he was very personable. He did have a Cambridge education and some athletic ability playing rugby, and we became tennis partners, though in singles I was his match. I enjoyed being with him and I thought I loved him. He asked me to marry him and I was encouraged to do so. We then were married. He was twenty years older than I. He had money and a degree in law, but did not practice law. We were happy but there were times when I wondered if we were right for each other. Sometimes I felt he was bored.

"It was his idea to come to America and get involved with ranching. Oliver Henry was an uncle of his, or maybe just a cousin. I'm not sure which. He agreed to take us in and learn the business and I think our families were glad to have us go. There were some financial concerns. I became bored. James didn't seem to be interested in children and it bothered me a great deal. He loved to play cards and we didn't do too much together. If I went riding, I went alone. There were other things we faced. When we took over the ranch it became even more difficult. Then he became ill, and we went back to England. The rest is . . . oh you don't want to hear anymore." She looked down at the table and was silent. Jakob felt at a loss for words and remained silent too.

"I'm sorry, if I pried. I didn't mean to. It sounds like you did have some very happy times, but then maybe things didn't turn out the way you expected. I guess it's part of life. I had my ups and downs too. At the moment I see all isn't lost. In fact, I see a way for both of us. I'm glad we met. Sometimes I have a need to have someone to lean on. It's still light out. Let's leave and go out for a while. I have another favorite place to show you." Geraldine's face lightened up and she smiled.

"Where to this time, Sir Jakob?" They left the Inn and watched some of the performers do their acts on the grass in front of the veranda as Bill Cody watched and directed them to perform. There was a lot of laughter and the booming voice of the colonel directing them.

"Want to stay here and watch more of this? I'll take you over and introduce you to him later. He's an interesting character."

"Oh no, let's do as you suggested. Take me to one of your special haunts. This day is too beautiful to waste our time here." Jakob helped Geraldine into the buggy and they were soon riding out of town along Big Goose Creek. They stopped at a rise above the creek with a view of the mountains. Jakob helped Geraldine out of the buggy and took a blanket and spread it on the ground. They sat and looked out on a pond watching a flock of ducks frolicking in the water.

"Do you like living here in Wyoming or do you miss England and your home?"

"Sometimes I'm not sure if I am happy here. Since I lost James, I get very lonesome for Suffolk. I'm here because I have to be. I've thought of selling the ranch many times since I came back, yet during these past months I have had some of my happiest moments."

"Well, that's good. Seems we're making some progress." Jakob chuckled and Geraldine broke into a big smile.

"You have given me something to look forward to."

"And what is that?"

"I expect a visit from you and BethAnn at the ranch, and I'll have you both all to myself."

"We'll be out to visit you. It will be good for BethAnn. I know she likes you and it will be good for her to become better acquainted with you. I still feel you have been so good to her and so generous. To see her so happy gives me great pleasure."

"Look, Jakob, the moon is starting to rise. Maybe we should go back now. As much as I would like to stay another day, I really should leave tomorrow." Jakob took up the blanket and put it in the buggy. He started to help her into the buggy when they suddenly came close together, and he momentarily stopped. Their lips were almost touching. His arms encircled her and he moved to kiss her tenderly. They parted with their lips almost touching, and she drew him close. They kissed again. Geraldine let her arms drop and climbed into the buggy. Both were quiet. Neither said a word but Geraldine moved close to Jakob as they rode slowly down the trail.

They stopped at the Inn and Jakob tied the horse to the rail, then helped Geraldine out of the buggy. There were still people on the veranda talking. He took Geraldine up to her room and opened the door for her. He again put his arms around her and drew her close to him.

She put her arms around Jakob and they kissed. Parting, Jakob said, "I'm going to miss you." She drew close to him and put her hands on his face and drew his lips to her and tenderly kissed them. Geraldine smiled to him and slowly closed the door. Jakob hesitated and walked down the hall and stairs, out of the Inn, and left for home.

Chapter 32

A Test of Courage

Jakob came home after seeing Geraldine to her hotel room. BethAnn was still up and waiting for him. She was thrilled about her horse and talked excitedly about it. Geraldine made a big hit with her. He could tell BethAnn really liked her. She treated BethAnn as a mother would relate to her daughter. Jakob realized his love and care for BethAnn could never replace what only a loving mother would give her. He thought about Liz. *If only you were here. BethAnn really needs your love, your care. It can't possibly be matched by mine. I see her growing and I see you. She is so much like you in every way* . BethAnn seemed to be growing so fast, as well as her acceptance of responsibilities at her age seemed incredible. Jakob and BethAnn talked about the fair and how proud he was she had won a ribbon for her raising the rabbit. She then asked Jakob about Geraldine, and if he had seen her.

"Did Geraldine ask about me, Daddy? She is so nice. Why did she give me Nelly? She didn't really know me. I guess you must have told her about me. Did you Daddy? I am so happy and I will take good care of Nelly. Do you think we can go see Geraldine at her ranch? She asked us to visit her. That would be fun. I would like to see her other horses. Do you think she will teach me how to do tricks with Nelly?" BethAnn talked incessantly; she was so excited. They sat on the porch swing, with BethAnn keeping the conversation going, as she cuddled next to him. The moon was up full and she turned her conversation to the moon. "Why isn't the moon as bright as the sun? Do you know why, Daddy?" Jakob would try to answer her questions as best he could. "Daddy, do you think Skippy will like Nelly? I won't be able to play with him as much now because I'll be taking care of Nelly." Jakob looked intently at BethAnn.

"I don't think Skippy will mind. He'll still knows you love him because you will also do things with him, and you won't be with Nelly all the time. Skippy will be with you in the house."

"Oh yes, Daddy, I will still be with Skippy a lot. Do you think Chucha will like Nelly?"

"I'm sure she will like her, but you could ask her."

"Oh, sure she'll like her. Why wouldn't she like her? She's friendly. But I will ask her anyway." BethAnn could hold a conversation with almost anyone and she loved to talk. Jakob patiently answered her questions. Chucha entered the porch and announced the time, and asked if BethAnn wanted some milk and a freshly-baked *kolacky,* a type of biscuit with fruit on it.

"Oh yes! Mmm, I'll have one."

"Well, Dolly, it's getting late and time for you to go to bed. You go have your milk and *kolacky*." BethAnn turned to Jakob and gave him a hug and kiss, then went into the kitchen to get her treat. "Don't forget to brush your teeth and I'll be up to tuck you in." Having BethAnn had been such a delight. He would often say, "She is my reason to live."

When he lost Liz he had gone into a depression, and BethAnn was the one to give him the motivation to go on with his life. It had been five years since he lost Liz, and now Geraldine entered into his life. He has some pangs of guilt and regret because she was there and he still couldn't forget the one he loved so much. There was still the lingering sorrow, he just couldn't shake. He fully knew his loneliness for Liz had to be put aside and he had to go on living but it was a challenge for him. Thinking about BethAnn made Jakob realize she too, needed someone to take the place of Liz. *Could someone like Geraldine do that? Would she have in her heart, the same feeling for BethAnn, as she would for her own daughter? She seems like she could, but how could I ever know for sure? I think I can control my feelings, but can BethAnn? She is just a child and I must protect those feelings. Geraldine once said she wanted children. Would BethAnn fulfill those desires?*

Jakob was beginning to realize Geraldine was getting to be more than just a friend, but did he know her well enough? *I better start controlling my own emotions,* he thought while sitting on the swing with the moon overhead; he was plagued with mixed feelings. As he sat their trying to make something of them, he looked at his watch, and realized he had to return to his office the next day, so he decided to close this day and go to bed.

The Sheridan County Fair was now in the past, and he could go back to his old routine. There was an older man waiting for him as he approached his office. Jakob could see by the look on his face he was in pain. Jakob sat him in his chair and proceeded to take care of him. It was just as he was finishing up, when Andy Meeks entered his office, distressed.

"Doc Kelly asked me to come over and get you. They brought a guy in his office in pretty rough shape and he needs your help."

"Okay. Tell him I'm be over as soon as I can." Jakob cleaned up and closed the office and then went over to Doc Kelly's. A small group was gathered in front of the office. He went inside the office and saw a man lying on the table who was bloodied up.

"They brought this guy in, just a short while ago. It looks like he has been worked over and is pretty rough shape. He's been in and out of consciousness. It almost reminds me of the war, when they used a rifle butt on someone. Besides the busted teeth and facial and head lacerations, it looks like he has a broken jaw. And, it's a compound fracture. We got to do something for this guy or we may lose him." Jakob went to the man and examined his face and looked inside his mouth. There were broken teeth, cuts on one side of his jaw and the jaw was obviously broken with bone showing through the gum. He shook his head. Jakob motioned Doc Kelly to the side of the room, where he quietly spoke to Kelly so the man couldn't hear, although he seemed to be unconscious.

"Hey, Kelly, this is a compound fracture. I've never treated one. I've seen them done over at Cook County Hospital by Doctor Logan, the surgeon, but I have never done anything like this. This is beyond my expertise." He shook his head. "Uh . . . uh."

"Listen Jake, we have to do something for him, or he could be terribly disfigured or even die."

"But, Kelly, don't you understand. I'm a dentist not a bone surgeon. I know what I can and cannot do and this is one place I shouldn't be."

"Listen, Jake, we can do it. You and me. We have to Jake. There is no one else. Do you understand?" Jakob was silent and shaking his head slowly. Kelly looking him in the eyes and exclaimed, "Well?"

"Kelly, you don't understand! I'm a dentist. I'm not a bone surgeon."

"Kid, I do understand. But, we got to do something for him. You don't understand what will happen. We did battlefield injuries, not knowing the result, because there was no other choice. I have some ether here and we can put him to sleep. Do you have any wire, to wire up the break?"

"Okay. Okay. We'll do it, but God help us, because I will need His help." Jakob went to his office to get some gold wire and a few of his instruments, then returned to Doc Kelly's. The man was now awake, moaning with considerable pain. They sterilized the instruments and the wire and got him ready for the surgery. Jakob was beside himself. He had looked over his surgery book while at his office and he knew what had to be done and how to do it, but wondered if he could do it. Kelly had his anesthesia mask ready for the either, which he would administer.

Jakob stood in the corner of the room. He was praying and asking for Divine guidance, then went to the table. Kelly had already checked the patient's vitals and motioned for Jakob to be ready to start. The ether dripped into the mask. The moaning stopped and his breathing was apparent. Soon the patient was asleep and Kelly nodded. Jakob took over. He opened the mouth and started clearing the broken pieces of teeth, dirt and blood out of his mouth. He found the break in the jawbone and made the first cut. He forgot his initial fear and trepidation and went to work quickly, opening the wound and removing bone fragments. He carefully removed the roots of the broken teeth and then joined the broken jaw parts together carefully, using the wire to hold the pieces of jaw in place. Having removed all the fragments of bone in the area, he was ready to close the wound. He quickly sutured the area after making sure there were no other broken tooth pieces.

"That it, Jake?"

"I . . . I hope so." Making sure the jaw was set in proper alignment, he wrapped a bandage around the jaw and head to keep the lower jaw in place and prevent it from moving. He sutured the other cuts and was finished. Kelly took a towel and wiped the perspiration from Jakob's forehead. It was a while before the patient opened his eyes and moaned a little. He moaned and mumbled something. Kelly told him to keep quiet and he would be all right. Jakob looked at Doc Kelly and raised his eyes in relief. Kelly grinned and checked the patient's vitals, and in spite of all he had been through they seemed good. He took a towel and moistened it and then moistened the patient's lips as he cleaned up the blood. The patient moaned on and off and drifted off into sleep.

"Well Kid, you did it. I knew you could."

Jakob stood quiet and just looked on. "You know Jake, we don't even know this guy's name." When he was brought in, he remained nameless. Andy Meeks, who was waiting in the background watching, went back over to the Lucky Lady and got some ice to put on the side of the patients jaw. He also brought back a bottle of whiskey and a couple of glasses. He poured each a drink.

"Here you are gents. I think you need this." They downed their whiskey.

Doc Kelly looked at Jakob, who still appeared completely stressed. "Sit down, Kid you did a good job. I knew you could do it. He'll be all right. If this guy doesn't get an infection, we'll be in the clear." The crowd in front of Doc Kelly's office started to leave, and Kelly said the patient could stay there until that night, when they would take him over to the Commercial Hotel to stay. Some of the ladies there would take care of him. Jakob stayed around Doc Kelly's office keeping an eye on the man, while Kelly saw his other patients.

He was pretty much awake and even sitting up, so Jakob went back to his office. Jakob stayed in his office the rest of the afternoon. No one came in except the banker next door who wanted to find out what had happened over at Doc Kelly's. Jakob then left for home. In a quiet moment after dinner, he silently gave thanks for the outcome of his surgery and prayed the man would fully recover. He realized he had needed Divine guidance and felt he'd received it.

BethAnn was ready to go for a ride on her horse. The day had been stressful for Jakob, and he wanted to just stay home, but BethAnn had been waiting all day for him to take her riding and Jakob could not disappoint her. She had Nelly saddled and readied, and waited for Jakob to saddle his horse. The day was beautiful and the sun was still high enough for a good ride before it would set. They started out toward Big Horn. BethAnn looked beautiful in her outfit: white blouse with her Levi's and a wide-brimmed hat with a strap under her chin. She sat straight and looked like a professional rider. Her blonde hair was in a pony tail. Jakob saw the image of Liz in her.

BethAnn had already learned to canter, as they moved along the trail. She excitedly talked as they moved along, walking and then cantering, but not working the horses hard. Jakob could see with the right training she would one day become an expert horsewoman. They stopped along the trail and Jakob pointed out various trees and plants, as well as birds and prairie dogs and rabbits. He warned her to be aware of an occasional rattlesnake that could spook her horse.

They didn't make it to Big Horn because the sun was starting to set and he didn't want to ride in the dark. They made it back home just in time. Chucha was waiting for them and had a snack ready. The ride with BethAnn was a stress breaker for Jakob. He forgot about his trials of the day and just enjoyed his daughter. Riding their horses together was another way of enjoying each other's company.

"Daddy, do you think we could take Skippy with us the next time we go for a ride?"

"We can try and see if he will stay with us and not be tempted to run off."

"That would be great. Then he might not feel left out." Jakob sat in his chair and picked up one of his Dental Journals to read while BethAnn mimicked her dad by reading one of her books.

As usual, Jakob had a visit from Skippy who noted it was time for Jakob to get up and let him out. He then put on the coffee. As he sat in the kitchen he watched Skippy frolicking in the yard. Then he noticed him stare at something before he backed and circled around it. Jake got up and went into the yard. As he approached the dog he noted Skippy had cornered a snake. He called Skippy but the dog ignored him, so he ran into the house and got his gun. He ran back to see the snake striking at Skippy but Skippy moved quickly back. It was a rattlesnake and Jakob immediately shot it. He took Skippy back into the house and left the snake to show to the others. It was the first such incident he ever experienced since living in Sheridan. He later showed BethAnn and Chucha what had happened and warned them such predators exist and could even be close to home. He later then disposed of the carrion.

Jakob left for his office but stopped first to see Doc Kelly. The patient they had taken care of the previous day in his office; he was now identified as Robert Sears. In spite of his previous day's experience and surgery, he seemed to be doing better than expected. He had considerable pain and swelling and was badly bruised. He had spent the night in the Commercial Hotel.

He was hard to understand because his mouth was closed shut but he told the story of how he had played cards at the Rocky Saloon and had won a considerable amount of money. When the card game ended he left, taking his winnings with him. He was riding out of town toward a ranch near Big Horn, when he found himself being pulled off his horse by a rope and knocked to the ground, with men surrounding him and beating him. When he regained consciousness, his horse was gone and so was all the money he had won. He lay there all night, and then some men found him in the morning and brought him to Doc Kelly.

Jakob examined Robert and thought he was doing quite well. He even said he was hungry.

"Eating is going to be hard for you. All you can eat are things that are liquid. Anything you eat has to be ground up fine. Nothing can be chewed. That bandage around your head has to stay there and you can't move your jaw around like you would when chewing. Your jawbone has to heal before you can chew, and it can take some weeks. And only one of us can touch the bandage. It's not going to be easy for you for awhile. I want you to stay in town so we can take care of you. Understand?"

"But Doc, I ain't got no money," he said, almost indistinguishably and muffled.

"I guess we are just going to have to help you because we need to follow your progress. That jawbone has to mend or you are in real trouble. Right, Kelly?"

"It won't be the first time I had to bankroll a patient."

The next few days the patient came regularly to Doc Kelly's office. "Jake, I had to open up the wound and drain it. I got a lot of pus out of it.

"I guess we'll have to watch it and drain it as often as it needs to be." A few days later the same had to be done, but there was less pus coming out and it was finally clean and healing. Doc Kelly got some cheap whiskey from Andy Meeks and cut it with water. Then used it to clean out Robert's mouth because he couldn't open it yet. Doc Kelly told Jakob, "His mouth really stinks but the cheap whiskey wash did the trick, except he now smells like an old sot. He's lost some weight because he can't get any real food in him. Jake, how long do you think we have to keep him here?"

"You know how long it takes for bones to heal. Jawbone is no different than any other bone. The book says four to six weeks. I guess I didn't tell you but I promised to take BethAnn out to see the Oliver Henry Ranch. Geraldine Widicker said she would give her some lessons in horsemanship. This might just be a good time to take her."

"Taking BethAnn out there to get lessons in horsemanship, eh? That's pretty far for her to go for lessons in horsemanship. You sure it's the real reason you want to go? I saw you hanging out with her at the fair and having dinners at the Sheridan Inn. She's not bad lookin' Jake. How long are you going to stay? Oh! None of my business, of course. Huh?"

"Kelly, you old dog. You always try to make something out of nothing. If it weren't that she invited BethAnn, I wouldn't be going."

"Okay, Jake, you've been working hard. You deserve a few days off. I can take care of your patient."

"What do you mean my patient. He's your patient and you conned me to take care of him for you."

"Not to worry, Jake. You just go ahead and I'll be okay." And he started laughing. "When are you leaving?"

"I think I'll head out next Saturday. I don't plan on being there too long."

Jakob came home from his office early. He was greeted by BethAnn.

"Daddy, you're home early today. Would you like to go out for a ride? I think Nelly needs some exercise. It's a real nice day and I don't think it will rain."

"Well, if you don't think it will rain, maybe it would be a nice day to take a ride in the country." BethAnn was off in a flash to get Nelly ready and saddled. Jakob changed into riding clothes and met BethAnn in the barn. He had told Chucha not to make dinner for them because he was taking BethAnn out to Big Horn for dinner. He and BethAnn rode side by side and they talked as they went along.

"BethAnn, I was thinking this weekend might be a good time for us to visit Geraldine at her ranch. What do you think?"

"Really, Daddy? I think it would be great. I was wondering when we would go. I was afraid we might not go at all. I know you have been busy but I felt you might enjoy a few days off. When do you plan on leaving? Tomorrow?"

"Oh, no. We have to get everything ready and pack our clothes, and I have to make sure everything is in order here. Chucha has to take care of Skippy and the house and all those things will take some time to arrange. We can leave Saturday."

BethAnn was really excited and even though Jakob would not admit it, he too was excited. Geraldine was beginning to occupy a good deal of his extracurricular thinking. They stopped and tied up in front of the Emma's Café, in Big Horn. Emma made the best fried chicken in the West, at least that's what Jakob always told her, and she was proud of her cooking. The cafe was not big and didn't have many tables, so it was always crowded. In fact, customers had to sit outside on a bench in front when it was full. Her daughter, Annie, waited on tables. With the fried chicken, they always served cornmeal biscuits, mashed potatoes and gravy, green beans, coffee and a piece of her pie. Fortunately there was room for them inside and they were immediately seated by Annie.

"Doc Miller, we haven't seen you for a long time. This must be your daughter. How nice to have you folks come in. I know, you probably want the fried chicken."

"Of course, it's the best in the West."

"Wait till I tell Maw you're here. She'll be happy you came in." And it wasn't long before Emma was there in front of the table. She bent down and gave Jakob a big kiss on the cheek.

"Doc, it's so good to see you. How nice of you to come out to see me. And this must be your pretty little girl. I just had to come out and say hello, but now I really must get back to work or you won't get any chicken. Thanks for coming." Emma was off to the kitchen.

Jakob first met Emma when she had come to see Jakob because of pain, when he first moved to Sheridan. She was almost toothless and Jakob took out her infected teeth and made her a set of dentures. It was amazing how her personality changed to the happy, vibrant woman she was now.

They ate their fried chicken and took the leftovers home in a bag. Emma gave Jakob a big hug before they left for home. A few hours later they arrived home just as the sky turned dark. BethAnn, of course, shared her experience with Chucha.

Later, after BethAnn was in bed, Jakob told Chucha they would be going to visit Geraldine at her ranch for a while. She graciously said she would take care of the house and the dog, and for him not to worry. Jakob had already sent a letter to Geraldine with one of her men which said that they would arrive on Saturday.

Saturday morning arrived. They left at sunrise on a clear, warm and windy day. Nelly was tied behind as they rumbled off. At first, the trail was good, with not too many ruts. But as they got farther away, the trail got lumpy, as BethAnn would say. At noon, they stopped at a stream with a few nearby trees and Jakob put a blanket on the ground and they ate the lunch Chucha had prepared. Then BethAnn left and took care of Nelly. She led her carefully to the stream so she could get her drink of water, then gave her a treat of a carrot Chucha had put in the picnic basket.

After finishing their lunch, they cleaned up and put everything away. BethAnn made sure Nelly was properly tied to the wagon and they started off. The wind had died down some but the clear sky and bright sun still made the day very hot. Both of them wore wide-rimmed hats to keep as much sun off their faces as possible, but they still felt a sunburn developing.

They would see occasional riders in the distance and the mountains were looming closer. Some hills developed and the ground was largely covered with short weeds. Occasionally, a hawk was visible above, and once they saw a bunch of buzzards circling. It was later in the afternoon when Jakob saw in the distance what he thought might be the ranch. It looked like it could be some miles away. BethAnn was excited as she stared at the buildings slowly getting bigger. An occasional cloud of dust indicated the presence of a rider.

They finally came to the entrance of the Oliver Henry Ranch, where they began to see some activity. Some buildings appeared and pens for the cattle were largely empty along with a large corral for horses.

Several riders approached and welcomed them. The big ranch-style building lay ahead. The front door opened and a figure came out on the big veranda. It was Geraldine, dressed in Levi's with a white puffed-sleeve shirt and stylish riding boots. Her hair was up in a bun. This was Lady Geraldine in the attire of the West, with a smile and a wave. The wagon stopped and BethAnn was off and running in leaps and bounds and into the arms of Geraldine before Jakob even got off the wagon and tied up the horse. Jakob mused at the display of friendship for a long moment. And then he slowly walked up the steps to the veranda. He approached

Geraldine and placed a friendly kiss on her cheek, as BethAnn looked on standing next to her.

"Welcome to the Olive Henry Ranch, Jakob and BethAnn." Jakob took her two hands, then squeezed them.

"It's nice to be here and we thank you for your gracious invitation."

"Come into the house. You must be thirsty after the long ride. I have some cold lemonade which was just made for you." They went into the large, breezy living area and sat across from the massive fireplace. Jakob immediately remembered the room filled with laughing people, with Oliver in the midst of his guests holding a bottle of Scotch. It was a different day then, and a different event they had attended. BethAnn quickly finished her lemonade and jumped up.

"Oh my. I forgot about Nelly. I have to take care of her." Geraldine laughed.

"BethAnn, you don't have to worry about Nelly while you're here. My men have already taken care of her. She is in the barn being watered and will soon be fed. You are a thoughtful young lady to have remembered. I'm so proud of you."

"Oh, I love her. And she depends on me."

"BethAnn, how old are you? Jakob, I can't believe this. BethAnn acts so responsibly. How did she ever get that way?"

"I'm seven, Geraldine, and soon I'll be eight. Nelly needs me and if I don't care for her she will be unhappy." Geraldine got up and went over to BethAnn, then hugged her and kissed her on the cheek.

BethAnn smiled. "Oh. Geraldine you are so nice. I love you." Jakob was taken aback by the display of affection between BethAnn and Geraldine. He just looked on and said nothing. He had hardly ever talked about Geraldine with BethAnn.

"I bet you two are tired from your long ride. I'll take you up to your rooms and you can clean up and rest if you wish before we have supper. Little Deer has prepared your rooms for you."

They climbed the big staircase to the second floor. BethAnn looked around the massive ranch house and said nothing as Geraldine took each one to their room. She had prepared BethAnn's room for a young lady. It had frilly curtains, a bed covered with stuffed animals, and a doll placed on the pillow. BethAnn looked around and smiled, then she looked at Jakob.

"Daddy, isn't this room pretty?" Jakob agreed. When he was here for the party he and Liz had slept in it, but it was decorated completely different. Geraldine took Jakob to his room. Opening the door, she walked in with him. It was tastefully decorated in English-style furnishings.

Jakob placed his suitecase on the floor and Geraldine came up to him. She put her arms around him and kissed him tenderly. A totally astonished Jakob was dumbfounded. "Welcome to my ranch, Sir Jakob. I've missed you."

Jakob was overcome by the moment but put his arms around Geraldine and drew her close to him, then looked into her eyes and kissed her. "You're welcome, Lady Geraldine. If I had known you were so lonesome, I'd have been here sooner."

Geraldine just smiled. "I'll see you in the great room before dinner for cocktails." And she closed the door behind her. Jakob crossed the room and turned facing the mirror. "Well, old boy, this looks like it may be an interesting trip." And he smiled, then loosened his shirt and took off his boots. He lay back on the bed and closed his eyes.

I wonder if she really meant it, when she said she missed me? The sun, the long ride and the early rising were enough for him to easily fall asleep.

There was a knock on the door. Jakob was startled and opened his eyes. Then there was another knock on the door. "Daddy! Daddy! Are you awake?"

"Yes, dear, come on in." BethAnn opened the door and came up to the bed.

"Daddy, this place is really something. My bedroom is just beautiful. I fell asleep almost as soon as I laid down. What time is it? It's so quiet here but I did hear someone in the hallway. Should we get up and go downstairs?"

"Sure, let's go. I had a nap and I feel great now."

"I wonder where Geraldine is?"

"I don't know, but I'll bet we can find her. Let me put on my boots and freshen up a bit before we go down, okay?"

"Take your time, Daddy. I'll meet you downstairs." And BethAnn left, closing the door behind her. *You know, I think she really likes Geraldine. At least she seems very comfortable with her.* He left the room and started down the stairs. He could now hear BethAnn giggling, so he followed the sound of voices and entered the kitchen. BethAnn was munching on a cookie.

"Well, looks who's here BethAnn, Sir Jakob of long nap. If you had slept any longer, we would have missed cocktail hour. I don't have Robert or William here, so I guess you will have to make the martinis. The gin is on the counter with the other items necessary to make them."

"I hardly slept, My Lady. And since when do you ask a guest to make the martinis?" As Jakob was at work making the martinis, a little lady with a white blouse, skirt and cap entered the room.

"Jakob and BethAnn, this is Little Deer. She does the cooking here. Later you will meet Maria who helps with the housekeeping. Little Deer, will you bring the drinks into the great room and also bring something for BethAnn." Geraldine led the way into the great room. After the drinks arrived, they sat and Jakob offered a toast. While they were seated, a big white cat slithered into the room and brushed by everybody, then finally settled in by BethAnn.

"BethAnn, I want you to meet Prince. He is the Royal cat here." BethAnn thought that was funny, as she stroked his soft white fur. He was the center of her attention. Jakob watched the cat until Geraldine spoke. "I'm so glad you were able make it here. I was wondering when you might come."

"I have been very busy and something came up that made it difficult to leave." Jakob told her about the man with the broken jaw he and Kelly had taken care of. "And I just didn't want to leave him."

"I thought about inviting some more guests and having a party, but I want to be able to get to know BethAnn better and I do want to help her with her horsemanship and teach her some of the fundamentals of riding for competition. I just know she will be good. She is such a fast learner." Jakob smiled.

"I have a question for you." Geraldine nodded. "I thought you ladies in England always rode sidesaddle." Geraldine laughed.

"Of course we do, but we are not in England. Here we ride of necessity and even for work. I will, in fact, teach BethAnn to ride sidesaddle, so when she goes to England she will feel at home. But enough of that for now."

BethAnn followed Prince out on to the veranda and left Jakob with Geraldine, sitting together on the couch, sipping their martinis. Geraldine was dressed in a flowing light-colored kaftan. Her dark hair was in a braid crossing her left shoulder. With her skin lightly tanned, she wore a light red lip rouge. Jakob studied her as she talked with just a bit of an English accent.

"You look pretty fancy tonight. I'm still essentially in my traveling clothes, which are not really correct for having dinner with Lady Geraldine."

"Oh, you silly. I don't follow the customs of those back in jolly old England. This is a different world. You look absolutely great to me." Just then Little Deer came in and told Geraldine dinner was ready to be served.

"Shall we eat now? We can talk more later. I'll get BethAnn." Geraldine left and went on the veranda and found BethAnn on a swing with Prince laying next to her. "We are going to have dinner now BethAnn. Won't you come in?"

They entered the great room and followed Little Deer into the dining room. They would be sitting at one end of the big table which was set with glass and silver on a white tablecloth. The candles in the silver candelabra were lit. Maria did the serving in her black uniform, with a white apron and white cap. "Will you have wine with dinner? I have some fine French Chardonnay."

"It's your party, Lady Geraldine."

"Then it shall be a French Chardonnay." Maria brought in the wine and carefully poured it into the large goblets. "May I then propose a toast to my dear friends?" Geraldine smiled at Jakob and then BethAnn. Jakob felt the implication and thanked Geraldine.

The dinner was exquisite with game hens and a chokecherry sauce. Jakob was impressed with Little Deer's cooking, which was culminated with a delicious chocolate mousse. They left the table and went back into the library. Jakob had not seen the library when he had visited Oliver Henry. It had a large window that faced the Bighorns. The shelves were filled with books and various small mementos. A large bust of Thomas Jefferson was among the furnishings. Little Deer brought in a decanter of cognac and two snifters. Prince took a liking to BethAnn, who asked to go back on the veranda with him.

This left Jakob with Geraldine, who found plenty to talk about. Geraldine referred to the problems she had with her husband's nephews. She had sent them back to England but wasn't sure whether she would recover her losses. The operation of the ranch became a challenge for her.

"I am grateful James made me participate in the operation of the ranch. If he hadn't I would never have been able to take over. As it is, it's really a man's job. I'm not sure the men have respect for me because I'm a woman. George, my foreman, is very important to me. He is older and has the respect of the men. I pray he will live long because I don't know what I would do without him."

Jakob could see Geraldine was an unusual woman. Coming from a sheltered background in an aristocratic family, she had to become an astute business woman. She was really more than just a taker. She was a doer. He had a deeper respect for her.

She asked Jakob about his background and his life in Milwaukee. When he had finished telling her, they both knew more about each other.

It had gotten dark and BethAnn came in, with Prince following her. She sat on the floor with Prince's head on her lap.

"I think Prince likes me. I wonder if he would get along with Skippy. Skippy doesn't seem to like other animals. He always chases squirrels."

Jakob answered, "That's the way it is in the animal world. Maybe if they took the time to learn more about each other, it would be different." And they all laughed.

"Daddy, you are so funny." BethAnn yawned and Jakob looked at his watch and noted it was ten, which is normally her bedtime.

"You have a big day ahead of you tomorrow. It's ten o'clock. Maybe you should get ready for bed." BethAnn looked a little exasperated.

"It's been a long day. I bet Little Deer will find you some of those cookies and milk before you go to bed," added Geraldine. BethAnn went into the kitchen, followed by Prince and Little Deer, who got her the bedtime snack. She finished her snack and went skipping up the steps to her room.

"I'm going to my room now and I will brush my teeth," she shouted.

Jakob followed by shouting, "And I will be right up to tuck you in bed." Jakob couldn't help but talk about what a good little girl she was, and then he went up the stairs to BethAnn's room. While being tucked in bed she lifted up her arms to hug and kiss Jakob.

"You know, Daddy, I really like Geraldine. Don't you think she's nice?"

Jakob kissed her. "Yes, I do think she is nice," and he left the room and went back to Geraldine. He sat next to her on the couch. She got up and got the cognac and poured some in their snifters. They touched their glasses and sipped some. Jakob looked into her eyes without saying anything. A smile slowly developed.

"What are you thinking, Jakob?" Jakob moved his head a little.

"I'm thinking . . . I'm thinking I'm falling in love with you. Can this be possible?"

Geraldine looked serious. She moistened her lips. She looked almost soulfully at Jakob. "Do you really? Are you sure?" She moved her lips close to his and slowly put her arms around his neck. At first her lips nearly touched his, but then they were in full contact. They parted. "Jakob, I do love you. I can't believe this is happening to me. I've thought about you since we first met that day at the Inn. I feared to believe it was true, but the more I saw you the more I knew it was true. I feared it could never be. When we were apart those weeks you were at work I feared I might lose you. I feared you might not be able to love me. But now today . . . " She held him tightly and pressed her lips against his. Jakob closed his eyes as they remained locked in an embrace. They parted and spoke softly.

Geraldine got up and took Jakob's hand. They embraced again and parted. Geraldine spoke softly. "I want you Jakob." Jakob's eyes searched hers and they moved up the long staircase to her room. The subdued lighting made the room seem almost surreal. She stood before him as he took off his boots and the shirt that she had already unbuttoned. She lifted the kaftan over her head and he saw her slender body grace the bed. He then lay next to her holding her soft body against his and they commenced making love.

Jakob awakened in the middle of the night with Geraldine's naked warm body still next to him. He kissed her softly and gathered his clothing, then went to his bedroom. His thoughts were of the grandeur of those moments spent in the arms of his love, and he soon fell asleep.

His eyes opened as he heard a soft knocking on his door. He thought for a moment.

"It's me Daddy. Are you up yet?"

Jakob smiled. "Well, not just yet, Dolly. Will you wait, so I can get myself together." He started putting on his clothes.

"That's okay, Daddy, I'm dressed. I'll meet you downstairs. See you later." Jakob lay back in his bed. His memory of the previous night was fresh. *Oh my God, what did I do?* His memory was erotically attached to thoughts of the previous night, but he felt ashamed . . . no, embarrassed. He felt he had lost complete control of his emotions. *What did I do? What did I say?* His mind went over and over what had happened. *But, I do love her and she did say she loves me and wanted me. But I took advantage of her. How could I have done it? What will she think of me? What will I say to her when we see each other?*

He got out of bed and got ready to go down, completely confused and yet feeling like he was ready to go down and reaffirm his feeling to Geraldine. Opening the door he walked to the stairs. Now he could hear laughter and conversation. Jakob walked into the kitchen where BethAnn was already eating with Geraldine sitting next to her. There was an elderly man standing nearby and Little Deer was working at the stove.

"Well, Sir Sleepyhead, glad you could make it down for breakfast. You remember George Roberts, my right-hand man and whatever it takes to run this place. I'm sure you met him when you came to Oliver Henry's party."

"Oh, certainly I remember him. It's nice to see you, George." George acknowledged Jakob and made some remarks about being happy to see him. He seemed short on words.

"George and I have a few things we need to take care of. Little Deer will get your breakfast for you. I have to go out with George to get them straightened out. I'll be back as soon as I can, then maybe I can get together with BethAnn, for some riding instruction. See you later, sleepyhead."

Jakob's concern for how to approach Geraldine after their night of romance would have to wait. *Now that the lady ranch executive is off to do whatever ranch executives do,* he thought.

Jakob finished his bacon and eggs, toast and coffee. He had to wait awhile for the coffee, as he didn't take to having English tea for breakfast.

Jakob and BethAnn then took a short walk around the ranch. They were watching her men brand calves when Geraldine rode up to them on a snow-white horse. She was quite impressive in her Levi's that were filled out properly, a denim shirt with a blue kerchief, and a white Stetson. She dismounted and went up to Jakob and kissed him on the cheek. Jakob thought, *Oh, we're back to that now, but a show of too much affection might not be right in front of those who are looking me over.*

"Sorry I'm so late. I thought I'd be back much sooner but there were some things I had to hash out with some of the men. So, now I am at your disposal." Jakob and BethAnn agreed it was not a problem and told her they saw the calf branding, something neither of them had ever seen.

"Well, I'm ready, BethAnn. How about you?" BethAnn was almost jumping up and down in anticipation of riding. "Let's go down to the barn and get Nelly." Geraldine, who had already dismounted, led her horse, with Jakob and BethAnn following. They entered the barn containing many stalls and some fine-looking animals, with BethAnn running ahead to Nelly. Nelly was already at the stall door and recognized BethAnn. She reached down into her pocket and came up with a carrot for Nelly. Geraldine looked in astonishment at what she had done. "Where did you learn that, BethAnn?"

"Oh, I read it in a book and I saw you doing it too."

Geraldine just smiled. "We have work to do. Jakob, you can watch, if you please, but from hereon we'll ignore your presence. Right, BethAnn?" BethAnn smiled and nodded her head. BethAnn opened the stall and led Nelly out. The saddle was nearby and she saddled Nelly all by herself. They led Nelly to the corral and from there on Jakob just watched, as Geraldine instructed and BethAnn followed. BethAnn mounted and dismounted, she led and she ran, leading Nelly. She started and stopped. The next hour Geraldine and BethAnn went through many maneuvers. BethAnn got occasional hugs and applause from Geraldine for her efforts. Finally, they came back to Jakob.

"She has had enough for today. Later in the afternoon we can all go for a ride. Now, let's get back to the ranch for some lemonade. I'm sure BethAnn is thirsty because I am."

They sat on the veranda and Little Deer brought out the lemonade pitcher with glasses. "BethAnn, I predict you will be a good horsewoman. You are a good learner." BethAnn just smiled. They talked the rest of the morning about the ranch and what Geraldine was doing. Little Deer came out and informed Geraldine lunch would be ready soon. Almost at that same moment the bunkhouse bell rang, loud and clear, and Geraldine laughed. "I'm sure the men have been waiting for it the last hour. If you want to freshen up, why don't you do it now." BethAnn ran into the house and up the stairs, with Jakob and Geraldine following.

Jakob thought this would be a good time to bring up the last evening together. Geraldine was close to Jakob.

"Geraldine, about last night, I . . . " Geraldine slithered close to him and their lips were almost touching. I . . . " She put her arms around him and placed her lips firmly against his, with her body pressing against him and holding him tight. Their lips parted, still holding him close.

"I love you darling." Jakob became tongue tied. "I love you Jakob."

"Geraldine, I love you too." They slowly let go of each other and went to their rooms to freshen up for lunch with Jakob's thoughts reviewing his last night's experience with Geraldine.

Later, Jakob and BethAnn met Geraldine at the corral to go for a ride. BethAnn had her Nelly saddled and ready. Geraldine had one of her horses saddled and ready for Jakob. It was a beautiful horse which had been bred there at the ranch. It seemed a little high-strung at first, but Geraldine assured Jakob he would be able to ride her. She called her own horse, Sir Richard. It was obvious she was experienced by how she handled her horse. She took them to an area of the ranch where Jakob had not been, always being careful not to expose them to any danger. The ranch extended to the foothills of the Bighorns. Jakob was a good rider and enjoyed being with Geraldine. They stopped in various places to take in the scenery and even saw antelope in the distance. Coming back from their ride they were tired but exhilarated. Little Deer had their cold lemonade ready, and they enjoyed the refreshment. They then went to their rooms to rest and freshen-up before dinner.

Jakob lay in bed but couldn't sleep. It seemed like his relationship with Geraldine was moving fast, maybe too fast. He realized he loved her. His thoughts of marriage and his physical attraction for her was very strong but—he wasn't sure he knew her well enough. She was an incredibly beautiful woman in every way, but thoughts of Liz began to interfere. He and Geraldine were both different in so many ways; just the cultural differences were somewhat concerning. And he had BethAnn to consider. That might be considered minimal because she and Geraldine seemed to be totally in love with each other.

I'm certain that Geraldine loves BethAnn, and likewise, BethAnn loves Geraldine, and yet I should meet her family to be able to truly understand her and their cultural differences. And then there's the matter of money. She undoubtedly has more than I do. I don't need or want anyone to support me and my daughter, but could we live up to her lifestyle? All of a sudden this love he had for Geraldine had some strings attached and it bothered him. *But I love her. I want to be with her. I am so lonesome since I lost Liz. In spite of everything, living without my mate has been hard. I love BethAnn so much but I need a wife and she needs a mother. Oh, what should I do?* He lay in bed but he was troubled. There was a knock on the door.

"Daddy, are you awake?"

"Yes, I'm awake. You may come in." BethAnn came bounding in and jumped onto his bed. He got hold of her and hugged and kissed her. She was his and he loved her so. *My love is big enough for both*, he thought.

"Daddy, Geraldine is in the kitchen with Little Deer. I think we should go down, don't you?"

"You're right, so give me a couple minutes and I'll be down." BethAnn wiggled free of Jakob and went down to Geraldine. Jakob cleaned up and changed his clothes, to something more appropriate, and stood in the doorway to the kitchen.

"Well, Sir Jakob, are you ready to assume your duties as maker of the martinis for your hostess?" He entered the kitchen and approached Geraldine, put his arms around her and kissed her. Saying nothing, he started the martinis. Geraldine was completely surprised. BethAnn looked on somewhat surprised but said nothing.

The martinis finished, Geraldine directed Little Deer to bring them into the great room. Prince followed BethAnn and jumped up on the chair next to her. Little Deer gave her a lemonade. Jakob picked up a martini and gave it to Geraldine, and taking his he toasted.

"My Lady, that you may love and be loved."

Geraldine smiled. Looking into Jakob's eyes she answered, "I could want no more." BethAnn left the room and went on the veranda followed by Prince. "Jakob, what are your thoughts?"

"I have so many thoughts, dear. When I told you I love you, I meant it. I am in love with you, but I fear we may have moved too fast. I do want you for my wife but we hardly know each other enough to undertake marriage. I have to consider BethAnn. I haven't talked to her about us yet. I believe she loves you and I feel you love her. Being her mother will be a challenge for you, maybe, and then maybe not."

"Jakob, you are a sensitive man, as well as a sensible man. Everything you have said is right and I agree. I believe our love is strong enough to prevail. I want you and I need you, but we have to control our desires."

Little Deer came into the room and announced dinner was ready. She left and they embraced. BethAnn came in and they all sat at the table. Maria served the wine, then they had a special beef roast for dinner and indulged in apple pie for dessert. Geraldine suggested they go out on the veranda to enjoy a special dessert sauterne. As the sun went down, some of the men built a fire in an area near the corral and sat around it. Then a couple of them brought out musical instruments and played well into the night until the skeeters came out to spoil their evening. Jakob was the first to speak

"Geraldine, this visit has been just great and I needed it. You are a perfect hostess, and when I think about the time you have given BethAnn, it was just wonderful. But I really should return to Sheridan and the office. I have some things pending there."

"Oh, Jakob, you can't leave me so soon. Can't you stay at least another day? And what about BethAnn? I need more time with her. Can she stay at least another week? I'll bring her back. I just love being with her. What do you say?"

"I have thought of staying with you perhaps another day, then I really should get back. And if BethAnn wants to stay longer, it would be all right with me."

"Oh, hooray! Yes, I would like to stay longer with Geraldine, Daddy."

"Then, that's what shall be. I think it's great you ladies will be together." BethAnn put her arms around Jakob and kissed him. He looked at a slightly disappointed Geraldine and smiled. Little Deer came out to tell BethAnn she had a bedtime snack for her, and BethAnn left for the kitchen with her new-found friend, Prince, following her. Geraldine went up to Jakob and put her arms around him.

"I'm going to miss you when you leave, but I understand. I'm happy you're leaving BethAnn with me. She is a delight and I truly love her. We'll get to know each other better and I'll help her with her riding. I think she is doing just great. I'll bring her back in a week and then we will see each other. And I will still have you tomorrow." Jakob put his arms around Geraldine and kissed her tenderly, as BethAnn entered the room.

"I'm going up to bed, Daddy. Don't forget to tuck me in. Night, Geraldine. Can I kiss you good night?" Geraldine went up to BethAnn and kissed her good night. BethAnn started up the stairs and turned around and smiled to both of them. Geraldine came to Jakob and put her arms around him and hugged him, putting her head on his chest briefly.

"I think I better go up and tuck BethAnn in." He went up to BethAnn and brought the blanket up to her chin. She looked seriously at Jakob.

"Daddy, you like Geraldine, don't you?" Jakob nodded.

"Yes, I do."

BethAnn smiled. "I'm glad." And she reached up and kissed him.

Jakob came down to the great room. Geraldine was curled up on the couch and Jakob sat next to her.

"What's on for tomorrow?" Geraldine moved closer to him.

"Nothing special. The men are going to move some cattle to a new grazing area. Would you like to see how it's done? We don't have to. We can just stick around here. I want to spend some time with BethAnn. She's fun to be with and just loves being on Nelly."

"BethAnn really likes you. I think you two are bonding."

"I do care for her a lot. She is filling in a void in my life. I missed having children, but I never knew what I was really missing until you brought her to me. I always thought my father loved me, but seeing you with BethAnn makes me feel like he never really cared. Oh, he would bend to my desires, and he was concerned about me, but my dreams or inner thoughts were unknown to him. He never knew them, or cared. Sometimes I think I was like a pretty fixture someone took care of, so my father could look at me and be pleased. He never tucked me in bed or played with me, or made me laugh. I see you with BethAnn. As a child, I never . . . " Geraldine looked sorrowfully at Jakob. "Can you understand me? Or am I just feeling sorry for myself because I see you enjoy her."

Jakob gently took her hands, and looking into her eyes, said, "Don't do that to yourself. What happened in your life we can't change. Every day we start with a clean slate. BethAnn asked me if I like you and I told her I do. She said she was glad. She recognizes there is something between us and she's happy. I will tell her one day there is more than just something."

She put her arms around Jakob and kissed him tenderly. "You are my knight in shining armor."

Geraldine was free to be with Jakob and BethAnn for the day They had their breakfast and Geraldine had Little Deer put together a lunch. Then they were off to see the Oliver Henry Ranch's vast holdings. They first went to see her men drive the cattle to new grazing grounds. After that, they went to a picturesque lake where she laid out a lunch for them. It wasn't a hard ride, but they were tired when they came back and took naps before dinner.

Jakob lay back in his bed and thought of the events of the day. *Geraldine is everything I could ever want for a wife and mother for BethAnn, and yet she is not*

Liz. Geraldine and Liz are different but with acceptable differences. So, why am I even concerned? His eyes finally closed as he fell asleep.

When he awakened, BethAnn knocked on his door and told him she was going down to help Geraldine get dinner together. Jakob got dressed for dinner. On his way to the kitchen, he heard a lot of chatter and BethAnn was giggling. He arrived to see BethAnn rolling out dough to make cookies from some special recipe of Geraldine's.

"If you had gotten here sooner, I could have given you a job too. But you have done quite well with the martinis, so you may proceed with them." Little Deer was laughing and referred to Geraldine as the boss of the kitchen, but it was Geraldine who was making a special dinner of Shepherd's Pie.

"I not hear that kind pie," remarked Little Deer. "Boss lady show me."

"I bet you thought I don't know how to cook, didn't you? I have other talents too."

"I'm learning a lot about you and I am truly impressed. However, if we don't sit down and have our martinis, they will get warm, and a tepid martini is not too good."

They all laughed as Jakob moved to the great room carrying glasses and the pitcher of martinis with Geraldine right behind him. BethAnn said she had to stay in the kitchen to work on the cookies. Jakob put down the tray and turned around to find Geraldine next to him. She placed her soft hands on both sides of his face and drew him close and tenderly kissed him.

"I like that and I love you," she said. Geraldine held him tightly as he put his arms around her.

Jakob looked into her eyes. "Sometimes I just can't describe how I feel about you. I can't believe this is happening to us." They sat down on the couch and taking the martinis in hand toasted and sipped their drinks. Jakob realized the aristocratic Geraldine was not typical. She was talented and capable. The dinner of Shepherd's Pie and BethAnn's cookies for dessert were a treat. The evening was spent playing card games which included BethAnn. Jakob had made plans to leave early in the morning. One of Geraldine's men would accompany him. He would be going to Sheridan to get ranch supplies. Geraldine was sober. She was disappointed Jakob was leaving and she would not see him until she brought BethAnn back to Sheridan the following week. They went to bed in separate rooms.

Jakob lay awake thinking about Geraldine. Their bedrooms so close, and yet so far apart. The temptation was almost overwhelming but he knew he had to remain resolute.

Jakob awoke at daybreak. He had difficulty sleeping the night. His belongings were packed and in the wagon. He met Geraldine in the kitchen and they embraced. Geraldine seemed sad and Jakob was melancholy. They had breakfast together. BethAnn came down and kissed Jakob. She too was sad. It would be the first time she and Jakob were separated for more than just a few days.

His wagon was waiting for him; Geraldine's man had prepared it. Little Deer had made a lunch for Jakob and Raymond, the ranch straw-boss who would be going to pick up feed and lead the way. It was good to have more than just one traveling together, even though there really was nothing to worry about. It was a relatively safe route. BethAnn and Geraldine followed Jakob down the stairs to the wagon. BethAnn hugged and kissed Jakob and shed some tears as Geraldine waited. She put her arms around Jakob and kissed him.

"I'll see you in a week. Take care, I'll miss you." She quickly looked away and went into the ranch with BethAnn following. Jakob watched them until they were inside and then turned around and climbed into the wagon.

Chapter 33

A Home Without BethAnn

After returning home from visiting the Oliver Henry Ranch, Jakob was anxious for a full day in his office. However, there was no one waiting for him, so he decided to visit Doc Kelly to see how their broken jaw patient was doing. Kelly, seeing him come in, started questioning him.

"Well, it's nice you came back. I didn't expect you for another week. Did the princess kick you out?"

"Come on, Kelly, Geraldine is not a princess and she didn't kick me out. I came back of my own accord. BethAnn is still there and she is learning horseback riding from Geraldine, who is an expert."

"What's going on between you two? I get the feeling there is something more I should know. She's is a helluva good looker. You sure know how to pick them. Besides that, she has real bucks. You could sit around for the rest of your life on a pillow if you hook up with her."

"All right, Kelly, that's enough. I'm not going to say anything until you talk serious."

"Oh, so that's where we're at—serious. Okay, kid, I didn't mean to pick on you. I'm glad for you. I don't know much about her, but she sure looks pretty damn nice. If you picked her, I got to say, she has to be pretty damn good, and lucky too. Go to it."

The door to Kelly's office opened and in came Robert Sears. He mumbled a plea through his teeth: he wished he could go back to the ranch where he was working, near Big Horn. The office smelled of him the minute he came in. He'd been washing his mouth out with the cheap whiskey mouthwash Kelly gave him. He looked sad, skinny and unshaven. Kelly looked at him.

"What you think, Jake? Let's take off that scarf and see if the jaw has healed enough to let him go home. He's been here almost six weeks now. It should be healed." Jakob carefully took off the scarf bandage. He tenderly held the jaw to try to move it and applied a bending pressure at the break. It seemed firm as he slowly opened his jaw a little. Jakob flushed it out with water and then he gave him a drink of water, that he pleaded for.

"Take it easy now. Let's see how far you can open. Now, see if you can move your jaw from side to side. Go slowly."

"Gol dern. That feels good, Doc, jes to be able to open ma mouth. Got some more of that water? Mmm, it tastes so good. You know, Doc, I don't think I'll ever drink whiskey again after using it to swish my mouth out with that rotgut you gave me. You know my jaw, it don't feel bad. Kin I get me a piece of meat to chew on? I'm hungry." Jakob smiled.

"Why don't you take it easy with your food and eat soft stuff to build up strength in those muscles. Everything looks good. No reason why you can't go back home." The man left happy for the Lazy D ranch. He thanked them and promised he'd be back and pay the doctors for fixing him up and paying for the hotel room. Jake looked at Kelly. "What do you think? He looks like it is going to be all right. And best of all, the jaw is in good alignment. He should be able to chew correctly."

"You're right, Jake, and the wound area is clean as a whistle. The bone seems to be healed. We did it, Jake. I wouldn't have taken any bets, but we got him fixed up."

Doc Kelly and Jakob shook hands. Doc Kelly looked at Jakob. "You know, Jake, any guy coming here who gets his jaw busted can count on us to fix him up." Jakob looked sternly at Doc Kelly.

"Forget it, Kelly. Maybe we were just lucky this time." Doc Kelly laughed and Jakob left for his office. He had a few patients and finished early. Jakob decided to see his old friend Andy Meeks at the Lucky Lady. He was behind the bar and gave Jakob a big wave.

"When did you get back, Doc? I thought you took your kid to the Oliver Henry Ranch."

"I got in last night. It was a long ride, but I made it back. You remember the guy they brought in with a broken jaw, don't you? Well, we finally sent him home. That poor guy is lucky everything worked out for him. Did the sheriff ever get a lead on the guys who almost did him in?"

"Naw, nobody in town knew them. Just tough luck for the guy. And, just another lesson: if ya play cards with someone, ya better know who they are. But getting back to the trip over to the Oliver Henry Ranch, are you still hanging out with the princess?"

Jakob laughed. "Andy, she's not a princess, but they do call her Lady back in England. I guess I better give you the straight story. I'm not sure what you mean by *hanging out*, but yes, we are more than just friends. She is a really fine lady and I care a lot for her."

"And she is one sweet-looking dish, Doc."

Jakob smiled and continued. "Yes, she is beautiful, isn't she? But more important, she is intelligent, talented, and she is a good person. Right now she is hosting BethAnn at her ranch, teaching her horseback riding. She thinks BethAnn is good and could ride in shows. She loves my baby, and I think it is just great. You'd be surprised how well she runs that big ranch. She's really a great gal."

"Sounds to me, Doc, like this is more'n jes bein' better than friends, and BethAnn could use a mother, if you know what I mean."

"You're right, Andy. This is just between us. I care a lot for her and I think she feels the same about me. She and BethAnn are getting on just perfectly. There is a lot to be considered but . . . nothing is simple. She will be bringing BethAnn back in a week. There is a lot for the both of us to think about. That's the story, Andy. Just between you and me. I wanted you to know, but I'm not putting it in the newspaper."

Jakob thought his friend should know something about what was going on, rather than being the recipient of a rumor. One of the things which was sometimes a problem around Sheridan, were stories about some of the ladies who would like to be romantically involved with Jakob. Up to now, he had no interest in anyone. They finished their conversation and Jakob was off to home.

Chucha was waiting with dinner for Jakob. She was glad to see him back but she really missed BethAnn, as did Jakob. Jakob had never been a worrywart, but he was always concerned for BethAnn's welfare. The house was quiet and her chatter was missed. Chucha's conversations were somewhat limited, though she did fairly well with the language now. Jakob knew her primary concerns were always those of BethAnn and him. He usually did daily checks of his property and made sure the animals were taken care of. Skippy was beside himself now that BethAnn wasn't around. He kept looking for her, especially since Jakob came home. Home was not home without BethAnn.

The following week was none too active for Jakob, but he did go to see his friend and pastor, John Binotti, at St. Ignatius Church. They talked about a lot of things associated with the church now being built. Finally he got around to telling him about Geraldine.

"Father, I've found a lady I think I want to marry." Jakob went on to tell him about Geraldine and everything he knew about her.

"Do you love her?" Jakob nodded. "And what about BethAnn? Do you think she will be able to share you with her?" Jakob went on to tell him about his experiences the past weeks and how he felt BethAnn admired and loved Geraldine; even though he had not talked to BethAnn about his desire to marry Geraldine, he felt she would accept it. "What about the money situation? She obviously has more than you do, and having too much can be just as serious a problem as too little. Would you be moving in with her at the ranch, or go to England to live?"

"Yes, John, I recognize those as possible problems. I don't know yet how they would be handled, but I definitely would not leave this country and the ranch . . . I don't know."

"You are an intelligent man, Jakob. I have no doubt you will do the right thing." And then he spoke again. "Have you slept together? You don't have to answer that, but . . . " Jakob nodded in the affirmative. "There are consequences to that." He raised his eyebrows and smiled. "God bless you, Jakob. If you do get married, I would like to officiate." Jakob smiled and got up to leave.

"Thanks John, I appreciate your input. I want to do what is right, and you will definitely be the one to officiate."

It was a long week since he left BethAnn with Geraldine, and he expected to see her today. He missed Geraldine, and over and over in his mind he thought about what he should do with his life and with Geraldine. His love for her was deep, but he was frightened they might not be able to sort out their differences, although they had not been really approached.

The day was perfect for travel: warm, sunny and windy, with a sky filled with cirrus clouds and the possibly of rain through the night. He had finished his day at the office and they had not yet arrived. Then he became somewhat apprehensive. He sat nervously in front of his office until he saw the wagon as it finally lumbered in, with Nelly trailing behind. Raymond was handling the reins, with BethAnn and Geraldine sitting next to him. When the wagon stopped BethAnn was almost instantly off and in Jakob's arms. Geraldine then followed BethAnn down from the wagon. She gave Jakob a hug and a peck on the cheek.

"I am sure glad to see you back. I got a little anxious because you came this late, but I figured you were bringing Nelly with you and it might slow you down."

"We had no problems, Daddy. I even rode Nelly for awhile."

"Jakob, your daughter is something else. She is doing real well with Nelly and could probably even handle a bigger horse. She has learned so much and could be ready to train for competition."

"That's just great. Are you going to be staying with us? We have plenty of room."

"No, I think not. I have some things to do in town tomorrow, so I will stay at the Inn. Raymond will be at the Commercial, but I'll accept dinner with you at the Sheridan Inn."

"Sure you don't want to stay at my place?" Geraldine declined and Jakob continued. "Your choice, but I'll buy you the dinner. What say I stop by about seven?" Geraldine agreed and Jakob and BethAnn headed home.

BethAnn talked continuously. She had a great time with Geraldine, but said she was glad to be home. She said she really missed Chucha and Skippy. When they went into the house, Skippy gave her the royal dog welcome. She later said she liked Skippy better then Prince, who she also became fond of. Chucha was glad to see BethAnn and she kissed and hugged her. Jakob got BethAnn settled in and got himself ready to meet Geraldine.

He tied up his rig and went into the Inn. Henry Clayton was at the desk and greeted Jakob.

"I don't think your lady friend came down yet." So Jakob decided to just go up to her room. He knocked on the door and Geraldine answered.

"I had hoped you would come up to the room. That little peck I gave you when I got off the wagon didn't satisfy me." She moved close to Jakob and he put his arms around her and drew her close to him. She placed her hands on both sides of his face and kissed him softly. "I missed you, Jakob Miller. I don't know what I'm going to do. This week we were apart seemed like a month."

Jakob kissed her and held her tightly. "You're right. I don't know what we're going to do. I missed you terribly." They held each other and finally Jakob said, "I think we better go down now or Henry may get the wrong idea of what's going on in here. You must be hungry after the long ride."

They entered the dining room and were greeted by Annabelle who then seated them. "I guess I know what you folks want." And she left to get them their martinis.

Jakob was the first to speak. "How was your week with BethAnn?"

"We had a marvelous time. I had such great fun with her. For a seven year old, she is so easy to be with, so mature for her age, and a quick learner. I bet she does well in school. She just loves being around horses. I'm really glad I gave her the mustang. I think she'll be able to enjoy her for a long time. You know, Jakob, she is a delightful little girl. I just love her."

"That's good because it is important to me for you to love each other." Geraldine agreed. Their drinks arrived and Annabelle gave them the menus. They both ordered Lukas's chicken in a wine sauce. Later, Jakob smiled and said, "Do you like fried chicken?" Geraldine said she did like it some, but the cook back home didn't really make it very often, and it was always too dry. "Well now, there is a lady out in Big Horn who makes the best fried chicken I have ever tasted. I've got to take you out there sometime. You would love it. And Emma, who makes it, is a great gal."

"That sounds good. Maybe the next time I come here we can go there. I have some news for you. My youngest sister and her husband will be coming to visit me. Eleanor is now married to Roger Allen, who comes from an old Suffolk family. They thought they would like to get into the ranching business. Apparently there is now a depression in England, so they want to see my operation. They will probably be with me for some time. Ellie is a great girl. I know you will like her. I don't know Roger, but Mama seems to like him. That could ease up things for me here. Jakob, I would like to take you back home with me to meet my family. I had hoped we could do it before the winter set in, but I don't think it will work out. And we definitely don't want to go in the winter. The trip would be too hard. This will put us into next spring. Oh Honey, can we wait so long?"

Geraldine started to sob and tears rolled down her cheeks. "I want you, Honey. Now that my heart knows you are the one each day will hurt until we are one."

Jakob saw the agonized look on her face. "Please, dear, we'll work this out. I don't know how, but we'll do it. I feel the same as you do. I want to meet your family and I want you to meet mine. I thought when we do go, we'll take BethAnn for a visit with my parents and then we'll go to see your family."

Annabelle arrived with the dinners and the subject changed. Lukas followed, and stopped by their table to welcome them. He had just stopped for few moments and was then back to his kitchen.

Geraldine's visit to Sheridan was short. She and Jakob had spent some time together, but not as much as both wanted.

Over the next few months she came to Sheridan and they were able to spend time together. Their love grew and their marriage was being planned. Winter arrived and travel was now near impossible. Each time Geraldine had planned to leave the ranch there was a storm or the bitter cold made travel impossible. Geraldine had her sister Eleanor and her husband Roger, living with her. They were learning the business and were helpful, but during winter there was not too much for them to do. Jakob had planned they would get together for Christmas, but two days before Christmas twelve inches of snow had fallen. With the strong winds the snow drifted to four to five feet deep in places. Mother Nature kept them apart. Both Jakob and BethAnn missed having Geraldine with them for the holiday.

It was March 10th when Raymond took a wagon from the Oliver Henry Ranch to Sheridan for supplies they were desperately in need of. For warmth Geraldine was buried under buffalo skins for the ten-hour trip. She registered at the Sheridan Inn. Jakob had been waiting for her for two hours, sitting in the bar. When she arrived, he helped her into the hotel where they sat next to the blazing fireplace with hot coffee and brandy to thaw her out. Geraldine's teeth were chattering and Jakob put his arms around her and held her tightly, with their lips together. Geraldine finally forced her way back from Jakob.

"Jakob, I think you can let go of me. I'm warm enough now. I can take off my coat, and we can go into the dining room." Jakob took his arms away from Geraldine and smiled.

"I didn't mind helping you warm up. Your lips tasted so good." With that said, Geraldine started laughing.

"And I thought you were just trying to get me warmed up from that bitter cold."

"Can't blame a guy for trying. We better skip the martinis. The brandy coffee has given you enough spirits for the day. You must be hungry after the long trip."

Geraldine laughed and said, "Jakob you have quenched my hunger with the long kiss."

"Do you realize how long it's been since we saw each other?" Annabelle was waiting for their order and they had to redirect the conversation. Lukas was serving his buffalo stew, which fit the cold Wyoming night well. Annabelle then brought them a bowl of potato and bacon soup to start with.

"Jakob, it's been too long to be apart. I missed you so. Your letters were not enough. We have to set a date to go to England. I know you want to meet my family. Let's do it next month. April will be a good month to travel."

"Yes, April would be fine. I was going to suggest next month but was waiting to see you first." They finished their dinner and continued talking holding a snifter of brandy.

"I'm very tired, Jakob. I think I should go to bed. After the long ride in the cold I just feel exhausted. Tomorrow morning I have some things which have to be done. Maybe we can get together for lunch." Jakob walked Geraldine to her room. She turned toward him and he put his arms around her and drew her to him.

"You still have some kisses left, don't you?" She smiled, put her hands on both sides of his face and kissed him. They stood holding each other. "I'm glad you came." She opened her door and went into her room.

Geraldine walked into Jakob's office before noon and found him waiting for her. They went out for lunch and had decided on Chinese food, so he took her to Son Lee, an old standby restaurant in Sheridan. Geraldine told Jakob she would be leaving the next day for the ranch. "I would like to stay longer, but I really have to get back." They started making plans for their trip to England. "England is beautiful in the spring, so if we leave early in April we should have good travel weather. And I know you will enjoy it."

Jakob said he would make arrangements for BethAnn to stay with her grandparents in Milwaukee. "It will be a treat for BethAnn and for my parents. By the way, BethAnn has been asking about you so I want you to come over to my house for dinner. You will meet Chucha who will make one of her famous dinners. I know you will love her." Jakob then took Geraldine to the Sheridan Inn and went back to his office.

His afternoon was not too busy and he was anxious to take Geraldine to his home. BethAnn was excited to see her, and when they entered the house she was there next to Geraldine, hugging and kissing her. They had really struck up a friendship during her visit to the ranch. Geraldine met Chucha who warmly welcomed her. They sat and talked, with BethAnn doing most of the talking. She sat close to Geraldine and wouldn't leave her side. BethAnn then took her on a tour of the house, and showed her everything she was doing. BethAnn now had an art class in school, and had her pictures proudly displayed on the walls. She couldn't wait to show her the picture she had done of Nelly.

Chucha had set the table in her finery, with a white tablecloth, glasses and silver. It was set with lit candles, which gave it a special festive look. She then invited them to be seated. She called Jakob Pan, meaning Mister, and BethAnn was Paninka, or young lady. Chucha had made her favorite chicken with dumplings, mashed potatoes with gravy, pickled beets, beans with crisp bacon crumbles, and her bread. The dessert was a delicious bread pudding laced with rum. When they were filled to capacity, she served a honey liquor that she had made. Geraldine thought her dinner was fit for the Queen, and she told Chucha she had never had such a grand dinner. Chucha just beamed from ear to ear.

The evening ended when it was time for BethAnn to go to bed. She hugged and kissed Geraldine and again thanked her for Nelly. Though she didn't ride her much in the cold weather, she assured Geraldine she was being taking care of.

Jakob took Geraldine back to the Sheridan Inn. She thanked him for the wonderful evening she had with BethAnn and Chucha. "You are really fortunate to have her with you. She is really a gem. I just love her cooking." They pulled up in front of the Sheridan Inn and then Jakob took Geraldine to her room.

"I wish you didn't have to go back. I'm going to miss you." He put his arms around her and pulled her close to him and kissed her. A tear slowly left her eye and went down her cheek.

"It gets harder and harder to leave you, but I have the trip to England with you to look forward to." Holding him tightly, she kissed him, then turned around as Jakob left.

Chapter 34

Stopover in Milwaukee

Jakob and Geraldine have been looking forward to their April 10th departure to England through the long, cold Wyoming winter. Jakob had already made arrangements with his parents to take care of BethAnn. He hated to take her out of school, but April was the best month for them to leave for England. Geraldine's sister and husband would be left in charge of the ranch while she was away. She had some concerns whether they could handle it, but George Roberts, the foreman, would be there to actually run the ranch and assist them.

BethAnn would have to leave school before the end of the school year, but she was well ahead in her studies and planned to take lessons with her. Margaret would be able to help her with them as necessary. Jakob had talked with BethAnn, about her visit with her grandmother and she was looking forward to it. Chucha would take care of the house and the animals. There was a great deal to do in preparation for the trip. A new dentist was now practicing in Sheridan and Jakob had made arrangements with Harold Brown, a graduate of Northwestern University, to take care of his patients who needed emergency treatment. Jakob thought the trip would take probably two months to complete. He and Geraldine were looking forward to it so they could get on with their wedding plans.

With much luggage, they boarded the train in Sheridan. They would be taking the new northern route, which had opened up and would save a great deal of time getting to Chicago. They would travel to Billings and from there, on to Chicago and Milwaukee. For BethAnn, it would be an exciting trip, because she had never left the Sheridan area or been on a train. She had not seen her grandmother since Liz's funeral and so she hardly remembered her. Jakob thought, *I hope Mother will understand her. Her life in Sheridan is considerably different from what it would be in Milwaukee. But BethAnn is a charmer and I'm sure she will do well. BethAnn will surely miss her Nelly and Skippy, but it won't be that long. I'm sure she will do well. How will Mother react to Geraldine? We aren't married yet, and here we are traveling to England together. I hope Mother's mores can handle that.* A group of Jakob's special friends, as well as Geraldine's sister, saw them off at the train station.

BethAnn was so excited about the train ride, as she looked out the window at the passing landscape and the different towns where the train stopped. Jakob and Geraldine had compartments, so the sleeping arrangements were taken care of for the long ride to Chicago. BethAnn had studied some geography about the trip before they left, and was impressed by the size of the Mississippi River, when they crossed over it. Jakob had been in touch with his mother and she had sleeping arrangements taken care of at their home. Geraldine and Jakob would have separate bedrooms, of course, and BethAnn would be using Margret's sewing room for a bedroom.

The train chugged into Chicago about mid-morning. Later they would transfer to the next Milwaukee train at 1:00 which would arrive in Milwaukee at about 4 p.m. The sight of the big city buildings of Chicago was beyond BethAnn's expectations. She couldn't believe such a place existed. Boarding the Milwaukee train out of Chicago to Milwaukee would be the last leg to their first destination. Jakob became somewhat apprehensive about the meeting between Geraldine and Margaret, yet Jakob knew his mother well enough to realize it probably would go all right.

There were now taxi cabs at the station in Milwaukee which would take them to Jakob's parents' home. This was early spring in Milwaukee, so there wasn't too much change from winter yet; the temperature was in the 40s. There were still small piles of melting snow visible in various places. The cab stopped at 2804 West Wisconsin Avenue. The grass and bushes did show some signs of greening and tulips and daffodils were starting to show. But it was still a very chilly spring. BethAnn was excited by the ride in the taxi. The taxi driver was amazed at the amount of luggage they had. He didn't know that Jakob and Geraldine had left most of it in a locker at the train station. They unloaded the luggage then walked up the steps to the large brown-stone house.

Jakob rang the bell and the door quickly opened. Bob and Margaret Miller answered. There was a chorus of hellos and Jakob and BethAnn were flooded by hugs and kisses. BethAnn received oohs and aahs, as they had not seen her for five years.

"Come on in. Come in." And the group entered Jakob's former home. BethAnn of course was immediately recognized and then Jakob presented Geraldine.

"Mother, Dad, I would like you to meet someone who is very special to me, Geraldine Widicker." Both acted graciously and put their hands out to Geraldine.

She clasped them and answered, "It is my pleasure to meet you." Geraldine looked attractive in her long, royal blue cashmere wool coat with a short fur collar, and chic hat and black kidskin gloves, which she had removed to shake hands. She smiled warmly as she spoke. "Jakob has told me so much about you, I already feel like I know you."

"I'm Bob and this is Margaret. Jakob has told us much about you. He said you are beautiful and charming." Then turning to Jakob he said, "But Jakob you did not say how beautiful and charming she really is."

"Dad, I left that for you to discover."

"Geraldine, welcome to Milwaukee and to our house. We are happy you are here with us." Jakob thought, *Wow, Mother is in great form today. I think she likes Geraldine.*

"Oh, you are so nice to say that." Then, looking at BethAnn she added, "This is our real charming lady, Miss BethAnn." BethAnn blushed as Bob took her hands.

"We're so glad you are all here. We have really been looking forward to your visit with us. I've wanted to see my granddaughter again, and now she is with us. You are such a pretty one and we finally get a chance to have you stay with us." Margaret, not to be outdone, showered BethAnn with her attention.

"Let's get you settled in first. I'll show you to your rooms and then we can chat briefly before dinner." Margaret took them to their rooms and told them to get comfortable and come down when they were ready.

"I'll be right down, Grandmother. It won't take me long." BethAnn was the first one in living room talking to her grandparents. Then Jakob and Geraldine finally came down.

"Here, you two, sit over here and Bobby will get you a glass of wine. He has Chardonnay or Cabernet Sauvignon." Bob passed out the wine-filled glasses and a special new beverage called Coca-Cola, for BethAnn. Margaret became especially interested in Geraldine.

"You and Jakob are going to England? How exciting. I have never been outside the United States, except when Bobby took me to the Niagara Falls, in Canada, on our honeymoon. Were you born there?" Geraldine told them she was born in England and had lived in the United States only since 1898. "What made you come to the United States and Sheridan?" She then explained she doesn't really live in Sheridan, but rather on a ranch not too far from Sheridan, and explained her reason for coming to the United States. Margaret was intent on getting as much information on Geraldine as she could until Bob reminded her they should be having their dinner soon.

"These folks must be hungry, Margaret. I bet they haven't eaten since noon. Right, Jakob?" Jakob laughed and told them they had fasted so they would be hungry and have plenty room for Mother's special dinner. Margaret was flattered and immediately went to get dinner on the table. Jakob's father was a very warm and gracious man. He showered his attention on BethAnn, but showed his interest in Geraldine, who reciprocated.

Margaret soon came in and invited them to be seated for dinner. The table setting was just perfect, and the food was prepared to the same standard. Dad cut the ham roast in measured slices, and with the sweet potatoes, salad, vegetables and breads, all feasted and shared in the conversation. The dessert of cheesecake and strawberries topped off a meal fit for royalty. Geraldine was very complimentary of the dinner and then remarked the table looked so festive with its linens, silver and burning candles. Needless to say, it flattered Margaret, who received the compliment graciously.

After dinner they returned to the living room and continued with the conversation until Jakob noticing BethAnn yawning.

Looking at his watch he remarked, "BethAnn, you are past your bedtime. We didn't even notice it. Maybe you should get ready for bed."

"Jakob, it's not that late and this is a special occasion," remarked Margaret.

"It's okay Gramma, I usually go to bed at ten. I am kinda tired. So maybe I'll go up and get ready for bed." And she went up to her bedroom.

"Jakob, I'm amazed. I had to fight you tooth and nail to get you to go to bed. She is adorable. You have done a good job with her." Later, BethAnn came down in her nightgown and gave all a kiss good night, then reminded Jakob to tuck her in. Jakob left to tuck her in, as the others carried on the conversation. When he returned, Margaret confronted Geraldine.

"Jakob mentioned your father is Sir Gerald Landry. Does it mean you are part of the English aristocracy?" Geraldine flushed somewhat, and smiled.

"Yes, I guess you might say that. My father is referred to as a baron. But here in the United States, I am Geraldine. I am a citizen here." She uncomfortably laughed, as did the others. There was much conversation during the evening until Jakob suggested it had been a long day for them, and he was tired. They all agreed to call it a day and left for their respective bedrooms. Jakob walked Geraldine to her room. She turned and put her arms around him and kissed him tenderly. "This has been an enjoyable evening. Your mother is a great cook. She said she made the cheesecake. It was great. I love your dad. Now I can see why you are the way you are." Jakob held her tightly and kissed her.

"And I can see why you are the way you are. And I love you for it. Good night, my dear."

Morning arrived in Milwaukee with bright sunshine, but it was still chilly. Jakob came down and found his father drinking coffee. Seeing Jakob, he took down a cup and filled it for him

"Good morning Dad. I thought you'd be getting ready to go to the office." He tasted his coffee.

"No, I canceled the appointments when I knew you were coming. You're not going to be here very long, as you will to be leaving for New York the day after tomorrow. I wish you were staying longer, but then you'll be coming back after England."

"I'm so glad BethAnn is going to be here with you. I thought of taking her with us, but I felt it would be good for her to get to know her grandparents better."

"I'm in full agreement. We hardly know the child and she is an absolute delight. I see Liz when I look at her. Jakob, your lady friend is a beautiful woman. I can understand your interest in her, and I truly understand your thoughts of marriage. It's been, what, six years since you lost Liz? A man needs a mate, and BethAnn needs a mother. Are you sure Geraldine is the right one?"

"Yes, I feel she is the right one. I've dwelled on this for a long time. I believe she loves BethAnn, and BethAnn loves her and will accept her as her mother.

There are some issues I must consider and this is why I must go to England." BethAnn arrived in the kitchen in her nightgown.

"Good morning, Daddy and Grandfather." BethAnn put her arms around Jakob and kissed him, then hugged and kissed her Grandfather. Grandfather kissed her and welcomed her. Bob asked her if she would like a glass of orange juice or milk. "Oh, orange juice. I'd just love it." It was just moments later when Margaret came into the room wearing a very perky house-dress. Her hair was brushed and neatly in place, and she wore earrings and even a short necklace. Margaret hugged and kissed BethAnn and acknowledged Jakob and Bob. She was followed by Geraldine who arrived in a long, silken housecoat. Her makeup was in place, and she too wore a short string of pearls with her hair neatly in place.

"Good morning, everyone, I guess I'm the last one up." BethAnn went up to her and hugged and kissed her. She kissed her on the forehead. "After sleeping on the train this past few days, the bed was really a luxury. Margaret, your bedroom decor is just beautiful. I admire your tastes." Margaret was flattered by the compliment and accepted it graciously. Margaret had baked a delicious breakfast cake everyone had with their coffee.

"Dad, I'd like to show Geraldine some of Milwaukee. Are you available to do some guiding? I understand you bought one of those Fords, I have been reading about." Bob was thrilled to show off his new Ford and did take them on a tour of Milwaukee.

"Geraldine, Lake Michigan is really great during the summer when we used to go down to the beach for a swim. It is cold water, but really refreshing on a hot day."

They spent most of the day on the tour. Margaret didn't go with them because she stayed home to prepare for the dinner party. She had invited some of the relatives to see Jakob and BethAnn, and of course to meet Geraldine. After the day on the town, they all took naps in preparation for the dinner party, except for BethAnn, who stayed in the kitchen with her grandmother. Margaret was thrilled BethAnn was interested in being with her in the kitchen. She put her to work doing some of the preparation. BethAnn was excellent at using a mixer or cutting vegetables for the salad. Jakob thought, *Why did I even wonder about how Mother and BethAnn would relate to each other? They get along fine.*

Dinner was to be at six and everyone was downstairs and awaiting the guests. Geraldine had asked Jakob how she should dress for the guests. He told her they generally dressed in taste, but not formally. Geraldine came down in a beige chiffon, above ankle-length dress with long sleeves. It had a v-shaped neck that extended just above the cleavage, with the back rounded. She wore several long strands of brownish beads. Geraldine looked beautiful. Her hair was parted in the middle and swept up on the sides and bunched on the top and back. Jakob thought it was a bit much, but she looked terrific. BethAnn wore a cute blue dress with a white collar. It extended to the calf with ruffles on the bottom hem.

Grandmother and Grandfather Miller were the first to arrive and were happy to see Jakob and delighted with BethAnn. Jakob had sent them a picture of her when she was six, but they were truly overjoyed to finally meet her. They were gracious in their meeting of Geraldine, who met them with her special charm. The others came in one by one: Aunt Jenny, Cousin Albert and his wife and son, cousin Nell, the Kramers, and to Jakob's surprise, the O'Malleys. It was a largely family group and their close friends. Margaret just loved introducing everyone to Lady Geraldine, who at first was somewhat uncomfortable with it, but Geraldine did look the part, and with her mild English accent and charm, she was a hit. They fell in love with BethAnn, who was also a charmer. She seemed so grown up for her age. The dinner table was filled with Margaret's best. Her glassware, silver and candelabra with burning candles showed elegance and taste. Dinner was Margaret's finest and consisted of a prime beef roast with twice-baked potatoes. Her mixed vegetables, and other complementary items, and a repeat of the strawberry cheesecake, made for an outstanding meal.

The table conversation was most interesting. When it was learned that BethAnn had a pony and had been tutored in horsemanship by Geraldine, all other conversation stopped and BethAnn and Geraldine were in the spotlight. Jakob felt a little uncomfortable the O'Malleys were there at first, but they were most gracious and mentioned Alice had sent her regards. She was now married and had two children. When the party learned Geraldine was the owner of a ranch that raised specially trained horses, it stimulated another group of questions to the aristocratic lady.

The evening lasted well into the night and it seemed no one wanted to leave. Margaret was complimented for the meal and all agreed they had a great evening. Grandfather Miller paid special attention to Geraldine and commended her for what she had done for BethAnn. With everyone gone, Margaret told them not to worry about cleaning up because she was having someone come by the next day to do it. Everyone had a full day of activity and all retired. Jakob took Geraldine to her bedroom and they embraced.

"Do you think your mother has accepted me as a daughter-in-law?" Jakob answered he thought she had. "I sincerely do hope so. She has been very nice to me and I do like her. Your dad is really very nice too. As I look at him I see you." They kissed again and Geraldine softly said, "Good night my darling."

Jakob awoke to a knock on his door.

"Daddy, Daddy, are you awake yet?" Jakob smiled and told BethAnn he was awake and she could come in. BethAnn entered and sat on Jakob's bed. "Daddy, Grandma said I could help make breakfast today. I was in the kitchen but she isn't up yet. Grandfather Bob is there and he made the coffee, so if you want coffee it's ready." Jakob laughed and thought, *BethAnn has made herself at home already.* He told her he would be coming down for coffee just as soon as he was dressed. "I'll tell Grandpa you're coming down. Meet you in the kitchen." And she was skipping off to the kitchen. Jakob put a robe on and soon followed her to the kitchen.

"BethAnn told me you had coffee made, so I thought I'd come down and join you two."

"Jakob, you didn't have to get up this early. BethAnn and I have been having a great talk. I'm learning a lot from her. She's told me all about Nelly, her horse, Skippy, her dog and Dilly, her rabbit. We're going to get along just fine when you go to England." Jakob laughed at BethAnn and admitted she was a great conversationalist. "You're leaving tomorrow, so I thought we must take it easy today. We'll go to the office and you can see what I'm working on these days. I did buy an X-ray machine. I can tell you, I don't know how I ever worked without one. They are expensive but they are worth it." Bob went into the details of how important the X-ray machine was and even suggested Jakob get one as soon as he was able to afford it. The subject was changed when BethAnn saw some birds in the tree next to the house. Margaret came into the kitchen to start breakfast.

"You men might as well go into the living room. BethAnn and I are going to make breakfast and you will just be in the way."

"Can I help, or are you afraid too many cooks will spoil the breakfast?" chimed in Geraldine, who had just arrived. Margaret thought she could help, but there wasn't much for her to do other than to make the toast and set the table. Jakob and Bob left, continuing with their discussion on the X-ray.

They finished their breakfast and BethAnn was proud to have participated in making it. Her grandmother gave her adequate praise for her assistance. Jakob said he was going to dress and then go to see his dad's office. They would be discussing business, but if anyone wanted to go along they were welcome. No one made any commitment, so Bob and Jakob went by themselves.

They rolled up to his dad's office in his new black Ford. He was very proud of it. "There's just a handful of us in town who have one," he proudly announced. Jakob thought it was great but didn't think it would be appropriate in Sheridan.

"You have good roads here. Other than Main Street and a few others, our roads are filled with ruts."

Bob's office was on the second floor of the building, with a large drug store beneath it. There was also a medical doctor in an adjacent office. The building was located at the north end of Racine Avenue, which was part of the downtown. Jakob noticed how meticulously clean and quiet it was in the building, although Racine Avenue did have a streetcar that ran on it. They opened the door and Jakob saw a modern dental office. His dad had just bought new S.S. White dental equipment. Instead of a pedal to pump the drill, it had an electric motor.

"You know, Jakob, I have stored my old equipment and it is still good. I can ship it out to you. You could add an electric motor to it, and have an electric drill instead of the old pedal drill you now use. And getting an X-ray machine would be a good investment. I want to show you mine and the X-ray pictures it takes." Jakob was impressed and vowed to upgrade his office, making it more modern.

By this time they were ready for lunch, so Bob took him over to the Elks Club. Bob proudly introduced him to his many friends before sitting down for lunch. Jakob was glad to be able to spend this time with his dad.

"Jakob, regarding your trip to England . . . does this mean you will be getting married to Geraldine?" Jakob answered in the affirmative. "Well, I can say she is lovely and she seems to love BethAnn. Taking that into consideration, and your love for each other, I'd say you could go on with your life as husband and wife. I have only one concern, and it is your social status."

"Yes, I know what you're thinking Dad. It's the only real concern I still have. That's why we are going to England to bring our relationship into the light. I believe our marriage can work. Does Mother have concerns?"

"Oh, you know your mother. Of course she has. But I wouldn't let it worry me if I were you. You have a good head on your shoulders. I trust your judgment. You will do what's right and I have a gut feeling it will work out well for you."

"Thanks, Dad, I'm glad we talked and I appreciate your confidence in me. Maybe we should get back home. I probably should have a heart-to heart talk with Mother and then start to get ready for tomorrow. We leave at two-thirty on the New York Central Twentieth Century Limited, out of the Randolph Street station. We will be in New York City, Grand Central Station in eighteen hours. A few hours later we'll board our ship, the White Star Line RMS *Oceanic*, for Southampton, England. After that, I'm a little fuzzy as to what we do."

"Sounds like you have an exciting trip ahead of you. There is one thing I forgot to ask you. If you decide to go through with the wedding, and I'm presuming you will. Will you get married in England?"

"That's one of those strings we haven't picked up yet. One thing is for sure, BethAnn will be part of the ceremony. And as to where we will be married, my friend John Binotti, at St. Ignatius Church in Sheridan, said he would like to officiate."

Bob shook his head. "That gut feeling is getting even stronger. Let's get going for home."

The home had been cleaned up from yesterday's dinner party. Margaret had filled in Geraldine and BethAnn on Jakob's early life.

"Jakob, you never told me about your athletic prowess—high school letters in football and baseball, and summer boys' camp lifeguard, I'm impressed. But I am also disappointed. You ran away from your mother on the first day in school so you wouldn't have to go to first grade." They all laughed. "And you were such a headstrong little boy." They continued laughing as Margaret mentioned a few other transgressions. The afternoon continued with much chatter until Margaret suggested they take a nap. Then looking at Jakob's dad, she suggested, "Maybe you will take us to the club for dinner tonight? That will save me from making a big meal." Bob graciously agreed to take them to dinner and they headed off to take naps.

Jakob stopped his mother and suggested they chat a little first. He spent the time discussing his plans. He questioned his mother on how she felt about Geraldine. She agreed she was charming and enjoyed her company.

Then she said, "Jakob, you will be having separate cabins on the ship, won't you?" Jakob smiled.

"Mother!" She looked incredulously at Jakob.

"Don't Mother me, young man. There are consequences you know." Jakob laughed, as he remembered hearing those words once before.

"We do have separate cabins, Mother. You don't have to be concerned." She seemed satisfied and the discussion ended. Jakob excused himself to take his nap. Lying in bed he thought, *See Jakob, that wasn't as hard as you thought it would be, was it?*

Bob was happy to take everyone in his new car and parked it in front of the country club, next to several other cars. They were ushered to a table in the dining room Jakob remembered: it was the one used for his wedding reception. All of a sudden a ghost from his past crept up on him and gripped him. He asked to be excused and left the table for the men' room, where he stood looking into the mirror at his image. A tear developed in his eye and rolled down his cheek. He was gripped by emotion and could see Liz in his mind. He remembered the glorious night of the wedding reception at the country club and how deeply he was in love with Liz. He didn't know what to do. He felt almost paralyzed and then Bob came in.

"I'm sorry, Jakob. We should never have come here. I wasn't thinking."

"I'm okay, Dad. Now . . . let's go back. I'll be all right." They left and returned to the table.

A sumptuous dinner was served, and several of the Miller friends stopped by to greet them and to meet Jakob and Geraldine. Jakob tried hard to take part in the gathering and soon managed well. It was their last night together and they all had an enjoyable time. He and Geraldine would be leaving early in the morning. Bob would take them to the train station to catch the 7:30 Milwaukee Road to Chicago, Union Station.

Bob managed to speak. "Jakob, we're sorry you have to leave tomorrow. It's been so nice having you here and meeting Geraldine. We are happy to have you both here, and best of all we will have BethAnn with us until you return." Thus, the evening ended on a cheerful note as they left for home.

Jakob and Geraldine arrived at the Milwaukee train station, in plenty of time to get their 7:30 a.m. train to Chicago. BethAnn was there for the send-off. She seemed unhappy to see them leave, but looked forward to being with her grandparents. Jakob told them he would keep in touch and let them know when they would be returning.

The train left on time. It was a sunny but chilly day. After making stops at Racine, Kenosha and Waukegan, the next stop was Union Station, Chicago. They retrieved their luggage from the storage locker and took a taxi to the Randolph Street Station, to catch the New York Central 20th Century Limited. They had some time to spare. They checked their luggage at the train and then Jakob took Geraldine for some sightseeing in Chicago. She got to see the State Street stores and Michigan Boulevard hotels. They had lunch at the famous Burghoff's Restaurant before leaving for the station.

"For its size Jakob, Chicago is not nearly as congested as London, and it seems so new." Jakob then mentioned Chicago had a big fire in 1871 during which a great part of the city burned down, so much of it had been rebuilt. Then in 1893 Chicago had what they called the Columbian Exposition, a world's fair. With it, much was built which changed the face of the city. Cultural things like museums and the latest in architecture, industry and science were added to Chicago's vastness.

They made it back to the station and found the platform with the famous plush red carpet which led to the train—New York Central Railroad's red carpet treatment for its passengers. They boarded the New York Central's best and most luxurious train. It wasn't long before they heard, "All aboard . . . All aboard." Then at two-thirty, a gentle tug could be felt as the train slowly moved out of the station, through switches, then into the sunlight. The sun shone through the tall Chicago buildings first, then industrial and commercial buildings, and finally through some of the residential neighborhoods and out of Chicago. They watched the passing landscape as they settled in for their trip to New York.

"Let's go to the dining car and get a cup of coffee. We can talk there," suggested Jakob. After passing through several cars, they entered the dining car and were seated by a white uniformed waiter captain who took their order. "What did you think of Milwaukee?" asked Jakob.

"I think it is a very nice city. I guess it is bigger than I expected it would be. Your parents have a lovely home, and I really enjoyed being with them. They were certainly very nice to me, but I expected they would be. However, you sprung me on them, before telling them much about me."

"No, not exactly. I let them know about us awhile back, so it didn't really come as a complete surprise. I felt they would accept you. My dad was very supportive in the talks I had with him and I know he likes you. My mother was also quite supportive, but she is not as demonstrative as my dad. I thought everything went fine. They are so thrilled to have BethAnn with them. I feel bad, she has not seen much of them up to now, but I think they will make it up with this trip." They finished their coffee and Jakob suggested they go back to their car. "I could use a nap. We got up early and I've gotten used to these late afternoon naps. What do you say?" Geraldine agreed and they went back to their car, reclined their seat as much as they could and took their nap.

There was enough noise in the car so the nap wasn't too long. Geraldine put her head on Jakob's shoulder and they held hands as the landscape passed by their window. This train was much faster than the ones they took from Sheridan to Chicago and the ride was more comfortable. The porter came by and offered them pillows, which they accepted. Daylight passed quickly into night and Jakob suggested they might go back to the dining car for dinner.

"I'm not too hungry after that big lunch. Maybe be we can just get a light dinner," said Geraldine. They walked back to the dining car and had to wait until there was a table available. They were finally seated.

"How about a martini to celebrate our red carpet trip?" Geraldine agreed and the waiter brought them their drinks. Jakob toasted their trip to New York. "It's not as good as the ones William makes, but it will do." They ordered a light dinner and watched the lights flickering by, as they ate. In the back of the dining car was a piano, with a man playing it. After they finished dinner, they went back and listened to the music. Some joined in with singing while others preferred conversation. One couple was on their honeymoon and another was going to visit their parents.

It was getting late, so they went back to their car. When they got there, they discovered the porter had already made up their beds, so they got ready for the night.

"We didn't get much sleep before. I do hope we will do better tonight. Do you mind if I take the lower bunk?" Jakob laughed and said he didn't mind climbing up, but if he fell down it would be her fault.

"Silly. A big boy like you shouldn't fall down, but if you do I'll help you get up." They kissed and took their places. Lying in his bed Jakob thought of the events of the past days, then he heard Geraldine's voice softly say, "Good night, Jakob. I love you."

"Good night, my dear." He closed his eyes and listened to the monotonous clickity clack of the train as it rode through the night, until he fell asleep. He slept intermittently, until he heard the soft melodious gong of the porter announcing it was seven o'clock and breakfast was being served in the dining car.

Chapter 35

Atlantic Crossing

The New York City traffic was slow and hectic from Grand Cental Station to the ship terminal. Jakob and Geraldine had plenty of time because the RMS *Oceanic* was scheduled to set sail at 2:30 p.m., but they were anxious to get settled in their cabins. The New York Passenger Ship Terminal loomed ahead. They soon saw the big passenger liner from inside the cab as they approached Chelsea Pier 62.

After checking in their luggage, they were ready to board at 12:15 with a few hours to spare before sailing. Their cabins were located on the promenade deck. They were none too big, but adequate. There was still time to get lunch before the grand send-off. Excitement prevailed throughout the ship among the passengers and crew who were moving about, in and out of the cabins. Finally, the deep sounding of the ship's horn indicated it was ready to cast off. Guests were then asked to leave.

Jakob and Geraldine found their way to the rail and saw the excited passengers waving and throwing ticker tape toward their friends below on the dock. The ship's lines were cast off the bollards on the pier, and they began to feel the movement of the ship as it started to leave from the dock. With the big tugs pulling and positioning the vessel, it soon was moved away from the dock area.

Some of the passengers remained at the rail still waving at their friends, while others like Jakob and Geraldine left for the other side of the ship and looked out onto the vast New York harbor to see the many boats, ships and tugs moving about. The *Oceanic* continued under the direction of the harbor pilot and the control of the tugs for some distance from the dock before the pilot left on his barge and the captain took over. Excitement prevailed throughout the ship.

"This is always so exciting. I just love it," exclaimed Geraldine.

"Yes it is. I have never been on a ship this big, or even on the ocean. I do remember once crossing Lake Michigan, from Milwaukee to Luddington, Michigan. Lake Michigan is a big body of water and the ferry we were on was big, but of course it was nothing like this ship. Then, one day one of my dad's friends had a sailboat on the lake, and he invited us on it. We went far out on the lake for a day of sailing, and I remember us losing sight of land. That was really a great day. But I can see this will really be exciting. I can't imagine, crossing the Atlantic Ocean." Geraldine moved close to Jakob, and put her arms around him and kissed him.

"I like being with you and I know I won't be lonesome when I'm with you. You know, Jakob, I do believe it is warmer out here, in New York harbor, even with the wind blowing. Oh, look! I can see the Statue of Liberty." Jakob held her hands and they watched the sights of New York Harbor pass them by. The steward announced the first seating for dinner would be at 5:00, but they would be eating at the second seating.

"Let's go inside and see if we can find a nice little bar. I'll buy you a martini to celebrate our trip. This is an English ship, so they certainly must be able to make one for us." Jakob asked one of the ship's stewards to direct them to a pub. In a dimly lit, cozy little bar they found an empty table, and were seated. A man in a waiter's uniform approached the table.

"What will be your pleasure, sir?"

"Does your bartender know how to make a good martini?"

"Oh, yes sir. James will make you a splendid one. Will Gordon's Gin be acceptable? We do have others but James favors Gordon's London Dry." Jakob nodded in agreement. "And how would you like it? Up tall, chilled, regular, dry or very dry, sir?" Jakob and Geraldine decided on up tall, chilled and regular. "Oh yes, sir. James will be delighted to make you his finest, and it will be with a stuffed olive if that is all right with you? I shall return promptly with James's finest, sir." Geraldine and Jakob looked at each other and muffled a laugh at the overly solicitous waiter. He promptly returned with the drinks on a silver tray, along with a small container of nuts. Placing napkins down first, he carefully placed an ornate martini glass on each one. "I trust you will find it satisfactory sir. May I inform you sir, when James makes a martini, it is truly an ambrosia, fit for the gods." He smiled, nodded and left.

"I say, old girl, I just can't wait to taste it. Should we sip it very slowly to receive the ultimate satisfaction, or shall we guzzle it down before it evaporates?"

"No, Sir Jakob. An English gentleman does not guzzle. You should know that. I shall propose a toast. Here's to a wonderful trip with you." They absorbed the ambiance of the bar and slowly finished their drinks. Geraldine, looking at Jakob, suggested, "Another thing you should remember, Sir Jakob, is a gentleman does dress for dinner, so we should probably leave now. If I don't have enough time to dress, you will be dining with someone who might look like a hag." Jakob responded that he would give Geraldine as much time as she needed to dress, rather than take the chance.

Jakob dressed in the formal attire he bought especially for the trip. He waited for Geraldine until the steward came by and announced the second seating was now available. Jakob knocked on Geraldine's cabin door.

"Is my lady ready yet?"

"Yes, she is, and you may come in now." Standing before him was Geraldine, dressed in an ankle-length black chiffon sleeved gown, with a deep v-neck short of the cleavage which continued over her shoulders and half the way down her back. A long double strand of pearls graced her neck. Her hair was parted to the side and swept back into a partial bun. The light fragrance along with a pale lip rouge, made her one step out of a fashion magazine.

"Geraldine, you look ravishing. My wait was well worth it."

Geraldine started laughing. "Jakob, you really look debonair. I love you in formal attire. But come to think of it, I love you in any attire." Jakob couldn't resist and took her in his arms. The fragrance of her hair was almost intoxicating and he kissed her. Geraldine broke from him.

"Let me come up for air, Sir Jakob. Are you sure you want to take me for dinner?"

Jakob smiled and raised his eyebrows. *Maybe not,* he thought. "You shouldn't have asked that question. Maybe we better leave now." They walked down the companionway and up to the dining room where they were met by the maitre d'.

"If you will follow me, Doctor Miller et Madam, I have a fine table for you next to the dance floor." He pulled out the chair and seated Geraldine, then one of the waiters did the same for Jakob. The band was playing soft dance music amid the voices of those already seated. As they walked through the dining room, Jakob noticed the turning of heads, as Geraldine passed through. The wine steward handed the wine list to Jakob, and stepping back he waited for their selection.

"What will it be, Lady Geraldine?"

"You know what I like, Sir Jakob. A Cabernet, or Chardonnay would be a fine choice." The steward came back with the right wine and poured the taster for Jakob, who accepted it. He then proceeded to pour the wine for Geraldine and Jakob, who toasted and sipped it. Geraldine soulfully looked at Jakob.

"Did I ever tell you I love you?"

"Yes, but you can do it again if you wish." The waiter arrived with menus and presented one to each of them. They studied the menu and placed their order. Jakob then looked at Geraldine. "Go ahead and tell me you love me now."

Geraldine just shook her head. "You spoiled the mood, silly."

"Geraldine, do you realize we have not danced together? This slow music is just great for starters. May I have this dance, My Lady?" He took her hand as he got up from the table. Geraldine rose from the chair and he led her on to the dance floor. She placed her hand his shoulder and brought her head close to his chest as they slowly moved to the music.

"If you still want to tell me you love me, you can do it now."

Then she softly spoke to him. "I love you, Jakob, but do you realize the music has stopped and we are the only ones left on the dance floor?"

"Oh, so we are. Well there is merit to that—no one will bump into us. Oh. Do you want to sit down now? Or perhaps we can just stay here holding each other, until the band starts to play again."

"Jakob, I believe they are taking a break."

As they sat down, the waiter placed a napkin on their laps and placed the consomme' in front of them. That was the beginning of a delicious gourmet meal. They finished their wine and waited for their dessert.

An elderly couple entered the dance floor, and danced near them, then stopped. They looked down at Geraldine and Jakob and the lady spoke.

"We couldn't help but notice how much you must be in love." Jakob looked surprised. "We can tell because we have been in love for fifty years. This is our anniversary. We wish for you to have many happy years." And they went off dancing.

Surprised, Jakob looked at Geraldine, who said, "Do we really look like we are in love?"

Jakob nodded yes and smiled. "You know, Geraldine, I enjoyed the dance before dinner. Will you dance with me some more? Maybe we can catch up with that couple. I want to congratulate them. Fifty years is a long time. Do you think we can make it?" They found the couple and congratulated them on fifty years of marriage before continuing their dance.

"I like dancing with you, Jakob." They continued dancing until the band stopped playing.

Jakob then suggested they go out on deck to see what the night was like. He opened the door to the deck and found the wind was strong. As they walked to the rail, they saw the moon and stars amid the clouds, but the seas were rough, with high waves.

"Jakob, I'm cold. Let's go back to the cabin so I can get a shawl." They went back into the ship to Geraldine's cabin. She searched and found the shawl. Holding the shawl, she started to leave, until Jakob put his arms around her.

"You know, you don't need the shawl. I can keep you warm." He was close to her and could smell the fragrance of her hair. "Hmmm, you smell so nice." His arms enclosed her body and their lips touched.

"Jakob, what are you doing to me?" He slowly unbuttoned her dress and put his hand inside it as they moved to the bed. Her dress slid down, leaving her partially disrobed. She helped him take off his jacket and shirt, and when they were completely disrobed they lay on the bed kissing and then making love. Geraldine lay in his arms as they slept through the night.

The sun crept through the shaded porthole and Jakob awakened, holding her soft body. He kissed her softly and thought about what they had enjoyed. *What am I going to do? I love her so much. How can I avoid this. It's inevitable*? he thought. Geraldine stirred. Her eyes opened, meeting his. She raised her head and kissed him.

"I love you so much Jakob." They lay there next to each other until they heard the steward announce breakfast was being served. "I don't want to get up Jakob. Let's just stay here all day."

Jakob smiled. "Not a bad idea, but I really think it is time for us to get up and have breakfast. You are fine here, but I have to go back to my cabin to dress."

"Well Jakob, I really didn't insist you stay here overnight, although I admit you did help me get warm without the shawl." Jakob smirked a little as he put on last evening's clothes. When there was no one in the companionway, he quickly left and entered his cabin.

Soon they both left their cabins and met in the middle of the companionway.

"Darling, fancy meeting you here," said Geraldine, as she giggled going to the dining room. They were seated with other passengers whom they had not met. There were introductions and small talk while they ate their breakfast. As they were finishing, Geraldine saw the couple they had met on the dance floor.

"Let's talk to them. They were so nice."

They approached them and Jakob spoke. "Look, Geraldine, the newlyweds." They all laughed. "Fifty years of marriage. Don't you folks feel kind of in a rut?"

All continued to laugh and the lady answered, "My name is Rosemary and this is John. We are the Andersons. We come from Cleveland, and I can definitely assure you we are not in a rut, but more in love than ever. Fifty years is nothing when it comes to love."

Geraldine smiled. "I am Geraldine Widicker and this is Jakob Miller. We are in love and are planning to get married just as soon as we can. We both lost our mates and God is giving us a second chance for happiness." They sat together drinking coffee and talking for the better part of the morning, and agreed they would be meeting again.

"It looks like a beautiful day. The sun is bright and the seas seem to be calmer. Let's look around the ship and maybe we can play one of those deck games, people play on ships—you know, shuffleboard."

"That would be fun, Jakob, but maybe I should go back to the cabin and get a shawl in case it gets cold out here."

"That would be all right, but if you remember the last time we went in for a shawl we didn't leave the cabin until the next day."

"Jakob it's too early for that kind of activity. Let's just go out, I can always go back in for a shawl if I need one." They walked the deck and even though it was windy, the temperature was comfortable. They stopped to watch some players for a while, then continued their walk.

"Look, Jakob, is that a ship out there?" It wasn't, but they continued watching the action of the waves as the wind picked up the water and caused a spray.

"Let's sit down on those deck chairs. Maybe one of the waiters will bring us something to drink. I'm thirsty." They pulled the chairs together. Soon one of the waiters came by. Drinks were ordered and then placed on the small round table between them.

"Jakob, we will be at Landry Manor in about eight days. I haven't told you much about my family history, other than my father was titled. Papa is a baron. As I told you, he is the third son of an earl, with a family history that goes back over two hundred years.

"When he was eighteen years old he joined the Army. Shortly after he joined, England became embroiled in the Crimean War. My father was big and strong and very athletic and a born leader. He soon became a sergeant of his company because of those qualities. Afterwards, he and his company were in the midst of the bitterly fought war. In one action his commanding officer, a lieutenant, was killed. There was no replacement for him and Papa was given a battlefield commission.

"His company was engaged in many dangerous missions. One was so dangerous that his regiment could have suffered grave casualties, were it not for the action of my father and his company. However, he was severely wounded and lost most of his men. He was in the army hospital there for almost a year, and then sent home to a military hospital in England. He remained there for the better part of another year before he was discharged. His left arm is barely usable, and he still has shrapnel in his leg. He has to use a cane to walk.

"For his valor, he received the Victoria Cross and was knighted by the Queen. His life could have been ended, were it not for his dauntless courage and strong will. By the action of the Queen, he became land-titled and named baron. Some of the land he received was not productive, but through his management he made it possible. During this period, many of those involved in farming went to the city to work and it was difficult for him to keep Landry Manor together.

"My mother's father owned a steel mill in Pennsylvania and while on a vacation to England, they had brought their daughter, Mary Sarah, with them. Somehow they met my father. I guess there was a romance of sorts. My father is fourteen years older than my mother, but they got married anyway. I guess there was a good amount of money involved, which helped my father, so they are more than just married partners. I am the first born, and as I told you, I also have a brother and two sisters. I believe my Papa, is sixty-nine years old now. And that brings chapter two to a close."

"Well, that is a fascinating story. Your father must be quite a person. I'm sure I can never match up to that."

"You are right when you say he is quite a person, but don't sell Jakob Miller short. There's more to tell, but I just heard they are serving lunch. Shall we go?"

"Sounds good. Do you need to go back to your cabin?" They decided to just go up for lunch. Everything looked different in the daytime. There was too much to eat, so they were served just what they wanted and received the same courtesy by the staff as the night before.

"I guess I don't really know much about England, other than what I learned in high school history and geography, the reading of some novels and of course,

Shakespeare. So please excuse me if I don't ask the right questions. It just sounds like your father was an amazing man. I don't know much about wars, except what the United States was involved in. The Civil War was terrible and we still suffer because of it. I can't even visualize being in combat. Doc Kelly sometimes talks about the Civil War. It had to be horrible. I guess I don't really know much about the differences between our governments. I was once asked to become involved in the politics of Sheridan, but I'm not really interested. I like what I am doing. Maybe someday I might change my mind, but not yet. Does your father have an interest in politics?"

"He certainly does. He is a member of Parliament and is very influential. Perhaps that is why he never tucked me in bed, as you always do with BethAnn, or go riding with me, or do the many things that you do with your daughter. Our family life was completely different from yours."

"I guess my life would be different if I were away from home in the politics of my country. My life is in Sheridan, and BethAnn and my profession are very important to me. How do you feel about the way we Americans live?"

"I guess I never really thought about it until I fell in love with you. My life with James was English. I don't believe I ever knew what it was like to be really loved." Jakob took her hands and held them, looking into her eyes. Then, looking up, he saw the Andersons approaching.

"I see you folks have had lunch already. We were thinking of joining you, but we'll just go on and do it another day."

"No. You just sit here. We'll have coffee with you and visit. Maybe you can give us the secret of eternal love," which caused all to laugh. Jakob asked John what he did for a living and found out he was a physician. That gave him plenty of opportunity to talk shop with him. In spite of the generational differences, they enjoyed being with the Andersons.

Jakob and Geraldine decided to again try their walk on the deck of the RMS *Oceanic*. The weather was beautiful, in the high 60s, with plenty of sun. The seas were still running six to eight feet, but the *Oceanic* plowed through them. They were now too far from land to have any birds following, and no other ships were visible. They managed to see all the sights of the ship which could be seen from the deck and returned to the cabins to discover invitations to the captain's cocktail party for, Tuesday, April 17, 1906, at 1700 hours. They also received an invitation for dinner at the captain's table for April 18 at 2000 hour, formal attire requested for both.

"Geraldine, do you realize we are now a part of the social elite aboard the RMS *Oceanic*? Don't you feel important? I don't have to worry because I will wear the same dinner clothes I wore yesterday. But how can you top what you wore yesterday? You were so lovely."

"Jakob, you don't have to worry. I'll be ready."

"I know you will, dear." And he placed a kiss on her lips. "Why don't we go to the library, to see what they have in the way of current books. Maybe I can find something on the aristocrats of England." Geraldine chose to go to her cabin and rest until the captain's cocktail party, so Jakob decided to go by himself. There were many books available on England, and he took one he thought would interest him. He sat in a large leather chair and opened the book. He started to read, but his mind wandered off to thoughts of the baron, Sir Gerald Randolph Landry. He became somewhat apprehensive. *What kind of a person is this man who will be my father-in-law?* he thought. He couldn't visualize any physical description. Somehow he almost sounded unreal. Yet, he was the father of the woman Jakob loved. He was almost gripped with a fear he might not like him. *What if this should happen? I mustn't even think like this. I've got to put these thoughts out of my mind.* He closed the book, put it back on the shelf, and returned to his cabin.

Jakob dressed in his evening wear with a white tie. He wasn't sure it was actually right, but most of the men dressed the same. *I wonder if Geraldine is ready? I'll give her a try and knock on her cabin door.* It opened, and standing in front of him was his Venus De Milo, in a calf length white chiffon dress, a v-neck with shoulder straps and a low back. A single strand of pearls graced her neck. White gloves extended above her elbows. Her hair was parted in the center and pulled to a bun in the back. She placed a kiss on his lips.

"Geraldine, what are you doing? You are going to make that captain drool with envy when he looks at you and having me at your side."

"He can drool with envy, but you are the one who has me." They made entrance to the captain's party and were introduced to Captain Roland Winthrop, a handsome bearded gentleman wearing a white uniform with a chest full of medals. His hat was adorned with gold braid on its visor. He held Geraldine's hand as he welcomed them aboard and briefly chatted with them, until one of the waiters with a tray of glasses offered champagne to them. They took their champagne, and the next couple stepped forward and was introduced to the captain.

Jakob observed the wandering eyes of those present as Geraldine moved through the gathering. She was the perfect conversationalist, and it set her apart from the crowd, especially with her slight English accent. It was an interesting cross section of people.

When all had arrived, the captain gave a presentation in which he proudly spoke of his ship. He described its various characteristics, and said it was considered the largest passenger ocean-liner of the day and with top speed to 19 knots, unheard of at that time. It had a crew of 349 for the 1700 passengers it carried, with 410 passengers in first class. He then introduced selected members of his bridge and invited those who wanted to visit the bridge to an escorted tour. Jakob and Geraldine stayed and chatted with their fellow passengers. Having already partaken of the hors d'oeuvres and champagne, they decided to leave.

It wasn't time yet for dinner seating, so they decided to stop by the ship's pub. The solicitous waiter was present and remembered them.

"Will it be the same, sir? Two of James's famous martinis?"

"That is correct. The ones that you said were made fit for the gods." Returning, he carried them on a silver tray and carefully placed each one on a napkin, along with some nuts. Bowing, he smiled and left.

They toasted and Geraldine said, "It was nice to be invited to the captain's cocktail party, but I would rather spend my time here with you."

"Did you say that just to make me feel good?" Geraldine laughed impishly.

"As a matter of fact, yes. But, I also mean it." Jakob beckoned her closer and reached over to kiss her. They talked about the cruise, but Geraldine said she was anxious to get to Landry Manor. She hoped Jakob would like it there and would enjoy being with her family. One of the stewards came by and announced seating time for dinner, so they left.

The maitre d' welcomed them and took them to their table near the dance floor. The wine steward came by, but they already had their fill of spirits, so they declined and ordered their dinner. Geraldine took Jakob's hand and led him to the dance floor. They danced until the waiter brought out their first course. After dinner, they went to the theater and were entertained with a cabaret. The ship provided them with food, relaxation and entertainment.

The next day they went up to the bridge and had an interesting visit during which they learned all about the workings of the ship. Geraldine was surprised to meet some people she knew who lived in Ipswich. They were coming back from a visit to New York.

On the fifth day of the cruise, the weather turned from bright sun to a gray dreary day which grew windy and cold. The seas increased and it started to rain. They were told to avoid going out on the open deck because of rain squalls, with strong winds. Everyone stayed inside, but there was plenty to do. Jakob and Geraldine had lunch with their friends the Andersons, and met others they visited with as well. The weather did put a damper on the cruise, but all were hoping it would get better. They went to the cabaret after dinner and turned in early.

WHAM! Jakob was awakened by a loud noise and the shudder of the vessel. He arose from the bed. As the ship seemed to momentarily quiver and items in the cabin fell to the deck, lights went out for a short time, and there was silence. Then he heard people in the companionway. The lights came back on and he left his bed. He opened the cabin door to find people milling around, some with life jackets on. Geraldine was next to him, frightened.

"What's happened?"

"I don't know. There was this terrible noise which woke me up. Wait, there's the cabin boy coming through, and he's saying something."

"Don't be frightened. Everything is all right. We just got hit by a giant wave. The ship is fine." Jakob spoke to him and he repeated the same story. He said the ship was not damaged, even though it was hit by the giant wave. Jakob then went up toward the bridge. The first officer was taking questions and related the same story: the ship sustained a hit by a rogue wave breaking on the foredeck, creating the noise, but the ship came through it fine. Jakob went back to his cabin and found Geraldine waiting for him.

"I guess we're all right. I spoke to the first officer we saw on the bridge the other day and he said a very large wave hit the ship, but it did not create any damage." It was 0530 and just starting to get light.

"Jakob, I'm afraid." He put his arm around her and held her. Geraldine was shivering.

"We're going to be okay. I know, the noise frightened me too. Here, let's just sit down." They sat down and then lay back on the bed, holding each other. Finally, Geraldine let go of Jakob and said she felt better.

"Why don't we get dressed and go to the dining room and get some coffee. I can't sleep anymore." Jakob walked Geraldine to her cabin, then went back to his and got dressed. He waited for Geraldine and then knocked on her door. She was ready and they went to the dining room.

Coffee was available, but breakfast was delayed because of damage done to the cooking utensils and dishes in the galley that went flying when the wave hit. They had their coffee while the passengers talked amongst themselves. One of the ship's officers explained the situation.

"The wave that hit the ship was huge." He thought it could have been forty or fifty feet high. "It just broke over the bow, sending tons of water on it." He said they had to slow down some, but they came through all right. "This is the North Atlantic and it is subject to bad weather, although such a rogue wave is very rare. A smaller ship probably would have sustained damage." The seas were still very high and the rain fell in squalls. In the meantime, the kitchen attendants brought out rolls and toast to start the breakfast.

"Jakob, this is the first time I have ever experienced such bad weather. I can remember storms, but they were over in a day. It seems interesting, how possible disaster brings people together. People who don't make any effort to talk to one another become friends when they share a common cause." Jakob agreed. He found it to be true as it happened on a number of occasions in Sheridan.

At daybreak the next morning, the sun came through and the winds had died down. The seas were still running high, but nowhere near as high as they had experienced the previous day. Jakob and Geraldine walked the decks and even stopped to play shuffleboard with some people they met after the wave hit.

The last day at sea, people talked to one another and wished them good luck and happiness during their visit to England. Several asked Jakob and Geraldine to sit with them for dinner, so they found themselves at a table for ten. The mix was interesting and it made for good conversation. They loved to hear Geraldine speak, with her English accent, and were amazed when she told them about her ranch in the foothills of the Bighorn Mountains. They couldn't believe, this voluptuous woman could rope a steer or break a horse. Jakob himself hadn't really grasped this until others recognized what she was capable of doing.

They danced and sang together. The ship's dining room staff built a pyramid of champagne glasses. Geraldine elected to climb to the top of the ladder to fill the top glasses with champagne, with cheers of the passengers. And, while everyone toasted each other they sang "Auld Lang Syne." The party started to break up after midnight and Jakob and Geraldine started toward their cabins, wishing they could stay for another day of revelry. However, their voyage would end soon when they arrived at the pier in Southampton the next day.

"Jakob, I have never experienced such a group of people in my life. They were so much fun to be with. Didn't you just love the group at our table? I wish we could see them again." Jakob held Geraldine and agreed the night had been great and he enjoyed being with the group. He told her the people in Sheridan were somewhat like that, and she would enjoy living there. They kissed and parted company, going into their own cabin.

Jakob awakened to the sounds of the cabin boy announcing breakfast was now being served in the main dining room. He looked out of the porthole and discovered the *Oceanic* was standing offshore, ready to head into Southampton. He got ready for breakfast and knocked on Geraldine's cabin door. She opened it and invited Jakob in while she was still getting ready.

"I guess this is the end of our voyage, Jakob. A pilot will bring the ship into port with the help of tugs. We still have a way to go before we dock. It is about ten miles up the channel before we will actually see Southampton docks. Shall we go for breakfast and see what's going on?" They went to the dining room and were served. There was lots of excitement among the passengers.

Both Jakob and Geraldine had most of their luggage ready and quickly finished the rest of their packing. The ship had been put in quarantine and will have to pass through Immigration and Customs before passengers could disembark. The pilot would take control of the ship, and they would move toward Southampton, assisted by the tugs. Geraldine told Jakob about the history of Southampton, the Roman occupation and subsequent occupiers. She pointed out the Isle of Wight that aided the protection of Southampton, making it useful for ships of all sizes.

"Actually, Jakob, the city of Southampton is still ten miles away. Once we get there, we will go through Customs then board a train at the Southampton station. It is very close to the water, and at high tide the water almost reaches the platform. Incidentally, you didn't pack your passports, did you? I did that once and had to go back through my luggage to find them."

"I'm not a world traveler, but I did retain my passports." Geraldine laughed.

The pace of the big vessel was slow as it was brought up for docking. The dock was filled with people. There was a lot of merriment as they waited for the passengers to disembark. The first-class passengers taken through Customs first, followed by the second and then third-class travelers.

"We'll get the train as soon as we get through Customs and have our luggage available." Luggage was brought up on the dock and debarkation began. Soon they were in line for Customs.

Looking at Jakob's new passport, the Customs agent remarked, "I say, this must be your first trip here, eh? Hope you enjoy it, old chap." Jakob smiled and thanked him.

Turning to Geraldine, he remarked, "Friendly fellow, the Customs agent." Geraldine smiled.

"That is somewhat unusual for Customs agents. But then maybe he was just in a good mood." Turning toward the train, Geraldine remarked, "The train will take us to South Central Railway Station. Tonight, we'll be in London and we'll stay in a delightful old hotel— The Great Eastern. It is near the railway station. Then tomorrow, we'll go from there to Ipswich."

They watched their baggage being loaded on the train and waited to get aboard. "I'm sure you will notice almost everything here is old. I guess that's the reason people in the states refer to England as the *old country*. But you'll get used to it, and hopefully you'll like it. Jakob, do you realize how old England is?"

"I guess I don't, but I'm learning fast."

There were a number of passengers from the ship who stopped by to wish Geraldine and Jakob well while in England. The Andersons came to say goodby and to wish them at least fifty years of love.

Rosemary kissed Jakob on the cheek and whispered, "God's Blessing on you Jakob, and love your wife." John did likewise to Geraldine.

"We hope to see you again." And they were gone.

"Jakob, those people were beautiful. I can't believe we were so fortunate to have met them and so many others on the ship." They were now on the platform getting ready to board the train.

"Geraldine, I like the idea of boarding the train and getting seats from the outside, as you do in England. It saves time going up that narrow aisle." They boarded the train and stowed their carry-on items above, then took their seats. "After the ocean voyage, I guess we are going to finish the day on a train. This one will take us all the way to London, won't it?" Geraldine agreed that it would, and said that the train ride would take about two hours. The door opened and two more passengers boarded, and sat across from them.

Soon the train started and they were on their way to Southampton which was some distance from the dock, and then on to London. Sitting back, they relaxed and closed their eyes, but didn't fall asleep. The train stopped in Southampton and took on more passengers before leaving for London. During the next two hours the train made a number of stops. Then it was announced London was the next stop.

Arrangements were made to take the baggage to the Great Eastern Hotel. Jakob was impressed with the hotel because it was so very old. They registered and were taken up to their rooms. They entered the "lift" that took them to the third floor. The bellman made sure everything was in order before placing the luggage in their rooms. The rooms were adequate but dated. Jakob gave the bellman a gratuity as he left.

Looking at Geraldine, he said, "This has been a hectic day. Shall we have our martini now or wait until later, after we have taken our naps and gotten dressed for dinner?"

"Maybe we should have the martini now. I know just the place we can go to recharge." They found a small pub and entered it. A charming waitress showed them to their table. Jakob ordered the martinis and they toasted to the first martini on the shore of England.

Sometime later they entered their rooms for their nap. Jakob lay in his bed reviewing the day. It had been a full one, between exiting the ship, going through Customs, and riding the train to London. In spite of the hotel's elegance, he was somewhat disappointed. He remembered the Palmer House in Chicago, and thought it was more opulent. However, the Palmer House was quite new compared to the Great Eastern Hotel. *I wonder if I will be much impressed with England.* His eyes grew weary and he fell asleep.

Noise in the hallway awakened Jakob, and he noted the time. He had slept an hour and was somewhat rested. It was time to dress for dinner. *How should I dress?* he thought *Maybe I should check with Geraldine.* He knocked on her door and she answered.

"What should I wear to dinner tonight? We aren't going formal, are we?" Geraldine said it was optional and a business suit would be acceptable.

"Did you manage to take a nap? I got about an hour."

Geraldine answered, "I did get a good nap and I'm ready for a grand night in London. I should be ready in about fifteen minutes."

Jakob was waiting at her door in fifteen minutes as she had suggested.

"I thought you were going to dress down from shipboard dress? You look beautiful. I do like you in that color." She wore an ankle-length lavender dress, with long sleeves and a lace collar. It was simple but elegant. The beads she wore were long and of a darker lavender color.

"You know, you always dress very tastefully."

"Jakob, you do know how to compliment, so I must compliment you too. You look like a professional businessman, and I like you that way. Now we are done with the complimenting, do I get a kiss? I have been waiting all day." Jakob put his arms around her and brought her close to him. He could smell the fragrance in her hair and held her before kissing. Then she put her arms around him and kissed him tenderly.

"I shouldn't admit it, but I really need two kisses."

They both laughed as Jakob remarked, "Any more kisses and we might just stay here and not make it to dinner. Now . . . for that martini I promised you. Will you lead me to that darkly lit bar?" After leaving the lift, they walked down one of the several walkways to an authentic English Pub. On one side of the room was a piano, with a formally attired man playing and softly singing. He acknowledged Jakob and Geraldine with a smile. They were seated and greeted by a young lady in a very short black skirt with a white apron.

"I trust this will be acceptable, sir. What may I get for you?" Jakob asked if the bartender knew how to make a martini, and she was quick to answer. "Of course sir. We actually specialize in them. Most of the gentlemen always come here to order them."

"Well now, what about the ladies? Do they partake of them?"

"Some of the more sophisticated ones do." Looking at Geraldine, she continued, "Pardon me, My Lady, if I am wrong, but I would expect you to indulge with your gentleman friend in a martini."

Geraldine just laughed and nodded. "Do you mean if I order a martini, I will be considered sophisticated?"

"Yes, My Lady."

"Then I shall order one."

The waitress left laughing. She returned shortly with the martinis on a silver tray. "Robin definitely prefers Gordon's gin, and would find it disgraceful to use a gin of lower quality. I am sure you will find his martini outstanding." She placed the frosted glasses of martinis on a napkin in front of them, curtsied and left.

"You know, I have an altogether different attitude about how the English treat the martini. It is with great respect." Geraldine laughed and told Jakob he was just jesting her. The conversation now took on a more serious note.

"Geraldine, I've been thinking about how should I address your father. He has a number of titles."

Geraldine shook her head. "Yes, there are a number of titles used to address him. As an American, you would be addressed as Mister, but because of your profession, you would usually be addressed as Doctor. You could call him Mister, but you might add some respect and address him as, Sir Gerald. Some may address him as Baron or My Lord, but if you addressed him as Sir Gerald. I believe it would be respectful. My mother could be addressed as, My Lady, and that distinguishes her from the daughters who are normally addressed Lady Geraldine, etc. Does that answer your question on etiquette? The English are peculiar when it comes to titles. I guess I have lived in America long enough and it doesn't bother me if someone calls me Missus. In England, they will undoubtedly refer too you as Doctor, certainly not Doc as they often do in Sheridan. We're not too far from Landry Manor and I know how you must feel, but don't worry, they don't bite."

Jakob laughed. "Is that a promise? It looks like my martini is empty. Maybe we should move on for dinner. I shall follow you, Lady Geraldine. You know, I like that title. It means that you are—kind of special."

They left the pub and found the London House, a very elegant restaurant. The maitre d' assigned a waiter to take them to their table. The service was exceptional and the beef roast dinner excellent. After finishing their dinner, they walked through the hotel, window shopping.

"Tomorrow we will leave for Ipswich and Landry Manor, the terminus of our trip," said Geraldine. Jakob was anxious to meet Geraldine's family. He felt he was more than ready.

Chapter 36

Landry Manor

Jakob and Geraldine checked out of London's Great Eastern Hotel after breakfast and were getting ready to take the train to Ipswich. Geraldine called Landry Manor and spoke with her Mama. She told Geraldine they would send a car and driver to pick them up at the train station in Ipswich when they arrived; Landry Manor was just a short drive from the station.

In his more quiet moments, Jakob missed BethAnn and would often think about her. He sent a wire to Milwaukee from London telling his parents they had safely arrived in England and would be at Landry Manor that day. He also asked them to be sure to tell BethAnn how much he missed her.

Geraldine mentioned she would have liked to spend more time in London showing Jakob the sights of the city, but was anxious to get to Landry Manor.

"We can always take a trip to London later, but right now, I would like to get to Landry Manor." Typical of London weather it was in the 50s and it was dreary. Their baggage was sent over to the station and Jakob and Geraldine were awaiting the 11:00 a.m. train.

Jakob wore the business suit and vest he had worn for dinner and Geraldine dressed in a long gray skirt with a white lace topped blouse and a short black jacket. Geraldine always dressed very well. She always looked the part of an aristocratic lady. Jakob was surprised to see how well many Londoners dressed while traveling, but he also saw the ugly signs of poverty, especially in the area of the train station where there were a number of vendors selling newspapers, flowers, fruit and various other wares.

They boarded the train and made themselves comfortable and holding hands. Geraldine was excited about visiting her former home and family, but Jakob remained apprehensive. He just didn't know how he would relate to the baron. As the train worked its way through London, he saw much industry and various kinds of living accommodations, some very poor. Much of it was very old. Geraldine talked about the different places she would like to take Jakob to visit, while Jakob kept thinking about his future relationship with her family. He had no idea of how he would be accepted. In Sheridan, Milwaukee, or even Chicago he had full confidence in himself, but here he was treading on completely unknown territory. Over and over, he kept asking himself if they would accept him, or would he be regarded a commoner, and therefore unworthy of a baron's daughter. The conductor announced the next stop was Ipswich, so they got their things together.

Ipswich station was crowded with people leaving the train, as well as those getting on. Their luggage was unloaded, and placed on a large cart, then taken off the platform toward the station. Geraldine was anxiously looking for the driver who was to pick them up. A uniformed man came up to her from behind.

"Lady Geraldine, I see you have arrived." Geraldine turned around and saw the driver.

"Sampson, I'm so happy to see you." Sampson was a middle-aged man in a greenish suit, boots and a visored cap who welcomed her. "We're a bit late because the train was behind schedule. I'm so glad to see you. I want you to meet Doctor Miller." Sampson acknowledged Jakob. The car was just a short distance away and Sampson started securing their luggage in place on a rack at the rear of the car. Jakob was taking quick glaces in all directions to see what kind of a place Ipswich was. It appeared very old. Its buildings seemed large and were made of wood and stone; some were bricked and weathered.

Sampson opened the car door for Geraldine and Jakob. Jakob couldn't distinguish who the car manufacturer was. It certainly wasn't a Ford or any of the American cars he saw in the States. It was black and shiny and was completely enclosed, not like some cars he seen which were open. It also had a lot of shiny brass on it.

They immediately left. The town streets were cobblestones and crowded, but when they got out of town they were on rough dirt roads, some with deep ruts and holes. There weren't any other cars, but there were many horses and various sorts of wagons and buggies.

"Jakob, we are almost there. Landry Manor is just over this hill." Ahead was an old red-bricked wall with a large black gate that was open. The wall looked to be about seven or eight feet high, with a weathered white stone cap. They passed through the gate and several hundred yards beyond was a large, three-story red brick building. As they drew closer, it too showed its age. The third floor had dormers and there were chimneys at both ends, as well as one in the middle. It looked to be in reasonably good repair, with white painted trim. The grounds were well landscaped and maintained, with trimmed bushes and trees flowering and greening. It almost looked like a park with a fountain.

The entrance to the building had a portico with a heavy wooden door and the many windows were shuttered and open. As they were driving closer, Jakob saw a number of people standing outside apparently waiting for Geraldine. The driver pulled up in front of the building, got out of the car, and then opened the rear door. Jakob got out, followed by Geraldine. Evidently the staff had come out to welcome them. Geraldine's father limped forward, leaning heavily on his cane, and was followed by her mother.

"Geraldine, my Joy, welcome home!" He put his arm around her and embraced her, followed by her mother doing likewise. Both kissed her on the cheek. The staff that lined up next to the door applauded. Jakob was standing to the side and behind Geraldine. She turned to Jakob, took him by his arm, and brought him forward so she could introduce him.

"Papa, Mama, I want you to meet the man I'm in love with, Doctor Jakob Miller." Her father was tall and handsome, with gray hair, a small bald spot on top, and a gray beard, neatly trimmed. His eyebrows and steel blue eyes gave him an impressive look. Her mother, a lovely lady was well endowed, with brownish hair pulled up in a bun. She smiled warmly. Jakob put his hand out.

"Sir Gerald, I'm honored to meet you and Lady Mary. It is so nice you would have me here." Sir Gerald placed his cane under his arm and firmly shook Jakob's hand. After he let go, Jakob bowed slightly to Lady Mary, who gave him her hand. He shook her hand and addressed her. Sir Gerald carefully looked at Jakob with a measured smile.

"Welcome to Landry Manor, Doctor." He had a heavy English accent.

Jakob gave his best smile. "I'm pleased to be here with you. And please, I would appreciate it if you called me Jakob, just as Geraldine does."

The baron smiled slightly and nodded. "As you wish, Jakob." He turned and invited them to go inside, but stopped before the staff. "This is my staff. They will do everything possible to make your stay comfortable and pleasant. Rutherford is my butler who is in charge of everything that has to do with Landry Manor." Rutherford smiled and nodded. "And this is Mrs. Wrightson, who will also be available to assist you, Please, don't forget to call on them if there is anything that you should need." She likewise nodded, as well as the rest of the staff, who all responded appropriately.

Geraldine was holding Jakob's arm as they entered the building. Beyond the small entry-way was a spacious room with a high ceiling that extended beyond the second floor. A large and ornate staircase on the right side of the room went to the second floor. At the rear of the room was a massive fireplace. There were two large crystal chandeliers that had been electrified, and at the left side of the room there were some large heavily draped windows. The walls were paneled in dark wood, with Victorian furnishings throughout the room.

"This is Landry Manor, Jakob. I trust you will be comfortable here. Rutherford will see to it, that your luggage will be placed in your room. In fact, it is probably up there right now. I'm sure you would like to freshen up. Robert will be your valet. Geraldine will show you your room, and when you are both ready My Lady Mary will have tea and crumpets for us."

"Come, Jakob, I'll show you to your room." They went up the large ornate staircase to the second floor. A wide hallway connected both sides of the second floor with a rail on one side. It was possible to look down onto the first floor from behind the rail.

"This is my room, and yours is the last room down the hall. I'm sure you won't have any trouble finding it." She opened her door and pulled Jakob in. Putting her arms around him, she kissed him. "It has been a long time since I kissed you, you know." Jakob smiled and held her close. "I'm going to be ready in about fifteen minutes and I'll stop by to get you, in case you should get lost." Jakob smiled and went on to his room which was quite large. It had a large, heavily draped window and a small fireplace, along with the usual bedroom furnishings. His luggage had been placed at the side of the room.

He lay down on the large canopied bed as random thoughts raced through his head. *So far so good, Jakob.* He looked around the room and then opened several of his suitcases, removing things he might need. Looking out the window, he saw expanses of fields with trees and bushes. He was impressed by the vastness of the place and the apparent age of the structure. *I wonder if this place was something else before it was a home,* he thought. Then he heard a soft knock on the door.

"Come on in." Geraldine entered and sat on the bed next to him.

"What do you think of my home away from home? Kind of old, isn't it? I'm glad it's not winter because it can be really cold and drafty here, in spite of the fireplaces. I think Papa was impressed with you. He can be cold and stuffy, but Mama is a dear, warm and loving and I know you will love her. Well, let's go down or the tea will be cold." Jakob put his arm around Geraldine and gave her a hug.

"I'm following you, Honey."

One of the footmen brought in a cart with the silver server, cups and saucers, and a large tray of crumpets, and slices of bread with meats. He served the tea and offered the crumpets and other items. They took what they wanted on their plates. He then moved back and stood in the background until called upon. Lady Mary was the first to speak.

"You must be exhausted from the trip. I have not been as far west as Wyoming, but for me, the trip from Pittsburgh to Landry Manor was unbelievably long. I was thoroughly exhausted."

Jakob smiled and answered, "Yes, it was long, but we made a stop along the way. We took my daughter to Milwaukee to spend time with her grandparents."

My Lady Mary expressed a wish. "You could have brought her to Landry Manor. We would have loved to see her."

"I thought about it, but she had not seen her grandparents for a long time, and I thought it better to leave her with them. If I had brought her, I know that you would have enjoyed her."

"Oh yes, Mama, BethAnn is such a lovely child. You would love her. She has a pony and I have been teaching her to ride. I am amazed how well she does. I too, wish she had come with us."

Sir Gerald chimed in, "Milwaukee! There are a lot of German people there, aren't there?" Jakob countered that there were a good number of Germans, but Milwaukee was a melting pot of all ethnic groups. "Don't they have a lot of breweries there?" Jakob told him there were a number of breweries Milwaukee was famous for, but maybe not as many as one might think.

"I have not been in the States but one time, and it was when I went to your

Capitol, Washington D.C., with a group from the Parliament to discuss imports. We didn't stay too long. We also saw your city of Baltimore. I guess it once was quite a hotbed. Our ships did mess it up in 1812. Too bad that had to happen."

The conversation went well and Jakob found Sir Gerald to be an opinionated man, but interesting. He enjoyed the scones and other items but only tolerated the tea. He would rather have had coffee.

Geraldine then took Jakob on a tour of the Manor, and described and identified the various paintings, pictures and artifacts. In the library were Sir Gerald's memorabilia and the Victoria Cross, all of which were very impressive. The tour took in the kitchen, and the servants' quarters on the lower level. Jakob was amazed at the number of men and women who worked there, but it was a big, old house. Everyone seemed to be very busy.

They left the kitchen area and Geraldine said on the morrow she would take him to see some of the outer buildings and the stable.

"Jakob, we could go for a ride. How would you like to do that? Oh, I'd love to. It's been so long since I have ridden here. What do you say?"

"I think I'd liked to, but you know I don't have any fancy riding clothes. I have my Levi's and boots. It's just plain old Western style."

"Oh, that would be all right. I think it would be cute. No one here has seen Western style dress. You might even start a new trend in riding for Suffolk. I have just the right horse for you. Oh, I'm excited. I'm really looking forward to tomorrow's ride."

"It's your call, Honey. Now we have tomorrow settled, what about dinner tonight?" Geraldine thought.

"Yes, tonight . . . Mama, has invited some friends over for dinner. They are old friends and I think you will like them. One is a soldier friend of Papa, and the other was in the foreign service. They will come with their wives, of course. I think the dinner clothes you wore on the ship will be just fine. Wear the white tie and your waistcoat. Papa and Jonathon may wear their dress uniforms—scarlet coats with medals, but Arnold will be in dinner clothes, so you won't be alone without any medals. Shall we go up? We can continue our talk in my bedroom."

Jakob and Geraldine sat next to a small table by the window in her room. "Jakob, this is going to be fun. I hope you will enjoy it. There is so much we can do and see. I don't know exactly what clothes you brought, but you could probably use a suit with knickers, for your more casual wear. There is a men's store in Ipswich that might have one for you, if you wish. You don't have to buy one but it might be nice. Think about it." They covered many topics and Jakob was becoming infected by Geraldine's excitement and was looking forward to doing the things she suggested. She also suggested Jakob could use Robert for his valet.

"Geraldine, I don't need anyone to help me dress."

"Well, he is available if you should need him. He will also take care of your clothes, cleaning and pressing them, as well as doing your other laundry. Do use him." Looking at the clock, she suggested they start getting ready for dinner. "The guests will arrive promptly at six and we'll start dinner at seven. A kiss right now would definitely be appropriate." Jakob took her in his arms and looked into her eyes. She kissed him tenderly. "I love you Jakob Miller. Now, let me get dressed for you."

Jakob left and went to his room. He took off his coat, shirt, and shoes and lay back on the large canopied bed. Lying there, he sifted through his thoughts. So much had happened in one short day.

He dressed in his dinner jacket and the white, winged collared shirt, waistcoat and white tie. Geraldine met Jakob at his room. She had a simple ankle-length black dress with a square neck and two long strands of pearls. Her hair was parted in the middle and braided, with the braid extending over her left shoulder. Jakob took a deep breath. Her fragrance was captivating.

They walked down together and met in the drawing room, just in time to hear the arrival of Major Jonathon Robertson and Mrs. Joanne Robertson, followed by Ambassador Arnold Willson and Mrs. Abigail Willson. Geraldine was right; the Army officers wore their uniforms and their medals. Geraldine and Jakob were introduced with much ado. Robert and Cedric, the footmen, took orders for drinks and Geraldine ordered martinis from Robert.

"You are absolutely right, Geraldine. He does make a splendid martini." She smiled.

Sir Gerald lifted his Scotch and toasted, "To my daughter, Geraldine, and her very good friend, Doctor Jakob Miller, our guests from the United States."

They all responded, "Hear, hear."

Jakob whispered into Geraldine's ear, "I feel like a fish out of water." Geraldine looked at him and grinned. But the guests were kind and engaged them in interesting conversation. They questioned Jakob about Wyoming and if the savages were under control. Jakob gave them a good explanation about life in Wyoming and told them the native Americans were making great strides, in spite of the vast cultural differences. Arnold Willson, the ambassador, was interested in the current political problems faced by President Roosevelt. Jakob answered as best as he could and hoped he wouldn't be asked any more such questions. But Mr. Willson was concerned if the United States was prepared militarily, should there be a conflict in Europe. Jakob answered that he hoped they were amply prepared, but didn't know. He hoped there would be no conflict in Europe. At about that moment, Rutherford stepped forward and announced, "My Lady, dinner will be served." And all moved to the large dinner table adorned in glistening glass, silver and white linens. The two candelabra with flickering candles gave the table a very elegant appearance. The table wine was a Bordeaux. A crab aspic was the first course served. The footmen then began serving the guests Tournedos Sautes

Aux Champignons, Potatos au Gratin, Carottes aux Herbes. The preparation was exceptional and the dinner conversation light. Jakob sat next to Mrs. Willson, and found her an interesting conversationalist. He learned something about the customs in India. After a dessert of Cherry Flan with a liquor, the party, filled with rich food, rose from their seats. Jakob left with the men, who were going to the library for a port wine and a cigar. The ladies congregated in the drawing room with their coffee. Jakob hadn't smoked a cigar since BethAnn was born, and saw his go out, after several puffs. The conversation was more on the politics of the Parliament that Sir Gerald would lead, which pretty much left Jakob out.

The evening ended at ten and Jakob was happy it did. The men left the library, took their wives and then bid their farewells. There was little talk after all were gone.

Sir Gerald and Lady Mary excused themselves and bid Jakob and Geraldine good night and started up the staircase to their bedroom. The staff was still cleaning up the dining room while Geraldine and Jakob sat in a love seat talking about the evening. Soon they decided it was time to go to sleep and they trekked up the staircase to their rooms.

"Poor Jakob, how did you get along with those men?" Jakob just smiled and kissed Geraldine good night.

It was a long day for Jakob and he slept well in the comfortable bed, only to be awakened by the crowing of a rooster nearby. At first he thought he was in Sheridan, until he opened his eyes. Light filtered through the heavy drapery. He just lay in bed mulling over the previous night and he wasn't exactly sure if he enjoyed the guests. They were all nice enough, but the conversation got boring when Sir Gerald started talking about the politics of Parliament. Sir Gerald seemed nice enough, but Jakob had a strange feeling about him. He felt comfortable with Lady Mary. She seemed sincere and loving, but Jakob didn't detect a deep love between her and Sir Gerald. There was a knock on the door and Jakob answered.

"It's Geraldine, may I come in?" Before he could answer she was in. "Oh, you're still in bed. It's going to be a beautiful day." Geraldine wore a beige silk lounging robe. She sat on the bed, then turned over and lay next to Jakob and kissed him. "Are you ready for an exciting day? After breakfast we can go outside and I'll show you the rest of the buildings. Then we'll go to the stable to get the horses and take a look around. There are some interesting things here to see. Papa likes to go bird hunting, but we won't go hunting. Get dressed and we'll go down for breakfast."

"Okay, that's fine. But what should I wear now?" She thought, then finally answered.

"Wear your Levis,' a shirt of your choice, and a coat if you wish at breakfast. When we go for our ride, you can wear your Wyoming-style riding clothes. I really think we should get you a casual suit in Ipswich. Then you will have something more fitting for daily life here."

Jakob went down with Geraldine for breakfast. Sir Gerald and Lady Mary were already there and eating.

"Normally, Lady Mary has her breakfast in bed," said Geraldine. On the buffet there were scrambled eggs, sausages, toast and marmalade, milk, tea and coffee. Rutherford asked them if they preferred a hot cereal, which neither wanted. Sir Gerald was deeply engrossed in his newspaper. He mumbled a good morning and kept reading. Lady Mary kissed Geraldine on the cheek and said a cheery good morning to Jakob. She asked if they both had a good sleep, then predicted a beautiful day, even though Jakob had looked out earlier and seen the landscape covered with a heavy mist.

The sun now seemed to be burning the mist away. Rutherford served Jakob and Geraldine the eggs and sausages and poured the coffee. Sir Gerald was evidently concerned with something he read, because he blurted out, "The unmitigated fools," and continued reading the paper. Lady Mary continued with a conversation to both Geraldine and Jakob.

"Mama, do you expect Mary Sarah back soon? I was hoping she would be here to meet Jakob and spend some time with us."

"She said she would be gone for a fortnight when she left for London to be with her friend Jenny Lynn, but I haven't heard from her. She was invited to some kind of event and wanted to visit with her. I suppose I could give her a jingle and see when she will be back."

"And what about Randy? Is there any hope he may be back while we're here?"

"I don't know when he'll return. He's with his regiment somewhere in India. I'm not sure just where, but maybe Papa knows. His tour of duty may be longer because there is something about us having problems with those people."

"I miss them Mama, Randy is such a funny one. I can't remember the last time I saw him. Is he still committed to Genevieve Raymond? She is so sweet. I hope he marries her."

"We both think a lot of her. She would make him a good wife, but this army business is so uncertain. He is a captain now, you know."

All of this conversation left Jakob out, but he patiently waited to get involved. Finally Geraldine suggested they go out and see the rest of Landry Manor. Sir Gerald continued with his paper grumbling at the news. Geraldine got up, went to Sir Gerald and pushed his paper aside. She gave him a kiss on the cheek and said she and Jakob would be going out, so she could show Jakob the rest of Landry Manor. Papa finally squeezed out, "Have a jolly time, you two."

They left by the rear exit. Just a few steps in back of the main building was a storehouse which was also used for baking breads and cakes. Next to it, a small building housed the generator providing electricity for the kitchen and first floor of the house. The second and third floors were not electrified yet. Farther on was a larger building the workshop Archer J. used for the various repairs necessary to keep Landry Manor alive. Archer was a funny-looking man, humpbacked, with a big black mustache, a lot of hair, and big dark eyes.

"Papa says Archer J. can fix anything, and without him Landry Manor would die. The building down the hill is the stable and where we keep the car. Sampson takes care of the car. Alfie is the stableman who takes care of the horses and all the equipment. He used to be a jockey, when he was younger. His young son helps clean out the stables and grooms the horses. You know, we do have horse racing, here in Suffolk."

They entered the stable to find there were enough stalls for ten horses, but they only had four horses now. "Three of these horses came from the Oliver Henry Ranch. If and when we ever need more horses, there is a livery stable nearby where we can get them." As she walked into the stable, one of the horses made a commotion. He saw Geraldine and recognized her. She came up to the door and gave him a carrot. He snorted and stomped and came up to her so she could stroke him. This was her horse and he recognized her. Geraldine pointed out another horse which would be ridden by Jakob, so he went to the stall to acquaint himself with the horse. He spent some time petting and rubbing its neck. The horse liked that. Geraldine gave Jakob a carrot he then gave to the horse.

The final building she showed him was a smaller one for the wagons, buggy and various pieces of farm equipment. They started back to Landry Manor as Geraldine filled in Jakob about the house.

"The house goes back almost one hundred fifty years. It was supposed to be a school for boys at one time. There was a fire and then it was abandoned as a school. It stayed that way until my father bought it and restored it into Landry Manor. The whole inside was drastically changed. It took several years before he moved in."

They returned in time for a lunch of a soup-like beef stew, a dark bread, fruit, juice and coffee. Cedric, one of the footmen, served the lunch. Sir Gerald was in a green suit, knickers with dark socks and black shoes. Lady Mary was in a plain dark blue dress, with some embroidery around the neck and in the front. Sir Gerald seemed quite sober and spoke little. He was upset about something he had read in the newspaper, while Lady Mary was quite chatty.

Geraldine talked about how she and Jakob planned a ride in the afternoon, and how her horse remembered her even after she had been away so long.

With lunch completed they sat and talked awhile. Geraldine and Jakob left to get dressed for riding. Jakob came down wearing his Levi's and shirt with his blue jacket, boots and his wide-brimmed hat: typical Western style. Geraldine came wearing a black riding coat over her black skirt and jodhpurs, a high white cravat, and a black top hat with a fine veil.

"Geraldine! Where are we going? To a fancy equestrian show? You look absolutely stunning. Are you sure you want to ride with an old cowpoke like me?" He laughed and put his arms around her and tried to kiss her except the veil was in the way. She picked up the veil and he kissed her but knocked off her top hat. They both laughed and admitted her outfit was not conducive for kissing.

They walked to the stable and discovered Alfie had the horses saddled and ready. Geraldine preferred to go sidesaddle. As she sat up ramrod straight, she was ready for any show.

Jakob laughed. "I thought you said you didn't ride sidesaddle any more."

"This is different." And they slowly moved from the stable chatting. Geraldine pointed out different things along the trail. She smiled at Jakob then kicked her horse. He moved out into a trot with Jakob following closely behind her. It was an exhilarating ride for both. As they neared a stream with ducks and various sorts of birds, she pulled up and moved her horse close to Jakob.

"You are right. If I tried to kiss you I would knock off my hat and have to get off the horse to get it. Or we could both get off our horses and I could take off my hat and kiss you passionately." Jakob got off his horse, then helped Geraldine get off hers. Immediately she took off her hat, put her arms around him and kissed him. As they stood there holding each other the horses started wandering away.

"Next time we decide to do this, we best tie the horses first." They walked down to the stream, leading their horses. Standing silently they watched the ducks frolicking in the water.

"Jakob, isn't this so beautiful? I just love it. Don't you?" Jakob nodded as he looked across the stream. They stood there admiring the view and Geraldine said, "Shall we go on? There is more to see." He agreed and they mounted their horses and continued their ride. They had ridden some distance and Landry Manor was no longer visible. They were high on a hill with a view of the entire area.

"Jakob, wouldn't this make a beautiful place to build a home? It's so quiet. Look over there. Later in the year you can see the field covered with heather and even smell it. It's starting to get late, maybe we should start back. Tomorrow we can go off in another direction."

They started back to Landry Manor. Geraldine said, "There's an archeological site out there. See it." She pointed out the site which existed back in Anglo-Saxon times. "There are many such sites here in Suffolk. Closer to the coast, and even in Ipswich, there are various Roman sites."

They walked the horses into the barn and Alfie took them. Then slowly walked to the house and up to their rooms. "We have about an hour before dinner. I'm glad we won't have guests tonight."

"You know, Geraldine, I just happened to think of something. This is Holy Week. Sunday will be Easter."

"Yes, I didn't forget it. I was going to mention it to you but it slipped my mind. You're Catholic, aren't you? We go to the Church of England, the Trinity Church in Ipswich. We'll be going there. Papa is on the church council. You can go there too, can't you?"

"Of course, and I'd like to. What time will the service be?"

"I think it is at nine. Oh, that would be great. We can all go together." Geraldine kissed Jakob before they went to their rooms.

Jakob dressed for dinner as he had before. Geraldine had a simple dress that was ankle length. It was beige with a high neck and lace down the front. She wore a long string of beads. Her fragrance was light. She met Jakob and kissed him, as they started down the stairs. Sir Gerald and Lady Mary were having a drink when they arrived. Sir Gerald lifted his glass in a toast.

"Have a good ride today? Did you go over to Moon Creek?" Geraldine said they did and Jakob acknowledged both Sir Gerald and Lady Mary. Robert came over and asked for their drink orders.

"Jakob, shall we indulge in a martini?" Jakob agreed and she passed the order on to Robert.

"Papa, will the car be available in the morning? We were thinking of going into Ipswich for some shopping."

"There is no problem tomorrow, but Thursday I will be going to London for several days. There are some issues to be ironed out there and I have to be present. I will be back either Friday or Saturday. Roy Brown is bringing up the issue of women voting and we have to nip it in the bud." Robert brought the martinis and Geraldine and Jakob took them. Sir Gerald shook his head.

"I don't see how you two can drink those. Why don't you have a nice comfortable Scotch? They are much better for you."

"Papa we do like them. I once read gin is good for you." Sir Gerald looked indignant.

"Bah, mendacity." And he walked over to Lady Mary and sat down.

"Papa, will you then be back for Sunday? It's Easter, you know." Sir Gerald, still irked, said he realized it was Easter and he would be going to church.

"Oh, that is great. We can all go together."

Looking at Jakob, Sir Gerald spoke. "I understand you are Catholic, Jakob. Will Rome accept you going to the Trinity Church with us? They have some ridiculous rules about going to our church."

Jakob realized he was now going into uncharted territory. "I see no problem, Sir Gerald, with me going to church with you. On Easter, we all pray to same risen Christ, as you do." Sir Gerald, looking at Jakob smiled and nodded his head in agreement.

Lady Mary, seeing an opportunity to change the conversation, asked about BethAnn and how she liked riding a horse. Geraldine continued with her thoughts of BethAnn until Rutherford came in and announced dinner would be served.

The table setting was for the four of them, but it was just as elaborate as the night before, with silver, glass, candelabra and footmen to serve. The menu was not quite as large but more than adequate, with courses of consomme', filet of turbot, roast duck, mixed vegetables, fresh baked rolls and a rhubarb pie.

After finishing dinner, Sir Gerald invited Jakob into his library for the traditional port wine and cigars. The conversation started out light, with Jakob asking questions about Landry Manor and about Sir Gerald's role in the Parliament. For a while Jakob was doing quite well keeping Sir Gerald talking on noncontroversial subjects, but Sir Gerald managed to bring up the subject closer to home, Geraldine. He said he loved his daughter very much and was concerned for her welfare.

"Geraldine has told me of her love for you, and I am glad she has finished her period of mourning for James. That went on much too long. They had a fine marriage but unfortunately he had this cancer thing, and passed away. I wanted her to stay here and forget about the ranch. But she insisted on going back to Wyoming . . . something about getting on with her life. She didn't really need to do that. She could have stayed here at Landry Manor. Geraldine is a most attractive and charming woman and there are plenty of potential mates for her here. Allen and Eleanor can take over the ranch, giving her plenty of income to live well. However, she now claims to love you. That's all very well, but do you feel you can care for her in the manner she is used to? Do you have the financial resources necessary? You are a dentist and I suppose you do financially well enough, for your type of living, but do you realize how much she pays for her dresses and other things she buys?" Jakob was seeing where the conversation was going and could sense disaster coming. He was trying to find a way to stop it.

"Sir Gerald, may I answer some of the questions you have brought up?"

"Let me continue, Jakob, and then you can have your say. I want—" and suddenly the door to the library opened and Geraldine and her mother came into the room.

"Papa, you and Jakob have been here long enough with your cigars and port. If you stay here any longer you both could suffocate in the smoke."

"Yes Gerald, why don't you two come out and join in with us?" Lady Mary handed the cane to Sir Gerald. Geraldine took Jakob's arm, leading him from the library into the drawing room.

"Papa if you want more of your port, you can have it while talking with us."

Lady Mary continued sternly, "Besides that Gerald, you have probably had enough. Remember what Doctor Bridges said about your drinking and smoking—no more than a single light Scotch. Your blood pressure has been too high. Now sit with us." Sir Gerald acquiesced to the demands of his wife and sat by her in the drawing room, while Geraldine had Jakob next to her, across from them in a love seat.

For Jakob, what had happened had to be an act of God. It gave him a reprieve because he could see where their conversation was going and it gave him time to mull over his answers to the baron. The rest of the evening, conversation was light and Easter church was settled.

Sir Gerald and Lady Mary excused themselves, as it was their bedtime. She rang for her personal maid, Anna, who met her in her bedroom. The baron would probably sleep in his own room.

"Jakob, how was your time with Papa? I thought I should rescue you. He wasn't in a very good mood today and I was afraid he might not be kind to you."

"It was all right. He was upset about this woman's suffrage thing. Then he got on the movement of the socialists. He referred to them as Marxists and said what they might do if they got too strong. Otherwise, our conversation was somewhat innocuous."

She put her arms around Jakob and kissed him on the cheek. "Jakob, are you sure it was all you two discussed?" Jakob didn't want to bring up the part of the conversation which had not been completed, lest it disturb Geraldine. "I know Papa, too well and he can be cutting. I wouldn't want him to hurt you."

Jakob smiled lovingly. "You are something else, dear. Maybe that's one of the reasons I love you. Just remember, Jakob's a big boy and can take care of himself. So, what are we going to do tomorrow? Get me a suit? I still don't know if I really need one and before I forget, will you tell Robert I don't need him to dress me. I'm okay with him making good martinis, but dressing me is not for me. Oh, he can do my laundry."

"We'll just go into Ipswich and stop at Barr & Roberts. If you don't like what you see, we'll just go on. But now it's time for us to get a good night's sleep." They started up the stairs, and when they were halfway up Geraldine stopped and took Jakob's hand.

"Jakob, when we get married will we sleep in separate bedrooms?"

Jakob started to laugh. "What do you think Geraldine?" And he continued laughing.

"That's not funny Jakob Miller. I want to know." Jakob took her in his arms and kissed her.

She drew away and coyly looked at him. "That is very important to me."

Chapter 37

Jakob's Dilemma

Jakob's after-dinner conversation with Sir Gerald left him with grave concerns. He prepared to go to sleep, but couldn't. The after-dinner custom of smoking a cigar and drinking port opened up something Jakob had not expected. Sir Gerald had opinions which deeply disturbed him. He felt his earlier concerns about Sir Gerald were valid.

Jakob thought, *Geraldine is a mature young widow, and should not be dominated by her father.* Sir Gerald evidently had plans for Geraldine other than the ones Geraldine had expressed for herself. Jakob believed Geraldine loves him. He had no doubts in his mind or heart, but he wondered if she would marry him without her father's consent. In the few comments Sir Gerald made to Jakob, he intimated there might be other suitors more qualified for her. His remarks about how much she spends on her clothes, and how much Jakob earned, could be somewhat valid. *Even though I love her deeply, maybe I can't afford her,* he thought. *The finery of her clothes might be more than I can afford.*

His thoughts drifted back to Liz, who dressed very well. But Liz also made some of her clothes. It was one of her talents, and she enjoyed doing it. Jakob liked to buy her clothes, and did. But he didn't even remotely spend what Geraldine must spend on her clothes. The awful truth came to him: maybe he was reaching out of his class. *But we love each other, and doesn't our love overcome all those things. I've got to stop thinking these thoughts. But I just can't lose her.* Fear gripped him. *Not only could, but I just might lose Geraldine.* He fell asleep with those thoughts clogging his mind.

After a restless night, the Landry Manor rooster awakened him. He knew very well where he was when he opened his eyes, and the thoughts that had haunted him were still there. He lay there immersed in a newfound reality. Then he heard a knock on the door. He knew it wasn't Robert the valet, because his knock was harder. It was Geraldine.

"Can I come in?"

"Sure, come on in." She came to his bed and kissed him, as he sat up.

"Good morning, Dear. Did you sleep well?" Jakob had fallen asleep in his robe. He smiled and nodded, he slept well. She smiled and kissed him again on the cheek. "Remember, we are going into Ipswich after breakfast. We'll go to Barr & Roberts and find you a more casual suit to wear here. It will be my gift to you. No, don't shake your head! I can buy you gifts. You do it for me, so why can't I do the same for you? You take me out for dinners all the time." Jakob continued to shake his head. "No, please stop shaking your head. I will do as I wish in this matter. Enough now, I'm going to get ready for breakfast."

Jakob laughed and kissed her as she left. He sat thinking about what she said. *Maybe we can work this out. Maybe I've been too negative on all this. I can't deny her the use of her own funds to do what she wishes to do. Don't give up Jakob. She loves you, as much as you love her. You know that.*

Geraldine and Jakob found Sir Gerald eating breakfast. He seemed to be in a better mood than the previous day and gave them a cheery good morning and told them Lady Mary was having breakfast in bed, as Robert served them their eggs, ham, biscuits and preserved fruit.

"Lady Mary said she will be going into Ipswich with you. She's going to the Child Welfare Center where she is doing volunteer work. I will be spending most of the day with Archer J. going over some things he will be doing in Landry Manor." He got up and left. Geraldine and Jakob finished their breakfast and Geraldine went to see her mama, and to find out when she would be ready to go to Ipswich.

Jakob sat in the drawing room waiting for Geraldine, studying the various furnishings and decorations. There was a large painting of Sir Gerald's father on a horse in full military uniform. It was located on the high wall going up the stairs to the second floor. On the wall above the dining room entrance was a portrait of Sir Gerald, also in uniform, with his Victoria Cross. There were various other pictures throughout the room, and a large coat of arms high over the fireplace. Multiple light sconces illuminated the darker areas of the vast room.

Then he heard Lady Mary and Geraldine coming down the stairs. Lady Mary was wearing a wide-brimmed hat with flowers and a bow to match her beige coat with big pockets. She was an attractive lady and Geraldine had a strong resemblance to her, though she was taller than her mother. Her two-piece gray suit and matching hat she wore tilted to the left side of her head gave her a very smart look. They both looked beautiful walking together.

Sampson had the car doors open and ready for the ladies to enter the back seat. Jakob would ride in the front with Sampson. The sky, with mixed clouds and a bright sun overhead, made it a perfect day. Sampson volunteered the temperature to be at 16 degrees Centigrade. The road to Ipswich was in use by many horse-drawn carriages and wagons hauling everything from hay and manure to animals. At one bend in the road, there was a cow with a farmer behind it carrying a switch. Sampson had to slow down to pass it. Once inside Ipswich, it was just a short drive to Barr & Roberts Tailors. The shop was in an older building and was quite small. Sampson told them he would be back after taking Lady Mary to the Child Welfare Center.

They entered the shop and a middle-aged man appeared from the back room. "Why, Lady Geraldine, what a pleasant surprise to see you. It has been a long time since we were able to serve you. You are looking just as lovely as ever. And what can Barr & Roberts do for you?"

"Mister Roberts, may I introduce Doctor Miller." Roberts bowed and extended his hand to Jakob. "Doctor Miller thought he might be interested in a rather casual suit, but he can better describe what he wants." Jakob took it from there.

"I am visiting with Lady Geraldine at Landry Manor and I failed to bring with me adequate clothes. I think I might be interested in something like a herringbone or tweed suit and waistcoat, in a four-button model and with knickers. I won't be staying here long, so having one tailored would be impossible. I thought perhaps you might have something ready made I might like."

"How interesting, I just might have something for you. Won't you step over here and let me get your measurements? I do carry a number of suits for just such an occasion as you describe." He left and soon came back carrying two suits, one in a medium green and the other in a lighter brown. They both were similarly styled; the green was a herringbone and the brown, a tweed. Jakob tried the coats and waistcoats on and stood before a mirror. He liked both but preferred the brown.

"Jakob, I'm in agreement, I like the brown better." The tailor took the knickers and led Jakob to the dressing room. Jakob put them on, then came out.

"I like it," he said, and Geraldine agreed; she liked it too. The tailor said he could do the alterations immediately if they wanted to wait, or they could come back on another day. Geraldine suggested he do it now and they would return later in the day. There was no price tag on the suit and Jakob asked for the price, which was given in pounds. Jakob was converting the price in American dollars when Geraldine said, it was acceptable and would be taken care of.

They left the happy tailor and met Sampson, who took them to a haberdashery just a short distance down the same street, where a shirt, cuff links, tie and socks were added to Jakob's outfit. Geraldine wanted to shop for more but Jakob said he felt his clothes were acceptable for the rest of his stay in England. He felt somewhat embarrassed. Geraldine had bought him the clothes, even though she insisted they were her gift to him for taking her out to so many dinners. They continued on, with Geraldine stopping in several stores for different personal items. They placed their purchases in the car and Geraldine told Sampson to take them down to the docks.

"You really haven't seen Ipswich until you have seen the docks. The docks here service shipping from all over the world. Ipswich has prospered as a port since medieval times. The Ipswich harbor extends eighteen kilometers downstream. We are at the head of the Orwell Estuary. The history of Ipswich goes back to the twelfth century and King John. Much English history has been made here. Do you want me to tell you more about Ipswich, or shall you take me for lunch at a famous pub?"

"My dear Lady, I'm going to have to take you to many pubs for several years to make up for your generous gifts to me." They passed the Great White Horse, one of the oldest inns, and went into a nearby small pub that served fish and chips. A big, bald-headed man with a white soiled apron took their order for a pint, and fish and chips. "I thought that you only drank martinis, and here you order a pint. I never cease to be amazed by you, Lady Geraldine."

"Oh, I would only indulge in a pint with fish and chips." Jakob shook his head and agreed it would be improper to have martinis with fish and chips.

Having finished their lunch, they went back to Barr & Roberts, for Jakob's suit. He tried it on and it fit perfectly. Mr. Roberts was excited with Jakob's appearance in the suit and on leaving he invited Jakob to come back to see other suits he carried. They spent the rest of the day shopping and touring in Ipswich until it was time to get Lady Mary at the Child Welfare Center. She came out and joined Geraldine in the back seat which was already filled with boxes and bags. On the trip back to Landry Manor, Lady Mary was chatty with the events of the day at the Center. Jakob felt Lady Mary seemed like a genuine person and Geraldine appeared to have a good relationship with her. They almost acted like girlfriends, rather than mother and daughter. They returned to Landry Manor in time for a nap before having dinner.

As was the custom, everybody dressed for dinner. Geraldine and Lady Mary dressed in ankle length gowns and wore above the elbow gloves. Sir Gerald dressed with a dinner jacket and waistcoat as did Jakob. They met in the drawing room. Rutherford was present, as well as Robert, the footman, who took orders for their drinks. Sir Gerald ordered his usual Scotch, and Lady Mary had her Chardonnay. Coming to Geraldine and Jakob, he asked if they wanted an olive with their martinis. He soon arrived with their drinks and before Sir Gerald could make the toast, Jakob raised his glass and toasted Sir Gerald and Lady Mary as grand-host and hostess. Sir Gerald nodded and Lady Mary thanked him and smiled.

"Did you get everything you wanted done today, Papa?" Sir Gerald related all the things he attended to, and felt his day was productive. He also said, one of the farmer tenant wives was sick and in bed.

"Geraldine, if you and Jakob are riding in that direction tomorrow could you stop by the Brothers farm and visit Mrs. Brothers? Just give her some kind of a greeting and wish her a rapid recovery. It would be a nice gesture on our part. I will be leaving for London early tomorrow and I want to catch the seven o'clock train. The House of Lords will be having a meeting at lunch, probably lasting the rest of the day. I expect to get back late on Saturday. We'll go to the nine o'clock service, on Easter Sunday. Mama will be having a dinner party on Sunday and we'll have some of our friends over. Lord Oliver Henry and Lady Abby may be with us for dinner. I'm sure you will be happy to see them. I understand you also know them, Jakob. It will be nice having them with us." Rutherford announced dinner would now be served so they moved to the dining room.

Following dinner, they went back to the drawing room for their after dinner port. Sir Gerald was not too talkative and excused himself because he would be getting up early to go to London.

Jakob got to know Lady Mary better. She talked about her early life in Pennsylvania and her family. Jakob wondered about how it was for her to pick up her life and go to a foreign country to live, and it was answered well by Lady Mary.

After Lady Mary left for bed, Jakob and Geraldine carried on the conversation about leaving your home of birth. Geraldine had done so when she went to Wyoming. She said it hadn't bothered her too much because she was at the ranch with her husband and other people she knew. The evening wore on, then both decided to go to bed. Geraldine reminded Jakob they would spend much of the next day seeing the Landry Manor farms.

Jakob decided to write to BethAnn and his parents before he went to sleep and relate some of what had happened at Landry Manor. Even though Geraldine kept him busy while they were at Landry Manor, he started to feel homesick. He missed BethAnn and wondered if he should have brought her with them. But he also missed Sheridan. His trip with Geraldine had been all he had expected. The more he was with her, the more deeply he felt about her.

England was interesting and even somewhat exciting, but the lifestyle he was introduced to left him with mixed feelings. *I couldn't live like this all my life. This is a shallow existence. I miss my friends and neighbors. I miss my patients. I am needed by the people I take care of. This has been all fine and I met Geraldine's parents, but I really should make plans to return. I just can't stay here indefinitely.* Jakob's letter wasn't finished because he started to fall asleep.

Jakob awakened to another bright, sunny day at Landry Manor. He stayed in bed until Geraldine knocked on his door. He invited her in and she came over and sat next to him on the bed. Pushing his hair aside, off his forehead, she kissed him.

"Good morning, Jakob. Sleep well?" Jakob said he did and she talked about getting ready to go out for the day. "I'll have the kitchen make a picnic lunch and I have just the place for us to go for a picnic. Let's get ready for breakfast. We'll probably eat alone, unless Mama comes down." Rutherford was waiting for them and greeted them as he poured their coffee.

"What would you like today for breakfast?" he asked as he poured the juice. Geraldine and Jakob made suggestions and he left for the kitchen. Lady Mary had come down and decided to have breakfast with them. Rutherford returned with Jakob and Geraldine's breakfasts and Lady Mary ordered hers. Rutherford left after he poured her tea.

Lady Mary was chatty and talked about a variety of subjects, but dwelt on her visit to the Child Welfare Center. She was concerned about the children. Since the economy in England was in a recession, many people were having a hard time making ends meet. Some, in the rural areas, were even moving into the big cities to seek work in industry or whatever they could find.

"It's the children who often suffer, and we must find ways to help them." She was truly concerned, and they were working on possible programs to help them. One was through school lunch programs. Lady Mary decided she would be going back to the Center today. The more Jakob saw of Lady Mary, the more he respected and liked her.

Geraldine dispatched Cedric, the footman, to inform Alfie to get the horses ready. After their breakfasts, they bid Lady Mary goodbye and left. Jakob dressed in his riding clothes and Geraldine put on a less formal outfit. Their lunch basket was brought to the stable and Alfie put it in Jakob's saddle bags.

They moved off in another direction from their first ride over rolling hills and fields, some recently planted. They passed farm houses and barns, some of which didn't look well kept. A few of the farms had sheep, while others had cows grazing. *Nothing like the ranches of Wyoming*, he thought.

As Sir Gerald requested, they rode to the Brothers farm first. There were some children in the field apparently working. Geraldine greeted Mr. Brothers who was behind a plow being pulled by a horse. The farmhouse was a hundred yards ahead and they rode up to the small farmhouse and barn. Jakob waited as Geraldine dismounted and went into the house. He watched a small boy feeding chickens. Geraldine was in the house for about fifteen minutes. When she came out, she mounted her horse and came up to Jakob.

"Mrs. Brothers is quite sick. I felt her forehead and it seemed warm. I made her tea and gave her bread that was on the table in the kitchen. She softened it in her tea and ate it. She seems weak, and should have someone helping her. I guess the little boy feeding the chickens is looking out after her. We should go back. I'll tell Mama to ask the doctor in Ipswich to stop by and see her. I feel so sorry for the lady." Jakob saw another side of Geraldine. She expressed sincere empathy for the lady, and took it upon herself to help her. They weren't too far from Landry Manor, and rode hard to get there. They arrived just before Lady Mary left for the Child Welfare Center. Geraldine told Lady Mary about Mrs. Brothers's plight, and they agreed she should be seen by a doctor.

"I'll take care of it. You two go ahead and have your picnic. I'm glad you came back. That poor woman has had too many children and works so hard to take care of the children and still help her husband." They watched as Sampson drove away with Lady Mary going to Ipswich.

"Jakob, I'm going to get some things in the kitchen and we'll take them back for her." She came out with a bag of food items she would take for the Brothers family. When they arrived, Mr. Brothers was in the house and Geraldine gave the bag to him. He seemed grateful and thanked her.

As they rode away, Geraldine told Jakob, "Those poor people are really having a hard time. The farm doesn't bring in enough for them to live on. I wish Papa would give them more land to work. They just don't have enough to survive on." Geraldine seemed really concerned.

They rode some distance without talking, then arrived at a rise overlooking the river. There were some boats on it going toward Ipswich. It was a warm day for April, with just a slight breeze, and the sun was high.

"Is this the place you want to picnic? It is an idyllic spot." Geraldine nodded and agreed. They tied the horses to some brush. Not too far off some sheep were grazing. Geraldine spread the blanket for them to sit on and they started nibbling on their lunch. They lay back on the blanket and looked up at the sky.

"Isn't this place just beautiful? It's so peaceful here. Jakob, do you think you could ever live here? I just love it here."

Jakob didn't answer. He didn't have the words just yet, and he wondered what Geraldine was leading up to. He had a sinking feeling. *Could Geraldine want to stay in England and not return to Wyoming?* He rolled over and kissed her.

"Why did you ask me that, Honey?"

"Oh, I don't know. I do love it here."

"More than Wyoming?" She hesitated and lay silent.

"Oh I get confused. Yes . . . but I do like Wyoming. I guess it's just this has been my home and my life. I was raised here."

"I understand—and I hope you can understand me. I certainly could visit here, as we are doing now, but I don't feel I could spend my entire life here. I truly love Wyoming. It can be cold and windy. But . . . you know my mother keeps asking me to move back to Milwaukee, and tells me I would have an easier life. I could make more money there. But, Wyoming: the mountains and streams, my patients, my friends, Sheridan—I couldn't give them up. I like our lifestyle there. In fact, I've been thinking we should really be making plans to go back to Sheridan. We've been gone a long time. I really miss my BethAnn. And I should get back to work. I need to work. I'm not just made to lounge around. I get satisfaction out of taking care of my patients. It's more than just the money. I look on them as my friends and they need me. Can you understand how I feel?"

"Yes. I guess I do understand. You need to be challenged and you thrive on achieving and helping others. But I'm not really too far behind you. The ranch. I guess I forgot about it since I've been away so long. But Papa wants me to come back to Landry Manor."

Jakob was stunned and hesitatingly continued. "And, what are your feelings?" She didn't answer.

"Geraldine there are things we haven't talked about. Maybe we shouldn't put them off any longer. You know I love you and I want you to be my wife, but I don't know how much longer we should wait. It's hard being with you but not having you. There seems to be a chasm between us, that has to be breached. Here in England, it is the social class. Here I am a commoner. In Wyoming we are equal, except . . . except on a monetary level. Your father asked me if I could afford you. Could I afford to buy you the clothes you wear, and support your lifestyle? If that is really important to you I know I couldn't do it. I am doing quite well financially in my profession, but I don't have the money Sir Gerald or you have. You have never told me what your assets are, but I'm sure they are considerably more than mine. You and I and BethAnn can live comfortably on my income, but it would be on a budget based on what I make."

"Jakob, there is no chasm between us. You are not a commoner. Neither of us is better or lesser. Please don't feel that way. I believe someday the concept will be completely lost here in England, just as it is in America. As to the matter of how much we each have, it doesn't really matter. I could live and be happy on whatever you make. The clothes issue is . . . is just part of this aristocracy thing. It is not really important. Is there anything else you are concerned with? Please tell me. Just as you want to marry me, I want to be your wife. We can bridge any chasm with our love." She moved close to him and embraced him. They held each other and then kissed again.

"You want to go back to Sheridan, don't you? I understand. When are you thinking of us going back?"

"I haven't set any date yet because we hadn't discussed it but we should really get our sailing reservations." They talked further and finished their lunch. Geraldine wanted to show more of the area to Jakob. She talked about going to the seashore to visit some of the fishing villages, the crumbling cliffs, and the estuaries with their various bird species.

"We'll do it next week. This is such a beautiful area to explore." They took their time going back to Landry Manor, stopping at some quaint villages along the way. They saw how hard the people had to work in the rural areas.

They returned before Lady Mary, and Rutherford served them tea out on the lawn. He told them Lady Mary had called and said she would be back in time for dinner.

"Mama doesn't usually spend this much time at the Child Welfare Office. I wonder what they're doing? This recession in England is definitely making it difficult for a lot of people here in Suffolk. We saw some of that at the Brothers farm. There are parts of London I wouldn't want to visit. I wish Parliament would solve some of these problems. Papa has his own ideas, but they are at odds with some members of Parliament. I guess I don't understand much of what is going on in government. He talks about the Marxists and Socialists,

Liberals and the Labour Party. But then, I also hear much I don't understand about government in the States when I am there." Jakob admitted he knew little about English politics.

Lady Mary had arrived from the Child Welfare Office and went to her room to get ready for dinner. Jakob and Geraldine were in the drawing room and Robert had just served them their martinis. Both were already dressed for dinner. When Lady Mary came down, she related what had been done at her meeting. Her committee had agreed there should be some kind of lunch or breakfast provided for the children at their schools, and they, as a committee, would lobby the Parliament to provide for it. She said she wanted to go to London with several other members of the committee to initiate the idea with the Parliament.

"Lady Mary, I commend you for what you are attempting to do. I think this is great. I don't know much about you English, but it sounds like American to me." That was all Lady Mary needed to boost her enthusiasm. Geraldine chimed in and added to the excitement for the idea.

"Mama, before I forget, did you get to see the doctor about Mrs. Brothers?"

"Yes, I did see Dr. Ingles. He will look in on her tomorrow morning. I'm so glad you went to see her. I'm sure Papa will be happy too." The discussion continued through dinner.

"My Lady Mary, I do like your spunk." She was delighted with the support she received. Jakob thought, *I wonder just what kind of support she will get from Sir Gerald?* The evening was the first he had really enjoyed, and saw Lady Mary as a typical warm American woman. The evening ended on a positive note and Lady Mary even gave Jakob a kiss on the cheek before she went up to her room.

Geraldine and Jakob came down for breakfast and were greeted by Lady Mary, who was still riding high on the previous night's discussion. She seemed so different from her initial sober and somewhat aloof mood. She was now looking forward to the Easter Day festivities which would include Oliver Henry. Lady Mary left to speak with Rutherford and the cook, Maggy, to make the arrangements for the Easter Day reception.

Jakob asked Geraldine if she had made any plans for the day. She suggested they might ride out to see another archaeological site, or maybe they could drive into Ipswich. Jakob suggested, "One thing I would like to do is see about getting steamship reservations to New York. Where would we go to do that?"

"There is an agency in Ipswich we can use. I'll make arrangements with Sampson to leave at eleven. You can wear your new suit. I want to see you in it." They both got dressed to go to Ipswich. Geraldine wore her two-piece gray suit and Jakob in his new brown tweed with knickers.

"Jakob, I like your new suit. You look like a fine English gentleman."

Lady Mary came by and saw Jakob. "Jakob, I just love the suit you're wearing. I haven't seen you in it before. It makes you look chic." Jakob laughed and said, he always dressed to please the ladies.

Geraldine answered, "And just what ladies do you dress to please beside me and Mama?"

Jakob laughed. "I retract the statement. I dress to please the ladies present."

Sampson stopped in front of the travel agency. Jakob explained to the agent they needed reservations to New York from Southampton. The agent asked for the travel date and Jakob indicated he would like it to be within the next few weeks.

The agent also indicated the first travel date from Southampton would be May 28th, but there are several sailings available from Liverpool earlier. Geraldine felt Southampton was more convenient to use. The agent said the ship sailing from Southampton HMS *Oceanic*, the same ship they had sailed from New York.

"Well, it would be perfect for us." They were able to get adjacent cabins in first class. The reservations were made for sailing on May 28th.

"That was easy Jakob. Sometimes, it can be difficult to get reservations when you want them, and especially in May or June. We can wire ahead for the train reservations. Now, Sampson can take us down to the docks, and I will take you to a very special sea-food pub." Sampson was waiting, and Geraldine directed him to a small pub in the area where the fishing boats came in.

"Beg your pardon, Lady Geraldine, but are you sure this is the place where you want to eat? Some of these fishermen can be crude and I wouldn't recommend it." But Geraldine was not to be discouraged by the appearance of the establishment. It was called The Ipswich Crab Limited. They went inside and were waited on by a big woman, who was difficult to understand. She mentioned a special crab dish and Geraldine ordered it.

"Did you understand what she said?"

"Yes, I did, with some difficulty. Some people in Suffolk speak with the Suffolk dialect. It's quite old, but some still speak it. It is almost like a different language. I learned some of it when I was young."

A basket of crabs was thrust before them, along with biscuits, and a small dish of a sauce for the crabs. The meat had to be removed from the shells. They also ordered a pint to go with the lunch. The ambiance of the establishment had much to be desired, but the food was outstanding when washed down with the pint of ale. They received side glances from other patrons in the pub, but they left satisfied with the lunch. Geraldine later pointed out various buildings with historical significance. They then returned to Landry Manor in time for the afternoon tea.

Lady Mary was waiting for them and was visibly upset. She told them Sir Gerald was taken to the hospital in London. He became ill at his meeting and the people there thought he should be seen by a doctor. They described him as having a severe headache. He was now in the hospital and she was waiting to hear more. Obviously he would not be coming back that day. She had talked to Earl Henry Bradwell who said he would call just as soon as he found out anything about his condition.

Lady Mary was very concerned. She said she would cancel the dinner party for Easter Sunday, but was uncertain as to whether she could find Lord Oliver Henry because he probably left Hereford already. The others nearby would be contacted by Mrs. Wrightson, who acted as Lady Mary's secretary, and would make the calls.

Geraldine tried to allay Lady Mary's apprehension but her mother was still quite fearful, especially since she had not heard from the earl. Lady Mary spent the time in her room and came down only for dinner. Geraldine was also concerned for her father, and worried about her mother who was so upset. They had a quiet and sober dinner, and Lady Mary promptly excused herself and went back to her room. Jakob and Geraldine sat in the drawing room.

"I wish I knew what to do, but we have so little information. Mrs. Wrightson got in touch with everyone and canceled the dinner party, but Lord Henry is somewhere in London and can't be reached."

It was later in the evening when Geraldine answered the phone. It was Earl Bradwell, who said he had no other news except that Sir Gerald was in the King Edward VII Hospital in Westminster. He said it was probably the best hospital in London, and he would call just as soon as he had any more information. Geraldine went up to see Lady Mary to relay the information. The evening went slowly and Jakob said he would go to his room and finish his letter to BethAnn.

Jakob didn't need a clock to wake him as the local rooster did it for him. He lay in bed thinking about the letter he wrote to BethAnn and his family. He was looking forward to returning to Milwaukee and Sheridan, but he too was concerned about Sir Gerald's hospitalization. He wondered if it would have any effect on his plans. He got up, and sat in his chair by the window, and looked out on the view of Landry Manor's landscape. He wondered if Geraldine was up yet when suddenly there was a knock on his door. It sounded like Geraldine.

"May I come in?" Jakob invited her in. "Oh, you're up already."

"Yes, the old rooster woke me up. I was just getting ready to come to your room to get you up."

"I should have waited for you." She kissed him, then sat on his lap and put her arms around him. Jakob couldn't resist, and they kissed.

"Jakob, I love you so."

He held her closly. "Can we get married when we get back to Sheridan?"

"Yes, Jakob. Let's do that. I need something to look forward to." And they embraced. Geraldine then got up and went to the door. "I'm going to see Mama, and find out what we are going to do about church. I wonder if she will want to go. She's waiting for a telephone call from Earl Bradwell. I'll be back."

She left and Jakob started dressing in his brown tweed suit. Geraldine soon arrived and told Jakob she didn't think Mama would be going to services unless she received a call first. But she thought they should go. "I'm going to dress and I'll meet you in the dining room."

Jakob entered the dining room and was greeted by Rutherford, who handed him the newspaper. He asked for coffee and told Rutherford he would wait until Lady Geraldine arrived before eating. Scanning through the paper he read some of the stories. There was a short article about the House of Lords meeting, but it give no details. Geraldine arrived and they ordered their breakfast. Just then the phone rang. Geraldine answered and it was Earl Bradwell. She dispatched Rutherford to ask Lady Mary to come to the phone. In the meantime, she spoke with him. He told her Sir Gerald was diagnosed with a stroke. Lady Mary arrived and Geraldine gave her the telephone. Geraldine and Jakob sat waiting as Lady Mary spoke to the earl. From the sound of the conversation, it appeared serious. After speaking to him she hung up the telephone and started to cry. Geraldine consoled her mother while she sobbed. Looking at Geraldine, she started to relate what she heard from the earl.

"Earl Bradwell said Papa was resting comfortably in the hospital after suffering a stroke. The left side of his body is paralyzed and his speech is affected. You can't understand what he is saying. The doctors think he will recover, but will be handicapped and will need care for the rest of his life. He will have to stay in the hospital for perhaps several weeks. I should make arrangements for his care, so I will go to London to see him tomorrow." She was very distraught and didn't know what she should do first.

"Mama, why don't you have your breakfast now? Rutherford can get it for you." She declined her breakfast and said she wasn't hungry. "You have to eat. Do it now while you're here. You can get dressed later." Words from Geraldine did help her make a decision to have her breakfast. Geraldine seemed distressed, but was calm and able to make decisions and help her mother. Jakob sat and just listened because Geraldine had things under control. Lady Mary sat looking, as if in space, and sobbed. Jakob had never seen any closeness between Sir Gerald and Lady Mary, but then he had not been there too long. He wondered if she realized what she had to face with Sir Gerald.

"Mama, there is a service at Trinity at eleven. Do you want to go to it? Maybe it will help you face what you are going through. We need prayer. Jakob and I will go with you."

"Maybe you are right. I should go. I can tell the Vicar what has happened to Gerald. I'm sure he would want to know. I'll get ready and we'll go. You'll come too, won't you Jakob?" It was the first time she spoke to Jakob since the call, and

Jakob wanted her to feel she had his support after this tragic event.

"Of course I will My Lady. We'll be with you and do whatever we can to help you. I believe prayers do help."

"Thank you, Jakob. I know you are right." And she left, followed by Geraldine who asked Rutherford to tell Annie to go to Lady Mary's room. Jakob sat in the drawing room and mulled over what had happened with Sir Gerald. He knew the prognosis for stroke was not good, and he wondered how this would affect Geraldine, and subsequently him.

Sampson stopped in front of Trinity Church in Ipswich. The 11:00 service was the second one of the morning, and it was crowded. Many were dressed in their Easter finery. An usher led them to their seats, close to the front of the church. Some of the parishioners acknowledged Lady Mary's presence as she walked up the aisle. It was evident they knew her. It was also evident Sir Gerald was not there, and they looked to see who the other gentlemen was.

The service was not too long. The choir sang beautifully, and the sermon by the Vicar was on Christ's Resurrection. It was, different service from St. Ignatius, but it was the same Jesus Christ he prayed to. On the way out Lady Mary stopped to talk with the Vicar and spoke of Sir Gerald's stroke. He consoled Lady Mary as best as he could. He recognized Geraldine, who introduced Jakob to him. He promised to pray for Sir Gerald and said he would make arrangements to visit him when Lady Mary let him know where he would be. Sampson drove them back to Landry Manor.

Lunch was served when they arrived from church, but no one really felt like eating. Maggy, the cook, made it a light fare. The telephone rang and Lady Mary took it immediately. It was Lord Oliver Henry. He had received word from his people in Hereford that Lady Mary had canceled the dinner party because of Sir Gerald's stroke. He was very concerned and said he would not want to impose on Lady Mary, but was grateful he was told of Sir Gerald's unfortunate medical problem. Lord Henry said he was sorry he could not be with Geraldine and Jakob because he was looking forward to seeing them. He sent his regards and told Lady Mary she and Sir Gerald were in his prayers. That took the stress off Lady Mary, who now didn't have to entertain anyone.

Lady Mary excused herself and went to her room. Geraldine and Jakob went into the drawing room.

"Jakob, I'm happy they we were able to contact Lord Henry. I was looking forward to seeing him and Abby, but Mama did not need to host a dinner party at this time. She is so distraught. I hope she is resting now." Jakob agreed she needs to rest to gain back some of her composure. "Jakob, I should really go with Mama to London tomorrow. I hate to see her go there alone, even though Papa's sister Allison is there and she can stay with her. What do you think?"

"Geraldine, I believe you should do what you feel is best for your mother."

"I'll talk with Mama, and see what she thinks, but I believe it would be best. I wouldn't necessarily have to stay there more than a day or two. I'm sorry I have to leave you, but I'll be back just as soon as Mama is settled in. Allison will look after her. She is Papa's sister. They have a nice relationship. She is widowed and has a big apartment with plenty of room."

"You don't have to be concerned about me. I'll find something to do."

"I'll tell Alfie to have a horse available for you if you want to go riding. And if you want to go into Ipswich, Sampson will take you. I'll be in touch and will miss you." She came up to Jakob and kissed him and then went up to see her mother.

They were all up early and Jakob went down with Geraldine for breakfast. Lady Mary greeted them. She seemed in much better spirits and was anxious to leave for London. They both had prepared their travel wear and Sampson put it in the car. Jakob said he would go with them to the train. They were early so they sat and waited for the train to arrive. Jakob wished Lady Mary the best and told her he would be praying for them. She seemed surprised and kissed him on the cheek. Geraldine put her arms around Jakob and kissed him again.

"I'll be back as soon as Mama is settled in." They boarded the train and Jakob watched as it left the station.

On returning to Landry Manor, Jakob sat on one of the lawn chairs. Rutherford brought him coffee and the newspaper. The day was bright, but with clouds obscuring the sun occasionally. He tried reading the newspaper, but thoughts of home or Geraldine kept interfering. He already missed Geraldine. They had been together almost constantly since leaving Sheridan.

I've been with her for more than a month and I certainly do know her now. I really want to spend the rest of my life with her. She has such a beautiful smile and it almost makes me melt with passion. Her brown eyes seem to twinkle. I see those long lashes and as she smiles, the small dimples in her cheeks show. Her skin is so soft and her hands so slender. I have to marry her. I can't live without her, and she loves my BethAnn. BethAnn needs a mother. She's getting older and she needs to be with a woman. I can't teach her all what she has to know as a girl. And BethAnn loves her too. He walked to the stable and chatted briefly with Alfie, then went back for lunch. He hated eating by himself, and he even thought about going down to the kitchen to eat his meals with the staff, but it would be unheard of. Besides, the staff was not too overly friendly with him. He spent the afternoon riding, following the same trail he had ridden with Geraldine. But it wasn't the same by himself.

He found himself bored, and discovered a book in Sir Gerald's library to read while waiting to hear from Geraldine. A volume of Shelley caught his eyes and he took it down. *We once read and studied Shelley. I forgot what he wrote.* He thumbed through the pages and read. *"Love's Philosophy." I don't remember that, but then, I guess I wasn't ready for it,* he thought. Time seemed to crawl and he didn't know how to use it. Dinner was served, but eating by himself was more of the same boredom he experienced much of the day. He waited most of the evening in the library. Sir Gerald's collection of books didn't excite him. He had been through the newspaper several times, and was thinking of going to bed but it really was too early. The telephone finally rang, and Rutherford answered it. He informed Jakob it was Geraldine and she wanted to talk to him.

"Jakob, how are you? I'm sorry I'm not with you but I have been busy here. We arrived on time and went to Aunt Allison's apartment, to get Mama settled in. I just don't know how long she will be here. We went to the hospital to see Papa. It took a while to find him because this is a big hospital. When we did find him the doctors were with him, so we couldn't go in to see him yet. As they were leaving the room, I stopped them. They were busy and didn't seem to want to talk, but I insisted they speak with us. They finally did. We were told his stroke affected the left side of his body. There had been a blockage of an artery on the right side of his brain. They said a lot of things I didn't understand. I wish you had been with us because I'm sure you would have understood. The doctor said they thought he was stabilized. I guess it means he will not get worse. But they said, they didn't think he will get much better. Oh Jakob, he looks terrible. He doesn't recognize me or Mama. My Papa was such a strong man and so vibrant. Now he is so weak. He had little use of that left arm but now he has no use of his arm or his leg." Then she started to sob. After she gained her composure she talked about her mother, who was having a difficult time accepting all of this.

"I'll be back the day after tomorrow. We have another meeting with the doctor tomorrow. Aunt Allison will look after Mama, although she too is having difficulty with all of this. I miss you so. I wish I had you with me." Jakob spoke with her and tried to help as best as he could.

The next day was difficult for Jakob, because he didn't know what to do with his time. Then he had an idea. He found Rutherford and told him what Geraldine related to him. Rutherford was upset and deeply sorry for the turn of events.

"I have been with Sir Gerald for twenty-two years." He was deeply distressed.

"Rutherford, I was just wondering if there is a hospital in Ipswich?"

"Oh yes, there is. Sampson will know where it is."

"Fine. I am thinking of going there to see if they have a medical library with books on stroke, its treatment, and the prognosis. The more information we have, the better we can cope with this. I fear this will be a long, difficult journey for Lady Mary."

Sampson drove Jakob to the hospital. It wasn't very big compared to hospitals in the United States. Jakob had taken classes in the Cook County Hospital in Chicago, which was one of the largest.

He introduced himself to an administrator and told him what he wanted to do. The library wasn't much more than a few bookcases in his office. Jakob was able to find several books that might have the information he was looking for. He sat in a storeroom thumbing through and reading portions of them to learn as much as he could. Very little of what he read was useful but there was enough to be helpful. He spent the entire afternoon with the books.

Before leaving, he thanked the administrator for the use of the books, and asked if could return at another time. The administrator was cooperative and said he could return any time he wished.

The afternoon had been fruitful, but more importantly Jakob was immersed in something he felt might be helpful to the family. After dinner he sat in the drawing room going through the notes he had taken, while waiting for a call from Geraldine. Her call finally came. She would be arriving in Ipswich at eleven-thirty. Jakob told her he would be there with Sampson. He thought about all he had read and realized life at Landry Manor would be changed considerably. It would never be the same again.

The train from London was a little late. The doors to the cars started opening and Geraldine stepped out. Jakob stepped forward and immediately had her in his arms. He kissed her and held her as she started to sob.

"I missed you so much. I never realized how much strength you give to me until I didn't have you there next to me." He took her bag and her arm and they went to the car, with Sampson waiting. Geraldine related all that happened while she was in London. "The hospital seems to be all right, but the people there seem so cold and indifferent. They recognized Papa for his status, but other than that he was just another sick person." They arrived at Landry Manor and Rutherford greeted Geraldine. He questioned her about Sir Gerald and was emotionally choked up by her answers. He told her he was truly sorry for his condition.

Rutherford served them lunch. Jakob told Geraldine he had spent the afternoon going through medical books at the hospital for information about stroke. He said he learned much.

"The prognosis was not good for the stroke victim. So much depends on the severity of the stroke. The length of time one might live can also vary." The doctors did not give Lady Mary much hope as to his quality of life. He could be released from the hospital in a matter of weeks and taken home, but he would need around-the-clock attention. Jakob questioned Geraldine.

"Has Lady Mary made any plans as to what she will do?"

Geraldine shook her head. "I don't believe she has made any plans or even thought that far ahead. I will have to help Mama make some of those decisions.

"I have finally reached my sister Mary Sarah, and she will be returning home. She had left to stay with her friend in London because there was a problem between my father and her. She was romantically involved with a divorced man and Papa would not accept the arrangement. She has seen Papa and he didn't recognize her. She is filled with guilt about the whole affair. I spoke with her and she will be coming back to Landry Manor.

"We have also been in touch with the Army. An effort is being made to get Randy back. He is in some god-forsaken place in India, and it may be awhile before he can come back home. I know we are going to have to convert Papa's room into a sick room and hire a nurse to take care of him. I can't see his valet Max will be of much help." Jakob could see Geraldine was living with a great deal of stress and had taken on all the responsibility for Landry Manor.

"Have you been sleeping well?" Geraldine shrugged her shoulders. "Maybe you should take a nap."

"No, I don't think I can sleep. Why don't we go down to the stable and take a couple horses and go off somewhere. I need to do something and I need to be with you. We can ride to the lookout above the River Orwell."

Alfie had the horses ready for them, and they rode out. It was a perfect day for May. As they approached the rise, they slowed down and stopped. They looked over the hills to the other side of the river. Geraldine dismounted. She took the blanket that was rolled behind Jakob's saddle and spread it on the grass. They lay back on the blanket, looking up at the sky.

"Last week when we did this I saw only the beauty of the day and this place, and we talked of our future. Today a dark cloud shadows our day." Jakob rolled over and kissed her.

"Don't let the dark cloud spoil your dream. Remember, all clouds are on the move, and dark clouds do leave and let the sunshine come through." Geraldine turned toward Jakob and lifted her head and kissed him tenderly and lay back. They lay quietly gazing upward as Geraldine fell asleep. Jakob's thoughts drifted off.

Sir Gerald's stroke was a dark cloud over all. Jakob wondered how the dark cloud would also affect him. He was looking forward to returning to Sheridan with Geraldine. It was just two weeks away and the thought came to him, *Will Geraldine go back with me or will she choose to stay here?* He watched her sleep peacefully and wondered whether their plans would be challenged by the turn of events they were now experiencing.

Geraldine's eyes opened and she smiled at Jakob.

"How long did I sleep? I can't believe I fell asleep so fast. Last night it seemed to take hours." The smile slowly melted away and tears came from her eyes and moved down her cheeks. Jakob took her in his arms and held her, then he kissed her.

"What's the matter, Honey?" But she just shook her head and kissed him.

"Nothing. I am just being emotional. I'll get over it." She got up. "Maybe we should start going back." They picked up the blanket and secured it to the saddle, then Geraldine went back to her horse. Jakob put his arms around her, and kissed her, and helped her up on the horse. They rode slowly back to Landry Manor.

The next week was quiet and with Geraldine in constant contact with Lady Mary. Geraldine and Jakob spent time together, but Geraldine was often occupied with the business of the Manor. They stopped to see Mrs. Brothers, the tenant's wife, who seemed to be doing better, and visited with most of the other tenant farmers. Geraldine was making all the decisions regarding Landry Manor, as Sir Gerald was completely incapacitated. Lady Mary was still in London and left everything to Geraldine. She was not sure when Sir Gerald would be returning to Landry Manor, and work was being undertaken to make his bedroom into a hospital room. Mary Sarah still hadn't returned from London, and Randolph Edward was still somewhere in India.

The day for Jakob and Geraldine to return to Sheridan was fast approaching. After dinner Geraldine and Jakob were sitting in the drawing room.

"We haven't talked about the trip back to Sheridan, Geraldine, and the time is fast approaching." Geraldine looked at Jakob and began to cry.

"I can't talk about it, Jakob. I just can't talk about it, because I can't go. I have to cancel my reservation. I just can't go." Her sobbing continued. "I know you have to go, but I can't leave. My life is owned by Landry Manor. My mother needs me. She can't do without me. There is no one else." And she broke into tears. Jakob sat next to her, put his arms around her, and held her tight, while she sobbed almost uncontrollably.

What Jakob had seen coming became a reality, and he could see no solution. When she stopped sobbing, he kissed her and patted her, and kissed her.

"You're a captive, dear. I don't know what else you can do. Our lives have become like pawns, and we have no way out. I have to go back to Sheridan. There is no other alternative for me." They sat for a while holding each other in silence, not knowing what to say. Then they walked up the stairs to their rooms, holding on to each other. Jakob took her into his arms and kissed her tenderly.

"Don't give up Honey. It's not over for us and our plans. It's a setback but we'll work this out. You just have to do what you must do." Geraldine nodded and went into her room.

Jakob lay in bed, his mind muddled in thoughts. He thought this might happen, almost since the day she came back from London, and yet he kept thinking something would save them. But it was ordained for her to assume full responsibility. Lady Mary couldn't do it because she didn't have the ability, but Geraldine did. Jakob felt it really should be Randolph, the son, to assume his role as Baron of Landry Manor, but wondered if he could because of his responsibilities to the Army.

May 27th had arrived and it was time for Jakob to leave for London. He had done all his packing and everything was ready for his departure from Landry Manor. He had his reservation at the Great Eastern Hotel in London to stay overnight. Sampson would drive him to the station in Ipswich. He was ready to leave, and Geraldine came out with a day bag. She had decided to go to London with him. Jakob was happy she would be with him.

"I'll have you with me one more day and then I'll stay with Aunt Allison and Mama. I can then see you off to Southampton." She was obviously distraught to see him leave and wanted to be with him. The 10:00 a.m. train was on time and they boarded it. It would be at Liverpool Station before noon. They talked as they had on the trip going to Ipswich and viewed the landscape, which had by now turned much greener. It was a perfect day with a bright sun until they approached London and then became overcast. The train made many stops before it arrived at noon. Jakob's luggage was put on a cart and taken to the Great Eastern Hotel, where he checked in.

"Have you got some special place to eat lunch, or shall we just eat here in the hotel? I have no great desire to go sight-seeing. I'd be satisfied to just stay around the hotel and maybe we can do some window shopping. How do you feel?"

"I just want to be with you, Jakob." And she snuggled up close to him.

"Then that's what it will be. We'll have our lunch in the smaller dining room and do some window shopping. We'll just play it by ear." There was a small pub near the dining room with some people sitting at the bar. There were several empty tables. They found a table away from the rest and sat down.

"Do you think it's too early for a martini?" Geraldine shook her head and when the server came by they ordered martinis. Jakob held Geraldine's hands. "Your hands are cold."

She smiled. "But my heart is warm." The server put the martinis on the table and they picked them up and gently clicked glasses. She looked forlornly at Jakob and said, "To us."

"It's not over Geraldine. We are just facing a roadblock. You have to do what you are doing before we will be back to together for good." Geraldine smiled and nodded her head.

"That's right, for good and forever." They finished their martini and left for lunch. The room was elegant in appointments with large chandeliers and mirrored walls. It was not filled but there were several parties at a few tables. The service and food were very good. The hotel had stores of all kinds and they spent their time looking in the windows or walking through the aisles.

"Have you had enough of this?" To which Geraldine agreed. "Shall we go up to the room?" and Geraldine nodded in agreement. "How far away from here is your aunt's apartment?"

"Oh, it's some distance from here." Jakob turned the key and they walked in. "It will take about an hour to get there."

"You could stay here if you wish." Geraldine smiled coyly.

"Do you think I should?" Jakob shrugged his shoulders and put his arms around Geraldine and brought her close to him.

"I don't have to stay here, if it will be inconvenient for you" He kissed her softly. "I'll stay if you want me to." He smiled and kissed her again. Then he left her and went back to the door and placed the Do Not Disturb sign on the outside of the door.

"Then it's settled. You may stay with me." He put his arms around her, then picked her up and placed her on the bed. He helped her to disrobe, before he took off his own clothes. They held each other and kissed passionately.

"Jakob, I want you. I can't let you go without having you."

"Nor could I." And they made love.

The sun filtered through the drapes as Jakob opened his eyes to a new day. He turned to the side and saw his Geraldine lying next to him. He watched her as she slumbered and remembered the night they had together. He had to kiss her lips so softly. Her eyes opened. She smiled and held his face and drew it to her lips. "I love you Jakob Miller. Do you know that? Now you know what to expect when we see each other again in Sheridan."

They finished their breakfast and checked out. Jakob's luggage was ready to put on the train. They stood on the platform waiting and holding each other. The train to Southampton arrived. One final kiss and Jakob boarded the train. He watched Geraldine, with tears in her eyes following the train, as it left the station.

Chapter 38

Homeward Bound

After passing through Customs, Jakob boarded the HMS *Oceanic*. The excitement of the boarding passengers was not shared by Jakob. He went straight to his stateroom to check it out. Removing his coat and shoes he lay on his bed. He felt tired, emotionally and physically. His thoughts of Geraldine moved about in his head. He had left her behind and it bothered him greatly. *I've been cheated. Why didn't I marry her when I had the opportunity? We could have been married in Sheridan and had our honeymoon in England. The trip to England didn't change my feelings for Geraldine, not one iota. I didn't learn anything different about her and now I am alone to wait. What if she changes her mind? She is the custodian of Landry Manor. Her mother can't possibly handle it. Her brother isn't there. What if he should be killed or die. It would be hers.* Shaking his head, Jakob looked in the mirror. *What in heaven's name am I thinking? Geraldine loves me and will do everything possible to get back to me. I have to get rid of these crazy thoughts.*

He removed his shirt, washed his face and combed his hair to freshen up, and then put his shirt back on. The ship's horn was blaring, and it would soon be time for the HMS *Oceanic* to cast off. The cabin boys were going through calling, "All guests must leave. All guests must leave." Jakob went on deck and stood by the rail to watch the goings-on. Happy people were shouting and waving. Then a long blast from the ship's horn sounded indicating the ship would be moving out.

Lines were cast off and hauled aboard. Finally the last bow lines were aboard. The HMS *Oceanic* moved from the dock. The tugs were backing until the ship was in the middle of the channel. Jakob walked toward the bow, along the rail on the starboard side. He watched the crewmen stowing the lines. The ship moved past the Isle of Wight heading west-southwest. The seas were running four to six feet, with a stiff breeze on the bow causing a spray. The coast of England was on the starboard side, with Plymouth lying some distance ahead. They were far enough off shore now, so land objects were not too visible. He stood watching the shore slowly move by. Some of the birds already had stopped following. *Funny*, he thought, *how vastly different this trip is without Geraldine. We were so excited looking forward to the visit to Landry Manor and here I am, going back alone. But then I too should be excited because I'm on my way back home and I'll see my BethAnn.*

Jakob stayed at the bow rail until the sun started to set in the west. Clouds started to cover the sky and the setting sun was a range of colors. Lights could be faintly seen on the distant shore, and the stiff breeze felt cold on his face. Turning around he looked up toward the bridge. There were several officers on the port-side wing, probably taking celestial observations on the stars as they appeared. He went inside and found his stateroom. *I might as well get dressed for dinner. I wonder if I should go formal? I'm going alone. But then,* he thought, *I guess it's shipboard protocol.*

He heard the cabin boy calling out it was time for the second seating, so he left his cabin and approached the maitre d'.

"Doctor Miller. You're sailing back with us! I don't see Lady Geraldine on my list. Won't she be with us?"

"No, she's not going back."

"Oh . . . then may I seat you with a small group?" Jakob nodded it would be all right, and he was promptly seated at a table for six, next to an attractive lady. Two English couples and a French lady were already seated. She was introduced as Madam Collette Aubert. Her English was definitely tinted with French, offset by her charm and beauty. Everyone introduced themselves and told something about themselves; Madam Aubert was a cosmetologist and going to New York. She became very attentive to handsome Jakob but he was cool to her charm. They all ordered wine and Jakob asked for a martini. This immediately left him out of the conversation about the wines they were drinking. Jakob did mention that his martini had a French vermouth in it; he didn't say that it was just a teaspoon of the wine.

The conversation went in another direction as soon as they learned he was a dentist from Wyoming. They weren't too interested in his dentistry, but rather in the Indians who lived there and the "shoot 'em up guys," as someone had said. The evening ended up "*Jolly well good,*" as one of the English described it.

After dinner, Jakob left the group and took a walk around the windy deck. By now, the signs of land had all but disappeared, except for what must have been a lighthouse far into the distance turning off and on. He later visited the little pub where he and Geraldine had their martinis. The same attentive waiter was surprised to see him alone. Jakob ordered a wine.

"The lovely lady won't be joining you, sir?" Jakob just said she wouldn't be. He sat alone with his wine listening to the piano player who had joined the bar for the late-night drinkers. He was playing ballads and love songs which reminded Jakob of Geraldine. Finishing his drink, he left for his cabin and lay in bed. Although he was tired, he couldn't seem to fall asleep. His thoughts were of the previous night in the Eastern Hotel making love with Geraldine.

The next days were much of the same. He sat with the same group and got to know them better. The couples were interesting. One of the men was an engineer going to Pittsburgh to visit a manufacturing plant, and the other man was chemist going to study for an advanced degree at the University of Michigan. Their wives were just going along for the trip. Collette Aubert was going to a meeting with some wholesalers of cosmetics she was selling. She was quite attractive and attentive with Jakob. She later invited him to a cocktail party she was hosting in her suite the next day. Jakob wasn't quite sure he would go, but then he thought, it might be interesting. He certainly wasn't interested in her.

The next day he took a tour of the bridge, even though he had done it on the previous crossing but this time he became interested in the navigation of the vessel and wanted to learn how the captain knew where they were as they crossed the vast ocean.

The ship's navigator took an interest in Jakob and his questions, and had him come to the bridge when he was getting his LAN. The Local Apparent Noon, was the reading on the sun at its highest elevation, at twelve o'clock, noon, using the sextant. By taking the celestial angle on the sun using the sextant and the mathematics tables from a special Nautical Almanac—the navigator was able to get the exact latitude of the ship which he plotted on an ocean chart. Jakob was told, even Columbus knew how to do that. To get the longitude of the ship, an Englishman made the first special clock which could be carried on the ship, called a chronometer. It was necessary when they took celestial observations on the stars to have the exact time at Greenwich, England. With a book of mathematical tables and the Nautical Almanac, it was then possible to get the correct longitude and latitude, to plot the ship's position on the chart. Thus, the captain could follow the progress of the ship across the Atlantic by using the stars and sun. The navigator even let Jakob use a sextant to make some celestial observations. Jakob started to enjoy the trip more than ever, as he was able to see the progress of the ship on a chart of the North Atlantic Ocean.

He decided to go to the cocktail party at Collette Aubert's suite. Walking into the large opulent suite he found a variety of people, most of whom he had not met. She introduced him to the group, referring to him as "ma che're Jakob." He wasn't quite sure what it meant at first, but it did raise some eyebrows. The two couples from the dinner table were also there. The rest were either French or some other ethnic group, and were often difficult to understand. A waiter passed out the wine and cocktails and a waitress carried the varied hors d'oeuvres. Jakob thought, *I better stick with the wine for this party. Martinis might be too heavy.* He ordered a Chardonnay. The party lasted until dinner was being served. Jakob insisted he leave for dinner; Madam Aubert appeared to be too amorous toward him.

He spent much of his time with the navigator which he enjoyed doing. That thwarted Collette's interest in him because he was always busy. He declined going to the captain's cocktail party. Collette asked him to escort her. But he did sit at the captain's table for dinner. Fortunately, he found out when Collette would be there and made his appearance another day. However, the lady sitting next to him at the captain's table was quite interested in him, and wanted him to sit at her table for dinner the next day. She was a widow, considerably older than Jakob and she made it a point to give her address and phone number to him so that he might visit her in Boston.

The cruise to New York was in its last day, and the evening would be the grand finale. Special food and drinks were on the menu and a farewell show in the theater with champagne at midnight. Jakob managed to always be with others when Collette was present, but the grand finale caught him by surprise; she snuggled up next to him and they kissed. Jakob still retained his vivid memory of Geraldine, and his last night with her. Collette lost, even when she invited him to her hotel room at the Waldorf for cocktails the next day.

He woke up in time to see the ship enter New York Harbor. It was a thrill to see the Statue of Liberty and realize he was back home in the United States. He met his friends for breakfast and they said their goodbyes. Jakob enjoyed their company.

It took much of the morning to dock the ship, but when finally docked it didn't take long to disembark. Going through Customs was not too difficult. His purchases were minimal, consisting mainly of gifts for BethAnn and his parents. After he got his luggage, it was a hectic taxi ride to the St Regis Hotel for the night. He had reservations for the New York Central 20th Century Limited the next day.

Being alone in a New York hotel gave Jakob a hollow feeling. He had no friends or business contacts in New York. Jakob found his way to the Metropolitan Museum of Art and spent the rest of the afternoon there. Arriving back at the hotel, he found a small cocktail lounge off the lobby and decided he would have a martini before dinner. He noticed a small group of people he had seen on the ship and had met at the captain's table. They invited him to sit with them. As he had discovered, the English were a friendly group and these folks were in New York for a vacation. Knowing Jakob was an American, they felt they might learn something about New York from him.

"I'm afraid I can't help you very much with New York. I'm a stranger here myself. If we were in Chicago, I could point you to all the good spots to visit. Or, how about Sheridan, Wyoming, the greatest city in the West?"

"Sorry, old boy. We're limited to the East Coast and New York City, but do stay here with us. We have something in common. We all just got off the HMS *Oceanic*. By the way, what were you doing in England?" They were interested in his trip to Suffolk and Ipswich. Although they were from Herefordshire, when Jakob mentioned Oliver Henry it struck a note with several who knew of him. They shared thoughts about Oliver Henry, most of them not knowing he once had a ranch near Sheridan. They had a "jolly good time" together and invited him to have dinner with them. Jakob had gotten used to their accents and idiosyncrasies, and found them to be pleasant people to be with. By time the evening was finished, Jakob was an old friend and was invited to visit them in Herefordshire.

The 20th Century Limited left New York City at five for Chicago. Like the trip from Chicago, he walked the red carpet to the sleeper car and settled in. He had picked up *The New York Times* and some magazines to read on the trip. The train was well out of New York City when he decided to find the dining car. He was seated alone and opted not to have a martini with his dinner. Jakob found himself thinking about Geraldine and wondering what she might be doing, and it led to the upcoming visit to his parents.

What am I going to tell my parents about Geraldine? I guess it will have to be about her father's stroke and Geraldine is left behind managing her father's Landry Manor. Our marriage plans are in limbo. That's essentially it. When everything is stabilized there, she will come back to Wyoming. The dining car was emptying out and getting ready to close, so Jakob returned to the Pullman car.

His bed had been prepared so he lay next to the window watching the night landscape go by. There wasn't much to see but a variety of lights. *We should be getting into Chicago by nine. I will get the twelve o'clock train to Milwaukee. It will be great to see BethAnn. I miss her so. I'll just stay a couple days.* His eyes were starting to close so he decided to turn in for the night. The clickety-clack of the train was enough to put him to sleep. He almost slept though the night, just awakening a few times, then falling back asleep. Streaks of daylight came though the edges of the window covering, and noise in the aisle awakened him. It was 6:30 a.m. and he couldn't fall back asleep again. It was time to get up and get some coffee.

The dining car was half-full. He was seated across from and older man, probably older than his father, more like Grandfather Miller.

"Where you headed mister?" he asked Jakob, with a nice smile on his face.

"Well, Chicago to start with. Then on to Milwaukee, and eventually Sheridan, Wyoming." The older man seemed surprised.

"Those places are pretty far apart. And Wyoming! You have a long way to go. This isn't a vacation you're taking, is it?" Jakob tried to explain he was going to his parents' to pick up his daughter and take her to their home in Sheridan, Wyoming. But when he threw England into the story it became quite confusing to the gentleman.

"I'm just going to Chicago where I live. I spent a week in New York City with my older brother, who is in bad shape." Jakob had his breakfast and they talked. The older man still couldn't quite understand what Jakob's trip was all about. Jakob returned to the sleeping car to get his things together. They had passed South Bend, Indiana, while he was in the dining car, and Chicago was less than an hour and a half away.

The train was about a half hour late as they entered the Randolph Street Station in Chicago. Jakob spent some time to get his luggage together and a taxi that would take him to Union Station. He telephoned his dad and told him he was in Chicago, and would be in Milwaukee about two. He knew his father would be in his office and he told him he would take a cab to their home.

"Jakob, we've been anxiously waiting for you. I'll be home just as soon as I can. BethAnn has been counting the days to see you." That made Jakob even more eager to see BethAnn and his parents. The last train ride to Milwaukee seemed to be the longest, because he was so anxious.

Waukegan, Kenosha, Racine and finally Milwaukee; Jakob hadn't figured out the exact number of miles he had traveled since England but it was a long way. The taxi driver was soon unloading his luggage in front of his parents' house, when the front door opened. BethAnn seemed to almost fly out of it, and was in Jakob's arms.

"Daddy. Oh Daddy. I'm so happy to see you. I missed you so." She showered him with kisses and hugs. His mother, smiling, was standing next to him and embraced Jakob.

"Welcome back, son, we all missed you." BethAnn started dragging a suitcase up the steps to the house. And then she turned around.

"Daddy! Where is Geraldine? Where is Geraldine, Daddy? Didn't she come back? Where is she? Will she be coming later?" Jakob nodded yes.

"I'll tell you when we get in the house." They took the luggage into the house, with BethAnn following close behind.

"Jakob have you had lunch? Come to the kitchen and I'll make you something."

"I'm fine Mother, but I will have a coffee if you have some."

"Daddy, please, where is Geraldine? I missed her so." They were seated, when Jakob realized he had forgotten BethAnn would also miss Geraldine. She sat next to him, anxious for him to tell her about Geraldine.

"Geraldine is still in England Honey. She couldn't come back with me."

"But why, Daddy?" And she started to cry. Jakob suddenly realized how important Geraldine had become in her life. He took her in his arms and kissed her.

"Why didn't she come back with you?" Jakob explained her father had become very sick, and she had to stay with him and her mother to help them.

"She wanted to come back with me, but she felt she must stay." BethAnn started to cry again. She was truly broken-hearted.

"Will I ever see her again? I love her. She is so good to me. I thought she would be my mother. Don't you love her anymore, Daddy?" Jakob was taken aback by BethAnn and her love for Geraldine.

"Of course I love her. She'll come back to us, but I don't know when. Geraldine does love you and me and said she will come back as soon as she could, but we have to patiently wait. I feel just as badly as you do because I want her to be my wife and your mother."

BethAnn was distraught and quietly sobbed. Margaret patiently waited until BethAnn stopped. She poured Jakob a cup of coffee and questioned him about what had happened. Jakob explained that Sir Gerald had a stroke and was incapacitated in the hospital, and Lady Mary was unable to care for him. Geraldine had to take over a great deal of responsibility, making it impossible to just leave them. Jakob showered as much attention on BethAnn as he could, to help get her over the disappointment of Geraldine not coming back.

Bob came home early from his office and greeted his son. He too was disappointed Geraldine did not return, but understood her reasons. There was joy amidst disappointment. Margaret made dinner and Jakob talked about his trip to England. They told Jakob about their visit with BethAnn, which turned out to be wonderful for the grandparents as well as BethAnn.

After BethAnn went to bed, Jakob tucked her in and had a heart-to-heart talk with her, hoping it would soothe her disappointment. He spoke more in details to his parents, who understood his plight.

He lay in bed that night thinking about BethAnn and Geraldine and realized BethAnn had already accepted her as her mother.

The next two days were spent with his parents, friends, and relatives. Jakob brought out the gifts he had bought them in England. A large box contained BethAnn's gift. She carefully unwrapped it and opened the box. Inside was an English lady's riding outfit, which also contained the traditional top hat. Jakob told her Geraldine had helped pick it out for her. He smiled and hugged BethAnn.

"I just can't wait to see you in that outfit riding on Nelly. You are going to look so great. The Sheridan County Fair is coming up and I'm going to make sure you are in it riding Nelly. We will have a picture taken of you to send to Geraldine, so she will see who is waiting for her." BethAnn was thrilled and immediately put on the top hat. They all clapped for her. He brought an English tea service for his parents, which they were delighted to have.

Following Jakob's loss of Liz, Margaret thought only she could raise BethAnn. As she now viewed her son, Jakob, she fully realized how wrong she was. Jakob had done so well raising his daughter. BethAnn belonged to Jakob and no one could have done better.

BethAnn and Jakob boarded the Milwaukee Road headed for Chicago. It was a difficult farewell for BethAnn and Margaret as they had developed a close relationship during BethAnn's stay. BethAnn had not known her grandmother. Memories of her mother were few, so this was very important for her. And it was a learning experience for both of them. Margaret's life took on a new meaning now that she was a grandmother. Jakob also realized BethAnn would have to visit her grandmother regularly to keep their relationship alive.

They arrived in Union Station and waited until they were able to board the train going west. There were now several train lines going to Sheridan but they stayed with the Chicago, Milwaukee, St. Paul and Pacific Railroad, better known as the Milwaukee Road. BethAnn was a good traveler. The trip was long and tiring: over thirteen hundred miles from Chicago to Billings, where they would get the train to take them to Sheridan. BethAnn kept Jakob alert with her many questions about what she saw along the way. They were both anxious to get home. The train made numerous stops as it traveled through five states with several changes of trains. Even though they used Pullman cars for sleeping, it was a tiresome trip. When they left Billings for Sheridan, they were elated.

The sound of the conductor calling out, "Sheridan, Sheridan, Wyoming," sounded really good. With the train whistle blowing, as the train started to slow down and the bell ringing, it was a sure sign they had arrived. They had talked to some of the passengers along the way and goodbyes were said.

"We have to get Wilbur Riggs to take us home," said Jakob. Sure enough, his son Little Henry was there and Jakob hailed him, as he got off the train. It took awhile to get all the baggage together. All loaded up, they were on their way home. BethAnn was so excited to see Skippy and her horse Nelly. Jakob told her the horses were at Wilbur Riggs's livery stable. It would be too hard for Chucha to take care of them this long. They had to be exercised and groomed, and Wilbur Riggs had the facilities.

It seemed like forever since they had been home, but it was actually two months since they left Sheridan. Everything had changed. The trees and bushes were green. The apple trees were filled with blossoms, as well as the dogwood and cherry trees. Summer had almost arrived to Sheridan, as well as Jakob and BethAnn. Little Henry brought the suitcases and boxes on to the porch. Chucha heard the noise, as well as Skippy and they were out of the front door to greet Jakob and BethAnn. Skippy was jumping up and down and Chucha gave them hugs and kisses. They went inside the house which was sparkling clean. Chucha had done a thorough housecleaning. As Jakob looked around, he thought of the magnificence and grandeur of Landry Manor, but it lacked the warmth and love of his home and his own Princess BethAnn.

Chucha soon had a cup of coffee in front of Jakob and a glass of milk for BethAnn, with a plate of *kolacky* to snack on. Skippy was still carrying on, happy to be with BethAnn. BethAnn was up to see her room which Chucha had spruced up.

"Happy to be back home, Honey?"

"Oh, Daddy, yes. I love my home. Being with Grandmother and Grandfather was wonderful and I love them, but it so nice to be in my home with you and Chucha and Skippy. When are we going to get Nelly? I miss her so. I hope she hasn't forgotten me." Jakob assured her Nelly didn't forget her and said they would be bringing the horse back soon.

She went with Jakob to do an inspection of the property and to check on BethAnn's rabbits. Chucha must have worked like a beaver because the property was groomed as well as it had ever been and Chucha even began planting the garden. Chucha had taken care of Jakob's home and property as well as if it were her own. Jakob brought back a gift for her. He knew she often used a shawl as a cover and so he brought her a beautiful English wool shawl she would make good use of. She was thrilled he had thought of her and thanked him and gave him a big hug and a kiss on the cheek. Then she asked him, "Pan'Jakob, nice lady, Geraldine. She no come back?" Jakob explained as best as he could why she hadn't returned as yet. Chucha pulled out all the stops and made one of her great dinners as a homecoming. She even had a cake in the oven.

That night some of the neighbors came over and welcomed them back home. Little Henry brought back Jakob's horse and Nelly. BethAnn was in the barn telling Nelly all about her trip to Milwaukee and Nelly didn't forget her. Jakob started making plans for the next day. He had a list of all he had to do. The next days would be hectic for him, but he was looking forward to getting back to work. He said he was not made for a life of leisure.

Chapter 39

Jakob Returns

It was Jakob's first day back at work and it wasn't an English rooster that awakened him, but the cold nose of Skippy. He didn't bother to look at the clock. Skippy wanted out to do his thing, and to re-establish his domain by chasing the squirrels and birds from his territory.

The sun wasn't up yet and the sky was a dull gray. *No use going back to bed,* he thought as he put the coffee pot on the stove and sat watching Skippy's antics. Chucha arrived in time to pour him a cup of coffee.

"What are you doing getting up so early, Chucha?"

"Dzien dobry, Pan. Oh, I so sorry, I forget. Good morning, Doctor Jakob. Forgive me for talking Polish. I forget sometimes."

"Don't worry Chucha, I understand. I know you try to speak English. Liz would be proud of you for how well you are doing, and I am too. You didn't have to get up this early."

"Dot's all right, Pan. I no can sleep."

"It looks like it is going to be a good day. I am going back to work just as soon as I take care of some things that have to be done first." The patter of soft footsteps coming down the stairs announced the arrival of BethAnn, who immediately sat on Jakob's lap.

"Good morning, Daddy." And that was accompanied by a big kiss and hug. "Are you going to work today?"

"I certainly am. I haven't worked for two months and I have to make up for a lot of lost time."

"Oh, Daddy, you always work. I thought maybe you would like to go for a ride. Nelly needs some exercise."

"She does, huh? She is going to have to wait because I have things I must do, and they comes first. But I just may find some time late this afternoon. How do you think that would work out for Nelly and you?"

"That would be just great. I have some things I must do too Daddy, and maybe Chucha might have things for me to do. I'll be ready when you come back and we can just go for a little ride. It has been a long time since Nelly has been on the trail." Chucha laughed at BethAnn, as she started frying sausage and eggs, which would be accompanied with her special breakfast cake.

They both were enjoying their breakfast as BethAnn enumerated the tasks she needed to do. Chucha chimed in, saying BethAnn could help her make noodles for that evening soup, which delighted BethAnn. She loved to work in the kitchen.

Jakob had gotten dressed, and after a hug and kiss from BethAnn, he was off to get his rig ready to make the numerous calls he had listed. His first stop would be the *Sheridan Post* to get an ad in the paper announcing his return.

"Hey, Doc, it's good to see you back. You've been gone a long time."

"Good to be back, Edgar. I have been away too long. Traveling is okay, but I'm not made for it. I'll tell you what, there's nothing like being back here in Sheridan."

"You went to England, didn't you? That should have been a great trip."

"It was, but . . . I'll give you the whole story when we get together with the guys for lunch next Monday. But for now, I want you to run an announcement in the paper saying I'm back. Run it for a week which should be long enough." This was the start of Jakob's day. He followed it up with a stop to see Harold Brown, the dentist, who took care of his patients.

"Welcome back Jake. How's it feel to be going back to work? Everything went fine here. I got a list for you, of who I took care of and what I did. You know Mrs. Winter, the tall gray haired lady. She was angry you weren't here to take care of her. I told her you were on a vacation, but she said it was no excuse. You should be around to take care of her when she needs you." Jakob laughed.

"Did she bring you a loaf of the homemade bread she makes?" Harold said she didn't.

"She didn't? Oh, then she really was mad." And they both had a good laugh. "Don't worry, she'll get over it." He stopped to see Doc Kelly who was outside sitting and talking to a couple of guys. He saluted Jakob as he drove up.

"Well, well. Sir Doctor Jakob is back to be with us commoners." Jakob laughed.

"That's no way to greet an old friend. I came here to bring glad tidings from the folks in England, especially to the famous Doc Kelly of Sheridan."

"Jake, you sure know how to put me on. Everybody was asking where is Jake, and I told them you were hobnobbing with them English." They all started laughing.

"I just wanted to let you know the only reason I came back was just in case you needed me." Kelly looked at Jakob and just laughed.

"Before I forget; Jake, remember the guy whose busted jaw we fixed? He stopped by the office the other day and told me his jaw felt good. And he gave me twenty-five, on account. Not bad. I figured his jaw must be okay. He looked good and he put on a bunch of weight. Remember how skinny he got?

"I tell you what, Jake, just because I'm your friend I'll buy you a drink tonight at the Lucky Lady, that is, if you have time for us commoners." Jakob was laughing as he rode off. He made stops at the bank and at Elmer Findley's, to announce he was back. While passing by his office he noticed someone sitting there, so he turned around and went back and tied up.

"I thought you would be stopping here today, Doc. I heard you were back. I got this old fang been killing me. It's been hurting since before you left, but I figured I could wait until you got back." This became his first patient since he returned. The office was pretty dusty, but Jakob took care of him, anyway.

Later he stopped at the post office and picked up a few packages and a whole bunch of mail. He put it in his buggy for later. It was now almost time for lunch, so he stopped to see his friend Andy Meeks at the Lucky Lady. Of all the places in town, the Luck Lady was always busy. As he walked through the swinging doors, Andy saw him.

"Doc! You're back. I heard you got back, but I didn't think you'd be stopping by this early." He put a glass and bottle in front of him. "Here, how about one on me?" Jakob shook his head no, and just shook Andy's hand.

"Okay. If you won't have a drink, I'll buy you lunch. How about it?" Jakob smiled and nodded okay. "Harry, you take over for me, I'm going for lunch with Doc." He slapped Jakob on the back. "Let's go over to Lee Wong's for some chop suey." Andy was one of Jakob's best friends, and they would talk about the goings on in town. Jakob told him Geraldine hadn't returned with him, but hoped she would return sometime soon. "Well Doc, I sure hope she gets back here for ya. She sure is one good-lookin' woman."

After lunch, Jakob went back to his office and found someone waiting for him, so it was back to work. Jakob did say he wanted to get back to work, but he didn't think it would be this soon. After finishing the patient, he started cleaning up the office, which had collected a lot of dust while he was gone. He looked around and remembered his dad's clean, neat office and thought, *Dad's office doesn't have Wyoming winds blowing dust all over.* The door to his office opened and closed frequently as others stopped by just to say hello, so Jakob was back to his usual schedule. He finished his cleaning and straightening the office and looked at his watch. He thought about BethAnn wanting to go riding. *It just might be a good way to end the day,* he thought.

Sure enough, BethAnn was already waiting for him to get home, with Nelly all saddled up.

"Hi Daddy, I'm ready to go any time you are." Jakob laughed.

"As soon as I can change, Dolly, I'll be out to get Jenny saddled up. Where do you want to go?"

"Any place you say will be fine with me. I think Nelly is anxious to get going." Jakob was in his room changing as he thought about BethAnn. *She is such a pleasant child and always so happy. She is fun being with. I hope we can get Geraldine here. She will be so good for BethAnn.* Then another thought came to him. *BethAnn has a birthday coming up. She will be nine. I have to give her a birthday party.*

He arrived at the stable and talked with his horse, petting and giving her a carrot. It had been two months since he had ridden her.

"I'm almost ready. Just a soon as I get Jenny saddled up, we can get going." They followed a trail near their house, just ambling along. It was a perfect day for riding and the sun was still high, with a fresh breeze. It really felt good to be back in Sheridan and among his friends. He thought about England and the trip with Geraldine. *It was great to be with her, but somehow it didn't feel like home. The people there were friendly, but not like those in Sheridan. I just can't explain the difference,* he thought. *Maybe it's just because Americans are a different breed of people.* BethAnn was excited to be out on her horse. She had learned a lot about horses and riding from Geraldine. It showed as confidence in what she was doing. For an eight-year old going on nine, it was amazing how well she could ride, and he enjoyed being with her.

They took the trail toward Acme and they slowly rode along. Acme was a different sort of community, with a variety of ethnic groups but they seemed to segregate themselves as Italians, Slovaks, Poles and even Japanese. They each lived in their own little areas. Working in the mines was dangerous and back-breaking work. Some would eventually leave Acme and come to Sheridan to find different work, such as Jozef, who was working in the bank and even Chucha who was working for Jakob.

They didn't go all the way to Acme but turned around and rode slowly back. Chucha had prepared a sumptuous dinner for them. It was their second dinner back home after their long trip. Jakob thought, *In spite of the extravagant cookery I experienced in England, Chucha provides some of the best cookery I have ever tasted. I guess that's another reason why I like Sheridan.*

After dinner, BethAnn went off with Skippy and Jakob sat on his front porch. *I should have heard from Geraldine by now,* he thought, *but maybe she's just too busy. Everything seems perfect here, except my Geraldine is several thousands away from me.*

He went through his mail, looking for a letter from Geraldine but found none; but he'd received a letter from his dad.

He's shipping the dental equipment he promised me. That will upgrade my office. I can get rid of that old barber chair and have a real adjustable dental chair with a headrest. His suggestion I add an electric dental motor to replace the pedaled one I'm using is a great idea. We now have electricity and maybe I should get an x-ray machine. It would really help. Jakob was getting excited about adding different equipment and upgrading his office.

There was a letter from the mayor regarding the coming Sheridan County Fair which brought him up to date on the fair. He hadn't forgotten about it, but realized it was coming soon.

Monday at eleven-thirty, the luncheon group met at the Sheridan Inn in the back corner of the bar-room. Lukas had a special lunch for the group. Jakob was a little late because his appointment ran over, but the rest of the men were already there. Harold Stevens addressed Jakob.

"Glad to see you could make it, Jake. We've been waiting for you to give us a blow-by-blow account of that trip to England. But before you do, I want to introduce you men to a couple of new gentlemen, you may not know. Lloyd Phillips, with the brewery, and Gene Rodgers, with Anderson Coal, have asked to meet with us today. They have something to discuss with us." Harold Stevens, from the First National Bank, continued. "Jake, you were gone for a couple months, so you should have a lot to tell us. What gives?" There were a few chuckles as Jakob stood up.

"Now I know you men are all wondering why I went to England. I really went as an unofficial ambassador from Sheridan. Yes, I was representing all of you gentlemen, as I was taking orders for the things you deal in. I took orders for all of you, even for money, Harold. But do you want to know what happened? The order book I had put all those orders in accidentally fell over the side of the HMS *Oceanic*, into the Atlantic Ocean, somewhere between Plymouth, England and New York City." That, of course, sent the group jeering at Jakob, who laughed with them. He then proceeded to give them a brief account of his trip. They asked some questions, he answered and then the discussion went on to the county fair and other items of importance. When that discussion ended Ernie Johnson, from the Johnson Drug Store got up.

"I suppose some of you are wondering why Lloyd and Gene are here but I'll let them explain it to you. Lloyd!" Lloyd was a younger man who had opened a brewery.

"Gentlemen. As you know there is a mayoral election coming up. Mayor Burns has been mayor of Sheridan for four terms. There's been some talk about maybe he would be retiring. Our main purpose here is to suggest we should be looking for someone to run for the mayor's office. We have to find someone who can take over as mayor of a growing Sheridan, someone who has the best interests of Sheridan in mind. Maybe, even one of us. We are all in business and have a responsibility to find the right man to represent us, as well as the other people who live here. This year, our first hospital is officially opening. Do you all realize how important that is to Sheridan? Most of you worked hard to make it possible. So, as business people, we have to be ready to assist, if and when Mayor Burns retires." It was a good talk and Jakob felt maybe he could do more to help Sheridan move on successfully. The meeting went on with suggestions of possible candidates and ended on a positive note.

Weeks had passed and Jakob still had not heard from Geraldine. Jakob was now preparing for the Sheridan County Fair. He had recruited people to assist him, most of whom had worked previously with Jakob. He had been working on the fair for some years, ever since Mayor Burns asked him, so he had the tasks well organized. He was looking forward to it, even though he was very busy at his office. The equipment his father had sent was just being stored, because he was too busy to install it.

Sheridan was already starting to fill up with visitors for the fair. The Indians usually set up along Goose Creek. Most of the out-of-town folks were camping close to the fairgrounds. The hotels were starting to fill up. There was excitement in town. Doc Kelly stopped at Jakob's office.

"I got some things to talk to you about, Jake. First of all, and very importantly, if you suggest to Mayor Burns that I judge cattle again this year, I'll get a couple of guys from that Hole in the Wall gang to visit you. Now, you wouldn't want me to do that, would you? Okay! You do understand how I feel about being a judge, don't you? I'm glad you agree with me." Jakob just laughed.

"Now, besides that, I got something else I want to talk to you about. You know the hospital has finally opened for business. I'm going to be on the staff, and they are needing to add other docs as well. I want you on the staff. If anyone gets a tooth or jaw problem which could end up in the hospital, I want you to be the guy to fix them. I know what you can do, but I don't know about the other guys. Understand? We'll be able to put people to sleep, when they need serious surgery. Like it would have been nice if we had a hospital when we fixed the guy's broken jaw, instead of doing it on the table in my office. Do you understand, Jake? I'm putting your name in for the staff."

"Okay, Kelly, I promise I won't tell Mayor Burns you are the best choice to judge cows. Not to worry. Remember, we're friends. You know, I once thought about working in the hospital with some of these bad accident cases we get. You're right, they should be taken care of in the hospital not in an office, even though we have been doing them there for years. I'm all for it."

"Okay kid, we'll drink to that at the Lucky Lady. Now there's something else I want to talk to you about. You got some kind a problem? You haven't been yourself since you got back from the big trip. I been noticing you moping around. What's the matter? There's something that's bothering you. Now you level with me Jake. I'm your friend."

"You think there's something wrong with me, huh? Does it really show?"

"Yes, it does."

"Okay, you're right, Kelly. I guess I can't help it but I'm worried. I haven't told you much about Geraldine, but the reason I went to England was to meet her family. I'm in love with her. I haven't told you but I planned on marrying her and now I'm worried I may lose her." He went on to tell Doc Kelly about his affair with Geraldine. Kelly, not with his usual bravado, related a story Jakob was not aware of.

"I know how you feel, Jake. I lost my lady twenty years ago. Just like you, but we didn't have a kid like you do. When it happened, I just wanted to die. I thought of different things I could do to end it all. But as much as I felt I wanted to die, I couldn't do it. I lived in Philadelphia then. I had seen plenty of personal loss in my time, and then I just felt I had to get away. So I packed up and landed here, where no one knew me. I should have married again, but I didn't. You got the right idea, so do it, Jake. You do it. That woman will come back. If she doesn't, she's crazy. You're a good guy. She'll come back.

"Enough of that stuff. I'll let them know at the hospital you will be on the staff. It's a good idea. You just hang in there. She'll come back. See you later. Don't forget, I'll buy you one over at the Lucky Lady tonight."

Jakob watched as Kelly got on his horse and rode away. He closed the office and left for home. It gave him something to think about. He thought, *That was the first time Kelly ever talked about his personal life. I never knew he had been married. He never, ever showed his feelings. He always seemed to have all the answers. I guess I learn something new every day.*

Doc Kelly's idea of including Jakob on the staff of the hospital was a good one and Jakob thought his patients could benefit from it. He remembered going to the Cook County Hospital as a student and watching his professors do complicated procedures and he was now excited about the idea of working in a hospital.

BethAnn welcomed him as he arrived home. She insisted on showing him the garden she and Chucha had planted. They walked around the property and looked at all the trees and bushes which were showing new growth. He had a sense of pride in what he now owned. BethAnn took him to the barn to show him how she had groomed Nelly. She would be riding Nelly in the opening day parade of the Sheridan County Fair and was excited about it. This would be the first time BethAnn would be riding in a parade and even though she was capable, Jakob was a bit apprehensive for her, but he would be riding alongside her. Chucha came out to the garden to get them, as she had dinner on the table.

After dinner, BethAnn stayed with Chucha to help her clean up and Jakob went to sit on the front porch. His thoughts were of Geraldine. It was almost two months since he left Geraldine at the station in London and he had not yet heard from her. He had written her when he got back to Sheridan and asked her what was happening at Landry Manor. Doc Kelly's words gave him some strength and hope, but he had an agonizing feeling. Geraldine might not be able to return. Her responsibilities at Landry Manor might prevent her from returning. He wondered whether her sister Eleanor would be showing at the fair, and if he would see her. If he did, perhaps she might know what was happening at Landry Manor. He went to bed at night still not knowing for certain, if he would ever see her again.

Opening day of the Sheridan County Fair began with a big parade that went down Main Street. It consisted of the marching bands, the Civil War veterans, a detachment from Fort MacKenzie, the fire department, some of Colonel Cody's group, Crow Indians in full regalia, and just about anyone else who wanted to be in it, which included the mayor, some of his commissioners, Jakob with BethAnn and some cowboys from the surrounding ranches. It was a rollicking group marching down Main Street carrying flags and banners to the fairgrounds. BethAnn did very well. She even showed off some of the things that she learned from Geraldine in the handling of Nelly.

The following days were busy for Jakob. He worked in his office in the mornings and at the fair in the afternoons. He judged some of the horse races, but had some trouble in one of the them where there was a close call between one of the Crow Indians and a local cowboy. It was finally resolved by running the race again, with just the two riders. The Indian rider won it, without a doubt, but the cowboy still sulked and claimed he had won the first time.

The following morning Jakob was seeing patients in his office when a lady came in who he had not ever seen before. Because of her dress, she appeared to be one of the English ranchers.

"Doctor Miller, we have never met. I am Eleanor Allen, Geraldine Widicker's sister." Jakob immediately saw a distinct resemblance to Geraldine.

"Eleanor, how nice to meet you. Geraldine spoke of you. Are you here for the fair?"

"Yes, I'm here for the fair, but Geraldine wanted me to stop by to see you. I see you're very busy. Maybe we should meet and can talk later."

"That would be fine. How would lunch be for you at the Sheridan Inn?"

"That would be excellent. I'm staying there."

" I should be able to get away at noon, but I could be a little late." He watched Eleanor leave, as he returned to his patient. While he worked, his thoughts were interrupted with the anticipation of learning something about Geraldine. Jakob arrived late at twelve-thirty.

"I'm sorry I was delayed in getting here. My morning was very busy."

"This is fine for me. I know you are a busy person and I had a chance to look at the menu." Annabelle waited on them and they ordered their lunch. Jakob was the first to speak.

"I am so happy to meet you. I was wondering whether I would see you here. Will you be showing some of your horses?"

"Yes, I am. But I really wanted to see you because I have received several letters from Geraldine." Jakob's immediate thought was, *Why didn't Geraldine write to me?* "Geraldine has been very busy with the business of Landry Manor. My father is completely helpless. He now has around-the-clock care from a nurse who lives there. Geraldine has full charge of everything. Lady Mary is very distraught with the turn of events and is incapable of accepting any responsibility or doing anything. We do worry about her. Randolph Edward has not returned from India, and no one knows when he will return. My other sister has married and is living in London. She is of no assistance to Geraldine. Geraldine is . . . stranded in Suffolk." She looked at Jakob without speaking and he slowly began to speak.

"I haven't heard from her since I left on the train to Southampton."

"Yes, I know. She is having a difficult time reconciling all of this." Eleanor waited for Jakob to speak, but he was having a difficult time putting his words together.

"Geraldine fears the worst and that she may not be able to return here—she is having a difficult time handling her plight."

Jakob looked away. He couldn't speak. What he had feared most seemed to be almost inevitable and he was stunned.

"I'm sorry but I guess I just don't know what to say. We were supposed to get married when we came back. We love each other. What am I to do? What can I do?" Eleanor found herself without words for Jakob and sensed his utter disappointment.

"Don't give up. Geraldine may just be depressed and is seeing the wrong side of the problem. A solution could come forward." They talked more but had nothing left but a slight glimmer of hope. She thanked Jakob for the lunch and tried to reinforce the hope that still remained as she left. Jakob sat at the table mulling over and over in his mind what Eleanor had said. He tried to convince himself not to give up hope. *Geraldine may just be overwhelmed with her responsibility. Maybe when her brother returns they can come to terms with Landry Manor. I can't give up hope.*

He returned to the fair and judged a horse race. The rest of the afternoon was a repeat of all he had been doing the past few days, and he found himself just going through the motions. He left for the day and went back to his office. He couldn't shed the thoughts of his conversation with Eleanor. He thought of writing to Geraldine, but he didn't know what to say to her. Jakob started several letters and gave up. Someone walked into his office in need of care. It took his mind off of his problem, at least for a while. Then he closed his office and decided to go home. *I'll take BethAnn and we can go for a ride. I don't want to stay around here.*

Jakob didn't have to ask BethAnn twice. She was ready to go and quickly had Nelly saddled. Jakob just wanted to ride, with no definite place to go. He listened to BethAnn's chatter and lost track of his thoughts; he just listened to his daughter's world. They ended up at Little Goose Creek where Jakob gave the ring to Liz, and his mind drifted off to that cold April day when he placed the ring on her finger.

Maybe this is all meant to be. I had my love with Liz, and now I have her daughter. Maybe I shouldn't expect any more. I have her.

"Daddy, you look sad. Is something the matter."

"No, Dolly, nothing is the matter. I'm really happy, I have you and we're out here together, but maybe we should return home now. Chucha will have dinner ready for us." They arrived home to find Chucha waiting.

Two days passed and the fair was over. Jakob was glad it was finished. He saw Eleanor once more but had little conversation with her. He was at a loss of words as they said goodbyes.

Jakob got back in the routine of his office. The equipment his father had sent to him was installed and he was happy with his upgraded office. The dental chair was a vast improvement over his old barber chair. He still hadn't gotten the electric motor to power his drill. His practice was busy and he almost forgot about Geraldine, except in some of his quiet moments.

Jakob was in the Lucky Lady on a Saturday afternoon with Doc Kelly when, at one of the tables, a ruckus started between a couple of card players. It ended out in the street, with guns drawn, bullets flying, and one of them fell to the ground. One of the bullets entered the victim's leg and the other went right through the mouth. There was a lot of bleeding and pain. Doc Kelly examined him and they took him to the hospital. The shooter was sent to the jail.

"Jake, I'm gonna need your help on this one." They both went to the hospital and found the patient in the operating room. The nurse got the bleeding almost stopped, but there was bullet in his leg and a hole in both sides of his mouth. The bullet had gone through both cheeks and some of his teeth were shattered. "Looks like I'm going to work on the leg, while you take care of his mouth, Jake."

"I asked the nurse and found out they don't have any dental instruments here, Kelly. I have to go back to my office and get what I need."

"Then get going, Jake, and we'll get this guy ready." Jakob went to his office to get his instruments, put them in a bag and went back to the hospital. The nurse met him and took his instruments to be sterilized, even though Jakob told her he had sterilized them. She directed him to the scrub room, where Kelly was already scrubbing up.

"You got to scrub up here, Jake. This is a hospital and you work by their rules." Jakob started the process of scrubbing in preparation for surgery. When he was finished, the nurse held up a gown in front of him. He pushed his arms in and she drew it around him and tied it in back. Next she held the powered glove open for him as he pushed his hands in. She tied a mask and pushed a cap over his head.

"Kelly, I can see this isn't going to be easy."

"Yes, I know, you're in a hospital Jake and they got rules." Jakob went into the operating room and found the covered patient on a table with a bright light shining on him and his sterilized instruments, on a tray to the left. Kelly was on the other side of the table. Another nurse had an ether mask she put over the patient and when Kelly nodded, she started dripping ether on it, until he was asleep.

"Go ahead Jake, you're first. Get going and clean up the mess in his mouth." He looked in and saw the crowns of two teeth on the right side gone and four on the left side smashed. He started cleaning out the broken fragments before he went after the roots. Fortunately the jaw wasn't broken, although he took out a large piece of bone. He moved fast and got all the debris out and started suturing. The bleeding was controlled and he looked up at Kelly.

"What we going to do with the holes in his cheeks, sew them up?"

"Up to you Jake. Doesn't look like the muscles are torn. You get the left side and I'll get the right. We'll just put a couple sutures to close the holes in the cheeks. Are you finished with the mouth?"

"You know Kelly, I like doing it this way. I get no screaming and groaning from the patient, he's quiet and holds still and I got the roots of the broken teeth out and cleaned up the blood."

Doc Kelly took the cover off the injured leg and exposed the bullet hole.

"Hope the bullet didn't go in too deep." He inserted a probe to find the bullet. "We're in luck Jake, it's superficial," Doc said as he quickly lifted it out with a hemostat. "Took a lot of these things out in my time." Finishing up, he put in a couple of stitches. "Well, that takes care of this guy. You can take over now nurse." They left the operating room taking off their gloves and gowns.

"Well, Jake, you did all right, considering this is the first time you worked in a hospital. Let's go back to the Lucky Lady and finish where we left off when all this happened. I think we deserve at least one drink."

Chapter 40

BethAnn's Birthday

Summer was rapidly passing for Jakob. The county fair was now history, but those who worked on it were still talking about its success and the different events which were memorable. The Monday noon luncheon group had not heard much about the mayor's retiring, even though there were numerous names suggested for his replacement. Jakob decided not to go to Buffalo to take care of those people. There was a hometown dentist practicing there, and even though many of Jakob's patients lived there, he decided not to go back. Jakob had plenty to do in Sheridan.

Jakob's staff appointment to the hospital gave him another way of taking care of his patients. Besides the need for hospital care for accident cases, there were those people who were so frightened of dental care pain, they avoided getting necessary care. It was now possible for Jakob to do some of the work under general anesthesia, and he was being asked to treat those people. Badly infected teeth were a common and serious health hazard and Jakob's skills were sought in Sheridan and from afar for patients who were hospitalized. His practice flourished as Sheridan grew.

BethAnn's birthday was not too far off. She was going to be nine and Jakob wanted to do something special for her. He knew a birthday party was definitely in order, but Jakob thought there was more he should do for her. She had mentioned on several occasions her desire to play the piano. *Maybe I should buy her a piano and let her take music lessons,* and then he thought of Harry at the Lucky Lady. *Maybe he could give her piano lessons or the lady at the church who plays the organ might be available to give lessons. Music would be something to expand her education. Liz would want her to have it. Liz loved music and I would often hear her singing or humming a tune.* Jakob felt BethAnn's love for music came from her prenatal days, when Liz would sing to her unborn baby, and the days after she was born when they both sang to her.

Her birthday was September 20th and Jakob made plans to have all her friends come to the house. They had a big yard where he could put up a tent and Jakob would even ask some of the musicians he knew to come and play. He remembered how her baptismal party was such a great success. Jakob was excited about the idea of having the party. He told Chucha and she thought it was a wonderful idea and was already thinking of foods she would serve. Jakob made a list of people he would invite. The plans were made and some of those invited started getting things together. Jakob initially wanted it to be a surprise party, but he decided to let BethAnn know shortly before the party, so she could invite her own friends.

After he came home from the office, Jakob asked BethAnn if she would like to take a short trail ride. School was already in session and BethAnn had homework she was required to do.

"That would be great, Daddy. I've already started my homework and I don't have too much to do. Let's go."

"We'll just go up to that little pond off Goose Creek and watch the ducks, while they are still around." BethAnn had Nelly ready to go as Jakob saddled up. They often would go for rides together. It gave him a chance to be with her and they could talk. It also broke up the stress of his day in the office. They arrived at the pond and, sure enough, the ducks were in and out of the water and having a good time. They got off the horses and led them to the pond so they could get a drink as they watched the ducks.

"BethAnn, I remember you once telling me how much you would like to play the piano. Would you really like to learn?"

"Oh yes I would, I love music, Daddy. I really would like to learn how to play the piano. I remember my mother singing to me." Jakob was struck by the thought. *BethAnn was two when Liz died. Could she possibly remember her mother?* "And, you too, Daddy. You used to always sing to me. Some were silly songs, but I remember them. In school they sometimes play music because there is a band. We have a piano in school and a teacher plays in music class. I would like to someday learn to play a piano for you."

"You know, you have a birthday coming soon, and I was thinking I would like to buy you a piano as a birthday present and you could take music lessons."

"Would you really do that? Oh Daddy, really! Yes, I would like to play the piano. I know I would have to practice a lot before I could play for you and Chucha. If I played good, I could maybe even play in church."

"All right, Dolly, you sold me. I will buy you a piano for your birthday." BethAnn was thrilled and hugged and kissed Jakob. "I'm so glad you want to learn the piano, because I love music too, and I can look forward to you playing for me. Well, it's getting late, maybe we should leave now. Our days are getting shorter and it will be getting dark earlier." They got back in the saddle and started for home. BethAnn was excited that she would receive a piano.

The next day Jakob stopped to see Harry at the Lucky Lady and told him about his idea of getting a piano for BethAnn.

"Hey, Doc, that's a great idea. Every kid should learn to play a musical instrument. Best thing you could ever buy for her. Tell you what, I'll even give her some lessons. You know I learned when I was a kid in grammar school. My mother taught me. You don't know it, but I was once in a symphony orchestra, when I was at Indiana University."

"I never knew you went to Indiana University."

"Sure, Doc, I once played some pretty fancy music. This stuff I play in the Lucky Lady gives me some kicks. Once I had a big job in Chicago, but . . . it was in another time. You know, I don't have to stay around here. I just like it here. Yep, Doc, I sure would like to give your kid some piano lessons. I think it would be great. Did you buy a piano yet?"

"No, not yet. Got any ideas?"

"Sure do. I can get you a real good deal on a very good piano. I know of a guy over in Ranchester who has one he wants to sell. Wife died, and he doesn't play. She was a real fine piano player. I'll talk with him and have a piano here before her birthday. You can count on me." Jakob left the Lucky Lady excited. *I didn't know Harry even went to college and to think her was in a symphony orchestra. But then, he did play for our wedding at church, and he did accompany Diamond Lil at the Cady. I'm sure glad I talked with him*, he thought.

His preparations for the party were going as planned. It was time for him to let BethAnn know, so she could invite her friends to the party. Jakob already started to invite his friends to come. It was the weekend and Jakob was doing some things around the house, with BethAnn following him around.

"BethAnn, next Saturday is your birthday. Did you remember?"

"Yes, Daddy, I'm going to be nine. I'm so excited you will get me a piano. Will Chucha bake me a cake?"

"I'm sure she will. I was thinking you should have a birthday party and invite your friends. What do you think about that?"

"A party! I think it would be just great. I wondered what was going on around here. Something seemed kind of sneaky." Jakob started laughing and told her to invite all the friends she wanted. He would also ask some of his friends and neighbors.

BethAnn now knew about the party and was really excited. She started inviting all her friends. It was the Thursday before the party and Harry had the piano delivered from Ranchester to Jakob's house and placed in their living room. He came over and set it up and spent most of the afternoon tuning it.

Jakob and BethAnn sat in the living room watching and waiting. When he was finished he sat down and played numbers by Beethoven and Chopin. They had a private concert given by the honky-tonk piano player from the Lucky Lady. Jakob couldn't believe his ears. BethAnn was inspired and couldn't wait to start the lessons Harry promised to give her. He even sat her down and started her out that day, which really excited her.

All was in readiness for the party. The tent had been put up and a neighbor lady decorated the house. Chucha was getting things ready and had baked cookies and was working on the cake. Jakob had seen Father John Binotti, and invited him to the party. After all, he had baptized BethAnn shortly after she was born.

September 20th had come and BethAnn put on the dress Jakob had picked out for her at The New York Store. It was white with light blue trim, and blue flowered ruffles on the hem that went to her mid calf. Her blonde hair reached her shoulders and had a ribbon on it. With blue eyes and a dimples in her cheeks, she looked adorable. BethAnn was excited as she waited for her guests who finally started arriving in mid-afternoon. She had invited many friends from school. Even the neighbors down the street came to wish her a happy birthday. They brought gifts she gratefully received, and they were placed on a table. She giggled and laughed, hugged and kissed the arriving guests.

Many of Jakob's friends came by, along with Harry who brought a concertina he would be playing. The other musicians who came played solo, or they occasionally got together to play a few numbers. Some of the ladies brought casseroles and various other dishes. Cookies and cakes were all placed on a table to be eaten later. The mothers helped with the children, leading them in games. There was dancing and singing and gaiety prevailed. Jakob's friends and associates came by. Some stayed but others left, leaving BethAnn a gift and good wishes.

BethAnn brought Nelly out to show her to friends and even helped some of her friends get up on her for a short ride. For BethAnn and her friends, this was a party to be remembered. Chucha had made other foods that were served and went into the house to get the birthday cake she had baked for BethAnn. While getting the cake ready to take out, she looked up and saw a lady standing next to her. She had just arrived. It was Geraldine.

"Pani—Lady Geraldine!" She put her arms around her and hugged and kissed her.

"Chucha! I've come back. I wanted to come back for BethAnn's birthday, and I made it." Chucha was delighted and excited to tell Jakob.

"Pan Jakob in yard with people. Wait, I go get him."

"Don't tell Jakob I'm here," she pleaded. "Just ask him to come here." Chucha smiled and nodded then went out to the yard and found Jakob amongst his friends. She went up to him and tapped him on the shoulder.

"Pan Jakob, lady in kitchen want talk to you." Jakob asked her who it was, and she just shrugged her shoulders, so he turned around and headed for the house. He walked up the stairs, opened the door and walked into the kitchen. Standing in front of him was Geraldine, who looked at him with a half smile and a soulful expression.

"Jakob, I love you. Will you still have me?" Jakob, momentarily startled, began to move toward her. As they met, she put her arms around him. He encircled her with his arms and picked her up holding her tightly. Tears flowed down her cheeks as she held on to him. She lifted her head up to meet his lips. They stood together locked in each other's arms.

As they parted he said, "Of course I will still have you. I love you Geraldine. I have missed you so much. I feared I might have lost you."

He held her tightly and they kissed. Geraldine faced him and said, "I'll never let you go again. I wanted so much to be here for BethAnn's birthday and I just made it. The train got in an hour ago. I didn't realize you would be having this big party."

"I had planned it for her, but didn't even dream you would be here. Are you really here for good? No more Landry Manor?" Geraldine nodded her head and kissed him.

"Everything is taken care of there, and now I'm yours, and you are mine." Geraldine looked into his eyes. "There is so much for me to tell you, but it can wait. Where is my BethAnn? I have to see her and wish her a happy birthday and kiss her. I have missed her so much." They opened the kitchen door and went out. BethAnn was with her friends playing a game and she looked up to see Geraldine. She ran to her and put her arms around her.

"Geraldine, you came to my party. You've come back. I'm so happy. I missed you so much." Geraldine bent down and they kissed each other. She hugged her tightly. By this time, almost everyone realized who had arrived. BethAnn insisted on introducing Geraldine to her friends.

"This is Geraldine. She is going to be my mother." Tears came down Jakob's cheek which he quickly wiped away.

The rest of the evening Jakob spent introducing Geraldine to his friends, as most had not met Geraldine before. She introduced an element of charm they had not experienced. The birthday cake was cut as they all sang "Happy Birthday" to BethAnn, and each received a piece of the cake Chucha had baked for her.

The guests left one-by-one, as they had come, leaving BethAnn basking in a glow she would long remember. The last to leave was Harry, who wanted to play something for them on BethAnn's new piano. He told them it was something new by a French composer. He began and the melody that stirred their deepest emotions. They sat in the living room, as the soft notes filled the night and when he finished, he told them he had just recently bought the music. It was called "Clair de Lune," by a French composer, named Claude Debussy. He felt sure it would one day be acclaimed.

Harry got up to leave and looking at Jakob and Geraldine he asked, "Hey, guys, am I going to be able to play at the wedding?"

Jakob and Geraldine started to laugh as Geraldine answered, "Nobody could do it any better than you Harry."

It was getting late and it had been a big day for BethAnn. She sat next to Jakob and thanked him for the party and all he had done for her.

"Daddy, you are so good to me. I love you so." Looking at Geraldine she added, "You gave me the best birthday present I could ever have. We missed you so." Putting her arms around her she kissed her. "I have had a full day. I'm tired. I think I'll just go to bed now." They all laughed as BethAnn moved off the couch and went up the stairs to her room. Chucha followed her and agreed it had been a full day. The ladies had helped her clean up the yard bringing all the foods inside, making her job much easier. This left Jakob and Geraldine on the couch with Skippy between them, until Jakob nudged him off the couch.

"I didn't ask if you are going to stay here with us tonight?"

"No, dear, they took my luggage over to the Sheridan Inn. I thought it would be best. We still should be discrete with our relationship."

"Then I'll take you over to the hotel. It is getting late." He got his buggy together and they started for the Inn. Jakob tied the horse to the post and they went inside. The Inn was quiet, with only Robert Johnson at the desk for the night. Jakob opened the door to her room.

"Can I come in for a while?" Geraldine looked at him and smiled. "We have some things to talk over." They sat on a small couch and Jakob continued, "Where do we go from here, dear? Are you going to stay here for a while?"

"What do you want me to do, Jakob? We do have a lot of plans to make. When should we get married?"

"I would say tomorrow, if we could."

Geraldine laughed and kissed him. "All right, serious now."

"Just as soon as we can make arrangements. We have waited too long. I can't live without you. Tomorrow is Sunday. Will you come to church with us?"

"Of course Jakob. It would be perfect. I met Father John and I want to see more of him. Is it he you want to marry us? Can we talk with him tomorrow? We can set our date. You are right, we have waited too long."

"I'll be here by nine o'clock." He got up, followed by Geraldine, and put his arms around her and kissed her tenderly. They held each other tightly kissing. Jakob slowly backed off. He smiled. "Nine o'clock. We'll be here." He hesitated . . . and then he left.

BethAnn and Chucha got into the buggy and they headed to the Sheridan Inn for Geraldine. She was waiting for them on the veranda, dressed with a flowered green dress and a large brimmed hat tied under her chin. Jakob helped Geraldine into the buggy. They sat very close as they rode to church. The buggy was made for three people. The church was now located at the north end of town, off of Main Street. It was designed to hold a large number of worshipers but it was already too small, making it necessary for John Binotti to hold two services on Sunday. Upon arriving, they were greeted by some of Jakob's friends and acquaintances from Sheridan. Some had been to BethAnn's party, but most had never seen Geraldine. They took their seats in a pew near the front.

For Geraldine this was a new experience, because she had always attended the Church of England. In the eyes of her father, the Catholic church was not even mentioned. She followed Jakob as he participated in the ritual. The sermon given by Father John was on the Beatitudes, and she carefully listened. When they went up to receive Communion, she stayed seated. They later met John Binotti as they were leaving the church. Jakob asked if they might meet with him soon.

He replied, "Do you want to do it today?" Jakob said he would like to, if it were possible. "How about your house, if Chucha will make dinner for us?" Jakob laughed and looked at Chucha.

"Did you hear what Father said Chucha? He wants to be invited for dinner today." Chucha laughed.

"I fix good dinner for him."

"You're on John. We'll look for you about two if that is all right?" They left so others might be greeted by him. Seated in the buggy, they started for home. Chucha was beaming because she would make dinner for the Priest.

John Binotti arrived promptly at two and was greeted by all. Chucha had pulled out all the stops and made what she called a hunter's stew. She said she was glad he came, because she had started this three days ago, as required by the recipe. It was real treat for all.

"How did she know I would be coming over today?" asked John, who laughed. "It was God's will." They looked at each other quizzically and John spoke. "Evidently, you didn't realize it is God who brought us together today." No one spoke but took those words to heart.

After feasting on Chucha's best they sat together to talk about what John had come for.

"Jakob, you and Geraldine and I have important business to discuss. BethAnn, you don't mind if we don't include you right now, do you?" She smiled.

"No, Father, I know you will make them one." And she left, smiling. Jakob thought, *How did she know we would be talking about our coming marriage?*

"Your daughter is a very smart little girl, and the family that comes from this union between you two will be beautiful." They talked at length and he quizzed them on all aspects of the coming marriage. He asked Geraldine if she would want to become a Catholic. She said she thought she would, but wanted to learn more about the faith. They decided to have the ceremony on the second Sunday in October. They had much to do in preparation for the great event. Jakob went to BethAnn's room and asked her to come down. She was all smiles and sat with them.

Jakob looked at her. "BethAnn, Geraldine and I are going to get married." She jumped up and screamed.

"Oh, Daddy, I'm so glad. Then, I can really call Geraldine my mother." She put her arms around Geraldine and kissed her and then did the same to Jakob. Father John got up to leave.

"I guess that settles things. BethAnn approves. We'll get together later to work out the details. Next Sunday I will announce in church, your upcoming marriage." Chucha started to cry and put her arms around Jakob.

"I so happy for you and my little BethAnn." Jakob looked around at those he loved, and thought, *Maybe this is God's will.* Father John thanked Chucha for the splendid dinner and said he would be back any time he was invited.

"We have much to go over in preparation for your wedding, so we will be in touch. I have other parish duties and must leave. It is God's will we have met," Father John said, and he left.

They left the house and sat on the porch, discussing the coming wedding.

"Jakob, I need to go to the ranch for a few days. Do you want to go with me? I know you are busy, and it's all right if you don't, but I have some business to discuss and I want to ask my sister to be my attendant at the wedding."

"I'd like to go with you, but I do have a busy schedule. Let me see if it's possible." Their happy event would require a lot of preparation, for both Jakob and Geraldine who were making lists of things they had to do.

The excitement of the day had obliterated the birthday of yesterday and BethAnn exclaimed "I have birthday presents I haven't opened." They all laughed as BethAnn went to the table that held them and started opening them. BethAnn was engrossed in her gifts as Jakob and Geraldine looked on. Skippy sat next to her as she opened the packages.

Geraldine got up and went to BethAnn's piano and sat down. She touched a few keys and then some more, as she started to put together a tune, and then began playing Beethoven's "Fur Elise." Everyone looked at her in awe, as the notes were played so well.

"I guess I haven't forgotten it." BethAnn sat next to Geraldine.

"Geraldine, it was beautiful. You know how to play the piano." Jakob was astonished.

"I love it. It's just I haven't played for, oh, so many years." BethAnn was excited.

"Maybe you can teach me to play that song, when I learn the piano. Maybe we can play together."

Geraldine smiled "Yes, we will."

The rest of the day was spent planning for the wedding and the future. It was getting late so Jakob took Geraldine to the Sheridan Inn. They stopped in the bar now partially filled with visitors, and sat at a lone table in the corner of the room.

"Doc, I didn't see you come in. Lady Geraldine, I didn't know you were in town."

"I got in yesterday, Annabelle. It's nice to see you."

"I know what you guys want." And she went to the bar and was soon back with two martinis. They picked up their glasses and touched them.

"Welcome back, Honey." She smiled.

"It's so good to be back with you. I know this is where I belong." They bent over the table and kissed. They went on talking about the wedding until the bar started to close.

"I guess it's time we call it quits for the night." Jakob walked Geraldine to her room. He opened the door and took her in his arms and kissed her. He held her tight and then let her go.

"Good night, my sweet Prince. I'll see you in my dreams." And he left.

As Jakob approached his office the next day, people stopped to congratulate him. *News travels fast,* he thought. His thoughts were between the work he was doing and his impending wedding. It seemed most people knew about his wedding. He finished his morning and was going to leave for the Sheridan Inn to see Geraldine, when in walked Doc Kelly. He had been at BethAnn's party but had left before Geraldine arrived.

"Well, Jake, I heard your princess came to the party. Why didn't you tell me she was going to be there? I'd of stayed to meet her."

"I didn't know she would be there, Kelly. It was a complete surprise to me."

"Well, Kid, I'm glad for you. I really am. I told you she would be back. Now, you got to introduce me to her."

"I will, Kelly. I'm also expecting you to be my best man at the wedding. By the way, it's going to be fancy. I expect you to get a new suit for it. The one you've been wearing for the last ten years is worn out."

"Now, Jake, we are friends but that's expecting a lot from me. I don't know if I can afford one."

"You can, Kelly. If you can't, I'll put you in touch with my banker."

"Okay, Jake. I'll see what I can do. Do you realize what a new suit will cost me?"

"Yes, Kelly, about the same amount you sometimes lose playing cards on Saturday night." Kelly left laughing. Jakob was about to close the door to his office when in walked Harold Stevens from the bank.

"Jake, have you and Geraldine set a date for the wedding yet?"

"Second Sunday in October, and I expect you to be there."

"Oh, that's good. Sunday. Then I won't have to close the bank." Harold left and Jakob started laughing as he walked down the street toward the Sheridan Inn. He was worried he'd have to close the bank. Jakob entered the Inn. Henry Clayton was at the desk.

"Doc, I heard the good news. Why didn't you tell me she was going to show up? I would have stayed at the party." Jakob explained he didn't know Geraldine was coming in. It was a surprise to him. "Well, if you're looking for her now, she left a couple hours ago. She said if you come by, she would be back after three."

The following week Jakob had a busy schedule and had lots of planning for the wedding. But he had developed a nagging feeling since he got up that morning, which was between elation for Geraldine who had come back, and depression. He now thought he knew what it was. When he saw Geraldine standing in front of him in the kitchen, his heart skipped a beat and he was happy beyond belief. She was back and now they could get married. But later that night, his beautiful Liz entered his mind. He felt he should go to the cemetery to straighten out things with Liz.

As he stood before her grave the next day, tears came to his eyes as he spoke.

"I still love you Liz. I can't ever forget you. I know you would want me to be happy and I know I will. Our BethAnn will have the mother she needs to help raise her. I will always have you in my heart Liz, except it will be along with Geraldine. You will both be my ladies." He felt justified and his life could continue with the women he now loved. Jakob left the cemetery and rode back to his office.

Chapter 41

October 14th

During the past weeks Jakob spent much of his time in preparation for his marriage. He and Geraldine were together as much as possible. However, some of her time was at the ranch which required her attention and he had his dental practice which he needed to attend to. The day of the wedding finally arrived. Skippy didn't have to wake Jakob up. His eyes opened with his realization this was the day he had waited so long for. He let Skippy out the door and got the coffee pot ready.

He sat watching Skippy with a squirrel chattering at him from the lower branch of the tree. The pot of coffee on the stove was bubbling softly. Looking at his watch his thoughts were about the wedding. *Six hours from now I will be in church getting married. Just four months ago I felt my world was shattered, and today a new chapter in my life begins.* He mulled over the events of the last month. It was hectic between trying to take care of his office and completing the preparations for this day. His emotions ran high. *I guess, I can't say I'm not nervous about all this, because I am*, he thought, as he filled his cup and took a sip of the hot brew. He arose from his chair, and carried his coffee into the living room, and sat in his favorite chair.

Chucha came down the stairs, and seeing Jakob sitting she smiled.

"Good morning, Pan. Today is important day for you. I happy for you to have wife. She be a good woman for you and BethAnn."

"Thank you, Chucha. I know she's a good woman. She will be a good wife for me and a good mother for BethAnn. I'm just thinking about how different our lives will be. I just want you to know you will still be a part of our lives, just as you have all the years you've been with us." Chucha smiled and nodded an approval, then went into the kitchen to start breakfast. Jakob picked up his coffee and went out on the porch. The sun was bright and the wind was brisk, a typical October Wyoming day and definitely too chilly to stay out very long. Coming back in, BethAnn came down from her bedroom.

"What's outside, Daddy?" He shrugged his shoulders.

"Oh, nothing. I just went outside." Jakob hugged and kissed her. BethAnn looked up at Jakob.

"Today is the day, Daddy. I'm so excited Geraldine will be living with us. I just can't wait. I'm going to wear the dress you bought me for my birthday party today. Geraldine said I look cute in it and she wants me to wear it. I'm so glad Grandmother and Grandfather Miller came for the wedding. They are at the Inn now, aren't they?" Jakob nodded they were.

Chucha had breakfast on the table and they sat down, with more talk on the wedding. Jakob ate some of his breakfast but couldn't finish it. He was obviously nervous. *I don't know what's the matter with me,* he thought.

The next hour was spent doing various things which could have been overlooked and were unimportant, but it kept him busy until Bob and Margaret Miller came in. They were already dressed for the wedding. Chucha offered them a full breakfast. They declined, but had coffee and her breakfast cake while sitting and talking with Jakob. They were obviously happy for him and filled the time with small talk. Margaret looked very attractive. She wore a beige dress that reached the calf of her legs, and a long pearl necklace adorned her neck. Her dark hair now had some gray in it but it didn't detract from her beauty. She appeared stately. Bob, whose hair now showed a fair amount of grey, especially at the temples, wore a dark blue pinstriped suit. He looked handsome. Geraldine asked him if he would walk down the aisle with her, which flattered him.

The Sheridan Floral Shop delivered flowers to the house for Margaret and BethAnn and boutonnieres, for Jakob, Kelly and Bob. Jakob had become increasingly quiet and sober until Doc Kelly arrived in his new suit which Jakob laughingly approved. Kelly made a point of telling him how much he paid for it. It was dark blue and had a vest. His gray hair and beard were neatly trimmed. He broke the solemnity of the group into laughter as he chided Jakob about his coming marriage. Jakob was now dressed in the formal attire he wore in England, with a white waistcoat, winged collar shirt and white tie. It was eleven and time to go to the church.

Kelly took Jakob in his rig and Little Henry drove the rest of the family in a carriage. Geraldine and her sister would come separately in a carriage from the Sheridan Inn. Jakob and Kelly arrived at St. Ignatius Church, which was now finished except for some of the incidental features. It had been decorated with flowers. Jakob and Kelly went into the sacristy where they were met by Father John. Between Father John and Kelly, they broke down Jakob's sober mood and had him laughing again in the confines of the church sacristy. John Binotti helped Jakob get through his most difficult period following the loss of Liz and gave him the encouragement he needed to get on with his life. They became close friends.

The church started to fill with people. Seats were packed tight and the aisles then filled with friends There were also people standing outside. This turned out to be the wedding of the year for Sheridan. Harry, in his tuxedo, sat at the piano and softly played until the church was filled. Then he played Debussy's "Clair de Lune" for the assembled. Jakob's mother was escorted down the aisle by Andy Meeks who also wore a tuxedo. She was seated in the front row. The mood was set.

Mary Romano, who sang in church during some of the services, stood by the piano and sang the "Ave Maria" with emotion. Subdued voices could be heard as they waited for Jakob and Geraldine.

Jakob and Father John walked from the sacristy, followed by Doc Kelly. They stood in front of the altar. It was a mature, handsome and genuine Jakob in his formal attire standing and waiting for his bride. Harry began playing the "Wedding March."

BethAnn stood waiting, in her pretty birthday dress and carrying a small bouquet of flowers. She slowly walked down the aisle, with a controlled smile and walked up to Jakob and put her arms around him until he bent down and kissed her, then she stood next to him. Geraldine's sister Eleanor followed, wearing a pale green dress that extended down to the calf, also holding a small bouquet of flowers. Eleanor was attractive. She resembled Geraldine, but was smaller in stature She stood at the left side of the altar.

The music stopped briefly as Bob, Jakob's father, appeared with Geraldine. Everyone in the church had turned to see them. Geraldine stood tall and stately. She wore a pale blue, floor-length chiffon dress, with a slight train. The sleeves were short and it had a rounded neck. A single strand of white pearls graced her slim neck. She wore matching satin gloves, that came above her elbows. Her dark brownish hair was back and in a bun, and a short lace veil secured by a white band extended just below her shoulders. She carried long-stemmed white roses.

Jakob just gasped. Her smile was controlled but you could sense she was happy walking tall, slowly down the aisle holding Jakob's father's arm, as the piano played the wedding march. She was like the picture of a Greek goddess. Jakob walked up to meet her in the front of the altar. Bob lifted her veil, kissed her on the cheek, and gave her hand to Jakob, then spoke with them briefly. Jakob embraced him and took her hand, and together they walked up the steps to the altar where Father John met them. He smiled and spoke a few words to them, then looked toward the congregation as the ceremony began.

"My dear friends, you have come together in this church so the Lord may seal and strengthen your love in the presence of the Church's minister and this community. Geraldine and Jakob, have you come here freely, and without reservation to give yourselves to each other in marriage?" They looked at each other in the solemnity of the moment and softly both answered yes.

"Will you love and honor each other as husband and wife for the rest of your lives?" They both nodded and answered they would.

And together they repeated, "I, Jakob, I, Geraldine do take you to be my wife, my husband. I promise to be true to you in sickness and in health. I will honor you all the days of my life." They placed rings on each other's fingers, as each spoke the words, "With this ring, I thee wed."

John gave them his blessing and then pronounced them, husband and wife. He introduced them to the congregation as Doctor and Mrs. Jakob Miller.

"And you may now kiss the bride." Jakob pushed back the veil and put his arms around Geraldine as she tenderly placed her hands on his face and drew his lips to hers. And they kissed, amongst the joy, laughter and applause of the congregation.

And thus, they began a journey they would take for the rest of their lives.

Acknowledgments

No author can write and publish a book without the help of others. This author relied on a number of people for assistance. My wife Norie read and often critiqued much of my writing. She was the engine that pushed me in those early days. Without the assistance of editors I am sure my book would not be publishable and for that I give thanks to Dennis Held and G. Washington for their expertise.

My knowledge of Sheridan, Wyoming came from several books. *In the Shadow of the Bighorns* by Cynde Georgen for the Sheridan Historical Society was invaluable. I found a copy of *Sagebrush Dentist* by Herman Gastrell Seely to give me some information on the early dentistry of Dr. Will Frackelton. I give thanks to the helpful people in the Sheridan Library for their assistance. My research into the English aristocracy was from many books on the subject.

I thank all those who took the time to read my copy and critique it. They gave me valuable assistance: Rick Jones, Jim Rodgers, B.J. Hosler, Bette Kinyon, to name a few.

About the Author

Stanley C. Parks: was born in Chicago, Illinois. He attended Loyola University and the University of Notre Dame. Stan was a Naval Officer in WWII and graduated from Loyola University School of Dentistry and did private practice dentistry in Chicago and Aurora, Illinois. He was Associate Professor at Northwestern University School of Dentistry.

Retirement was spent on water, cruising the East Coast, Florida and the Bahama Islands on his boat the Lady Norie III, with his "Only Mate." He has a professional captain's license. When not on water he was on stage performing local theater and television. He is a sculptor and writer and now lives in Spokane, Washington.